The GREAT Faerie Strike

Stink Eye Books is an imprint of Broken Eye Books dedicated to celebrating the influences of popular culture on speculative fiction—in our odd, strange, and offbeat way.

Broken Eye Books is an independent press, here to bring you the odd, strange, and offbeat side of speculative fiction. Our stories tend to blend genres, highlighting the weird and blurring its boundaries with horror, sci-fi, and fantasy.

Support weird. Support indie.

brokeneyebooks.com

twitter.com/brokeneyebooks
facebook.com/brokeneyebooks

The GREAT Faerie Strike

Spencer Ellsworth

THE GREAT FAERIE STRIKE
by SPENCER ELLSWORTH

Published by
Stink Eye Books

Stink Eye Books is an imprint of Broken Eye Books.
www.brokeneyebooks.com

978-1-940372-39-6 (trade paperback)
978-1-940372-40-2 (hardcover)
978-1-940372-43-3 (ebook)

Praise for The Great Faerie Strike

"A rollicking adventure told with Pratchettesque wit and compassion. This is an Otherworld as real and as strange as our own, with characters you can't help but root for and an economic system you can't help but recognize. This book is a delight."

—**Kate Heartfield**, author of *Alice Payne Arrives*

"Wacky, satirical, and downright hilarious. With sharp writing and a rollicking pace, Ellsworth will throw you down the rabbit hole and into the Otherworld."

—**Sean Grigsby**, author of *Smoke Eaters*
and *Daughters of Forgotten Light*

"Charming, rakish, and a rollicking good time."

—**Tina Connolly**, Nebula-nominated author
of *Ironskin* and *Seriously Wicked*

"Spencer Ellsworth's *The Great Faerie Strike* is Dickensian fantasy that punches the soot off tradition with a cunning female lead and a dastardly fun world. Must read for those who love fantasy but need a revolutionary fix."

—**Jason Ridler**, author of *Hex-Rated*
and *Harvest of Blood and Iron*

"Ellsworth's feypunk Victorian fantasy is *A Midsummer Night's Dream* meets *Underworld* with a dash of Dickens, featuring a heroine who is Lois Lane as imagined by a slightly drunk Jane Austen. While full of humor and fun fantasy adventure, it doesn't shy away from also exploring the darker side of capitalism or the struggle between finding your place in the world versus making your place in the world versus making the world the place you want it to be. A fitting tale for our times."

—**Randy Henderson**, author of *Finn Fancy Necromancy*

The GREAT Faerie Strike

(or Puckish Luck)

An Account of the Upheaval within the
Otherworld of 1851 and the Strange Creatures,
Conflicts, and Consequences that Attended Such

Chapter One

In Which our Vampire Faces the Trials of Madness, Memory, and Filial Duty

JANE LEANED OUT THE CARRIAGE WINDOW AND LOOKED BACK, FORCED herself to stare at the asylum as it disappeared into the distance.

The windows each had their own set of wrought-iron bars. Evenly spaced trees framed the perfectly square building. And the gate at the end of the driveway, also wrought-iron with massive black bars, looked like a smiling mouth—that had closed on over a year of her life.

She burned it all into memory with that gaze. Her seventeenth year of life, a year of bare rooms, steam baths, restraints, and Bible readings.

And she whispered to herself, "I am not mad."

"Jane, close the window." Her mother pulled the drapes. "You mustn't take a chill!"

"I wanted to see the countryside."

"Too much excitement for right now, dear. Rest. Next month, we will retire to your aunt Rebecca's house in the country, and we might take some long walks— oh, but not too long—and learn to play whist! You'll love whist, dear. Sharpens the mind. Unless that sounds like too much excitement? No, it's a dangerous pursuit, whist. Interferes with relaxation."

"Whatever you think is best, Mother," Jane said.

Her mother's eyes glimmered with tears. "From your mouth to God's ears.

How many prayers I've said, Jane—" She pressed Jane's hand in hers, unable to continue.

Jane leaned her head on her mother's breast. The heart beneath thundered, outpacing the clip-clop of the horses.

She remembered old Doctor Lark frowning, eyeing his stethoscope as if he suspected it of foul play after pressing it to Jane's chest. *Every time, the same thing. I'd swear to Providence, I've heard but one heartbeat in all the time I've attended to her.*

It was how Jane knew she was not human.

She whispered the words again like a catechism, sounding each syllable clearly to her own ears. "I'm not mad."

The stink of London reached them soon enough: the rot of cesspools, the dry stink of coal smoke, the too-sweet smell of broken gas mains. Jane carefully inclined her head to peer past the drapes without her mother noticing. In the distance, new rows of smokestacks and buildings rose along the skyline, obscured by coal dust that turned the sun into a red dot. By the roadside, sewing women walked, sharing around tins of hand cream. A phossy girl from the match factory, abscessed jaw wrapped in rags, limped behind them. Men stained ochre from the brickyard groaned and massaged sore backs.

"Jane!" her mother called. "Close the drapes! It's quite disturbing you!"

"London changes so quickly." A woman on the corner, holding three babes, cried to passersby that she had been turned from her home by her landlord.

Her mother yanked the drapes closed. "This 'progress'. . . our Lord must surely return this year to end such wickedness."

The carriage rolled to a stop in Shoreditch, and her mother put on a broad, overeager smile. "Upstairs we go! Rest before dinner, then a little rest after, and then bed!"

The house had changed. The fires weren't lit. End tables were missing favorite knickknacks. Jane touched the banister, and her hand came away dusty. "Mother, where is the servant girl?"

"Dear, you needn't worry about such a thing, not now!"

How much had that asylum cost? There had been no servants here in months.

"Rest!" Her mother prodded Jane upstairs, opening the door to the bedroom. Jane's four-poster, chest of drawers, and washing table stood dusty and neat as before. "Just as you left it." Her mother sat Jane on the bed, raising a cloud of dust, and pressed Jane's hand. "Such prayers I said. And now you're home."

Jane's eyes strayed to the chest of drawers. "Mother, I . . . I'll need that rest."

"Of course, of course!" She kissed Jane on the forehead and left the room, calling back, "I'll get the fire lit."

The door closed.

Jane sprang up from her bed.

She yanked out the bottom drawer in her chest, tossed old, camphor-smelling petticoats aside, and felt for the small box. "Come now, come now, you're there. I know you are—" The box came away in her hands. Just an old matchbox, but inside . . .

Jane clawed it open, shook its contents out. The wrench and lockpicks clattered to the floor from her trembling hands, and the tiny vial, no bigger than her pinky finger, landed in her palm.

It was real.

"I'm not mad," Jane said and giggled to herself, a high piercing giggle. "I'm not mad!"

Witchwater was real.

Jane took a deep breath, gathered up the picks, and shoved them into the bun of her pinned-up hair. It took a few tries as she was shaking. "No time," she muttered to herself. "Must go." From another drawer and carefully tucked into a corset, she withdrew a box of folded papers, wedging them down the back of her shirt, bracing them against the corset she was already wearing.

Once downstairs, she saw her mother bent over the fire, grunting as she scraped out yesterday's ashes and wedged kindling into the grate. Jane felt a strange pang of sympathy—*Mother* was laying the fire?—but she crushed it. The woman had spent her money to put Jane away, and she would get no sympathy. "Mother," Jane said.

"Oh, Jane, dear!" Her mother turned around, her face now soot-blackened. She stepped away from the fireplace. "Dear, you must rest. Believe me, it's best—"

Jane threw the witchwater.

The few drops splashed on the bridge of her mother's nose, leaking trails down through the soot. "Jane, what . . ."

And then, following the trails of water, the color leaked right out of her mother's irises, pooled along the bottom of her eyes. She stood frozen as a wax figure.

"Mother, listen. I've been back a while now. Several months."

"Several . . . months?"

"I've got a job. I work at a newspaper, writing stories."

"A newspaper?" Her mother twitched and spoke in a muddled voice as if she were chewing on wool. "One of those horrific rags, proclaiming the evils of the world? Dear, you are better than—"

"You approve, Mother."

The old woman's jaw tensed and then relaxed. "I approve."

"I've got to go out now. Business for the newspaper."

"Yes."

Jane let out a great breath of relief, started for the door, but turned. She leaned in close to her mother and said, "Who is my father?"

Her mother shook violently, doubled over as though a snake were twisting around inside her guts. "I-I-I cannot say! I cannot—"

"Never you mind, Mother." Some secrets were buried too deep for witchwater.

Jane put on her sturdy thick-heeled boots, threw the door open, ran into the stinking street, and bellowed as loud as she could, "I'm not mad!"

Horses, a herd of pigs, and men and women all turned toward her.

Jane yelled at all of them, "I'm not mad!"

"Oy, yeah, little bird. Sane folk, they bellow at me pigs all the time!" said a nearby swineherd.

Jane grinned at him. "I'm glad you agree."

She ran down the London street, dodging carriages and cattle, leaping over piles of horse dung and puddles. She just had to find the door and reach the Otherworld—and never be caught again.

It had all really started with the new doctor, five years ago. He'd entered the house, taken one look at Jane, and his eyes had widened. While her mother complained of Jane's hunger pangs and longing for rare beef, he looked in Jane's mouth, and, strangely, touched her teeth. And then stood up and changed Jane's life.

"In the interests of the girl, I think it's best we be frank. Jane's father was a vampire, was he not?"

"What?" Jane's mother replied. "I'll thank you not to spin fancies!"

"Madam," he'd said, "the Otherworld has been part of my trade for some time. I can tell you this is clearly Hecatian anemia." He smiled and patted Jane's leg.

"You mustn't believe the stories of vampires, dear. They won't turn you with a bite or change into bats. They're living creatures, same as you and I, though their hearts are notoriously shriveled and weak and beat but once a day." He turned and reached into his bag. "Now whilst they are notoriously secretive, I can tell you that a vampire does need to eat flesh, uncooked. I've got—"

That was when Jane's mother swatted him with her umbrella.

"Ow! Madam, I—"

"Out! Out of my house!" She beat at his face with the umbrella. "Take your heresies from this house! We fear God here!" Thump went the umbrella. "We fear God!"

For all that he fled the raging umbrella, he didn't go far. The next day, Jane went out to fetch a few flowers from the market, and a voice called from a nearby shopfront, "Jane."

The doctor stood there, holding a small stoppered bottle, smiling at her.

Young Jane had swallowed, found her gaze drawn to the bottle. There was something about it. "Mother says I'm not to mention you."

"Well, Adam got us all here by doing something he shouldn't. Don't you fret." He came forward, crouched next to her. "I've got to get back to Blackpool, but I've brought you something to put peaks in those cheeks."

"Is that blood?"

"Cow's blood. Thinned of course with water and a small amount of alcohol. The butcher at the Fields Market has been paid up for the month to supply you with such. Try some."

He unstoppered the flask.

Young Jane wanted to say no, to back away, run to her mother—but then the smell hit her, and she went dizzy. She'd always liked the smell of fresh beef, and this was like that but richer, intoxicating. She took a drink.

Strength flushed along her limbs immediately. Jane couldn't help it. She took a few more deep, filling draughts. For the first time, she didn't feel sickly. Her weariness, her dizziness, all replaced by a surge of energy. "Thank you, sir. It is—thank you!"

"I can't imagine what led your mother to take up with a vampire. Either he was an extraordinary fellow or . . . well, this is more germane to you." He handed her a slip of paper with an address on it.

"Your practice?" It was a strain to stop drinking long enough to ask the questions.

"A school. One more suited to you. I make a generous donation each year, so they should be quite willing to cover your first year's tuition. Perhaps your mother will be more pliable by then—easy, you'll choke!"

Jane gulped the rest of the drink, coughed, sprayed blood all over her chin. The doctor dabbed his handkerchief on her face with a laugh. "There, now you look a proper vampire!" His face grew serious. "Now remember, you mustn't consume human blood, merely livestock. One doesn't want to be put away as rabid."

"Yes sir." She sucked down more blood. "Yes of course."

That was how it started that magnificent day. Then three years at Guldenburg School in the Otherworld, learning the hidden world from goblins, fooling her mother into thinking she was at a private finishing school. Excursions into the wild wood and the City Beyond.

And then . . .

Then she'd become tired of secrets and confronted her mother. *I know my father was a vampire, and I know you weren't assaulted, for a vampire would rather* eat *a human than violate her. Tell me, Mother. Who was he?*

Her mother's normally strained smile vanished, and pink cheeks went pale. Promising to answer after tea, the damnable woman instead slipped laudanum into Jane's drink.

Jane had awoken to find herself pressed into bonds by her mother's churchmen, her mother sobbing, "She's gone mad, she's seeing fancies, she cannot be reasoned with!"

Never again.

Now, Jane ran down streets, cut across alleys, around carriages and herds of cows, ignored the cored-out feeling in her stomach. London grew dimmer, the gas lamps beginning to glow.

Jane was startled to see a green ring, drawn on the brick of a nearby building in chalk. Peering down the alley, Jane just made out a tiny golden keyhole set in the air. No human's eyes would have caught the sight.

"So quick! Oh my!" She lifted her skirts and trod into the alley, out of breath. There were a half-dozen doors to the Otherworld in London, but they moved around, and Jane had spent whole days wandering the city trying to find the ring-symbols that would denote an entrance. "It's as they say," she said to herself. "Puckish luck comes to all who walk the City Beyond." And a moment later, "I shouldn't talk to myself. I'll sound mad."

There had been talk of a newspaper for the City Beyond London, just before she went to the asylum—a newspaper that paid in pounds sterling, not faerie gold.

A newspaper where she could work answering questions.

Jane gently pressed her finger against the floating keyhole.

The air shivered. A terrible screaming whistle like a thousand trains running at high speed echoed in Jane's ears. Jane stumbled backward as a round door appeared, the shape first and then the details. It was all metal, burnished and riveted.

Steel? In Faerie? Who would work with iron in a realm where it was poison?

An impossible thing stuck its head through the door.

"Proper authorization?" It was a round, metal ball, riveted together with two glowing bulbs like gas lamps wired to its head—two gleaming gas lamps like eyes. Its automated voice rang, rumbled, all gears and mechanized clattering.

"Goodness me," Jane choked. "I come . . . I've come from ah, Guldenburg School, and I'll answer any riddle—"

"No riddles! Proper authorization needed." The voice was like a wounded dog's howl, mixed with the scratch of breaking charcoal. "Do you have an appointment?"

"No, but . . . I heard about a newspaper and—"

"Ridley Door Co. respectfully denies your entreaty!" The door slammed back into place with a great clang, and the whole door shivered in the air and vanished.

"No!" Jane ran forward, trying to seize the door, and ran right through it. Glimmering motes hung in the air, the only traces of the gateway. "No! I need to get to the Otherworld! I need to find work not with humans. They think—" An ugly sob worked its way up Jane's throat. She fought it down. She would *not* cry, and she was *not* mad!

"Old Pedge still keeps his door. No metal men. In Regent's Park by and by."

A short man, dressed in a vivid green suit, stood at the end of the alley. It was difficult to make out the man's face, even though his hair seemed unusually bright—vivid shades of white and orange, dancing like flame.

"Oh, thank you, sir," Jane said. "You know of the City Beyond London then?"

But between two blinks, the fellow was gone.

Did I just imagine all that? Did I . . . oh, dear, am I still in the asylum? Am I having visions? Am I—

No. The smells of London were real. The filthy alley was real. And Regent's Park was merely a three-mile walk. "I'm not mad, and I'm not giving up."

Night and rain both increased in Regent's Park. She was soon enough soaked, walking the sports pitches and the horse paths, looking for anything that resembled a faerie ring, till a rough male voice shouted, "Oy, yeh mad bird, out of the way!"

Jane spun around. "I'm not mad! I'm not—" A small figure ran right around her.

Murgalak's Fun Human Facts

Humans worry a great deal about maladies of the mind and insanity. Historically, only a few wise humans have figured out that it is better to simply remove the offending head and grow a new one. We goblins do hope for the rest of them.

Despite the darkness, the figure bolted without pause as if he could see perfectly.

Despite his height, his deep voice rumbled like a man's.

Neither of which were entirely human traits.

She ran after him.

The short man stopped at a stand of trees, bent down, and touched something on the ground. Jane just made it out now: a barely discernible ring of mushrooms, sprouted in the humus under that tree.

"Pedge! Open up, you! Well coopered, I am! Been a long night, but we've got your cheese."

Of course. Cheese. It made a pixie, a boggart, or a redcap drunker than all the whiskey in the world.

The short fellow was definitely an Otherworlder.

The air shimmered. The smell of a wild, windy heath came through the door. An uneven, spreading circle of warm light appeared in the air.

The Otherworld opened again. "Oh," Jane muttered, "this is the sort of door I recognize." She steeled herself.

A madgekin merchant stuck his head out of the circle of golden light, a great hairy head, thickly mustached and without a nose but clad in great dark goggles. Two hairy, spidery legs reached out from Otherworld to human world. "Give it here."

The small figure replied, "Hand over the hoof and let us in, Pedge."

"The cheese first, gnome."

The short fellow was a gnome? What sort of gnome stole for a living?

"It's raining like Oberon's piss!" the gnome said. "I'm no leg. One shilling!"

The madgekin produced a dirty shilling and pulled the gnome through with one hairy arm.

Jane bolted. No time to ask about gnomes—or why fey creatures were now using human money. She ran to the shrinking circle of golden light that marked the door and leapt through.

She seemed to hang there, suspended for an eternal second. The smells were suddenly sharper: the cheese a distinct, rich curdled smell overlaid on the reek of spices too rich and dizzying for the human world. The light, deeper and brighter than the human world, enveloped her, warm like a blanket.

Then Jane crashed into the madgekin, bounced off him, tripped over the gnome, and as her first act in the Otherworld in a year, knocked over a stack of crates.

"Ow. Oh dear." Shaking her head to clear it, she opened her eyes to see a madgekin's lair, packed with human items, stacks and stacks of cloth and crates, boots, and barrels.

And a very angry madgekin standing over her: a great swollen furry creature clad in a vest and hat, one of its furry spidery arms raised, holding a cudgel, its golden eyes burning above thick mustachios.

"You never paid for passage!"

The gnome picked himself up off the ground and swore, muttering something about great clumsy vampires.

Jane stumbled to her feet. "I'll answer a riddle, sir, I'll—" She ducked the cudgel. "Please, I'll pay passage—"

"You'll pay, yeh suckabucket!" The madgekin swung the cudgel, again and again, and Jane danced away from it until she knocked over a pile of crockery that went crashing to the ground. "Git! Git!"

"Sir, I—" *Oh, bother this.* Jane bolted out of the madgekin's lair, stumbled through a stand of trees, and clambered up a rise to get away from the raging furry arms.

The sky came into view, the eternal twilight of the City Beyond, littered with smeared, flaming stars. She let out a great, heaving breath.

It was real.

She was home.

She wasn't mad, the witchwater had worked, she'd found a door, and she breathed at last the sweet, unreal air of—

She doubled over, hacking and coughing. Something burned, made her feel as though her lungs were coals. Jane coughed so hard that her vision burst with stars.

When her vision cleared, Jane's breath caught again, not from the air. And she realized she'd missed some things on first glance.

Smokestacks rose on the horizon.

They poured green smoke into the gray sky, obscuring the flaming purple stars. And below them, squared-off buildings made a row, just like those marking warehouses and mills. In the distance, more smokestacks and towering buildings, glowing with a light like gas lamps.

The gnome came around the corner. "You got old Pedge well in a hugger-mugger back there, miss. Best get scarce."

"What happened?" Jane whispered, staring at the horrid horizon. "What happened to the Otherworld?"

"You been away?"

She nodded, not trusting her voice.

The gnome made a noise somewhere between a sigh and a groan. "Progress got us too."

Chapter Two

In which the (un)Gnomish Spirit of our Gnome is Introduced and Many a Word is Said, some Shameful, some Shaming

CHARLES THE GNOME BROKE OFF A CRUMB OF CHEESE AND HANDED IT TO the mad girl.

She ignored it, staring straight ahead, looking right heartbroken by the horizon.

Well, that was no surprise to anyone. The sight of Ridleyville, the collective warehouses and factories, was enough to make any Otherworlder spit. And he worked there every day.

Take today, when he would spend ten hours pouring the alchemical substances that captured seven leagues from the air and funneled them into seven-league boots—all so the rich could fly off to Paris.

"What happened?"

"The werewolves happened."

"Werewolves? What have werewolves to do with industry?"

"You heard of that old Malcolm Ridley fellow? What studied out his condition, grannied out how to be a wolf whenever he wanted?"

She frowned. "Oh yes. There were rumors in my last year of school. A rich man who could transform into the wolf at will and control his urges in said form by the help of potions."

"That's the dodger," Charles said. It made him angry just to say it. "Fellow bought up the whole Otherworld. A whole group of them, all werewolves and alchemists and humans who're in on the secret of the City Beyond. Found and shut down most madgekin doors. Pedge, back there, he squeaks by, but he's about the only one left, sitting on an unmonitored gate. They've made a right slap-bang job of it, factories turning out amulets and alchemical salves, shirts that won't rip or wear, seven-league boots, invisibility cloaks to sneak around on the missus. But we've got coin in our pockets."

"That's . . . that's mad!"

"We're all a bit mad now—"

"I'm not!" She turned a furious face on Charles. "I'm not mad!"

"Eh, of course not, miss. Sorry. We're all well on our chump." Mad as a boxed hare, this one.

She had yellow eyes like a vampire but faded, and her skin wasn't quite the full ashy gray of a true suckabucket.

Whatever the case, she weren't too awful-looking. Charles held up the last crumb of cheese. "I got a few minutes before work. Why don't we see what kind of fun there is to be had?"

Her glare was hot as cannon shot. "You forget yourself, sir. A gnome shouldn't—"

"Oy, then be on your way." Should've known. "A gnome shouldn't enjoy life? Shouldn't like a drink and a bricky lass?" Always they asked that. *What kind of gnome are you?* "You get any more huffy, you'll pop your corset."

"I am trying to find a newspaper office—"

"Cross the river. In the Towering Market. Off!"

She looked in the direction of the Black Fork, the river steaming with alchemical waste. "I suppose it costs a good bit to ferry the river," she said as though talking to herself.

Charles couldn't help it; he had a soft spot for the mad ones. He dug out the shilling Pedge had given him for the cheese. "Here now."

"What? I don't need—"

"That'll get you across the river. Get you something to fill the belly too."

Her lagging face softened. "Thank you, sir, and I'm sorry. I do not mean to seem ungrateful—"

"Off with yeh." Charles tromped in the other direction to work. This had better be a nice, uneventful day.

"Attention!"

The voice rang out from behind the iron gates of the workhouse.

"What's this now?" Charles's head snapped. They'd been waiting outside the factory, a full twenty minutes late. Down quota from yesterday too, a right rotten combination. He exchanged a confused look with the boggart to his right.

A human stepped out of the factory, walked up to the factory gates. The human was dressed all in finery, crowned by a hatless head of red hair thinned with gray. On his lapel, a pin of a wolf worked in silver.

That's Malcolm Ridley himself, the old werewolf tycoon. The very swell Charles had been talking to that odd girl about, who owned half the Otherworld. What was he doing here? And why were the factory gates still closed?

Murgalak's Fun Human Facts

Progress is the great goal of humanity, and its pursuit tends to make most humans miserable. This confirms the well-known theory that humans are a kind of depressed ant.

Behind him, oddly enough, came a whole pack of gray-skinned, knobby-headed vampires.

Other Otherworlders crowded the outside of the gates as close as they could be without getting burned by wrought-iron. Charles went down on his belly and wriggled under a massive badgebear's legs until he could see.

Ridley spoke. "In the interests of progress, the Ridley family has come to an agreement with the vampire clans of the Otherworld. Left without any access to the human world, they starved. No ready supply of blood was available. Our alchemists have been hard at work on a substance that mimics blood, and I am pleased to say we have created an excellent replica that will satisfy their need for nutrition."

"We gotta work with suckabuckets now?" a badgebear grumbled.

"The vampires will take over the cotton mill and the seven-league boot line. Those of you who have an excellent work record will be reassigned. For now, please make your way to the Ridley Center for the Deserving Otherworld Poor—"

The crowd grumbled. Charles, forgetting himself, leaned so far forward that he touched the iron gate and swore, yanking himself away from the burning metal. "What is this?"

"I told you," the werewolf swell said. "Progress."

Charles couldn't say how it happened. He reached down to the paving stones, found a loose one, snatched it up. He could only think about that shilling he'd let go, his aunt and uncle and cousin waiting on Charles's wages to bring home dinner, and he lifted the stone and yelled, "We're being sacked!"

Charles threw the stone.

It shattered next to Malcolm Ridley.

The werewolf didn't move. Didn't move even when pixies shouted and flew up over the walls and fluttered at the vampires, tossing what few tiny rocks they could carry. Didn't move when a badgebear threw herself against the gate, growling and shaking it, ignoring the burn of the iron. Malcolm Ridley walked forward and said, cool as the sea, "I have called Iron Riders for those who will not go in order." His red sideburns bristled, grew longer, and his voice deepened, grew ragged and growling as a wolf's. "Best you run before I too get a hunger."

Iron-shod wheels rang on stone nearby.

Charles bolted. He ran around the side of the workhouse, toward the shore of the river and the hill to the shipping docks. He ducked into an alley between two warehouses, and his eyes widened.

Another worker hid in the alley next to him. A wood-nymph in a dress stained with the alchemical substances used to treat wood products.

"Charles?" she said, her voice trembling. "Oh, Charley, I knew it! I knew you would come back to me!"

"Hullo, Elmina," Charles said to his old flame. Backing away, he stopped himself just at the mouth of the alley. "Oy, and not a minute to talk. Shame."

"Charles, wait! You need me! I saw it in my roots! Now that you're quit of that hussy—"

Charles turned around to run and crashed right into a fellow—a human. They tumbled to the ground and down the hill with Elmina's voice echoing as she chased them, the sound of steel-shod wheels clattering over her wails.

"Excuse me, sir," the fellow said as he picked himself up, dusting off his fine linen trousers. He was dressed up, all cotton, a right square-rigged swell just like Ridley. "All is chaos and violence, but I'm trying to find Ridley Ent—"

"She'll know!" Charles said, and just as the fellow reached out a hand, Charles shoved him at Elmina.

Swell and wood nymph went down in a heap, him muttering, "Oof, so sorry, miss," and her wailing, "Wait, Charley!"

Charles nearly bolted until he noticed something had fallen from the fellow's pocket. He picked it up. A heavy box of some sort of metal—but not iron as that would make his skin sizzle.

Charles turned the box over in his hands. A stylized *R*, the symbol of Ridley Manufacturing, had been emblazoned on the other side.

Some good news at last. Charles tucked the box inside his jacket pocket and muttered, "You'll get this back, swell, for buckets of coin!"

The fellow, trying to extricate himself from Elmina, couldn't answer.

Above, at the crest of the hill, glowing gas-lamp eyes appeared, and bulbous, spidery metal bodies on wheels. Like wheeled metal spiders, Iron Riders sprouted multiple arms, crackling at the ends with alchemical fire.

One hundred percent steel-forged iron. Ridley's enforcers.

Charles ran to the round hub of docks folks called Coins-Teeth. Ahead of him, a badgebear seized the crates destined for the ferries and threw them down on the pavement.

Charles scrambled through the fray, his short stature keeping him out of reach of most blows, and clambered up on the dock. It was all broken crates, drifts of sawdust and splinters, but come on, come on—

Charles seized a seven-league boot from a pile of packing sawdust. He felt around for its mate. And then the badgebear screamed, a great, high-keening roar.

Charles turned around to see the Iron Riders. One seized the badgebear in iron spidery arms. The badgebear's orange-black hide flashed green with the shock of alchemical fire, and then it fell, a smoking body, into the river shallows.

Another Rider clambered with its scuttling arms up the docks and, touching down, wheeled straight for Charles across the planks. Its gleaming lamp-eyes fixed Charles, and its spidery arms gleamed with alchemical fire.

Charles wedged himself into the single seven-league boot. "Away! Anywhere! Away dammit!"

Green fire crackled nearby, so close his beard smoked.

The seven-league boot launched him right up into the sky.

He careened like a madman through green smoke, beneath the twilight sky and the flaming stars. The whole of City Beyond gaped under him: the Black Fork, the river steaming green, the orderly warehouse streets of Ridleyville, and then the vast expanse of trees and vines and faerie lights that was the Choke, his home—

"No, too far, too far!" Charles yelled.

That only led him to spin faster. Charles sicked up the cheese, fragments of vomit flying through the air. The boot flew him down, spinning right toward a massive tree, in a vicious loop over and over, and Charles shouted, "Back, back, stop, stop—"

He crashed into a tree, bouncing through branches, off one great bough that rattled his bones, and thudded into a swath of grass, rolling a good ten paces across the ground.

"Bloody Puck's guts," Charles groaned. Everything hurt. "Bloody Puck's guts!" He spat out a thick wad of phlegm and muttered to the gnome god, not that the fellow listened. "I always heard gnomes were durable, but I'm not balmy enough to test it!"

Charles took a deep breath of the stinking air. Alive. Alive, and the Iron Rider with empty hands.

Alive and . . . full skint. No work.

"Whole game's a dodge!" he muttered, clambering to his feet. "Whole Otherworld barely gets by, all so alchemists and werewolves can have fancy parties! Seven-league boots for holidays! Invisibility cloaks to sneak around on the missus!" And here was Charles, no job, schooling unfinished, poor as Puck's donkey . . . and nothing else, except maybe his uncle.

Uncle.

Thinking of Riordan, Charles briefly wondered whether he could go back and beg forgiveness for starting a riot, get some more work in the factories.

Suppose it was too late for that once one threw a brick.

"Uncle," Charles breathed again. "Oy, this'll be the right end to the day."

Charles faced the massive, hoary oak where his family lived, its branches hanging over the Black Fork. It had taken three hours to find his way home through the wilderness of the Choke. The seven-league boot, as they did in time, had shrunk to fit in his palm, and Charles pocketed it next to the box.

He was bruised, scratched, had barely escaped a couple of hungry vines, but this he dreaded more than Iron Riders.

"Nothing for it." Charles started up the stairs.

His aunt Susan sat engrossed in her knitting—the glittering carded wool of a unicorn yak. Due to a leg injury, she couldn't work, and her blankets sold for only a few pence with the manufactured blankets to compete with. His little cousin George stared straight ahead, little black eyes intensely focused on the opposite wall. George had been working in a factory, but Charles had managed a few funds to send him to school two days a week.

And Uncle Riordan sat in his preferred chair, smoking his pipe, absorbed in his daily study of *The Gnome God's Reliable Prayer Book*. He glanced up at his nephew, frowned. "Charles, you're filthy. And home early."

Charles opened his mouth to say it and found he couldn't. "Ah, well, we're up quota and . . . I had a bit of a tumble in the Choke on the way out of work."

"Punctuality is the glorious sheen of reliability," Uncle Riordan quoted, one of his many aphorisms from the *Reliable Prayer Book*.

"George," Charles said, flopping down on a chair next to their small table. "Would you fetch your cousin Charles a bit to eat?"

"But Uncle Charles, I'm playing guard. I have to stand at my post till William gets back. I've been here four hours already."

Riordan put down the prayer book. "I stood at my post once for sixteen hours when I was your age, George."

"Really, Father? The best I've managed so far is six hours, but William says I'm getting better."

"Those heady days of childhood." Riordan gave his son a measured smile and turned his gaze back to Charles, and his eyes narrowed. "You've vomited, Charles! And what's this on your fist? Blood?"

"Ah, about that . . ." Charles swallowed. He couldn't say it was his own; gnomes had to go under a hacksaw before they'd even shed a drop. "Footpads, Uncle. I had to defend, and me stomach . . ."

"Heed not the flirtatiousness of untruth, you gnomes."

Charles couldn't say it. They needed his funds. Charles's factory pay came more reliably and at a higher wage than Riordan's servant pay, paid for George's schooling and the wool Susan needed.

"Do not tell me you were in a fight at work. Such a thing will little impress your employer and stinks of the lesser creatures who do not know reliability."

"I'm out me wages, Uncle." Charles put a hand to his mouth. Oh, blooming hell, he'd said it.

"What?" Susan said.

"For fighting?" Riordan said. "Charles, I told you there would be severe—"

"Whole factory was let go! The werewolves made up some kind of blood mixture and are paying the vampires in it. Don't know what on earth it is, but the suckabuckets have my job now and not a shilling left, and I'm . . . I'm well sorry, Uncle." Charles self-consciously shoved his bloody hand under his trouser leg. "They didn't throw us out kindly."

Silence. Aunt Susan exchanged a glance with Riordan, their expressions troubled.

"I'll get you a meal, Cousin Charles," George said and left his self-appointed guard post. George returned with a plate of yellow eggs faceup and a few strips of liver turned distinctly green. "Liver and eggs, just as reliable as ever from our reliable kitchen, Cousin Charles."

"Thank you, George." Charles spooned the liver and eggs in his mouth, trying to ignore the fact that the liver had gone green lately.

They needed a new enchantment on the oven, and he'd been planning to cover the cost. That wouldn't happen now either.

"Charles, come with me," Riordan said, standing. He walked out the door, along the branches of the great tree in the gleaming green light that steamed off the river. "We must talk."

"Oh, thirteen hells," Charles whispered to himself and followed his uncle.

Riordan waited on an upper branch of the tree, the Black Fork steaming green below him. Pixies littered the branches below their perch, giggling, tossing bits of cheap fake cheese made of milk and straw at each other. Faerie lights drifted up from the pixies, illuminating the dour creases in Riordan's face.

"Charles, what am I to do with you?"

Charles slumped down against the tree and didn't look at his uncle. "Oy, Uncle, I've a sour chivvy already. And it en't me fault!"

"Truly? You mean you were forced to engage in fisticuffs and given no hope of future work?"

It hurt how easily Riordan saw the truth. Charles could have followed the werewolf swell's rules and still had some hope of a wage. But there'd been a brick there, and he'd picked the thing up . . .

Riordan raised his face to the heavens as if making sure the gnome god heard. "To think I brought you to London to be a clergyman. To finish school, Charles! The clergy would have given purpose and direction to this fire of yours, employed it in the service of the gnome god in His Eternal Reliability. Here you are, school incomplete, a year into your work, your future traded for pliable women and cheese?"

"It's me hot head," he said weakly.

"God gave you the agency He has given every other creature."

Riordan was right. No one forced him to pick up the brick or to toss it. His hot head hadn't forced Charles to chase the ladies and skive off his schoolwork till he flunked out.

"The reliable gnome can stand at the center of a forest fire and only take a bit of char. The less reliable will burn away in the fire of passion." Riordan stepped past Charles. "I must go to work. Mister Eddington will attend a party and requires additional help. I was going to ask you to accompany me. It would be well for you to acquire some experience as a manservant; I am too old to acquire a full butler's position, but you might yet do so and earn far better wages than manufacturing. Now, I think your evening would be better spent in prayer."

Charles stumbled to his feet, nearly falling out of the tree with haste as Riordan walked away. "Wait . . . Uncle. Hang on. I'll go with you. We need the wages. I'll compose myself reliably. I swear it on the gnome god."

"You need not swear by Providence, for Providence is reliable without provocation," Riordan quoted.

"Right," Charles said. "Let me come."

Riordan's dour face, lit bright green by the river below, softened. Charles thought he saw something, a ghost of the hope his uncle'd once had for him. "Both my suits are hanging. Take the spare and use pins to account for size. Wash well." He started back toward the house and stopped, pivoted slowly to give Charles the most disapproving look he'd ever seen from under that wrinkled brow. "This is the last test, Charles."

"Aye," Charles said. "Where's this party, Uncle?"

"Ridley Manor."

Chapter Three

In which our Vampire is both Heartbroken and Challenged and the Joys of Verbiage are Discussed

THE FERRY WAS EASY ENOUGH FOR JANE TO FIND. AND FOR THE FIRST TIME she could remember in the Otherworld, no one even commented on the human coin, just took the shilling and gave her ninepence back.

Just like London. Just like dirty, overcrowded London.

She stood at the railing of the ferry and closed her eyes to the sight of a polluted river and smoky air. She knew what she would see when she opened her eyes. White walls. A wrought-iron grill over the window. Her cold bed frame and the Bible on the nightstand. *I am . . . I am . . .* She must have been mad. This could not be the Otherworld.

She opened her eyes.

The green-tinged, stinking river splashed around the ferry bottom as the boat docked. But almost, if she squinted, she thought she saw white walls and . . .

"No!" she bellowed. The creatures near her jumped, scuttled away. "I am here to find work at a newspaper!"

The Otherworld seemed more solid now. If strange.

The ferry docked.

She didn't recognize this dockyard—a mess of crates and ropes—at all. "Excuse me," Jane asked a nearby madgekin, an enormously hairy fellow carrying a half-dozen knapsacks in his eight hairy arms. "Excuse me. I'm trying to find the Towering Market—"

The madgekin jerked a furry thumb up. "You want to see the humans come to buy the Otherworld off our backs? There they are!"

Jane followed his gaze. A vast, black tower rose above them, sprouting bridges to other black towers, bridges big enough to have row houses built along them.

"Oh!" Jane said. "That's the Old Towers!"

"You been away?" the madgekin grumbled. "No one calls them that."

There'd been a bit of scaffolding and talk of construction there, last she was in the Otherworld, but this—this was enormous. They'd built an entire miniature city between those towers on bridges and platforms. "My word."

"Your word indeed. More like their trick, their great, old trick on us!"

The stairs were easy enough to find. Jane followed the surge of Otherworlders up the stairs, looking up at one of the bridges. It staggered the mind. Massive pylons. Steelwork that hardly belonged in the Otherworld stretched the lengths of the towers, braced with beams bigger than three houses.

Jane peered out through one of the openings in the stairs.

There were—or *had been*—four districts to the Otherworld. The Choke, that wild wood where most of the boggarts, redcaps, gnomes, and other creatures, and presumably the secretive vampires, lived. The Haunts, that ancient, crumbling city where sidhe came on business from their manors in other realms. The Under-Market, where anything in two worlds could be bought. And the Old Towers.

A glance along the east bank of the river showed the Choke was still there, a thick mass of trees, riverside paths thick with Otherworld folks. Although the trees glowed a strange bluish-green color she hadn't seen before, from the alchemical waste no doubt.

The Haunts were gone. Where there had stood miles of crumbling, ancient city, archways and domes and towers, there now stretched row after row of even, square factories under smokestacks pouring out green smoke.

The Under-Market was still there but mostly wide, empty squares and streets with a scattering of shopfronts instead of the bustling mass it had been.

She reached the first bridge and stepped into the Towering Market.

Stalls crowded the sides of the bridge, stacked with wares. A thick river of finely clad people walked through the street. It could have passed for a London market. Tobacco smoke hung in thick clouds, joining that weird green haze. Pastries gleamed on tables, fresh-baked, and a butcher hung prime steaks.

Oh, it became Otherworldly at second glance. Wine shone purplish-gold from sidhe grapes, but one had to look carefully to even see the difference. The prime steaks glimmered with a golden sheen, the flesh of rare white elk.

Dancing water nymphs splashed in a fountain for onlookers' coin, twirling back and forth. In a nearby bakery, a plate of day-old bread tried to leap for freedom, and the troll baker smacked it with a rolling pin.

But the patrons . . .

Far more humans than she'd ever seen in the Otherworld. Pendant-draped alchemists. Arab merchants with tame djinn. Men speaking in brash American accents, pointing at the goods. And many of London's upper class, all of them wearing a curious silver wolf pin.

"What happened?" Jane said again and felt foolish for talking to herself. "Where is King Oberon? Queen Titania? How did a human take over the Otherworld?" A few tall, hairy fauns walked among the humans, wearing police uniforms, and gnomes spoke on behalf of their human masters to the vendors.

There were no sidhe to be seen.

"Sir!" Jane called to the nearby faun. "Sir, what has . . ."

The faun glared down at her. "Vampire? Vampires are ba-a-ad news. Git to your people! Don't make me ca-a-all the Riders!"

"Ah, I . . ." Jane drew back. "I have an interview. At the newspaper?"

"Read the signs then!" He pointed and waited, slapped a baton into one furred hand with the other.

Jane turned, saw several posted boards bearing the legend Mercantile Guide. They stank of alchemy to keep them from growing a personality and wandering off. The News-Paper Distribution Centre was two bridges up among a cluster of houses and offices.

"Thank you very much. I've found it," Jane said and hurried past the disagreeable faun. Checking over her shoulder, she saw him standing there, openmouthed.

"Not enough that they've all gone mad." Jane said to herself. "They also think I'm an illiterate lout!"

Jane paid a troll butcher sixpence for a bottle of blood and sucked it down, her stomach finally calming. It was easier to ignore the hunger pangs after the asylum but still a great relief to put blood in her belly.

She went up two more bridges, through a banking district with the legend Otherworld Investments on every window, past what appeared to be a prison and police station, before she found it.

"The Otherworld Voice: The Finest News and Occurrences of Two Worlds, Tokk-a-Lokk, prop." It was painted on the window in gilt lettering. The lettering twitched, and the *E* in *Finest* twisted around, leapt from the window and scurried along the sill like a roach.

Jane took a deep, labored breath. "It doesn't matter what has changed. You can still answer questions." She knocked.

The whole door rattled with a great, booming roar. "Come in!" The words vibrated Jane's feet, made her wonder if the scaffolded bridge she stood on would fall.

Jane swallowed and opened the door. And jumped back into the street.

The editor of the *Otherworld Voice* was a wood troll, big as a train car, rust-colored with spiky skin like some cross of a lizard and a hedgehog. An empty aisle of clerical desks led to his single large desk—well, large if anyone else were sitting in it. He had wedged himself between chair and table and had vainly attempted to put on something like a newspaperman's suit, yards of black wool over a cotton shirt, all shredded by his spikes.

He held a human-printed book, the size like a beetle to a horse. The book's binding bore dozens of tears and scars, apparently from the troll's handling.

"Madness! Drivel!" the wood troll rumbled, and Jane backed up again before she realized he was speaking to the book in his hands. When he spoke, enormous fangs and a green tongue flashed, and the floor shook again. "You foolish old man, can you not see that Heep will ruin you?"

"Hello, sir, I—"

The troll stood up, and the desk clattered violently forward, nearly toppling. He held up the book, waved it at her, the front cover and pages flapping. "Have you read this Dickens?"

"Ah, no, sir. I prefer fiction from Faerie—"

"A factory by all accounts. Sensationalism, sentimentality! Vomiting words onto the page at some meretricious rate!" He threw the book down onto his desk and turned around, running one massive clawed hand across a row of tattered books on his shelf. "The human mind is a peculiar thing, dear. Like their children, they will throw filling fare to the dogs and eat the empty sweets instead. Where is that? Where is it? There it is." He turned around so fast that he bumped the desk and sent it skidding another pace outward. "Thackeray. Blessed Thackeray. Now here is a *writer*!"

"Uh, sir, I came to see if—"

"Listen." He held up a finger twice the size of a sausage roll. "Listen, dear girl, to the most sublime prose in English." He cleared his throat, a sound like ten dogs growling. "*The moral world has no particular objection to vice, but an insuperable repugnance to hearing vice called by its proper name.*" He raised the book in a spiky fist. "Does it not make you cry out to the heavens, 'yes, yes, this is truth!'" Knocking that fist against the joist of the ceiling, he sent a splinter flying.

"Uh . . . Mister . . ."

"Tokk-a-Lokk. Editor of the *Voice*. And you are?" His tone changed. Perhaps he had finally realized a stranger walked in on him.

"Jane. Jane of the Guldenburg School, raised in the human world, and ah . . . sir, I'm seeking work."

"Work?" The troll's tongue flicked out, a massive, green forked thing, tasting the air. "Work. Can you set type?"

"Er, no, but—"

"Have you operated any steam-powered device in the human world?"

"Sir, I am, ah, not unhopeful that I might . . . write. Write stories for your paper." She dug into the back of her dress, yanked out the papers she'd folded up and shoved into her corset. "I wrote this about the mating habits of Scottish dragons. It won an award at Guldenburg, the goblin school."

He took the papers carefully, trying to keep them in his relatively soft palm, though his claw caught the edge of one and ripped it. Spreading out the papers on his desk, Tokk-a-Lokk began to read.

Jane waited, her breath catching in her chest.

"They say it is mad, you know." Tokk-a-Lokk looked up from the page, tongue flicking between those razor teeth again. His breath hit Jane full in the face, bringing tears to her eyes. "That starting a newspaper for the Otherworld is a mad endeavor, but I say that, be that so, then writing is mad, that capitalism is mad, that the hope for a better world is mad. And perhaps we are all mad! Don't you think?"

"I'm not *mad*," Jane snapped.

"Indeed." He peered back at the paper.

Jane couldn't stand this, not any longer. "Sir, do forgive my directness, but what think you of this piece?"

"For what it is, it is very good," Tokk-a-Lokk said, and just as Jane's head went light, he added, "considering it is sensationalism of the first order. Exaggeration in abundance. Oppressed adjectives, slaving away to their unjust masters the adverbs!"

"What?" Jane stammered. "That paper won an award—"

"Frippery!"

This was ridiculous. She snapped off the words she'd practiced. "Sir, I can pass in and out of both worlds without suspicion! I have a dedicated history of writing, an award-winning style, and a hunger for story!" When he opened his enormous, toothy mouth again, she yelled, "I will find the answer to any question! Any question, sir!"

Tokk-a-Lokk tapped a huge black claw against a spike on his chin, not answering.

"I must be paid in human coin, I should add."

He gave her something that she thought might be meant as a grin—a great leering show of teeth. "I will tell you something I did *not* tell the last ten fools who came here with their writing samples. There is a tease of great writing here. A spark that after years becomes the flame. I say to go home and master your pen. Give yourself every day to the muse, and write whatever She puts upon you."

"What?"

He coughed, rattling the floor. "I mean, in the way humans speak of the muse. As Thackeray would say it. If you find a living muse, well, I myself dream of the noble novelist's life—"

"I must answer questions! I must!" That damned asylum, the whole twisted Otherworld, and now this? Her mind raced, all the news of this morning swirling in it. "What about these Ridleys? These werewolves who have taken over the Otherworld? What do you know about them?" Jane seized the papers from his desk. "I'll . . . I'll go seek out an interview with the old Ridley himself or one of his compatriots, and we'll discuss why the Otherworld has become some horrific wasteland as bad as London, and—"

The troll laughed, rattling the floor and bringing tears to Jane's eyes, both from the sentiment and his breath. "The Ridleys? The red-maned wolves of industry? They do not speak to newspaper-men, young lady."

"They will speak to me!" Jane shouted. She slammed the papers down on the table. Let him keep the paper. She would be back for it. "Where do they keep their manor? Here, in this Towering Market? In their factories?"

"They don't dwell in the Otherworld! To human London you must go.

Kensington is their manor if I recall. I sought an invite to their soiree tonight, but as I said, they do not—"

Jane turned and stormed toward the door. Fine. To Kensington. To crash a werewolf's party. "I will bring you a story that will break open the whole Otherworld!"

Chapter Four

In which an Old Friend is Met, our Vampire Bedevils our Gnome, and a Secret is Uncovered

CHARLES SCRUBBED UP AND CHANGED INTO RIORDAN'S SUIT. *IF IT'S A typical swell party, there should be enough people coming and going that I won't lock eyes with old Malcolm Ridley. Gnome god willing.*

And if he did?

Can't turn down the wages either way.

Laying out his torn work clothes, Charles went through the pockets. And found the box. He turned it over in his hands, feeling the fine inlaid design.

"Well, I've a chance to give you back now and be reliable," Charles said. "That ought to make up for lobbing that brick, right, Gnome God?"

Charles could swear the thing grew warm in his hands.

"Charles! Time approaches!"

He also plucked the seven-league boot, now shrunk to palm-size for easy carrying, from his tattered work jacket and tucked it into the pocket of Riordan's jacket, next to the box. Best to leave all his stolen items somewhere that they could be reliably found.

He followed after Riordan who stood in the entryway. Riordan gave Susan a reliable wave and tap on the heart as did Charles, and Riordan nodded to George, now back at his post. "Guard the house well 'gainst all things un-gnomish."

"Take care now," Charles said to his aunt and cousin.

George, still at his post, gave the briefest of nods.

They crossed the Black Fork at one of the vine bridges, leading across to the Under-Market. Walking through the Under-Market, Charles couldn't help a pang of sympathy. The Under-Market had been bustling, the busiest spot in all the Otherworld, two years back.

Now shopfronts were shuttered. Madgekins hawked cheap cheese made of straw and milk melted together. Boggarts sold serums made from bits of alchemical potions, potions they'd blagged off the vats at factories. These were the sort of serums that might cure your hair loss by melting your head.

All the respectable patrons had gone up to the Ridleys' new Towering Market or been driven out of business by that place. There'd been a time when the Under-Market was the busiest place in all the Otherworld.

Riordan headed for the stairs to the Towering Market. "We'll be going through a new door then?" Charles asked.

"The law is the refuge of the reliable," Riordan quoted. "The old doors have been declared a nuisance, and I have a pass to take us through a Ridley door."

"Right. The law." Human-made law for Otherworld creatures, but Charles didn't say that.

These stairs took them up the side of an Old Tower, right to one of the new Ridley doors between the Otherworld and the human world. Once there, the iron doorkeeper wheezed and groaned green steam at them, but after taking the pass in its massive metal claw, it wheezed, "Authorization granted."

Charles didn't like the way the doorkeeper leered at them. Those inhuman gas lamps gleamed, and the metal jaws ground their iron teeth back and forth. It was all made to tear apart Otherworld creatures. The doorkeepers were of the same make as the Iron Riders who would have minced Charles proper today if he hadn't gotten that seven-league boot on.

The new door whistled, steamed green, and flew open, revealing a muddy stretch of riverbank outside London. Charles and Riordan stepped through.

For a moment, they were caught in a scream like a thousand sobbing children mixed with a thousand roaring trains, their ears afire—

They passed through into the human world. All around them stretched a gray expanse of brown water, reeds and smoky sky, the fens west of London.

For a fey being, it was always like going underwater. Charles's hearing grew dull, and the whole world washed out, all the grayer after the brighter, warmer light of the Otherworld.

Riordan put a hand to his head, quavered dizzily. "Your hand please, Charles." Riordan took Charles's proffered hand and stood up straight, holding his head.

"You all right, Uncle?"

"It is difficult to become adjusted to that. Must be easier for the young." He coughed, shook his head. "Despite the noise, the reliability of the Ridley doors is much to be admired. They always open in the same place in the human world, on the same timetable."

Of course, Riordan would admire that. "How do you suppose the wolves made so many of these doors so damned quickly? Been a year now, and the old doors near all shuttered"—*save Pedge's, but Riordan needn't know that*—"and the only passage is through a metal man at a Ridley door."

"No one knows how they've done so. Might as well ask why the Ridleys can transform into wolves whenever they wish instead of waiting on the full moon. Or when Puck and his masters, Oberon and Titania, will return to restore the Otherworld to glory."

Charles snorted. "Sound like a preacher, Uncle."

"Godliness in a gnome will shine through in his conduct, not only his verbiage. Come, Elmont will be just up the road," Riordan said, and hitching up their pants, the two gnomes clambered up a culvert, stepping between ashy, soupy mud on clumps of grass, and onto a road.

A carriage waited there, driven by another gnome of Riordan's age, the knots and gnarled features of his face carved deep. The other gnome let out a dignified smile at the sight of Riordan and Charles and came forward at a steady but vigorous pace.

"Elmont!" Riordan seized the fellow gnome's arm, pumped it in an exacting handshake. Elmont was the driver for the Ridleys and a friend to Riordan since childhood. "Let the memory of a boon companion keep the gnome steady."

Elmont quoted, "A friend's presence is a balm comparable to prayer."

Riordan laughed and quoted back, "A gnome without companions is a shorn stump indeed."

"A fellow gnome's words strike the heart when any others' may fall deaf."

"The elder statesgnome's advice is the map to a pleasing life."

Elmont frowned and, after creasing his brow, quoted, "No gnome gains respect by fashions."

Riordan was puzzling over a reply when Elmont said, "This must be your nephew Charles."

"Reliably good to meet you, sir," Charles said, shaking Elmont's hand.

"Riordan has often spoken of your verve and potential for wisdom," Elmont said.

"Oh, he has?" Charles stuttered. "He, ah, must be telling tales."

"Charles," Riordan said. "A gnome's compliments are not lightly given and should not be lightly received."

"Shall we go? You are the last to arrive," Elmont said. "Punctuality is—"

"The glorious sheen of reliability indeed," Riordan said. "Let us go."

They clambered into the carriage next to a half-dozen other gnomes wedged together and respectfully nodding to one another. Charles shifted to keep the box in his pocket from pressing up against Riordan.

Riordan muttered, "He always has to have the last word that Elmont."

"What's this now? I thought you two were friends."

"We are. The greatest mark of friendship is silent ignorance of a gnome's flaws."

Charles laughed. "That was hardly silent!"

That proved to be a fool comment as Riordan didn't speak for the rest of the trip.

Charles watched the human world pass outside their window as they drew up into the suburbs of London. They went from bleak moors, where boys sifted through garbage heaps looking for rag and bone to sell, to lawns and wrought-iron gates and stone walls to gleaming gas lamps lighting up the dim, foggy air, thick with the smell of gas and coal. Not so different than the pass between the Under-Market and the Towering Market. The poor and the wealthy, living right on top of each other.

He couldn't help thinking of how that brick had felt in his hand today.

It shouldn't have felt so damnably good.

Ridley Manor looked none too different outside from the others: a high stone wall and massive wrought-iron gates. If a few faerie lights drifted above the roof, well, the neighbors might think they were seeing sparks thrown off a bonfire. Few enough humans had ever accessed the Otherworld throughout history; the Ridleys' inner circle that bought all the goods Charles and others had slaved over was still a small fraction of humans.

But who could say? They'd brought quite a circle of humans in on the secret, hundreds, maybe thousands. Might be the Ridleys were going to trumpet their secret to all the world one of these days. It wasn't as if any creature in the Otherworld could stop such a thing.

They filed in through the stable entrance, toward the back stairs and down into the basement. Below-stairs, the whole Ridley Manor was aflutter with gnomes, living up to their servile reputations. Several venerable gnomes in butler outfits directed others, passing in and out of the kitchens. Platters of roast pheasant, chicken, and boar rushed out of the kitchen with intoxicating smells. Charles and Riordan donned the frocks meant for all servants this evening.

Twelve gnomes groaned as they maneuvered a massive platter through the kitchen doors. On it, a great white elf-elk, purple antlers rising high, crouched as though still alive. Cooked whole.

But Charles's eyes went to the platter following it, a less massive platter that only needed five gnomes to carry it. The platter was spread with a hundred different sorts of cheese: hard cheese with ash rind, soft buttery mounds of crumbling Greek cheese, and—

"Charles!" Riordan snapped.

He forced his gaze onto Riordan, away from the platter. "Sorry, Uncle. Won't happen again."

"We're to refill wine. Fetch a platter of cups and make your rounds of the party. Do not speak under any terms. Merely take the empty cups and provide them with new cups. Clear?"

"As the Fountain of Youth, Uncle." Charles walked into the kitchen and, with Riordan, took a platter of wine glasses swirling with the gold-purple streaks of sidhe wine and started for the stairs.

He walked quickly, reliably, balancing the platter perfectly.

Out in the ballroom, folks—humans all—danced to the music of goblin musicians who sat playing strange, whirling gold instruments in a corner. Charles walked among the guests congregating at the edges of the dance floor, dodging massive skirts and flailing tails from the suits. Folks took full goblets from his platter and replaced them with empty cups without a word to Charles.

Charles focused on keeping his face as composed and reliable as anyone ever had.

Blooming Puck, I think I'm being reliable.

He went back for another platter, and this time moved out onto the wide, stone veranda, lit by cheery green alchemical fires, where folk had congregated under the trees, looking out on the vast gardens of the Ridleys. The evening breeze stirred Charles's hair, and laughter floated up from the lawn.

He recognized the game of elfstones: swooping stones, floating in the air, and the rich folks chasing them with nets. Charles had worked at an elfstone factory last year. He'd dipped the stones in vats hissing with alchemical potions. A poor boggart had fallen into one of those vats once and burned all his skin off.

Charles circled the edges of a wide crowd, even better dressed than the others, pearls and lace gleaming in patterns along the massive skirts, and caught snatches of conversation.

". . . the trouble we have with these lower races! The badgebears don't like the madgekins who don't like the boggarts who don't like the redcaps—it was pandemonium in those workhouses, sheer pandemonium. The whole thing is solved now very neatly with this arrangement we've made with the vampires." The speaker darted between a couple of women in wide dresses like bells, said, "Excuse me, ladies," and plucked a wine glass from Charles's platter. "Just stay there, little fellow," he said. "Till we're well and drunk and can't see a hole through a ladder!" The man raised a toast. "England. And Ridley!"

The crowd roared and toasted back.

"So, John, this whole business today, that was part of your plan?" asked an older, white-haired woman.

"I won't say I anticipated everything, Elizabeth." The speaker laughed merrily, and Charles chanced a quick look without moving his head. The speaker bore a head of bright red hair and a thick mustache. A young man, old enough to be wed, but Charles knew he was not. *John.*

This must have been John Ridley. The Red Prince, they called him. Old Malcolm's son and heir to the whole empire, all the factories and the doors into the Otherworld and the money they sucked up from the lower classes.

"We always knew there would be disputes."

Charles knew that voice as well. He froze, rooted to the spot. *Puck's chumpy tricks.*

Malcolm Ridley, the old wolf himself, looking none the worse for wear given he'd been at the center of a riot a few hours back, strode through the crowd, and plucked a cup of wine off Charles's platter.

The old man never glanced at Charles.

Charles's breath rattled in his lungs like a wind vane in a storm.

Malcolm Ridley took a deep draught of wine and stood next to his son. "The vampires were a scourge. Despite the regulation of the doors, they found ways into the human world, and we continually hear tell of children disappearing, of savage murder in the streets of London that could only be the deeds of vampires. Now their clan heads have agreed to cease such things for patented Ridley New Blood."

"I hear the whole of Otherworld is aflutter, John," said a young lady. "An uproar over being sacked!"

"That's exaggeration," John Ridley said. "Most were reassigned or will be. Those who caused trouble are now safely in prison and workhouse, thanks to the Iron Riders."

"To the Riders! Swift enforcers of justice."

Another cheer and round of drinking.

Charles had to swallow the word *bollocks*. His hands hurt from keeping them flat and upturned, holding the platter instead of making a couple of fists. *I will keep reliable, I will!*

"I haven't heard a thing about the ingredients in this new blood, John!" another fellow called.

"Don't crucify me because I won't reveal a business secret, Gregory!" the younger Ridley said.

They all laughed as if it were a great joke, the crowd congregated around old and young Ridley.

Charles moved on when it seemed everyone had refreshed their wine, and giving one surreptitious look back at Malcolm Ridley, sighed with relief. The gnome god had surely blessed him back there. *Must be showing some signs of reliability, right?*

"Excuse me! You there! Little fellow! From this morning?"

Charles whirled around, but he didn't see anything. From this morning? Had someone recognized him from the riot after all?

"Down here!"

The voice was coming from below the veranda. Charles peered down.

There in the bushes, her hair a mess of twigs, dressed in a fusty dress at least five years out of fashion, was the mad vampire girl who'd leapt through Pedge's door.

Charles was too shocked to speak.

"Hello! It is you. I thought so! Give me a hand if you'd be so kind."

Charles backed up. He could hardly look reliable talking to a slum like this, but throwing her out by her scruff wouldn't look near reliable either . . . Riordan would . . . *oh, hell, what would Uncle do?*

It was too late. The mad girl clambered up to the railing, peered around, and as everyone in the crowd was entranced by Malcolm and John Ridley, she was able to slip over the side, stand up, and brush herself off. "That'll be all right," she muttered. "I look just fine, don't you think? Wish I'd had time to wash, but if wishes were fishes . . . oh, I've quite forgotten the rest of that saying."

Charles turned and began walking, but she came right up to his side, snatched a cup of wine from his platter, and said, "Reliably good to see you again, as your people say. I've come here investigating these Ridleys. A story for the newspaper, which I thank you greatly for directing me toward. Point me in the direction of a Ridley please, little fellow?"

Charles tried to keep walking, but the damned girl put a hand on his shoulder, rooted him to the place. *Bloody suckabucket wench, get that blooming hand off my shoulder—*

"Excuse me?"

Two women in massive dresses, gleaming with inlaid pearls and diamonds, their hair in towering curls, walked toward Charles and the mad vampire.

One of the women, Charles noticed, bore red hair much like Malcolm and John Ridley.

That'd be Beverly Ridley, twin sister of John, daughter of old Malcolm. Blooming hell, he had all three parts of the devil's trinity nearby.

"Miss, who are you, and why are you bothering the help?"

"Terribly sorry!" The mad girl snatched up two wine cups from Charles's platter, lifted one to her lips, and offered the other to the red-haired women. "I am, ah, Jane of, ah, Madmabia. A princess, though the castle's a terribly drafty and fussy place, so you'll understand when I say we stay in Shoreditch. My father is a king among vampires in our old country." As she spoke, she shifted into something that might have been an attempt at a Prussian accent, though it sounded closer to a drunken centaur. "So nice of you to invite me."

"Who invited you?"

"Why . . . Malcolm Ridley. I'm a vampire princess after all."

Beverly Ridley's green eyes narrowed. "My father invited you."

"Oh, you are a Ridley as well?"

Her companion, a blonde woman who appeared to be far drunker, laughed.

"Of course, you silly girl! You don't know the Red Princess herself? You must be mad!"

"I'm not mad!" The vampire girl snapped—then returned to her fake accent. "I am so sorry. I did not mean to show a temper. Here. Let us all drink to the ingenuity of the Ridleys, makers of doors and factories and . . . changers . . . of the Otherworld."

The blonde woman, already drunk, toasted and drank deep. The mad girl—Jane, she'd said, and Charles would reckon that really was her name as all her other lies had been proper fimble-famble—lifted the cup to her lips, making a motion of drinking but not imbibing.

Beverly Ridley clutched the goblet and glared.

"Amazing wine!" Jane said, leaning into the accent and sounding now like a high-pitched puppet show. "A rich vintage!"

Beverly Ridley said, "My father and brother have never dealt with vampiric royalty. Only clan heads. And we have had many dealings with vampires recently."

"Ah, yes, clan heads are what we call them now. It's a new term, for in England, all vampires are equal before God, are they not?"

"Vampires don't speak of God. They're children of the devil and proud of it." Beverly Ridley's lip twitched, reminding Charles of a dog, snapping at the gate.

"Yes," the girl Jane choked. "The devil. One gets confused, you know, devils and gods. Well. Tell me then, as you are so close to your father and brother, are the rumors true? Have the Ridley men had—how shall we say—dalliances?"

"How dare you." Beverly Ridley said, half a growl.

At the same time, her companion laughed drunkenly. "Oh, come now, Beverly! Every werewolf knows about Elizabeth Unsworth. And that succubus's memoirs! You cannot say there was no truth in that. It's in the wolf's nature!"

"I have a mind to show you a wolf's nature right now," Beverly Ridley said.

"Mayhaps some more wine," Jane said and turned rapidly, so rapidly that she upended Charles's platter.

He gaped in horror as it flew out of his hands. Diving, Charles managed to catch four of the empty crystal goblets. A fifth goblet flew high in the air and came down on Charles's head.

It was the last full goblet.

Sidhe wine splattered purple and gold all over Riordan's spare suit, and the goblet crashed to the stone in front of Charles, shattered.

"Oh no!" Jane said. "Poor little fellow! I'm so sorry!"

Charles regarded this mad girl tormenting him, that nervously smiling face, and he couldn't help it. The words came rushing out of his mouth, "Suckabucket, just call me a little fellow again and—"

He cut himself off. The Ridley woman and her compatriot stared in horror, both at Jane and Charles.

Charles turned around, snatched up the platter, and ran for the stairs.

He clambered downstairs, past other gnomes, all staring in horror at him, bolted into the servants' room, laid down the platter and the goblets he'd managed to save, shoved his face into the wood of the table and roared, "Puck's balls!"

Riordan's nice suit was now ruined. And Charles looked more unreliable than if he'd planned it. "Witchsoap'll get this lush out."

Elmont would know where that was. As the Ridleys' driver, he'd have cleaned hay and horse dung from any number of suits.

Charles emerged from the servants' back stairs into the darkened yard. To stay out of sight, he walked along the line of the hedge below the house. And heard Riordan's voice.

Charles reversed direction, ducking behind the hedge.

"Come now, Elmont," Riordan said with an audible groan. "Give us a hand with this wine barrel, as the reliable do?" Riordan grunted, and Charles peered around the bush to see his uncle and another one of the gnomes in the servant frocks, struggling under the weight of a great barrel.

Charles turned and ran back downstairs. Riordan was on his heels. Oh, Puck's tricks played right on Charles, kicking him proper in his gnarled buttocks—Charles glanced up right in time to avoid running into a woman. "Miss, I—" He skidded to a halt.

It was *her*.

"You! You glocky suckabucket wench, causing all this trouble?" Charles fumed. "What are you doing downstairs?"

"I'm sorry," Jane said, "I'm very sorry, little fellow. I didn't mean to spill on you. It's just . . . it's been a day. Truly. I just thought there might be a way down here into a different portion of the house. Mayhaps the bedrooms. I'm investigating something for the newspaper, you see."

"Get. Bloody. Out."

"No need to be impolite, good sir."

"Out now, before I call the wolves!" Charles pointed.

Jane's voice went high and shrill, sounding more than a bit mad. "I can't leave! I have to find a story!"

"Go!" Charles threw decorum to the wind and seized her by the sleeve, yanking her along the hallway.

"Ow! Stop it. Let go. How is such a little fellow so strong?"

He yanked her, but she had the advantage in height and pulled him backward. She stumbled against the wall, and her hand flew up and hit the corner bunting at head height. It swung upward as though it was meant to, and the wall swung open behind her, a door just big enough for a person.

For half a second, they both just stood there, and then Jane darted away from Charles and into the secret passage.

"Get out of there!" Charles stopped at the edge of the passageway. "Out, yeh chumpy, daft blower! You—"

Riordan's voice carried down the stairs, distinctly calling, "A bit further now. There's a reliable fellow. All right, I've gotten stuck on this step—just a tick. There we go."

Uncle was nearly to him.

Charles ducked into the passageway, closed the secret pivoting door in the wall, and ran after Jane into the depths of the Ridleys' manor.

Chapter Five

In which, after a Revelation of Important Events, a Great Horror is Overheard, and our Gnome and Vampire are Caught in a Great Tumult

JANE, HER LEGS WORN AND STRETCHED FROM WALKING ALL OVER LONDON, stood just inside the gate of Ridley Manor under the eyes of a venerable old gnome.

The gnome, his face a mask of dour service, eyed Jane in her out-of-fashion dress and muddy boots and said, "Invitation, please."

"I fear I've lost it," Jane said, "but I am invited—vampiric royalty. I . . ."

The gnome gestured to two enormous stone trolls at the side of the gatehouse.

Jane quite suddenly found herself back in the street.

She kicked a clod of mud in frustration, sent it flying till it spattered on a gas-lamp pole. "Well, there are other ways in."

She'd gotten back to human London through one of those metal doors by posing as a choleric girl, and she'd snuck out in her best dress while her mother was off at Bible study, and she'd walked all the way to Kensington; she would not stop now.

Peering around to make sure she was unobserved, Jane approached one of the walls, slipped past the hedge, and put her hands to the stone to climb over it. And promptly yanked her hands back. "Providence!"

Her hands burned as though she'd pressed them to a hot stove. Some alchemical substance had been woven in this stone to keep Otherworld creatures from climbing it.

"Always having trouble with doors then?"

Inside the hedge, a few paces from her, a fellow stood. She could make out few details of him. Only a green suit and hair like flame.

"You?" Jane asked. "Sir, I believe we met earlier—"

"So much trouble with doors. I, on the other hand, have never had trouble passing between places. Yet you are like me, a wild thing like the wind, always moving upon the worlds."

The wall groaned and opened up, like a great smiling maw, to show the long dark lawn of the Ridley Manor.

"Why, sir, I—" Jane turned back to the gentleman and stammered. "Did you do this? Can you open any such door? I-I work for the *Otherworld Voice* and am seeking—"

"Go to the party. Enjoy yourself. I have an agreement with the wolves, but it pleases me to make a jest of them. "

Jane didn't need a second prompting.

The passageway sloped down. The rocky dirt caught at her sore feet. Behind her, she heard the gnome. "You chumpy bird, get back here!"

Jane ran along the passage, stone floor and wooden walls. This was one of those passageways from stories, the sort where the wealthy went for secret rendezvous.

"A sexual indiscretion is always good to sell papers, no doubt," Jane muttered to herself and bit her lip. She really needed to stop doing that if she was going to be taken seriously as someone not mad. "Or perhaps another secret vice—an uncontrollable opium habit?"

There she went again.

A crack of light showed through the wall up ahead on her left. Beyond it, the stone floor was piled

Murgalak's Fun Human Facts

Many humans rather like the idea of becoming werewolves. They will stalk the great wolves on the moors, offering themselves up for a tasty bite.

Most are eaten whole. Werewolves rarely turn other humans and hate to waste meat.

with dirt—an area under the foundation of the house. This must have been the end of the tunnel. Jane ran up next to the area, pressed against the wood, and felt it shift, just a bit. She pushed harder, throwing her shoulder into it.

"Oy! Get back here!"

The gnome was at her very heels. Jane squeezed through into a bare room lit by a single candle to reveal a bed and a ladies' toilet table on which rested a basin of water, a mirror, and tins of cream and tinctures. She turned around to shut the wall door on the gnome, but he pounded the section of wall, throwing her back against the bed.

His face fumed with fury she'd never seen on a gnome. "Chumpy blower! Look what you've done to me dunnage!" He motioned to his suit, swirled with the incandescent gold-and-purple of sidhe wine. "You're answering to Ridley if I have to drag you out!"

"No, please—" Jane kicked him and immediately regretted it. It was like kicking a knotty oak stump.

He yanked her by the dress and pulled her back toward the door. The old dress loudly tore, exposing her petticoats, and the gnome was left standing with a quarter-yard of pleated linen in his hands.

Jane clambered under the bed. It was the least dignified thing to do, but he'd have a harder time getting her out. "Go on! I'm not leaving!" she said. "It'd be indecent to see me now!"

"I'll pull you out by your ankle if I must, yeh glocky—" He ran around the bed and grabbed her shoe, but this time Jane held tight to the frame of the bed and—

Voices echoed down the tunnel.

"Quicker. Move! You've caused a stir already. In here!"

The voice had a strange effect on the gnome who, instead of yanking Jane out from under the bed any further, let go of her leg and—oh dear, that was terrible—he clambered under the bed with her! She shifted away from him; he was pressed up against her in quite a scandalous way. "What are you—"

"Quiet!"

"This is indecent—"

A knotty, hard-as-oak hand clapped over her mouth. Jane bit down and once again regretted it; even her sharp teeth rebounded from the hard surface. "That'll teach yeh," the gnome muttered and kept his filthy hand there. Jane couldn't maneuver into the right position to yank it away.

Footsteps clattered into the room, but she saw no boots, but then something swirled, an incandescent blue, revealing three sets of boots. Invisibility cloak. Of course. They were mass-produced now, no doubt, in those same factories Jane had seen earlier.

"The door's open."

"Beverly was in here earlier. She should know better." A man spoke. An older man by his cold, seasoned voice. "Why did you fail in your delivery?"

"I don't know what happened, sir—" a younger man said, apologetic and scattered. "I just . . . I was accosted in that riot by a hysterical wood nymph, and when I checked my pockets afterward—"

"He's useless, Father," said another voice, more robust, again without the rattle of age. A third man.

"So he is, John," said the older man's voice.

The gnome's hand twitched on her face.

"Now, John, Malcolm, I apologize dreadfully, but if we return to the area with the services of an excellent tracker, equipped to smell out such things, we will surely find it. The whole area is a wreck after the rioting. The object will have been quite overlooked, I think."

John? Malcolm? Jane's mind raced. Of the three men, two were named John and Malcolm and Malcolm the older man. Was she really hearing a conversation between the Ridleys?

And another fellow, a sort of failed messenger. Who lost something. A wood nymph had been involved. Interesting. A story for sure that might even impress that conceited troll.

For some reason, the gnome's hand shook.

"Let me tell you," said Malcolm Ridley, "something of stewardship. Providence has given man the stewardship of the animals, the Englishman the stewardship of the lesser races, and the Ridleys alone the stewardship of the fey creatures. We must honor our stewardship that we might go before God with our trust fulfilled. We sought your help for our stewardship in bringing the device from the far regions of the city. You failed."

"I . . . I understand I will not be compensated, and perhaps you will wait to turn me—no . . . wait—"

Clothes tore, and an odor like a great dog filled Jane's nostrils. Shreds of wool and cotton settled to the ground. Leather groaned and split. Great red paws tore through the boots.

The third man, the failed messenger, asked with a note of hope in his voice, "I'm to be turned after all?"

And then the bed rattled; booted feet kicked. Someone clambered over the bed, fell off, and screamed. A horrific rending sound and a vicious stench like an opened carcass.

Blood rushed across the stone floor, coated Jane's dress, ran around her elbows.

They ripped him apart!

She'd never known a man had so much blood in him. Oh, God, oh Providence save, they were tearing apart the man, they were ripping into him like butchers with some animal, they took as much care as dogs with a carcass, oh God, it was—

It was rather pleasant-smelling, all this blood.

Jane's mouth watered at the same time her heart thundered.

Her tongue flicked out, brushed the gnome's hand in an effort to get at the blood. *No!* She forced her tongue back in her mouth. This was ridiculous, entirely improper. *They just killed a man! Quiet and listen!*

Jane forced herself to focus despite the ache in her stomach. The sounds of feeding werewolves came to them; more fluids, stinking bile and urine, much less appetizing than blood, ran across the floor. She just caught a glimpse of the gore—a severed, bloody leg, a half-chewed hand—and two massive, red-furred bodies, snarling and snorting.

The werewolves ate for what felt like an eternity: an age of Jane keeping her tongue in her mouth, away from the blood soaking her, an age of the gnome's hand shaking on her face, and an age of her stomach howling like it was going to leap out of her throat.

Eventually, the red-furred figures shifted, the fur diminishing as if it were being pulled backward through a comb, and men's legs, white and only dusted with red hair, began to appear.

"I've lost my best suit, Father," the younger man said. "I'll have to have a new one made."

"We've lost far more than that. We are brought to the edge of ruin," said Malcolm Ridley, his steely voice carrying a deeper note as if he had taken more of the wolf back from the transformation. "That device was my sole hope for advantage over . . . you know well whom."

"God help the Otherworld. I'll tear it to pieces to find that box."

That *box* must have been the thing the messenger lost. Interesting.

"You smell something off in here?" the older man asked.

Jane's spine stiffened, ran cold.

"I thought that I had smelled something that could not have come from our meal."

John Ridley took a deep sniff and said, "Naught but this fool's guts far as I can tell. Come on, Father, we'll have it cleaned later. Let's find new clothes and return to the party."

"You settle the party. I'm headed immediately to the Otherworld. I'll expect this clean by morning. Do it yourself. Don't even trust the gnomes with this."

"The gnomes won't say a word."

Malcolm Ridley's voice rumbled with the deep growl of the wolf. "Clean it yourself! Any of the help find out, John, and I'll eat them! You're lucky I keep my stewardship well, son, or I might eat you."

John Ridley's voice trembled as he answered, "Yes, Father."

They swept the invisibility cloak over themselves, hiding their legs from Jane's view, and left the room.

After an eternity, Jane scuttled out from under the bed, and she winced, turning away from the sight. The dead man's blood still smelled enticing, but the body, torn and savaged from neck to crotch, was a horrific thing to behold. "They truly gutted the poor fellow," Jane said to the gnome who had now clambered out from the other side of the bed. "So there is an object, and this fellow lost it, and it's to aid the Ridleys in gaining an advantage over some other fellow and—can't exactly tell everything we saw here today without a great deal of risk, can we?"

The gnome didn't answer. His little black eyes had gone wide, and his mouth hung open. He shoved a hand in his pocket and seemed as though he had been struck.

"Little fellow?" Jane asked.

The gnome ran from the room into the tunnel, back toward the servants' quarters.

"He knows more than he's letting on." Jane couldn't say if that was journalistic instinct, but it wasn't madness.

She bolted after him.

Chapter Six

In which a Heart-Rending Insult is Given, Mysteries Deepen, and Death Takes a Hand

CHARLES DIDN'T BOTHER LOOKING BACK AT THE MAD VAMPIRE, DIDN'T bother looking at the ground, but ran up the secret passageway, across the uneven, rough stone, pushed on the section of wall, and clambered out into the servants' hallway, past a number of gnomes on the steps to the second floor, all of whom turned and stared. He didn't hear what they said. The blood and wine made him sticky and flushed worse than he already was.

He clambered into the hallway of the Ridleys' manor.

Down the hall, an end table waited, covered with carved wooden tigers from India. Charles ran to the end table, pulled the box from his pocket, and slammed it down, throwing the Indian tigers to the ground. He stepped away.

The carved metal shone in the faint gaslight of the hallway as if it were just another knickknack.

The man ate a fellow. Over . . . that box. The box he'd carried around all day!

Out of his hands now and back in the wolves'.

Charles turned and bolted back down the hallway toward the servants' entrance. He reached the top of the stairs, looked behind him to confirm that the box was still on the table, and turned around—

Uncle stood not three paces away.

Riordan was still immaculately dressed although for some reason he held, not a platter, but a single clay pitcher of wine. His eyes were wide. "Charles? Whatever is going on? What has happened to my suit? Charles!"

Charles couldn't even find anything close to the words for his day. *I nearly got et.* That wouldn't do.

"This is wine and"—Riordan's face furrowed—"blood?"

Charles found his voice. "Wine, oy. Drunk girl. Spilled all over me before I could say boo."

"But the blood, Charles. Where did all this blood come from?"

"Excuse me?"

Oh, by all the spirits of Hades. The vampire girl—Jane—had followed him up the stairs. She stood in the stairwell, her own dress sodden with blood.

Riordan caught a glimpse of her. "Miss, this is quite improper. If you are a party guest, I will show you to the floor."

"I only sought to speak with this little fellow, and—"

Charles stormed toward Jane. "Bugger off right now! I en't got cause to speak with you or any of your sort, and I'll find the trolls to crush you if you don't—"

Another voice. "What is this?"

Charles turned around, leaned past the top of the stairwell to catch a glimpse of the source of the voice, and near let go his bladder.

John Ridley, the younger of the two men he'd just heard do a murder, walked down the hall in a fresh suit, his face bearing signs of being hastily scrubbed. There was still blood in his mustache, little bits of dark red dripping from the orange-red hairs onto his white shirt collar.

Charles darted farther into the stairwell, tumbled down two stairs, and Jane caught him, kept him from falling any farther. She pressed him against the wall next to her, inside the lip of the wall that kept the side of the stairwell out of sight.

Charles nearly kept running, but then he saw Riordan, waiting obediently in the hall to speak to the werewolf.

No, Uncle, get away! He couldn't speak.

"I pop into my chambers, out of sight for barely five minutes, and I come back to gnome layabouts?" the younger Ridley said. "The others should have kept you new help in hand!"

John Ridley seemed content to lay into the only gnome in his way, which was Riordan. He didn't even glance at the stairwell.

"Wine in a clay pitcher? Standing about in the hallway? What has happened to you gnomes? Utter shame!" John Ridley paused, and then said to Riordan, "Before God, you must be the most unreliable gnome I've ever seen."

Riordan's whole frame shivered, and Charles, with everything, still nearly forgot himself to say, *you bastard swell!*

John Ridley's hand came into view, snatched the pitcher from Riordan's hands. "I can thank you for that at least." He sucked down the pitcher of wine, gulping like a thirsty dog.

Riordan didn't move. From his face, he could have been stabbed in the gut.

John Ridley stalked down the hall, away, roaring at every servant in his way.

When Charles was sure the werewolf had vanished down the hall, he crept up the stairs. Riordan stood at the top of the stairs still, hand trembling on the now-empty pitcher.

"Oy, Uncle Riordan, come on now. Don't pay it no mind. He's out for blood. And a swell to boot."

Enormous tears welled up at the wrinkled edges of Riordan's eyes.

"He called me un-un—"

"Shh, shh, no call to repeat an obscenity, Uncle."

The mad vampire bird, Jane, left the stairwell, came to stand by Riordan, and Charles was too distracted to tell her to bugger off. "Your form as a butler was excellent, sir, and I believe your service was reliable as Gibraltar. That fellow was merely in great distemper."

Riordan raised an angry eyebrow to the mad girl. "Charles," he coughed, "perhaps we should go if this is what comes of the night."

"No, Uncle, no!" Charles gestured to the gnomes still rushing around them, reliably serving. "You keep on serving; I'll find Elmont and get cleaned up. And you—" Charles glared at the vampire girl. "Cut your stick! Blag off! Right this minute!"

"I thought we might exchange notes, little fellow, on what we heard—"

Charles was proud of himself, even at his height of unreliability, that he didn't knock her down the blooming stairs, only turned his back and walked Riordan out toward the ballroom. "Forget what that swell said. There's bound to be some cups to gather up out there, and you'll go back to work while I get myself clean—"

"No, Charles." Riordan sighed. "The Ridleys are known to eat disobedient servants. Let's go."

"They won't eat you. All gnomes look the same to these swells."

Riordan pushed Charles's arm away. "Come with me, stay and be eaten, or go to the ends of the earth. I no longer care." He walked away. Instead of walking out toward the ballroom, he turned just before the main servants' entrance and walked along a hallway toward a side entrance.

"Puck's three balls on a pike," Charles cursed.

"Little fellow?"

Charles turned around and raised a finger to Jane. "Don't you come near me again now!"

"What do you suppose they spoke of down there when they—"

"I mean it! You're mad as the sea is deep!" Charles stalked away after Riordan, shaking with fury, not hearing if the girl called after him. Let the blower blow; he cared no more. Charles caught up with Riordan, now walking out the servant's door. They scuttled down a staircase and went around the side of the veranda.

Riordan appeared to be heading for a different exit than where they'd come in, walking through the long hedges of the backyard, perhaps for the gardener's entrance in the rear gates. Which meant Elmont wouldn't be driving them either. It'd be a long walk home then, all through London to get back to the door they'd come through.

Charles couldn't help it; he opened his mouth, about to say, *Uncle, it weren't me, and I swear it by all that's reliable! That vampire girl caused all the fuss.* He'd done so well for a few moments there.

A terrible scream rang through the yard.

Charles turned around.

The crowd on the veranda parted for a running figure, a man who reached the edge and doubled over, clutched the very railing Jane had crawled over just a few moments ago.

Even from here, Charles recognized young John Ridley.

The Red Prince's skin gleamed, a sheen of sweat in the enchanted torchlight. He pressed his belly to the stone railing, put a hand to his mouth, and let out a high whine like a kicked dog.

And then he vomited down the side of the veranda. All the gore and guts he'd consumed as a wolf, not half the hour back, came up, and Charles was glad he stood too far off to make out the details.

"Serves yeh right, yeh bastard," Charles muttered. "Eating a poor fellow."

But John Ridley kept vomiting.

Charles had never seen a man vomit so prodigiously, endless rounds of gagging and hurling until he was heaving and croaking and clutching his throat, and he reared up and tried to speak, but now he was gasping as if for air, and he fell backward onto the stone of the veranda.

The crowd closed in around him. Screams and cries of "Murder!" echoed in the air. And then, "Poison!"

Riordan didn't move.

"Uncle, let's go," Charles said. *Looks like that fellow they ate wasn't quite the meal they expected. Couldn't've happened to a nicer set of werewolves.* "Uncle?"

"Gnomes!" Someone else shouted. "Get the gnomes!"

"A gnome must have served him!" came a voice out of the crowd. "Get all the help up here, pinned in the ballroom! We'll need to question them all!"

Riordan took a deep breath and started back toward the veranda.

"Uncle! What are you doing? Uncle, turn around! You don't need to—"

"Charles, the law is the refuge of the reliable. You go. Tell Susan I'll be home anon, soon as this matter is straightened out."

"No, Uncle!" Charles ran around Riordan's other side, stood in his way, held hands up. "No! You don't need to talk to the wolves! They'll be out for blood! They'll eat you alive like you said!"

Riordan didn't answer but walked right up to Charles.

"I en't letting you—"

With an astonishing amount of strength, Riordan shoved Charles to the ground.

"Go, Charles!" he spat.

Charles fell to the ground and scrambled back up, looking after his uncle who had emerged into the light at the edge of the veranda and now approached the stone steps. Some of the swells and ladies saw Riordan approaching. They ran down, seized him by the arms, and lifted him off the grass, carrying him up the stone steps.

Charles couldn't help himself. He ran back toward the veranda. Running, running, not looking, and collided right with another gnome carrying a cheese platter.

Charles tumbled to the ground and stood up. He was all-over splattered with cheese. Soft and hard, Greek and English, enough cheese to get a full year's wages from Pedge.

More humans pointed down on him from the veranda. "That gnome's trying to filch cheese! That must be the one!"

Charles ran back toward the hedge—*but Uncle!*—and damn it, he turned back around, ducking under a carefully trimmed bush. He stuck a hand in his pocket.

There was the seven-league boot. If he just snatched his uncle, they could get well across London before they—

Hang on a tick.

There was something else in Charles's pocket, next to the boot. His fingers closed around a familiar boxy shape.

Charles shrunk, groaning. "Oh, thirteen hells. Oh, Puck. Oh, no, I know I put you on that table!"

At least he could trade for Riordan. Charles heard a growl, turned.

Where there had been folk on the lawn, there were now three wolves big as ponies. Their backs hunched up like bison, and their manes were thick and black, their snouts enormous, dripping with slaver, and their red eyes gleamed.

Their jaws were the size of steam presses, big enough to snap even a gnome in half.

Almost everyone was shouting "Gnomes! Gnomes! Round them up in the hall!"

He moved without thinking. Ran, and while he ran, shook out the seven-league boot from his other pocket. Hot, stinking wolf breath reached the back of his neck. Charles leapt into the boot and yelled, "Away!"

The boot soared up into the London sky, carrying Charles away from the party, away from werewolves, away from the mad vampire Jane, and away from his uncle.

But not, as his hand gripped the thing inexplicably back in his pocket, away from the box that had gotten a man killed tonight.

Chapter Seven

*In which our Vampire Achieves the
First of her Many Goals and is Much
Complicated in Other Endeavors*

JANE RAN ALONG THE BRIDGES OF THE TOWERING MARKET, THE PAPERS
clutched in her hand. The hot wind off the river below brought tears to her
eyes with its alchemical stink, but she did not stop. Her whole body ached,
exhausted from two full nights without sleep, but on she ran through shopfronts
just beginning to roll out, past sleepy fauns grumbling "maa-aa-ad girl," and
she didn't even stop to correct them.

She thudded into the door of the *Otherworld Voice* and caught herself on the
knob. "Mister a-Lokk?"

The door vibrated, rumbling along with the inhabitant inside. Tokk-a-Lokk
was in there, speaking to himself. Pacing as well by the way the ground shook.
His voice rumbled through the door. "He walked—no. He *descended*—yes—
descended the foul street, his soul a twisted mire—no. A *loathful* mire, full of
agony. No, not agony. *Entropy!* Yes! A loathful mire of entropy! Ah, it sings!"

Jane hammered the door, but the old troll kept right on talking to himself. It
was like trying to be heard over braying elephants.

"I don't suppose you're around again?" Jane asked the air.

Her mysterious green-suited benefactor did not answer.

As that strange gnome would have said, "Bugger this." Jane reached into her
bun and yanked out her lockpicks.

She'd taught herself this particular footpad's art within a few weeks of starting at Guldenburg. At the time, she'd anticipated her mother locking her away from the school or locking up her schoolbooks. Jane hadn't imagined her mother would be clever enough to drug her and go through her hair to remove her lockpicks. "But, Mother," Jane said to herself as she set the wrench and fiddled with the rake, "you didn't think I'd keep a backup set, did you? I've outsmarted all of you yet, and this story—"

It only took a matter of minutes, and the troll's proudly human metal lock swung open.

The door opened to reveal Tokk-a-Lokk, pacing the floor, hunched over, it seemed, to avoid taking divots out of the ceiling. "And he pondered—no. He *ruminated*—"

"Mister a-Lokk!"

"You?" The troll growled at her, and the whole floor shook. "You have interrupted the muse! Get out. Get—"

Jane held up the bundle of papers. "Look."

The troll looked her up and down, now noticing her torn, stained clothes. "I . . . see?"

"I went looking for a story, and oh, oh-" She was so excited she could barely speak. "I found one." She shoved the papers into his hands. "A story that will break open the Otherworld as I said."

"You cannot—" He raised one spiky eyebrow at Jane's choice of scrip—the backs of stolen party invitations. They were the same invitations that had convinced those mechanical doorkeepers to let her back into the Otherworld. "You really went to this party?"

"Read!"

He glanced over the first page and growled, "Would you make the great English sentence a trapeze?"

"Keep reading!"

He did so and not ten seconds later let out a startled growl, picked up the papers, scanned rapidly through the rest of the story. "Poisoned? John Ridley poisoned?"

"They're blaming the help. A Welsh gnome in particular, name of Riordan."

Tokk-a-Lokk stood up, now forgetting to hunch, and crashed right into a ceiling joist above him, a joist already splintered. He rubbed his spiky head. "We'll need to start before the press staff come in. Type'll have to be set for an early edition, out to all the Towering Market within the next hour if we can manage it. You can—"

"I'll do whatever's needed, Mister a-Lokk. Once I'm hired."

Tokk-a-Lokk's rumbling groan filled the room. "Yes, yes, I'll pay you for the story."

"Not just the story. I am a full-time employee now. These are my conditions." Jane's blood rushed through her like a raging river, making her feel light. "Fifty pound a year with a bonus to be agreed on for future stories. Permanent employment unless, of course, I am derelict in my duties. Which I will not be."

"Bribery! Extortion! Criminality of the greatest cheek!" He snarled at her but turned back to the story and back to Jane. "You really stole into the Ridleys' party?"

"Yes."

"You can pass as human, despite your clearly vampiric proclivities?"

"Most of them think I'm just a sickly girl."

He tapped one great claw on the desk, sending wood chips flying. "I have several madgekins who bring me gossip, but . . ."

"I am as much at home in London as the City Beyond, sir."

"You can go anywhere in both worlds. And you can—almost—write. Very well. Help me set the type and start the press, and we'll sign these extortionist, barbaric terms. What is your name, girl?"

Jane reached out to shake his hand but fell over the desk. Once on the ground, she realized that she quite couldn't stand. "Oh! Sorry! Sorry, sir, sorry. My name's Jane. Jane of the Guldenburg School, though I was raised in Shoreditch, sir."

"Welcome to the *Otherworld Voice*, Jane."

Jane, now in the back of a cab in human London, pulled the items from her purse. In one hand, a pass, good for a month's worth of travel between the Otherworld and the human world. In the other, five pounds.

Five pounds sterling.

It would cover her tuition at Guldenburg for half a year, allow her to finish her studies.

Murgalak's Fun Human Facts

The human brain is much smaller than a goblin's, so they are naturally held in place by interest in the news. A human (or an aberrant Otherworld creature) can overcome this tendency by having their skull opened up and adding a generous portion of cow brain to their own. Cows, as one might know from observing them, are much more philosophical creatures.

"An investment," Tokk-a-Lokk had said when he gave her the money. He'd held up the day's paper with her freshly printed story "John Ridley Poisoned!" emblazoned across the masthead. "For a story as dashing as this."

"I could look for the missing Puck. And Oberon!" Jane had said, "Or perhaps infiltrate the ranks of footpads, or—"

"I want exactly one story, dear. One."

"Yes. All right. One."

"The Ridleys have, on the same auspicious day that John was poisoned, fired half their staff and replaced them with vampires. Word has it that those vampires are being paid not in guinea nor farthing but in some kind of new blood. You are to discover the ingredients of this concoction and if this new policy has any connection to the death of Ridley."

Jane had nodded and said, "It should be easy enough to infiltrate vampires as I'm half . . . half—" She was so exhausted, she quite lost the thought.

"Go home and rest. Your mind is my greatest investment." He closed her hand over the five-pound note. "For the new blood. And a kinder treatment of the sentence."

Now, as she sat in the back of the cab, she could hardly credit it.

She unfolded the paper and read again. Jane had warred with herself over how much detail to put into the story.

John Ridley's poisoning and the accusation against Riordan were a matter of public record now. The gnomes had all, barring that strange one, lined up reliably and determined that the clay pitcher the young werewolf drank from had been his most recent drink before his untimely end, and though Jane had been in a hurry to sneak away, she'd heard Riordan admit in that familiar tone, "Yes, I gave the master a drink not a few minutes ago."

Her heart panged for the poor fellow Riordan if not his boorish nephew.

But Jane had left the secret chamber, the man's death, the conspiracy among both Ridleys to murder, out of the story. For now.

"Perhaps more," she muttered, "when I know more." Perhaps a follow-up with a gnome. Given what she'd heard under the bed, she might need to follow up with that brutish lout.

"Oy, you heard me?" the cabbie asked. "Where *to*, love? Most folk shout at me from inside the cab!"

Jane blinked and gave the man directions to her mother's house in Shoreditch and, unable to help herself, read through the story again. "I've quite captured the tone of the Ridleys," she muttered, "but oh, I must be more careful with adverbs. Mister a-Lokk is quite right . . ."

"What you reading there, love?" the cabbie asked, his voice coming in the open window. It was another hazy, dung-and-coal smoke day in London, little threatening her with a sunny sky.

"The newspaper! I write for the newspaper, sir, and this is my story. It's the noblest profession of all."

"A writer, eh?" the cabbie asked. "I love Mister Dickens. The wife reads him to me as I can't read myself. We were right old messes at the end of the last one, we were. All tears when David wised up and married Agnes who was so faithful to her father."

Jane imagined Tokk-a-Lokk chasing this fellow down the street, the spiky, towering monster waving about a copy of Thackeray, yelling, *Now this is a writer!* She giggled to herself but then stopped. *Don't sound mad.*

"Five pence that'll be, dearie," the cabbie said as they drew up to the door of the house in Shoreditch. He clambered down and opened the door, revealing a round, ruddy face. "Knocked it down a bit for Mister Dickens's sake—God above!"

"Excuse me, sir?" Jane held up the banknotes from the pocket of the massive coat she'd borrowed from Tokk-a-Lokk. "Can you change one pound, sir—"

"Don't hurt me, marm! I'm a good Christian!" He backed up, past the horse. "Jesus save me! Don't take me children, please! Don't take any more of the little ones!"

"You've seen a vampire before then? They've gone after children?"

He bolted away down the street, leaving both Jane and his horse.

Jane stared after him. The man was the first human to ever react so to her looks. Many commented on her sallow skin and her eyes, but only Otherworlders ever made the connection to vampires. A human doing so . . . that was peculiar.

"I'll need to write it down." Jane started after him, but her feet nearly gave out, and her vision blurred black.

She'd find this fellow again. After she got some sleep. Yes.

She crossed the street to her mother's house, leaving the whickering, annoyed horse and cab.

The door was ajar. Had her mother been expecting company? "Mother?" Jane said. She kept the cloak she'd borrowed from Mister a-Lokk tight around her to keep the sight of a blood-stained, ruined dress from her mother's view.

She stumbled into the main room but realized her mother was talking to someone. A squat fellow in a dingy hat.

"Not enough, oy. Couldn't buy the milltag off me back with this."

"Listen here, sir, if you insist on aggravating a poor woman, perhaps we ought to call the police to mediate this—"

"Go on! Call the bluebottles, and tell them you're down on the hoof a year now, and see whose cause they—"

"Excuse me?" Jane said, walking into the room.

Her mother faced a squat, red-nosed man who immediately brightened up at the sight of Jane. "Oy now! This is the girl? The daft one who's off her chump?"

"I beg your pardon, sir," Jane said. "What are you doing here, intimidating my mother like this?"

"Intimidating?" The fellow laughed. "Woman owes back rent!"

"Rent?" Jane turned toward her mother now. "Mother, you sold the house? We're renting now?"

Jane's mother wrung her hands. "Merely a loan against the house, Jane, to free up a few spare funds."

"Call it what you like, marm, you're behind on the hoof."

Jane stepped forward, right up to the debt collector. "Just try and intimidate me," she said, "after my night. You'll find that quite impossible! How much does Mother owe, you miserable lurker? Five pounds?"

"Ten."

Ten. Jane's heart twisted and sank.

Her hand tightened on the banknote.

I don't need to save Mother. This is all her fault because she put me in the damned asylum. I can take these funds, find lodging nearby or in the Otherworld, and be spared all the trouble of dealing with Mother . . .

She turned her gaze from the blaggard to the woman who'd raised her. Her mother shivered, eyes twitching, just like she had when Jane asked about her father.

A father who, no matter who he was, had not been there for Jane ever, and her mother always had to make do.

Jane raised the banknote and said, "I've got five pounds sterling for you here today, you vile blackguard. Come back in a few months more, and we'll settle up."

"You've got the hoof?" He held out a hand, and Jane, her whole body shaking with fury, pressed the five-pound note into it. He cackled. "We'll settle up right soon, we will. None of this 'months' business. You give me the five now and next week—"

Jane, hardly realizing what she was doing, bared her teeth and hissed.

The man stumbled backward, nearly tripped over her mother's overstuffed chair. "Blooming girl! What's that? Going to blooming eat me?"

"Out," Jane growled.

The fellow stumbled toward the door, grabbed his coat, and went out into the street. He did not, much as Jane wished it, drop the banknote she'd pressed into his hands.

Jane collapsed into the chair. "Mother," she said. "Mother, the house? You had to take a loan out?"

Her mother didn't answer. "Let me light the oven to get you some tea, dear. You look exhausted! I was terribly worried! You've only been back a . . . a . . ."

"A month," Jane said.

"Yes, a month." Her mother said it oddly. The witchwater would be wearing off. Soon enough, she'd need more. In that Towering Market, Jane would bet a small vial of witchwater would fetch more than a few shillings.

"You needn't have dealt with him, dear," her mother said from the other room. "I've got fifty shillings in a jar here. He was just being such a . . . well, it'd be impolite to say."

Jane waved a hand. "It's all right, Mother. I broke a big story. The death of John Ridley." She was so tired, it was hard to talk. "I'll take a few shillings though if you can spare . . ."

"John Ridley? What is this horror?"

"Land magnate. He was poisoned."

"Oh, the Ridleys. Yes, I heard of their strange machines at the exhibition. Mrs. Lowding from the church spoke much of them."

Jane blinked and sat up. "At the exhibition? Mother, what's the exhibition? Why are the Ridleys showing machines there?"

Her mother came back in the room, sooty from lighting the oven. "Oh, dear, I worry it would excite you. And to think, a poisoning—far too troubling. Let's speak of other things like . . . like your job. Wait . . . your job is far too exciting. Why is your job so exciting when you are but back a month?"

"Mother." Jane took her mother's arm. "What are the Ridleys exhibiting?"

"The Great Exhibition. Everything is on display. Goods and machines and all the ingenuity from the Empire and from other lands. The massive Crystal Palace in Hyde Park. All the devil's work of progress, no doubt. Don't you . . . well, perhaps it would be too exciting for you, and that is why you haven't studied it at your paper."

"Hm." Jane sank back into the chair. She wondered why a family that gained all their riches from the Otherworld would need to exhibit at a human trade fair, however grand. Perhaps it was connected to the vampires. Or that strange conversation in which the elder and younger Ridley killed the man. Or . . .

Her mother reached over to the table. "There were a great deal of pamphlets at the church today. Why not report on some of these? This tells of the need for charity, and this of the great hope of Jesus—oh, dear, what's this?" She held up a pamphlet. "A Communist manifesto? Someone at the church has troublesome leanings."

Her mother slapped the pamphlets back down on the table.

Jane surreptitiously slid the offending pamphlet up her sleeve. Rabble-rousing could be useful for . . . for . . . she was too tired to remember what for.

A man in a green suit flashed in her mind. *You are like me. A wild thing like the wind, always moving upon the worlds.* Sleep took her.

Chapter Eight

In which our Gnome and Vampire Have a Reckoning over the Chaos of a Labor Dispute and Determine Greater Conspiracy Afoot

PEDGE, I'M BLOODY BEGGING YOU."

Mud, blood, and worse soaked Charles's clothes. After two days of hiding under hedges, trying not to let any of the human parkgoers get a good look at him, blagging food and drink, the door was open and the madgekin wouldn't let him in.

"You brought that mad blower vampire through," Pedge said, the fur on his madgekin face rustling.

"I've got to get home! My aunt and me cousin need word! Back here tomorrow to blag all the cheese in London, I will. Same time. Don't have any other plans."

Pedge raised a fuzzy eyebrow. "This time tomorrow."

"Word of honor. You ever know a gnome to lie about that?"

"Yes," Pedge grumbled. "You." But he moved to let Charles through. "This time tomorrow!"

"Right grateful, I am, Pedge."

"Tomorrow!"

Charles ran along the path from Pedge's, clambered over a rise, and kept running, even as he realized he was going right to the Ridley warehouses. The Otherworld's richer sounds, lights, and smells felt like a slap this time.

He ducked around the corner of one of the workhouse gates into an alley. And then Charles noticed something at his feet.

It was a tattered newspaper, one of the new regular pamphlets that were always crying the bad news of the world. Charles picked it up, uncrinkled the pages, and immediately swore.

"John Ridley Poisoned!"

And right under that, the byline: *Jane, of Guldenburg.*

"You damnable mad vampire dollymop!"

The girl had done it. She'd gotten her story. Only bit she left out was how they'd hid in a secret room while the Ridleys chomped a man right up. But Riordan was in there. *The most recent gnome to service Ridley was one Riordan, a Welsh fellow by origin*—"Herefordshire!" Charles growled—*who identified the pitcher Ridley drank from.* "Oh, Uncle . . ." Charles groaned, putting a hand to his face. "You just had to tell them! You had to be that blooming reliable, did you?"

The poison, according to that mad girl, had been maradoth root. Near impossible thing to find as it only grows under a sickly birch in the dark of a new moon. Only gnomes might have the patience to cultivate such. A few grains of ground-up maradoth root was a good purgative for too much dairy for Otherworld folk. One grain would make a human purge their guts right out.

Jane nattered on, throwing out all sorts of conspiracy rot, but at the last, said, *This reporter, though, heard by sheer coincidence John Ridley berate the gnome as unreliable. Those who have made a study of the little fellows, as I have, know that this is as vicious an insult as can be given to any in the Otherworld.*

"No time to poison that bloody pitcher, you mug!" Charles shouted, crumpling up the paper and tossing it across the alley. "Three blooming seconds between that swell's insult and drinking the wine! Where's that in your glocky story?"

"Settle down, mate. We're all here for the same thing!"

The whisper came from over his shoulder. Charles looked behind him and saw the alley was now full of pixies, the light of a large group just visible under a heavy coat. And two boggarts, their normally gleeful, warty, sharp-toothed faces now serious. The whole crowd crept along the brick wall to Charles.

"That's the gnome who threw the brick at Ridley not two days back!" said a pixie.

"What are we doing here?" Charles asked the nearest boggart. He thought he recognized the fellow. They'd been on the seven-league boot lines together.

"Waiting on the suckabuckets." The boggart gave Charles a wide, horrifying grin full of needle-sharp teeth. "They've got themselves a reserved ferry." He pointed down the hill at what they called Coins-Teeth, the main dock, where not three days past Charles had run from the Riders and stolen a seven-league boot.

There, cobblestone streets ended in a wide, round plaza, jutting out into the river, stone and concrete forming a hub for the docks where Ridley goods came in and out of the workhouses.

"All the suckabuckets go home together on the same ferry. Going to make them sorry they took our work, the blood-slurping legs!"

"What about the Riders?" Charles asked.

"They only roll the suckabuckets up the dock and leave. We've got a couple of minutes."

Charles's eyes wandered back to the crinkled newspaper at his feet.

Vampires were the source of all his problems. Oh, the werewolf swells started it, but his life couldn't have been so hugger-muggered without vampires.

The nearest boggart pressed a club into Charles's hand. "Old Neddy here, a right and trusty cosh! That'll give the suckabuckets something to remember you by."

The club felt good in his hand. And Charles couldn't imagine anything he'd done in the last few mad days that felt as good as putting his fist in a vampire's face. Hell and damnation, the vampires deserved it.

"Oy, here they come!"

No. Be reliable. You threw the brick, and look where it got you. Don't make Uncle ashamed. Charles set down the club.

"There they are! Oy, look at that. They've even got a pretty dame."

A crowd of black-clad vampires, hunched against each other, walked down the street toward the ferry landing. On either side of them, the Iron Riders clattered along.

But that wasn't what drew Charles's eye.

A pretty dame. And there she was: visibly less hunched, not bald, but with the same sallow skin and yellow eyes as the rest.

Jane.

She leaned over to the vampire next to her, whispered something to the fellow, and made a note on parchment with charcoal.

Writing down more business nobody needed to bother with. Framing up Uncle. Charles yanked the club from the ground. "Let's get the suckabuckets."

The vampires reached the dock. The Iron Riders turned and wheeled away maddeningly slowly up the cobblestoned streets back toward the warehouses. The group of vampires were left huddled at the edge of the river near the greenish mist rising from the water. Even from here, he made out Jane's voice, talking to the other vampires. "Excuse me, sir, I only have a few questions—"

"There they go," Charles found himself saying as the Iron Riders disappeared around the corner, rolling back to the factory. "Count it down a minute."

Sixty breathless seconds later, the boggarts bellowed, "Get 'em!"

A host of Otherworld creatures rushed from the alleys, and Charles raised his club and bellowed, running right at the group of vampires, though he had eyes for only one of them.

Roaring badgebears, chirping pixies, grunting boggarts, and squealing redcaps all rushed for the vampires waiting at the hub of Coins-Teeth.

Charles went first, at their head.

Charles didn't see who threw the first rock, but it struck a vampire and knocked the fellow right off the dock into the water. Vampires bellowed and cried and backed into a cluster, but another group of Otherworlders hit them from the shallows, yanking them off the docks. All around them, Otherworlders tossed vampires into the water, beat them with cudgels. The vampires, for all their teeth and claws, shrieked in horror and covered their faces.

And Charles ran right for Jane, but she disappeared in the hubbub. "I want words with yeh—"

A young vampire, no older than George and no taller than Charles, stumbled into Charles's way, and Charles raised the club before he caught himself.

The little vampire screamed in horror.

"Oh, thirteen hells," Charles said and threw down his cudgel. "Come on, you little blighter." He grabbed the little vampire's hand, and the creature squeaked, but Charles pulled him through the hubbub toward the ferry, now throwing out green waves as it reached the dock. Charles yanked the little vampire forward. "I won't hurt you! Go on now! Get on that ferry!"

"What's that, gnome?" Cheese breath washed over them. A turf troll, a great, hairy and muddy thing, stormed up behind Charles and the little vampire, waving his own massive cudgel. "Nits make lice, don't you know? Don't go being a shirkster! Toss the suckabucket in the soup!"

Charles stepped in front of the little vampire and muttered, "Jump for the damned ferry!"

The little vampire, thank Puck, took his advice and leapt from the edge of the dock into the outstretched arms of an elder vampire on the ferry.

"Gnomes! Yeh're the trouble too! I ought to throw you in the river with them vampires, going and poisoning folk!" The turf troll roared, raised his own cudgel, and brought it down on Charles's head.

It broke into splinters over Charles's noggin.

"Ow!" Charles yelled. "I bloody felt that!"

The troll yanked Charles off his feet, swung him high in the air, and Charles saw only the vast expanse of the rushing water—water he hadn't the least idea how to swim—and had only enough time to think, *I'm going to die unreliable—*

"Ow!"

The troll dropped him just in time for Charles to come down on the dock, roll to the edge, and catch himself, hanging off right over the edge of the water.

The deep, rapid green water swirled right under him.

His breath came ragged as he clambered back up the dock. *Gnome God, I apologize for everything, and I'll—*

"Off, you blackguard! Leave my best source alone!"

Charles had to blink.

Jane had saved him.

She stood with a long hairpin in one hand, jabbing it at the turf troll. The troll roared and swiped at her. She ducked and jabbed again, backing up the dock toward dry land. "Come on, little fellow!" Jane yelled. "Away from the water. There's a good lad!"

"My name's not little fellow, yeh—" Charles scrambled to his feet. "Leave 'er alone!" Charles grabbed one broken end of the cudgel that had splintered on his head and jabbed the turf troll with it, right in his hairy calf. The troll turned and roared, clawed at Charles. Charles bobbed and wove, ran right between the turf troll's legs and straight past Jane.

Jane turned and ran with him back up the street away from the dock.

Three things happened at once.

The troll tripped over a loose stone and went down on his face.

The Riders, iron-shod wheels ringing on the cobblestones, sped out from the complex of warehouses and factories, their great spidery arms crackling with green-and-white alchemical fire as they rushed down the hill.

And something in the air reacted to the fire of the Riders.

The ever-present green haze, as constant in the City Beyond as coal dust in

London, turned white and gleaming, crackled with black lightning, and all of a sudden, all the air between Ridleyville and the river was one bank of fog, thick as a wall.

Angry fog, cackling and screaming.

"In here, little fellow!" Jane seized him by the arm and yanked Charles behind a stack of crates piled next to the loading dock of a warehouse. Charles didn't argue. Huddling behind the crates, he peered out at the horror.

The fog, in concert with the Riders, ate the Otherworld creatures alive.

Screaming rang out from the innards of the deadly cloud wall. Flashes of black lightning revealed skeletal forms, running and screaming. A finger of fog touched the turf troll that had just been after Charles and Jane, slithered up the troll's leg like a snake, twisting round the hairy body, and the smell of burning hair filled the air as he screamed.

"It's a witchfog," Jane said. "Most interesting."

"Don't know if *interesting* is quite the word," Charles said.

"I've never seen such a thing in action," Jane muttered, and Charles couldn't say whether she spoke to herself or to him. "A defense mechanism, used by witches in the human world to discourage pursuit when their covens were persecuted. It is best to create a defense that mimics a natural effect—a fog too thick to keep pursuing women into the woods for instance. But at times, the fog can be—oooh." Jane winced as the fog overcame the troll, and his roaring screams became gurgles of death. "Defensive."

"No witch-make, that!" Charles said. "That's the Riders."

"I have a hard time believing those mechanical monstrosities could summon such complex magic. I think this is merely a strange consequence of alchemical smoke and fire."

More fingers of fog, like an octopus's tentacles, crept along the ground and the walls of the buildings.

Charles and Jane pressed themselves against the crates, barely daring to breathe.

The fog crept on past their hiding place. It seeped out onto the river, split into several different segments, and crawled away down the water over the Black Fork.

It left only the Riders. And the remnants of a good number of Otherworld creatures. Bones, fur, clothes, but no flesh, the whole riot now turned to grisly remains on the dock and the street that led to it.

"That's a horror to run screaming from," Charles muttered. "Bloody blooming Puck's guts."

"Incredibly interesting. I wonder if the Ridleys predicted such a thing when they began producing magical material in their factories." Jane coughed. "It is not un-Providential that you and I keep meeting, little fellow."

"You could say that," Charles muttered.

"Perhaps you could help me with a follow-up story on your uncle? I don't believe we were ever properly introduced. I am Jane, formerly of Guldenburg School, and you are a gnome of Welsh stock whose name—"

"The cheek!" Charles could hardly keep his voice down, even with Iron Riders within shouting distance. "You think I want to help you spread your rot and gossip-mongering? Look what you've done to me uncle with your mad story!"

Jane's face wrinkled in confusion. "My dear little fellow, I've only reported the truth."

Charles didn't know where to start with this bird. "It would kill you to stop saying *little*, wouldn't it?"

"And I suppose you are going to stop saying *mad*?"

Both of them realized at once that they had raised their voices, and Charles forced himself back to a whisper. The Riders were only fifteen paces off. "I'm not helping you with a thing."

"Not a word when I just saved you from the wrath of a troll?"

Blooming Puck, she was right about that. She'd saved his life, what there was of it. "I . . . that was well done." Charles exhaled, letting out the tension that had been in him since the beginning. "But Bredwardine en't in Wales. It's in Herefordshire proper! Some truth wouldn't hurt the news!"

"Oh dear," she muttered to herself. "Mother's map had it in Wales."

The mad bird had saved him. Worse than that, she would blather about Riordan no matter what he did. *Maybe I can help her get a few things right.* "Me uncle wasn't capable of misplacing his cufflinks, much less murdering his employer. Put that in your damnable paper."

"John Ridley did call your uncle unreliable. That is motive, is it not?"

"You think me uncle is some kind of sleight-of-hand master who can slip maradoth into a pitcher of wine while he's under his employer's eye in a matter of seconds because he's so blooming ready for vengeance? And yet you believe me that he's reliable as the rock under England?"

"I'm not mad," she hissed. "Don't you imply that!"

"That's surely the way to convince folks you aren't mad, that is, growling at them."

She grimaced at him but didn't answer.

Charles tried to keep it to a whisper despite the rage in his head. "All right then. When would me uncle have poisoned that pitcher?"

"I don't know. Perhaps that was not the first time John Ridley called him unrel—"

"No need for that kind of language. You and I both know why Ridley was in a fit." The damnable box in Charles's pocket felt weirdly hot. "His father'd just given him a right drubbing."

"Yes," Jane said. "That conversation in that room and the murdered man." Jane half-spoke to herself. "I do wish I could put the sense of it together. Some fellow lost a very important item and was gravely punished for it."

The box was so warm in Charles's pocket that he had to pull the coat away from his chest. Why couldn't the damned thing have stayed where he left it? He set it right on that table.

Jane felt about her person. "Lost my charcoal and my paper. Have you any scrip, little fellow?"

Charles banged a fist against the wall. "Will you muzzle that? My name is Charles! *C*! *H*! *A*! *R*—"

"And my name is Jane, not *blower* or *bird* or *mad girl* or whatever worse epithet you've been saving—"

Both of them cut off speaking and peered over at the Riders.

The metal monsters were not moving.

"There, some paper." She reached up her sleeve, withdrew a pamphlet. She propped the pamphlet against her knee as if she were about to begin scribbling. "I don't suppose you have a writing implement?"

"Oh, yeh, I'm one for writing, I am."

"You spelled your name, and you read my story. I assumed you had your letters."

Charles nodded. "Aye, I came to the clergy school in the city when I was but ten. Left school last year . . . to work."

"I had to leave school as well," Jane said. "Not of my own choice."

There was an odd silence—the sort of moment, Charles thought, where he felt like he had a bit too much in common with this girl. Both of them trying to rub two shillings together, forced to leave school, and fate unkind.

Course, Charles weren't mad as a baited badger.

"That's very strange," Jane said.

"What's that now?" Charles peered out at the dock.

Of the ten or so Riders, five had wheeled out on the docks of Coins-Teeth to meet a boat. A very strange boat. Like the Riders, it was made of riveted steel, and as Charles watched, a strange round head, alight with gas lamps, lifted from the water, a Rider head on a barge.

Riders began unloading great crates from the back of the barge. It was some sort of trade, but Charles'd never seen Iron Riders involved in any of the unloading or loading that went on at the Ridley docks. They were made to enforce the law in Ridleyville, keep the workers from causing trouble. And they were hardly made for unloading—the clawed spiderlike legs didn't grip the crates terribly well.

But then, Charles saw, they didn't need to. The first Rider took a crate, broke the top away, and tipped it on its side. The others followed.

"They're dumping something into the river," Charles said.

Jane crept away from their hiding place even as Charles hissed, "No! Girl, look, they'll burn you alive, they will—"

Jane huddled by the loading deck and gasped, "Oh, dear heavens."

Charles crawled out away from the crates to where she was, and he gasped as well.

The Riders were dumping bones in the river.

From the shape of the skulls, they were human bones. But they were all so small. As if they were the bones of—

He and Jane exchanged the same horrified glance. "Children."

Chapter Nine

In Which our Vampire Connects, however Tenuously and Stressfully, with her Distant Relations

C HILDREN."

Jane didn't realize she'd said it until she had, and Charles had spoken it as well. These metal men were disposing of the bones of children. Hundreds— no, *thousands* of children. The horrors of the last few days paled in comparison to this. Jane's voice caught, and for once, she could not speak.

One of the Riders perked up. Its metal head twisted around on its hinge, inhumanly reversing its direction to look right at Jane and Charles.

"We're right in view, aren't we?" Jane asked and wondered why she said such an obvious thing aloud. "Have you an invisibility cloak?"

"They see right through those," Charles croaked.

The Rider's wheels creaked, and it began to move away from the pack, up the street from the water and toward them.

More gas-lamp eyes lit up across the dock, more Riders coming toward them. Spidery arms glimmered with alchemical fire, the same fire that had lit that horrid fog. Wheels rang out on the roughshod cobblestones.

Jane got to her feet, clutching at the brick behind her. "Charles, perhaps your madgekin would let us through his door again?"

"Got something better if there's any grit left in it," Charles said. He yanked something from his pocket, whipped it open like a handkerchief—was that a boot? It appeared to have tripled in size with a flick of his wrist.

"What's the boot for?"

"It's a seven-league boot! Get your arms around me waist."

"What? That's indec—"

"One boot, two of us, so you'd best hang tight!"

Jane saw what he meant and got to her knees and clutched the gnome around his waist. It felt a great deal like clutching a clothed tree stump. "Tight now!"

Charles wedged himself into the boot. "Wait—" Jane said. This wasn't quite right. "Where's the other boot? And are you sure it will carry both— AAAAAAH!"

They went sailing up into the air.

The boot faltered after the initial push, carrying them just above the trees of the Choke, over the canal through Ridleyville, and down, and then Charles yelled something, and up they went again.

Jane's arms ached horribly, and her grip was going to fail any second now. The single boot swayed and tossed them around. "Not in the water, not in the water!" Jane called as they sailed toward a dark, muddy pool where the canal drained. The boot lurched up, pointed above the trees, and Jane's arms simply couldn't take another second and—

The boot ripped itself in half and dropped them in the shallows.

Splat. Jane tumbled away and landed in shallow, mucky water. She spluttered as she stumbled up and out, soaked in the stinking foul drainage.

"Charles?"

There was Charles, a good twenty paces off, merely a pair of stumpy legs sticking out of the mud and wriggling.

"Hang on there, little fellow!" Jane ran through the mud, locked her arms around Charles's legs, and pulled to no avail. He was fairly heavy for how small he was. "Come on . . . little . . . fellow . . . sorry . . . Charles!" She yanked, and he finally came up with a spurt of black water.

Jane deposited him on the bleak, ashy mudbank and clapped him on the back. He coughed and hacked, spitting up mud through his muck-choked beard, until he could finally croak, "N-no more travel."

"If you mean no more travel by that boot, my good man, I don't think you need to worry as it tore itself in half."

They had landed in the most desolate place she had ever seen. The Otherworld's gray sky and flaming stars normally cheered her, but here the stars seemed all the more far away and the sky all the grayer. Immense trees of bizarre shapes rose on the horizon, a line of massive black trunks ending in great bulbous growths instead of a sprig of branches. Otherwise, mud and spiky black reeds intertwined as far as she could see.

"Do you have any idea where we are? Some forbidding country on the far side of hell?"

"Bog-builders," Charles said, pointing to the high trees along the horizon. "We're on the canal's drainage."

"Ah."

"Still in the Choke, just not in a bit of it where anyone would like to go." He coughed one last time, checked his pockets and seemed relieved. "I can find a way home. You saved me life, I got us away from the Riders, and then we're even, yeah? I don't need to see you ever again."

"That's a rather disagreeable way to say thank you, fellow," Jane snapped.

"You got your piece on me uncle, and we're square!"

Jane sighed. "Yes, I suppose we are." She couldn't help feeling that Charles knew more than he was letting on about that conversation in the secret chamber. But prying information from this disagreeable fellow was like trying to play cards with a badgebear.

They clambered up a soupy bank, and it took the better part of an hour just to press their way through reeds and mud to a path under scraggly trees.

Jane's mind went back to the bones of children. The Iron Riders, metal men built by the Ridleys exclusively to enforce their operation, were disposing of the bones of children. "Is that the secret of the new blood?" she muttered to herself. "Human children?"

No vampire would dispute a diet of human child. They'd line up and pay top dollar for such a thing, the same way humans would with veal or lamb, and they'd count it their best meal in months. London was a cold, unfeeling place where many children vanished between ignoble, illegitimate births and the workhouse.

Still, that was a great deal of children to go missing.

"Looks like some folk live here after all, eh? Glocky place to call home." Charles pointed to some shapes in the distance.

The cabbie had mentioned it. Of course! Perhaps vampires were going through to the human world to do the deeds? And Riders disposing of the bones?

And yet the Ridleys' whole purpose in making new blood and adding to their employ had been to confine vampires to the Otherworld.

It didn't add up.

"Lass, didn't know you had it in yeh to be so quiet."

"Hm? What's that?" Jane asked.

Charles waved to something ahead of them. "Hey there. No trouble. Just passing through, friends."

Ahead of them, a cluster of forbidding trees. Behind them on a rise, clusters of huts and thatched houses like a village from some bucolic scene in a novel. And under the trees just ahead of them, figures. Shadowed figures whose features Jane couldn't quite make out—save for yellow eyes.

"Oh my!" Jane said. "It's vampires! The day isn't wasted after all!"

"Puck's tricks," Charles swore. "Quick now, lass, get behind me. They'll crack their teeth on me."

"*I'm* a vampire, you forget, dear fellow."

"I didn't forget," he said. "You en't the standard make."

"They won't eat their own kind," Jane said.

"Oh, you know that, do you?"

The group of vampires crept forward. The day wasn't a complete loss, for all that she'd been tossed halfway across the City Beyond. "Hello, my compatriots!" Jane called. "It is excellent to see you. I've come to ask some questions of the vampire community, having been estranged—"

"Daemons bless me! A gnome!"

"Good eating, 'tis!"

The vampires rushed forward. Jane stepped in front of Charles. "Hang on now!" she said. "The gnome is a friend, and I am one of you, so you cannot—" A vampire shoved her aside, slavering. "Run, Charles!"

Right as she said it, more vampires appeared from the direction they'd come. A big one bolted forward, tackled Charles. Charles kicked the big one in the shins, but more of them yanked Charles off the ground. Jane ran to help, but another big vampire shoved her away. She went flying over a tree stump and fell on her buttocks.

A cry of glee sounded from the mass of vampires. And then a distinct scream of pain, "My tooth!"

"Take that, yeh suckabuckets!" Charles bellowed. "Not so easy to eat a gnome now!"

"Me tooth! Ah! Hard as rock like!"

"Bedivvah," one vampire shouted, whatever that meant. "I know just the thing. A saw, it do be, and then a gooseneck bar to open him up. Cracks the gnome just like a crab."

"Hang on now, dear fellows!" Jane called, clambering up, cursing her heavy linen skirt. "You cannot just—"

"Don't go telling us our business, English!" One of the vampires near her spat. "No alleluia lass needed round here now!" The others shoved Charles to the ground, and one of them tied his hands and set to kicking him forward up the hill toward their village.

"Hang on!" Jane rushed alongside the vampires who seemed disinclined to drive her off with force, though neither inclined to listen to her. "Steady now, Charles! I'll get you out of this."

Whatever answer he gave was lost in the roar of the vampire crowd.

They came over the hill into a hastily built vampire village. Rock and wood and a variety of already built structures had been employed to make thatched-roof huts; a larger building loomed in the center of it all with fresh thatch towering well overhead and a half-completed spire. The center of the village bore, instead of a village green, a vast fire pit ringed with stones and broken cement blocks. The vampires carried Charles into the pit and one bellowed, "Off for the saw!"

"Divvil save, a proper meal!"

"You going to watch, English?" one woman snapped at Jane. "Haven't given us enough trouble, have ye?"

Something registered with Jane. She'd heard their accent as a variant of Charles's rough cockney, but it wasn't, not now she got a good earful. "You're Irish!" Of course! Her mother was always complaining of "Papist Irish." They fled the terrible famines in their home for factory work.

"You come to gloat, English, over our hunger?"

"No," Jane said. "But you cannot eat that poor fellow, he's—"

The vampire spat on Jane's shoes and turned away.

"Knife-work, knife-work, a daemon's day never to shirk!" The vampire who had discussed sawing Charles open returned from his hut, brandishing a saw. The others sent up a gleeful cheer.

Charles turned a very light shade of his usual knotty brown. "Jane," he said.

"Jane, look, two things now. There's a thing in me pocket. Don't let them have it. And if you speak to me uncle, don't tell him about riots or cudgels or none of that. You understand? Just let him think I went out reliable please, Jane."

"I'll get you out, Charles. Don't you worry!"

"Ah, see?" He gave a sad little smile. "That was easy now. Not little fellow, just Charles."

The vampires crowded around Charles. Another vampire shoved Jane away, and two more elbowed her, pushing her out of the circle, the contempt for "English" apparently going around the group. "Good heavens, I'm one of you—" Jane started to say.

"Bedivvah!"

A vampire stood in the doorway of the large building. At the sight of him, the crowd hushed.

He was old and large, round in the belly, but from his sagging jowls and his eyes, Jane suspected he had once been larger. Dressed in a great black frock, he wore an inverted star on a golden chain around his neck. His age had emphasized his enormous, tufted ears, and his fangs jutted from beneath thick, crusted lips.

He looked, for all the world, like a Catholic priest bearing the devil's sign rather than God's.

He moved into the now-cowed crowd. "Daemon Perrick's day, and ye're eating a stumpy one?"

"Ah, come off it, Father!" yelled the vampire with the saw. "We're after five days and nought to eat but mudclots! The wolves said, they did, fair play to ye within your own borders!"

"Do the wolves dictate the conscience of a vampire, Billy Mac Baal?" The vampire priest came forward, limping, leaning on a cane, and shoved a great crooked, claw-topped finger at the speaker. "Here you are, offending our lord the divvil and bringing the gnome to the fire on Daemon Perrick's day?"

The other vampires quieted now, quiet enough that Jane could hear Charles's racing breath.

"Not at all, Father, but I—"

"Does not the Holy Book tell us of Daemon Perrick? Garfin the gnome, blessed among stumps, found the dead donkey lying beneath the lee and thought it a shame the meat would go to waste so brought it to the followers of the Universal Hellhouse, he did! The gnome is most beloved of Daemon Perrick, so it is said in the Book of the Slurping of the Legions and again in the Book of the Gnawing of the Emperor's Liver!"

A wave of signs went through the vampire crowd, fingers tracing reversed stars on their chests.

The one identified as Billy did not make the sign. "Are we to starve like? That's the way of it?"

"Best kneel in prayer, Billy Mac Baal. Your pride won't fill a belly, though you seem to think it will."

Jane pushed her way forward, and though several vampires cursed her and muttered about the English, she got herself within view of the vampire priest.

"A sister?" The priest smiled, showing enormous, chipped fangs. "A sister come back to us?"

Think quickly. "Sir, I must take the blame here. I came here with this gnome, seeking only . . . only to reunite myself with glorious faith and fervent prayer and—"

"All fall to our knees and say thanks, for we're after a great hard time!" He took Jane's hand in his, an enormous gray paw, and he sank to his knees in the mud. All the figures around them, including Jane, did so.

Only Charles remained standing, visibly shivering, in the middle of the firepit.

Now that Jane got a good look, there was more in the firepit than just coals. Torn packets were scattered about the mud, and Jane could just make out the words *Ridley Enterprises*. Was that the "new blood"?

The priest let out a loud, rumbling prayer. "Cur divvil, who art in hell, angels' tasty parts be fed to thy three heads. Thy kingdom come, thine gaseous horrors emanate, in Otherworld and human. Lead us not into the sunlight and deliver us from the eaters of garlic . . ." The young, big vampire named Billy snarled, got up off his knees, and sneaked away. "For thine is the kingdom and the power and the sweet, sweet slurp of the man-guts. Amen."

"Amen!"

The priest put out a hand for Jane to help him up, and she stood, braced herself, and let him pull himself to his feet, nearly pulling her down. "Now then," the priest said. "We're all after a long day and naught but mudclots to eat. The good divvil will bring a fine meal tomorrow, so he will. Go be blessed in your faith."

"Bless me, Father!" a young vampire said. Several others crowded around.

Jane worked her way around the group of vampires, now mostly crowding in for a blessing. She reached Charles. He stood in the center of the fire pit, breathing heavily, looking around him. Vampires still surrounded him for the most part, but they seemed to have lost interest in eating him.

Charles shuddered. "That fog, and now this. A fellow shouldn't have to worry about getting et twice in one day."

"At least it's proven itself a reliable fear," Jane said.

Charles smacked her leg.

"Oh! Do you suppose that's the new blood?" A vampire, apparently urged by the priest, appeared from the door of the church, carrying an armful of paper packets. The priest opened each packet and gave them to the supplicants, all of whom eagerly bowed for the priest's blessing on their forehead. Less eagerly, they took the packets, opened them, and choked down the meal inside.

"Mudclots," one vampire near her muttered.

"That's the new blood! Hang on one jot," she whispered to Charles. "I've got to see what this tastes of."

Jane got in line for a blessing, despite the sound of Charles snapping at her under his breath. She reached the vampire who drew an upside-down star, muttered something in what sounded like Latin, if Latin possessed more growling, and gave her one of the packets. "Only mudclots, Sister. We're after hard times all around."

"Thank you, Father." Jane hurriedly opened the packet to reveal a dark-colored mealy glob. A whiff of horrible smells hit her: gamey meat, slightly off, and a strange alchemical smell. She put a dab of it on her tongue.

It was disgusting. Like cottage cheese and blood pudding left to go rancid. All the promise of the smell and more.

That was no baby's blood.

She took another dab, and something grainy met her tongue. Jane isolated it and pulled it out—a bit of bone. "Then the bones are ground into meal as well," Jane said.

What on earth had they seen then?

The priest finished his blessings, but several vampires lingered close by, eating. They were only a little intimidated by the disgusting new blood, and the children gobbled it up hurriedly and looked anxiously at their parents for another packet. More than one parent, Jane saw, took only a few bites and gave the rest to their children. One saw her looking and said, "The wains must eat, ma'am, no matter how wretched the meal."

"Indeed." Jane picked up a half-finished packet from the ground, folded it carefully, and tucked it into the front of her dress. There would be time later to study it.

"I took you for an English heathen, so I did!" The priest cheerfully put two ham-sized hands on her forearms, clasped her elbows in the thick, callused, clawed hands. "And you've come back to the Universal Hellhouse, what we still respect and honor in Ireland, in the name of the Holy Father!"

"Blessed be," Jane replied and drew her best upside-down star on herself that she could. Satanic Papism. Her mother's head would come off. "I have been terribly remiss, Father, I . . . so you call these mudclots? How long have you been eating them?"

He groaned and settled into a seat next to Jane on the rocks and stumps that the vampires had put around their central village fire. "We're after a week of eating them, I reckon. The wolves sent their men through all our villages with their message—work for new blood. We took it a great bargain, so we did. Can't find a madgekin that'll let us through to poach blood off the humans, can't get a pass through those fancy Towering Market doors, so we can't eat!"

"So no one's gone through to the human world?"

"Not any of my parishioners, no, lass. Left Tír na nÓg under Ireland because there was no food to be found there with all the humans after years of famine." He grasped his enormous belly. "I've got a bit to spare, so I do, but the wains?" He waved a hand at the small vampires crowding around the area. "The mudclots are foul, but they fill the belly."

"The Ridleys never told you what's in this?" Jane asked. "No talk of ingredients?"

"They promised food, so they did, and so we agreed. No talk of ingredients, but we reckon it's dregs. They're buying whatever the butchers leave on the floor."

It was a reasonable theory but not convincing. This wasn't pork, beef, venison, or any other creature Jane had eaten. It was rather hideous meat in texture and taste both.

Charles finally spoke up with a squeak. "Well, Father, I'm mighty grateful, and the family'll want word, so I'll be on me way. Bless the divvil and all that and old Perrick—"

The priest gestured, and all of a sudden, three vampires rushed forward and seized Charles. They had him in hand so quickly he couldn't move to fight back, and they began carrying him toward the church.

"Bedivvah, it do be hard times. I can't turn away a meal in our very laps once time is right."

"I say, sir—" Jane said.

"Wait now!" Charles said. "What're yeh doing? Remember old Daemon Perrick? I was going to get et, you stopped them, and now you want a bite?"

"Not on Daemon Perrick's day, no, by hell!" The priest sounded scandalized. "You'll keep well, so you will, in the larder till tomorrow. That's Daemon Ganzig's day. As I recall, he never owed a thing to a gnome. We'll eat you then."

Chapter Ten

In which a Great Conviction is Discovered

SUCKABUCKET SCATLICKER, YOU OPEN THIS RIGHT NOW!" CHARLES hammered on the door, shaking it violently with his fists, but the hinges and the bolt held, barely moving under the impact.

The vampire priest's voice cackled back. "Pound all you wish, gnome, but that's good witchwood and an iron Yale lock, so it is."

He was right. Charles's fist nicked the iron of the lock mechanism, and he swore at the immediate burning in his flesh. "I'll kill yeh, every one of yeh, minute I get out of here! Yeh mugs!"

The priest laughed, his cackling disappearing into the distance.

"Charles." Jane's voice carried through the door, only just. "You need to calm down."

"Oh, you like this now? You come to gloat?" Charles snapped. "You'll get a fine story out of this for that paper!"

"I will get you out," she said, keeping her voice low, "but you'll have to give it a little time please. Here." Jane shoved something under the door. Charles bent down and felt a candle and a matchbook.

"I ought to be able to see me bits before they get chewed off, is that it?"

"Don't be callow! I thought you would prefer not to sit in the darkness. Something to read even." She slid something else under the doorway.

Charles felt the shape of a pamphlet. "Ah, just blooming perfect. You want me to read about the evils of alcohol and the joys of the Temperance Movement?"

"Cheeky again? I've saved you once today and will do so again."

"Right," Charles said and stopped the smart remark he was about to make. Jane was indeed his only hope. "I . . . I apologize."

"What? What on earth did you just say? You apologized to the mad blower causing all your troubles who is nothing but a gossipmonger. Perhaps you yourself feel a bit—what's the word—*mad*?"

Oy, she was milking this. "No cheek, all right? I promise I will get you an interview with me uncle. I will get you an interview with the Puck himself if you can just keep me from getting et." He forced himself to sound cheery, as if he'd sat down to a fine meal. "All's forgiven and forgotten once I'm bloody well out of here."

"There's a good fellow," Jane said. "Be patient. I'll be back."

Charles lit the match, the burned-garlic smell of phosphorus filling the enclosed space, and then lit the candle.

Nothing in here but a great stack of those "mudclot" packets—and one much-gnawed skull. "Blooming Puck's blooming tricks. I almost sympathize with those blood-sucking lurkers," Charles muttered.

The skull lowered its bony brow, narrowing its eyeholes. In the manner of human objects in the Otherworld, the skull had begun to acquire a personality. "You come here to mock me? I can move under my own power, you know!" It squirmed, fell on its side, and lay there, its jaw now disconnected. "Momentum," it said, a muffled word now without the jaw. "Momentum ish ah problem."

Charles bent down and reattached its jaw.

"Patronizing!" the skull said.

"Suppose I'll be here just like you if she fails," Charles said to the skull. "We can be two old skulls together."

"Who says I'd talk to you?" the skull asked.

Charles turned the pamphlet over and read the front: *The Communist Manifesto*. "This a political tract? Religious? Blooming hell, you couldn't have had a penny blood on yeh?" He sat down, crossed his legs, and set the candle upright. "Gnome God, this is a right laugh, isn't it?" Charles muttered. "Here I am in the most unreliable of situations, all because I sought to be reliable for one night. Can't get rid of the girl who ruined that blooming night. Fact is, I owe my life to her. I'm beginning to think you've got an un-gnomish sense of humor yourself."

If the gnome god heard, he let such a dubious comment pass unacknowledged as was the gnomish thing to do.

Charles opened the pamphlet and peered at the first page. Charles hadn't read much since leaving school.

But it came right back on the sight of those words.

The history of all hitherto existing society is the history of class struggles.

"Huh." Charles said. "Well, that's the truth then." There was those that had and those that hadn't, or hadn't much, and it had always been so.

"You reading about Temperance? Mania! I demand a drink! Thirsty as bone, I am!" the little skull yelled.

"It's not Temperance," Charles said.

He kept reading

The fellows who had written this—he flashed back to the cover and discovered they were named Marx and Engels, which sounded more like a couple of goblins—went on about the bourgeoisie, which was some rot word to mean the upper-class types like the Ridleys and their ilk, and the proletariat, which meant folk like Charles and the Otherworlders.

The discovery of America, the rounding of the Cape, opened up fresh ground for the rising bourgeoisie. The East-Indian and Chinese markets, the colonisation of America, trade with the colonies, the increase in the means of exchange and in commodities generally, gave to commerce, to navigation, to industry, an impulse never before known . . .

"Puck's tricks," Charles muttered, looking up from the page. "They're talking about the Otherworld."

Charles didn't know much about the English empire overseas, but he knew that cotton and tea and sugar weren't being grown on this rainy muddy island. Same as the Otherworld, they'd found other places to tell folks what to do— just as Ridley had said at the party. They assumed they were stewards because naught told them otherwise.

He talked to himself as if he were Jane. "They find folks what are minding their own business, and they tell 'em, we'll put coin in your pockets, and you give us everything you make, and then there en't near enough coin, and everyone's worse off."

"What's that now?"

Charles motioned to the skull. "And what can you do when you need coin in your pocket and food on the table, and the Ridleys string you up like a pheasant?"

He was surprised how easily the words came. Blooming hell, all of this today—the riot, the fog, the vampires' hunger, his own situation—

In the same proportion is the proletariat, the modern working class, developed . . .

It was all of the Ridleys' make.

Even the riots were of their own make. They'd created this world.

These labourers, who must sell themselves piecemeal, are a commodity, like every other article of commerce, and are consequently exposed to all the vicissitudes of competition, to all the fluctuations of the market.

"Bloody right!" Charles stood up. "They used us up and figured out they could pay the vampires in kind, so we were just another bloody commodity! The very workers who make their nonsense, and we're a commodity to them!"

"Babbling like mad!" The skull rattled from the floor.

"I'm sane," Charles muttered, reaching out to stroke the skull like it was a cat. "I'm the only sane one in the Otherworld."

And why didn't folks do something about it? Why were *humans* writing pamphlets about this when Riordan languished in a prison just for being in service at the wrong time?

Charles knew the answer, at least for gnomes. *Be reliable. Be steady.*

It was a strange feeling. All over, he chilled, hand trembling on the pamphlet. His vision trembled, blurred black, and then focused, and the clarity of anger came over him.

Charles turned a furious gaze at the wooden ceiling. "You en't listening, are you, Gnome God? Because it's the madness over being reliable that does it. We are so focused on decorum, on dignity, that we never stop to think how the bourgeoisie are laughing at us." He thought of Uncle Riordan, turning and walking back to that party, to his own death, never stopping. "What then, Uncle?" Charles whispered. "Did you never ask yourself whether industry itself was reliable? Whether this existence, where we're scraping for coin while the Ridleys throw a party with fifteen sorts of cheese, was reliable?"

It wasn't Charles that was unreliable. Oh, he was. But the Ridleys had taken everything, sucked up all their labor and coin, and given them dribbles in return.

That was so far from reliable it didn't come near the word.

"What's got you so worked up?" the skull asked.

"Fellow, neither you nor I need to be in here," Charles said. "Only the Ridleys really want us here."

"Who's that?"

Charles picked the pamphlet up again.

If Marx and Engels could granny out a solution to this madness that he— and the whole of Otherworld—found themselves caught in, Charles would be a Communist, whatever that meant for fey folks. He'd be the leader of the whole Puck-blessed party.

Reliability be damned.

If he got out of here, he would pull the Ridleys' house down around their ears.

Chapter Eleven

In which our Vampire Outwits the Other Vampires but must yet Allow for our Gnome's Conviction

JANE CLEARED HER THROAT. "I FEAR . . ."

"Go on now. Confession is fine for the soul, so 'tis."

"I have been remiss in my . . . meals."

"Oh, aren't we all poor eaters after the last few years? Say three Hail Liliths, and were times better, I would tell you to eat three cats."

Jane sat in an improvised confessional booth and tried to imagine what constituted a sin for a vampire.

They'd carried Charles into their church, which was thus far just a large thatched hut with a lot of room to sit on the floor, a larder where they'd locked Charles, a rough-wood lectern, and this curtain-draped confessional. The smell of sulfur filled the room, burning outside the booth as "incense."

It was hot in here, oppressively so, and stank of the "mudclots" and the sulfur, and Jane had been here for hours.

She hoped to distract the priest with a litany of sins. A dreadfully hasty plan, but despite the permanent gray twilight of the Otherworld, they were well into the night, and she should have been able to put him to sleep.

"I . . ." What sort of sin could a devil-worshiper expect? Jane could only think of the one sin she had been warned about continually at the asylum. "I have not been un-tormented by thoughts. About men."

The priest chuckled. "M'dear, you're a young woman, so you are, and there's no shame in that."

"But I . . ." Oh dear, this one wouldn't work either? Perhaps something ridiculous. "I have thoughts about . . . about badgebear men, Father! About their fur! I want to do . . . *things*. With their fur."

Mister a-Lokk had better appreciate this.

"Are you after an indiscretion, young lass? God forgives such a thing, for it is in our nature to fall, but you must leave off the lad and turn your thoughts to the divvil in His Eternal Reeking—"

"Wait," Jane said. "You mean to tell me that chastity is still a virtue among followers of the devil?"

"We're not uncivilized, miss."

Well, that was peculiar enough that Jane could have spent a whole day inquiring after it.

"Did your mother never tell you the truth of the divvil and His glories?"

"No," Jane said. "Not knowing the devil—that is something I am also guilty of, Father! Tell me of His glories."

"Well, once you are to know—"

"Truth of the matter is, Father," Jane interrupted, "my mother never spoke of my father. I didn't even know I was half a vampire until I was nearly thirteen years of age. I thought I was sickly, and the terrible hunger pangs I suffered, the cravings for blood, were some sort of disease!"

"Bedivvah, that is truly a tale o'woe! To have been kept from the knowledge of the divvil who liberates all vampire souls!"

"She put me in an asylum, Father! Did you know that? I spent four years at Guldenburg, you know, the goblin school—"

"Aye—"

"And all those years, I had to deceive my mother. Oh, I know it's against the will of Providence . . . or, ah, the devil, to deceive your mother, but I had to. Witchwater or compatriots, everything you can imagine to keep her paying the tuition. Once I brought a goblin under a glamour to talk about the school, to try and maintain the fiction that it was a human school. That was a terrible mistake. The goblin grew very interested in our knickknacks and was convinced that the ivory elephant could speak the language of its kind."

"Bedivvah—"

"And then—*and then, Father!*—I could bear the deceit no more. I had to learn of vampires from a goblin. Of my own kind, I learned in a classroom! I went to Mother, and I was determined: no more deceit. She turned quite pale when I mentioned vampires and said that she feared I was mad, and I pressed her, and finally she ran upstairs, and I could not talk her out.

"That was when I thought of the newspaper, you see, as a career. Perhaps I could go about the Otherworld answering questions, and while doing so, I could grow closer to my great answer. But then . . . then my mother came out and said we would speak after a bit of tea, and she *doused* it with laudanum, and I . . ." She closed her eyes, kept back a very frustrating feeling in the throat. *I am not mad, and I will not weep, not here!* "I was carried off to an asylum." Jane's voice fell, lower in the quiet. "She forced more laudanum down my throat and employed every man in church with a strong arm to pack me off, said I was quite mad, that I was seeing things, that my school had only encouraged my delusions. And in that asylum . . . oh, may our Lord bear witness, Father, I knew I was not mad, but who would not think they were mad when the task given one was to sit quietly for hours? To occupy the mind only with blank walls?" Jane forced back the rawness that kept creeping into her throat. "I could not bear it! I thought I was mad for days, for weeks at a time. I feared I had imagined the whole Otherworld."

The floodgates had opened. She went on. She told him of the asylum garden where Jane thought she'd seen phookas and redcaps frolicking but then, blinking away the phantoms, had seen just the garden. Of the way the white walls seemed to resolve themselves into her mother's weeping face. "It wasn't until I stepped through the door into the Otherworld that I knew I wasn't mad, had it confirmed. But the Otherworld has become . . . has become . . ." She trailed off.

The priest didn't answer.

In the silence, Jane recognized the rattling breathing and wheezing through the nose of snoring. She swept aside the curtain and revealed the priest, head drooping onto his robe, a bit of pink drool trailing down his chin.

Jane barely restrained herself from shouting. "I have never told anyone that!" she whispered angrily. "And you fall asleep?"

It took a moment to remember that this had been the plan all along.

Jane clambered to her feet, her disused legs aching from sitting, and crept along the corridor to the larder set into a high stone wall.

No vampires were to be seen in here or beyond the doorframe of the church.

If they worked in the Ridleys' factories, they must have been abed, for there would be another long day of work tomorrow.

"And I don't suppose you'd like to help out?" she asked the empty air, just in case a certain green-suited fellow was listening.

Nothing answered.

She pulled the tension wrench and rakes from where she kept them tucked away in her hair and went to her knees, set the wrench and began testing for pins on the heavy iron lock.

The lock buzzed like an angry bee, but it couldn't close on her tension wrench. Jane propped her wrist against the knob and thanked God, or the devil, whoever might be listening, that iron didn't bother vampires.

And she tried to forget what she'd just said. Even now, bent over a lock to free a gnome from a vampire's clutches, there was a strange temptation to imagine all this as but a mad fantasy, a bit of madness that rattled the back of her brain, crept up from some dark basement of the mind.

"No," Jane said. "I am not"—the tension wrench sprang back, and she pressed it again—"mad! Not!"

From inside the door, she heard Charles speaking. No doubt he'd heard and prepared some cheeky reply.

Inch by agonizing inch, the bolt turned, and Jane was able to press the door open. "Whatever you're about to say," Jane said under her breath, "I hope you'll temper it with some gratitude—"

But Charles was not speaking to her.

By the light of her candle, nearly burned down, he stood in the center of the larder, holding a much-weathered skull.

Brows lowered, Charles spoke as intently to the skull as any Hamlet-in-the-park. "You see, the bourgeoisie has created the problem, but only the proletariat can create the solution. The bourgeoisie is a bloody predator by nature: it must consume, it must create goods for consumption. Nothing without an obedient, unthinking proletariat at its command. You and I, mate, we're the coal for their fires."

"Will I get a proper burial?" the skull asked.

"In the new world, all will be communally well-treated—in food, in burials—"

"Charles!" Jane hissed. "What are you doing? Let's go?"

He looked up and smiled broadly as if he hadn't even heard her come in. "Jane! Excellent. We were just having a discussion about Communism."

"Let's go! Before you're eaten!"

"Right." Charles pocketed the skull in one part of his jacket, and in the other, she saw the pamphlet she'd slid under the door. "Good idea. Get a nice early start on the matter."

"Quiet!" What on Earth?

They snuck along the wall of the church, right past the confessional where the priest still slumped, his snores pushing around the black curtain that covered the booth.

They reached the door and saw the vampire village still in the formless gray twilight of the Otherworld, and with Jane taking the lead, they ran from one hut to another, the only sound their breath. At the last hut, Jane nodded to Charles, and they ran across the wide-open stretch of mud between the village and the nearest trees.

Jane let out a great heaving breath when they reached those spindly, black trees, relieved beyond measure.

"Where are you taking me?" the skull in Charles's pocket snapped.

Jane turned and motioned with her hands for Charles to toss the thing away, but instead, he lifted up the corner of his jacket and whispered, "Keep quiet now! We're going to challenge the bourgeoisie once and for all!"

"Charles, shhh—"

A vampire stepped out from the trees in front of them.

"It's that priest's folly, so it is." It was the one the priest had named Billy. "Running like? Lass, I'll thank you to carry on, but this gnome goes to me belly."

"Run, Charles!" Jane said. "The other way! Go, I—"

Charles did not run. In fact, the damned fool walked right past her with his arms open. "Mate," Charles said. "Isn't this what the Ridleys want?"

Billy the vampire leapt at Charles.

The gnome stepped aside, quite nimbly, and Billy went sprawling in the mud.

Charles just stood there in arm's reach! "Look at us. Fighting amongst ourselves, reinforcing the prejudice of the bourgeoisie. What can that prove, other than that we are as uncivilized as they claim?"

Billy got to his feet, turned, and tried to seize Charles, but Charles dodged, slipping in the mud and going down on his own buttocks. The skull tumbled from his pocket and landed at Jane's feet.

Billy loomed over Charles. "I'll tear your eyes out, gnome!"

"That won't make a difference to the—"

Jane swept up the skull and threw it, hard as she could, right into the vampire's face. The old bone shattered on Billy's noggin with a great crack. Billy staggered, dazed, and went down on his knees.

"Oy, Jane!" Charles said. "I promised that skull a burial!"

"Let's go, Charles! You'll get yourself killed!"

"I do appreciate your gesture, Jane, but the longer we fight among ourselves, the longer we prolong the Ridleys' dominance." Charles hunched over Billy, now clutching his face and moaning in pain. "Listen, mate. I'll be speaking on Communism and the responsibility of the proletariat in the Under-Market tomorrow evening. I'd love to have you and your fellow vampires represented, so we could all take control of our own destinies together."

Billy, deliriously, flailed around, trying to strike Charles. The gnome dodged nimbly and clouted the vampire on the head with his oaky fist. "None of that."

The now twice-struck vampire groaned, clutching his head.

Charles returned to Jane's side, and she held her hands up in exasperation. "Will we run then? I thought perhaps you'd like to stay and have tea!"

"Don't be cheeky, Jane."

"Don't tell me you found religion in that larder, my good fellow."

"Much better." Charles's black eyes, bristly beard, and knotty cheeks lit up in the grin of a child presented a new toy. "Communism."

Chapter Twelve

In which our Gnome Returns Home and Much Explores his New Conviction for Better and Worse

THE BOURGEOISIE FEAR THE PRESS, AND THAT'S WHY THAT PAPER OF YOURS, it's an equalizer." He'd been speaking for hours and barely scraped the depths of Communism. "See, Jane, the proletariat—"

"You're not really going to speak tonight, are you?" Jane asked. She walked alongside him, a little slumped and tired, looking full coopered after her night. "Cheers for inviting that Billy fellow, but if he shows with a horde of vampires, they'll just eat you."

"Let them," Charles said.

Jane raised an eyebrow.

"Not let them *eat* me," Charles clarified. Jane was a lovely girl but a bit obtuse. Of all the folks in the Otherworld, she should know why Marx was right. "I'll preach to a great mixed crowd. Badgebears, pixies, vampires, the Ridleys if they bother!" He held up the *Manifesto*, tried to hand it to Jane, but she only eyed it suspiciously. "They're ripe for Communism!"

"Ripe is a good word for those vampires at least."

"Don't be cheeky, Jane! It's a bourgeois insult to call the proletariat unwashed."

"How thoughtless of me."

They walked along the banks of the Black Fork, toward Charles's home. Faerie lights drifted, shimmering over the steaming green water. Water sprites sang discordant tunes. Pixies congregated by the hundreds, their groups making clouds of glimmering blue along the branches of the trees, passing around the cheese.

Imitation cheese made of straw and milk, just enough to get an Otherworlder glocky. The cheese was a trick. A quick quiff to get their coin, and that coin was a bigger quiff to reinforce the bourgeois system.

"You mentioned something in your pocket back there—"

Charles coughed. No need to talk about that box. "We were talking about Marx, Jane."

"All right then, how will you explain such a concept as this, er, bureau-juice—"

"Bourgeoisie!" Charles didn't know how to pronounce it either, but he thought he had the gist: *bur-jee-OY-see*? Had to be.

"Yes. How on earth will you get the Otherworld to even learn such a word?" In that odd manner she had, she spoke half to herself. "It is an excellent story if they don't eat you. While Mister a-Lokk is waiting on the new blood, I can write on the hopes of Communism. The slavery of the shilling. Hm . . . and a gnome, the very nephew of the fellow suspected of murder . . ."

"Oy now," Charles said. "You can't bring me uncle into this, Jane." For the first time since he'd cracked Marx's pamphlet open, that soaring feeling faded. Riordan was already in danger, and here he was embracing a radical philosophy. "Just stick to Commun—"

"My dear fellow, if I don't report on your connection, I'd be quite undutiful. All the help at that party know that your uncle brought his nephew and that said nephew did not report in after the poisoning. You've a terrible choice. Be silent and keep out of your uncle's business or make a stink about Communism and confront the Ridleys directly."

She was right. Charles's innards squeezed into knots at the thought. There was no going forward without putting Riordan in danger.

"So is this when you tell me that I'm mad and I've got no business and I've ruined everything?" Jane said.

"No." Charles peered up at her. "Where'd you get that idea?"

"That's all you've said to me thus far, my dear fellow, even after I saved your life."

Oy, she was right about that. "That was before I read the *Manifesto*, back when I let the bourgeoisie get me down. You've got a good way of putting your words together, you do."

"Gracious," Jane said. "I think that was almost a compliment."

Jane's acquiescence did nothing for the stress in his gut. He had to accept the risk to Riordan if he was to start a movement. And strange as it sounded, he had to trust Jane.

They reached the family's tree, hanging over the Black Fork, the knotty branches shining in the greenish light from below. "Me aunt and cousin will have heard by now," Charles said, looking up at the house.

"I'll leave you to it," Jane said, "and see you tomorrow night—"

"Stay! For a mug of ale, Jane, and an exclusive interview with the gnome who's going to pull the whole bloody Otherworld down."

"You are asking me to stay with you?" She sounded faintly scandalized. "After I 'ruined everything'?"

"Come on now, I've apologized. We'll let it go and have us a good talk." Charles started up the stairs but turned back. "But keep it quiet now. Don't try to interview me aunt and cousin or make a fuss of aught else. Just say your propers while I get cleaned up." Charles turned again, and then said, "And don't say *reliable*. Or . . . its opposite."

"Excuse me?" Jane bristled.

"You're not a gnome. It en't your place to say *reliable* to other gnomes."

"I will speak to the denizens of the Otherworld in whatever way best suits my stories, Charles of Bredwardine."

There was no discouraging this one, but damned if she weren't growing on him. "Mad as a bugbear you are, Jane," he laughed.

"I'm not mad!" Her yellow eyes blazed. She bared her teeth, showing the sharp fangs that jutted up just beneath her bottom lip.

"Ah." Charles held his hands up. "Apologies, Jane. I didn't mean to prod yeh."

She sagged, hunching over as if the air had been let out of her. "Perhaps I should tell you that you are not, ah, the first to accuse me of madness. It was not un-problematic in the human world."

"Well, the bourgeoisie would like all the proletariat to think they're mad."

Jane didn't answer. Weirdly, she didn't seem comforted by Marx's words. Charles couldn't think why.

Charles walked up the stairs to his home. Familiar smells of fresh-carded unicorn yak wool, slightly off liver and eggs, and stout, gnomish ale greeted him.

Aunt Susan and George both sat where they had two days ago when he'd left for the party. They both gaped when he came in.

"Oh my! Cousin Charles!" George wavered at his post. "You're here! You—

what happened to your clothes? How did you end up like that?"

"Long, long story," Charles said. "I've come with news of Riordan—"

"Reliably good to see you, young man."

Charles turned and noticed, in his own chair, a familiar figure. "Elmont!"

Somber-faced, the driver for the Ridleys stood, walked to Charles, and took his hand, one knotty set of fingers closing over another. "In times of sorrow, reliability 'tis the rock upon which we stand."

"How's Uncle?"

"I have only seen him briefly, but the master has agreed to keep him in the cells by the North Tower door in the Otherworld at my urging, so his family may visit."

"Puck's—" Charles cut himself off. "You talked the Ridleys into a kindness toward him? That's excellent news."

"Where did you go on the night of the party?" Elmont said. "You know the master has passed?"

"John Ridley has died?" came Jane's voice.

Charles closed his eyes. This girl and her timing.

He turned and motioned to the new arrival. "Elmont, this is Jane, what writes for the *Otherworld Voice*—you know, the news rag. She's come to get some information about Riordan, to write about his reliability so all the Otherworld can hear of it." He motioned around the room. "Jane. Susan and George, my aunt and cousin."

"Reliably good to meet you," Jane said.

Charles closed his eyes. *Blooming hell.*

"Reliability is not to be found in the crying of news and horrors but in the steadiness of hearth and home," Elmont said. "How did you encounter . . . each other?"

"Oh, she saved me from getting et by a pack of vampires," Charles said. "I've had a time, I have, getting home from that party." Charles felt every inch of his dirty suit under Elmont's gaze, well aware of the *Manifesto* thrusting from his pocket.

"You should have remained," Elmont said. "All the help were needed to determine the source of the master's distemper."

"I saw three great werewolves coming for me, jaws like alligators." Charles put a hand on the *Manifesto* to strengthen him. "Can't blame a fellow for running."

"Hm," Elmont said, a syllable that clearly said he clearly would blame Charles for running. "Riordan asked that I send you to see him as soon as word came." Elmont turned to Susan. "I must take my leave as morning in the human world approaches."

"Thank you, good sir," Susan said and, with some struggle, rose on her hurt knee to clasp Elmont's hands.

"Priscilla will be by tomorrow to pass on her own good cheer and reliability."

As he passed Jane, she extended a hand as well. "I'd love to interview you, sir, on your thoughts regarding the—"

"The reliable need not speak to be heard."

"But sir, one good gnome's word is the worth of all the less-reliable."

Charles had to stifle a laugh. It seemed Jane, among the other strange things in her head, bore a gnome aphorism or two.

"No, thank you," Elmont coughed

"Go on," Charles said. "We'll work this out."

Elmont left. "Don't you worry," Charles said to Susan as soon as Elmont passed out the door. "I've got it well in hand, Auntie."

"I remain steady," Aunt Susan said, clutching his head. "But it is so difficult, Charles. Sometimes I think I cannot be reliable for one more second. I want to toss the wool in the river and . . ." Her oaky hand shook in Charles's. "He was such a good gnome, Charles! He was so reliable! What poor fortune is this from this world . . ."

"You stay steady for Uncle, Auntie," Charles said. "I've got this figured out, I do. Fortune and all. He'll be home in no time."

"Oh, Charles, my poor heart sings to hear that " She put a hand on Jane's wrist, and unlike Elmont, there was a good bit of hope in Susan's face as it beamed at the reporter. "And the newspaper might help?"

"I will represent the character of your husband faithfully. I promise," Jane said. "Both worlds will know of his great reliability."

"Come on now," Charles said. "You wait for me out there, Jane, and we'll talk after I get some drink. Susan, George, I'll be back after I give her the facts about Uncle."

Normally, beer from the enchanted barrel had the same problems their food did, tasting old and off. Tonight, Charles could have sworn it tasted sweet as wine just for him. He took a deep draught, holding another cup of ale for Jane, and walked out along a thick, vine-wrapped branch till they were well above the river and the rest of the Choke—the same place where he'd spoken to Riordan not a few days back.

Murgalak's Fun Human Facts

The human mating ritual is quite complex, involving horses, carriages, and the little-used retractable tail of the female, which contains the pollen necessary to become priggant. The only more-complex ritual is that which might take place between two Otherworlders of different races.

The green glow of the river lit up the whole world. Charles didn't mind a bit. Truth to tell, the light made Jane look rather pretty, even with those permanent question lines between the eyes. And truth to tell, that constant questioning had its own bit of charm. He handed her a clay cup, and she took it wordlessly, not looking away from the river, flowing green far below.

Charles took a deep drink of the fine ale and then set it down. He found himself rubbing his hands together as if he were about to tuck into a great meal. Time to talk Communism, the only solution for all of this.

And then Jane spoke. "My mother had me committed to an asylum."

"What's that?" Charles asked.

"Oh yes. She thinks the whole Otherworld is a figment and won't admit that my father was a vampire. She drugged me with laudanum, and all her churchmen dragged me to the asylum."

"Ah." So that's why she was so sensitive about the word *mad*. And that made Charles a right mug. "Apologies again then, Jane. I didn't mean it in any manner like that."

"Oh, you did mean it," Jane said and gave a strange laugh. "But how could I blame you? I seem mad. I should be mad . . ." She let out a strange sniff as if she were about to weep. "Those were good years in Guldenburg School. The goblins thought I was terribly persistent, always wanting to know the exact details of Titania's ruling policy or of Puck's great deals. I always made them stray from the topic, but I had to know everything. I took quite as many courses as I could. I was in the running for Head Scholar for a bit there."

"Not the usual path for a girl."

"Goblins don't care much for reproducing, and they've got little concept of gender as you or I do. I could advance at the school in ways I never could in the human world." She stared into the ale. "And yet in the asylum, I almost believed that I had imagined it because they kept telling me so."

She went silent. Charles took a deep draught of his ale. "You know," Charles said, "madness en't the sort of thing you sit down and granny out, measuring part and parcel. We're all mad by someone's standards."

She glared at him. "Are you saying my mother's right?"

Oh, hell. "No, Jane, course not."

"Don't be diplomatic. Of course, you think I'm mad!"

"I don't, swear on Oberon! I'm just glad it's you, answering these questions, writing these stories for the paper. Don't matter what folk think. You're made for this sort of work."

"Thank you." She passed her ale to Charles. "Here."

"You taking up Temperance now?"

"You'll not help the cause of Communism with drunkenness, dear fellow," Jane said.

"Now that's a bit too far," Charles began, "telling a fellow about his beliefs and his drink at once and—"

But she was off on another subject. "You may be able to get the vampires' ruff up," Jane said, half to herself, "for that new blood was absolutely wretched to taste. It's quite unlikely that it was made with the blood of those children we saw."

Charles quaffed Jane's ale. "Those bones are some other Ridley dodge, you think?"

"I cannot imagine what would lead any man, werewolf or no, to risk the deaths of hundreds of children. But they have not been unwilling, as we've seen, to resort to murder." She trailed off. "Perhaps it's connected to that conversation we overheard. What secret would be worth such bloody deeds if not the deaths of children?"

Charles's pocket felt warm again with the object. Blooming hell, they were in this together no matter what. "I . . . I might know something about that conversation." He took the box out of his pocket. "Had to do with this bit."

Jane's eyes lit up. "A well!"

"A what? No one's digging for water around here, Jane. River's right there."

"Not that sort of well, my dear fellow." Jane held out a hand. Charles, despite the bit of him that screamed not to show the cursed thing to anyone, put it in her hand. "These objects store things—magically. At Guldenburg, they kept books. Goblins do tend to write an awful lot, and goblins sorted out printing centuries before humans did, so they put whole libraries in these things. You could put a herd of elephants in one if the spell is done properly, by a licensed witch." She held the thing up, began pressing different places on the surface as if feeling for something. "What has this to do with our conversation?"

"You remember hiding under the bed and the fellow what got et? And his story?"

"I doubt I shall forget it anytime soon."

"This is the thing he lost."

Jane's eyes widened, lighting up with the green glow from below. "This?"

Charles couldn't help himself: he checked over his shoulder, checked below them, and even though no one could possibly hear them, he leaned closer to Jane and whispered, "Fellow dropped this not two feet from me earlier in the day. I pick it up, see the Ridley seal, and I figure I'll exchange it for a bit of coin."

Jane didn't answer, her mouth hanging open.

"We heard them eat the fellow, and I ran right up the hall and put this on an end table, left it there, happy to be done with it. In the space of a dog's meal, it's back in my pocket. Can't say how or why."

Jane opened her mouth three separate times to speak, furrowed the lines between her eyes, and finally said, "Charles the gnome, you have a strange sort of luck."

"That en't Puckish luck you talk about. I've got the kind of luck always lands a fellow in the fire. What do you reckon they created it for?" Charles said. "From what we heard under that bed, I'd say old Ridley must have a rival. Said the box was an advantage over 'you know well whom.'"

"Perhaps an industrial rival?" Jane said. "And perhaps this is part of a great scheme to destroy that rival." She kept fiddling with the box. "There was a logic to opening these things at the school. It's not un-simple. Anyone could open them if they had the proper sequence. Hard, soft, middling, soft, index finger, third finger . . ." She pressed several different places and then several others. "Not the sequence I'm used to, but perhaps they could open it at Guldenburg."

"Naw, don't show it to the goblins. They'll stick it in a vault and say it's the theoretical significance of mum-gubbledy."

"That is not and has never been a word," Jane replied as she continued meddling with the box.

She tried so many combinations for so long that Charles was about to tell her to leave off . . . and all of a sudden, a noise surrounded them, a great hissing like thousands of steam trains all at once, mingled with a thousand screams, rising to high heaven. The whole world seemed to quiet except for that scream.

Charles covered his ears, and his vision blurred with the roar. When it finally faded after an age of skin-scraping, nerve-rattling screams, he opened his eyes, and the box lay open in Jane's hands.

And inside, set on a soft satin lining, a single, small piece of dried meat.

"Blooming hell," Charles said. "What is that?"

"Looks like a dried heart," Jane said. "Odd. I expected more."

"Not a herd of elephants in this one." Charles touched the innards of the box and pulled his hand away fast as if he'd touched iron. "Ow! Blooming thing bit me!"

"Hm." Jane touched the inside lining of the box. "Yes, it is uncomfortable even for me, as if it irritates my vampire side. I wonder what sort of magic this was made for? It's certainly not keeping books."

"Or elephants."

"I really think I should take this to Professor Murgalak."

"Suppose you can if yeh must," Charles said. "But don't let the goblins hold onto it, yeah? Bring it back here."

"I'll have it with me at your vampire meeting tomorrow evening."

The river hissed, and steam began to rise, a hot and oppressive steam. Charles and Jane exchanged glances, and Charles knew she was thinking, as he was, of the killer fog from earlier.

He scrambled down a branch, and Jane followed him until they stood on the other side of the tree.

It was still bloody hot, even away from the river, and Charles's mud-and-blood-caked suit was turning to a soaked mop. He stripped away the jacket and vest and undid the shirt, leaving it open to his bare chest.

"Oh, put that back on!" Jane said, flushing and turning away. "It isn't decent!"

"Come on now, woman, it's me own tree," Charles said.

"Here I hoped you had ceased being a boor! Button your shirt, and cease forgetting yourself!"

Charles took a good look at Jane, flushing and holding a hand up over her face.

Her hand twitched, and she peeked just a bit.

Now here was a mystery this girl hadn't investigated. He buttoned his shirt but left the jacket off. "Better?"

"No! It isn't decent to go without a coat, in just your sleeves!"

"Are you sure you wouldn't like me to take the shirt off again?"

"Oh goodness me! After everything we've been through, you're acting a true blaggard!"

Charles swung the jacket over his shoulder and felt the *Manifesto* through the pocket.

Marx and Engels wouldn't approve of carrying on like a randy old drunk. About that, Jane was right.

He put on the bloodstained vest. "Ah, apologies, Jane. I got a bit carried away in the heat. You go on. Take that thing to your goblins, and see if they can't granny it out. I'll go see me uncle, see if he's amenable to an interview. Be in the Under-Market tomorrow evening, and we'll see if I can speak of Communism to these vampires without getting et, eh? Sounds a plan?"

"Yes, well . . ." Jane flushed as she started down the tree. "It has been an interesting evening."

"Puckish luck now," Charles wished her.

As she walked away, Jane called, "Ah, Puckish luck to you as well, Charles."

Hell and Puck's tricks, she was growing on him.

Chapter Thirteen

In which our Vampire Explores the Depths of Academia, the Heights of Commerce, and the Unexpected Features of Maritime Trade

JANE NEARLY FELL AS SHE CLAMBERED UP THE FEW STEPS TO THE DOOR. SHE had been up late last night writing at the *Voice* after leaving Charles's house, made it to her mother's in the wee hours, and was up again at an early hour to make this appointment.

"Sleep deprivation appears to be a hazard of reporting. And it can join," Jane said tiredly to herself, "vampires and werewolves and utterly boorish gnomes . . ."

She swallowed as she remembered Charles's unbuttoned shirt from the night before.

With that, she was quite awake.

"It doesn't bear thinking about!" Jane said sharply to herself.

She stood on the front step of Guldenburg. The bronze knocker above her head was shaped as a goblin's face. Sunken eyes glared down from under long, tufted ears, and spectacles perched at the edge of its huge molded snout. Instead of knocking, Jane gently pushed the brass spectacles up the brass face.

The door opened.

A dustpan flew through the door and bounced off Jane's face with a painful thud. Its companion broom swept along to her right, and then Jane lunged to the side to make room for an end table bucking like a horse. A flash of enchanted light followed it, froze the end table in place, and it tumbled down the stairs into the street.

"Drat and blast!" A goblin, dressed in an ill-fitting, loose wool suit—the image of the door knocker with his spectacles balanced on a great scaly snout—peered up at Jane. In one hand, he clutched a glowing amulet, the source of the light. "Hello? Oh, it is Jane?"

"Hello, Professor Murgalak," Jane said, her heart aching with the sight. "I've missed you dearly!"

"Fascinating! That you should appear just as I pondered the lateral movement and state of world-straddling, those who cross both . . ." He blinked. "Were you gone?"

Jane sighed. *Goblins.* "Yes. Gone a year."

"Come in then! Welcome back from . . . where you went!"

Jane stepped into the hall, a great, high-ceilinged, dusty place. The smell immediately hit her, and her heart ached. Guldenburg. The school. Endless books and papers, dried ink and long-burning candles, and witchlights made to burn to the very last of their enchanted oil. Her home. *Far more than Mother's house.*

And then she darted out of the way as an end table crab-walked down the hall, fast as it could. "Do control yourself!" Murgalak yelled at the table and yanked an amulet from his coat, sending a flash of alchemical light to freeze the end table in place.

"A purge?" Jane asked. The goblins, despite being Otherworlders, preferred the calm of the human world where objects did not come to life.

"That is the theory," Murgalak said, glaring around the hallway for any more possessed objects. "Are you still writing on the subject of the Scots' dragons? Fascinating, that, and so few students take a steady interest in such . . ." Murgalak trailed off as he often did.

"I'm actually writing for the newspaper now, sir," Jane said. She thought of the account she'd left for Mister a-Lokk. *To describe the taste, one must think of meat that was never terribly worth eating, now gone off.* She'd tasted the "mudclot" she'd kept one more time just to describe the taste accurately. It was even worse than she remembered.

"Ah, the newspaper! Humans do love those. They are a favorite food of the working class."

"I'm . . . not sure that's right, sir."

"I'm sure I've read such attested in the scholarship on humans!"

The hall ended in the great central pit of Guldenburg. Here balconies and stairways wrapped their way around an endless abyss, rails and stairs like a tangled nest descended and ascended endlessly. Chairs and tables, lamps and books, leapt up and down the stairs, chased by cursing, wool-clad, bespectacled goblins.

One huge door dominated this wing. The library. Jane's heart leapt at the sight. It had been the greatest haven of her life. In school, she hadn't made many friends—goblins made excellent study partners but weren't much for social life—but she could have studied the history of the Otherworld forever.

On another wall, a great map of Guldenburg gleamed, a central well with different pathways snaking away toward London and the other cities. The school was built on a nexus within the Otherworld. Unlike the City Beyond, which existed only as a reflection of London, Guldenburg had entrances in multiple places: the original entrance in Frankfurt and then entrances in Paris and Berlin as well, and there was talk of opening a channel to Istanbul, catering to the ifrits.

"My office! A haven from maddened furniture." Murgalak led her from the stairway through one heavy, wooden door into a room dominated by a huge desk and an overstuffed chair, which he climbed into, looking like a child in a mother's seat. His footrest reared up and barked, and Murgalak blasted it with the amulet.

"Have you completed your great compendium of human activity?" Jane asked. Professor Murgalak's life goal was to assemble a guide to humans for Otherworlders. But he tended to rely entirely on the opinions of other goblin scholars for his sources rather than speaking to actual humans.

"The work goes on! I doubt I'll ever be done, you know, with many a theory to go through and many an observation yet to record from the greats. Why, I've barely started into Bungilik, and squaring his theories with my own, well . . ."

He would go on like this if left alone. All her professors babbled to themselves. It was a terribly annoying habit. "I imagine it's a great amount of work."

"I've had great luck with my *Fun Human Facts*. A penny per, and each one a delightful truth about humans!" He handed Jane a small card. "They're a great hit among children!"

"Probably not human children," Jane replied. She held out the box that she had tucked into the crook of her arm. "I came to ask you to look at this."

"Oh my!" Murgalak pushed his gold-rimmed spectacles up his scaly nose, sniffed, and took the box from Jane's hand. "A well! Have the Ridleys begun manufacturing these for general sale?"

"It fell into a friend's hands, and I am not un-puzzled about its origin and nature."

Murgalak pressed it over and over in a similar sequence to what she had done last night, but he had not the luck Jane had. "Hmm. It does not follow the same sequence as those in the library spectralizer room. I was at the spectralizers yestermorn—a Surturian fire-gem was the subject of study. The patterns were fascinating, as if it generated a new wavelength along the aether, willfully incendiary and . . ."

Mum-gubbledy. Jane chuckled to herself. Charles was clever, she would give him that. "Try opening it again and doubling the middling sequence."

He did so, and the sound rang out like a dozen trains running at high speed just outside their ears, and the box sprang open, revealing only the little dried bit of meat.

"A dried heart," Murgalak said. "Fascinating!" He held it up. "Why, this practically validates Bungilik's theory of the significance of the mundane!"

"Oh, you know what this is?" Jane said. *We are brought to the edge of ruin by this. That device was my sole hope of advantage over . . . you know well whom.*

"No, I don't know the function of this specifically," he said. "But it is fascinating to see a whole well prepared yet to have no magic within it whatsoever!"

"What?"

"Oh, yes, this object is quite mundane!" Murgalak raised the well in the air gleefully. "Nothing magic about it at all."

Jane pointed. "That bit of meat is not magical at all?"

"Merely well preserved."

And men are willing to kill for it?

"You know the saying, dear. Flesh for flesh, blood for blood, both for magic."

"No, I don't know what that means, I'm afraid," Jane said.

Professor Murgalak pushed his spectacles up his nose and harrumphed. "Check your Magical Theory notes. Traditionally, magic takes a great toll on the soul. One can avoid this toll by enlisting the flesh and blood of others to generate magical powers. It is human sacrifice, much like the Matholics practice in their Maths ceremonies."

"That's not . . ." Jane hesitated, not wishing to get distracted by correcting him on Catholics. "Would one be able to give up one's blood and flesh and leave the bones?"

The professor blinked, tufted eyebrows twitching. "I've never had opportunity to observe the phenomenon myself."

Jane muttered to herself, "Why on Earth would the Ridleys be willing to murder over a device that isn't even magical?"

"Speak up, dear. I won't abide mumbling to oneself."

"Sorry, sir," Jane said. "I am disappointed in the results of my questioning thus far." *I could have had that much more sleep.*

"I have heard that the Ridleys are showing something at a trade fair. Perhaps these wells are connected to this item?" the professor asked, and Jane's interest piqued again. Murgalak continued, "The humans have all gathered there because the human queen is there. They all bring their larvae, so the Queen Victoris may let them slurp of her royal jelly."

"My dear professor," Jane said, "I think you have your types of queens confused."

Murgalak blinked. "Oh, no, I'm quite sure it is. I've printed up a *Fun Human Facts* on the subject. This is why the madgekins report so few cats to be seen at the docks because the queen eats them at her great feasts to prepare the jelly."

"Truly . . ." Jane paused. "Wait, no cats on the docks?"

"Yes, I've just heard."

"Why are cats gone from the docks? Have they not plenty of rodents to feed on?"

"As I said, the queen has requested them for her great corpuscle. Bungilik wrote a whole treatise on the subject."

Interesting. Was a lack of rats connected to the Ridleys' activity as well? "I hope to see you soon, Professor. I'm . . . I'm saving to complete my schooling, and I thought to apply to the fund for needy students again, and . . ."

The professor was hastily scribbling some thought that had just occurred to him.

Jane inhaled deeply of the smell of the school. One day. Soon.

It was strange, how a smell could affect one. Jane's eyes blurred with tears as she left. She would not think of school until she had the funds. She would think of . . .

Charles's chest muscles just visible between the folds of shirt came into her head.

"I will not think of that either," she muttered.

Jane stood in Hyde Park, staring at the Great Exhibition.

"Oh, my word."

She had to check for humans on all sides to ensure she hadn't somehow wandered into the Otherworld.

There stood a crystal palace made of square glass panes, jointed one to the other in a great grid and set in archways and corners and high walls. Every facet of it glowed, even in the gray London rain, a gleaming square of glass. From inside came the roar of massive crowds.

Murgalak's Fun Human Facts

The human queen, Victoris, was appointed Queen of England in 1837 after a long pupation period where she was fed the royal jelly of the previous queen, called Bloody Mary because she preferred blood over all other foods. A strange one even for a human.

"God's newest miracle, that," a fellow said to her right.

She could hardly argue. Even the Towering Market paled in comparison to this. "Clever little humans," Jane found herself saying. "You've made something that outshines the Otherworld."

Before she got in line, Jane visited a stinking, spattered privy, and once inside, plugging her nose with one hand, she held the box with the other. "Can't have you anywhere that you might be seen," she muttered.

She pulled her dress up. For lack of an expensive crin au lin underskirt, Jane's mother had sewn scraps of stiff, old tarry rope around the inside of this dress to help keep its shape. Jane worked a piece of the rope free, bent it until it would flex a bit, and tied it around the box, and then she worked it back in under the dress, tying it around one of its mates.

"There," she said to the box. "It's terribly awkward to have you thumping my backside, but you'll stay well hidden under there, I should hope."

"A shilling!" the doorman thundered when she reached the entrance to the Crystal Palace. He peered at her, but all he said was, "You a bit choleric for this, my dear?"

"I must see it, sir," Jane said, trying to sound an impressionable girl. "I've been so looking forward to it!"

"Suppose the air's as bad here as anywhere. We'll take your shilling. Come on love."

Interesting. So far none of these Londoners—mostly middle-class folks, women in wide dresses and men in tailed suits—had been shocked by her appearance. That cabbie who recognized her as a vampire had been of the lower working class.

The same class that could lose any number of children without a great outcry.

"Don't the factory workers get to come see the exhibition?" she asked the doorman as he waved her through.

"Oh, aye, there's a special day when the poor can come, pay a rate what they can afford. By the queen's command."

"Is there an exhibition here by the Ridley enterprisers?"

"You know a man of business, he's here. Check you the guide. There's a girl!"

Inside, it was not so much that the Towering Market paled before this place—it was more as if this was the ideal that all other markets, human or no, strove to reach. Crystal fountains gleamed in the light of gas lamps under spreading trees, marking the original paths of the park here. Statues festooned the hall—marble visages of women bathing and men dancing, massive horses. Jane went by every household good she could imagine: lovely china, spoons, bolts of cloth, wooden toys, clothes, rows upon rows of shoes displayed by trained milliners as if they hadn't been made in a factory.

"Come see Hobbs, the escape artist!" Jane turned to an announcer bellowing over the crowd. "The greatest escape artist of his day! See him pick the great Parautopic Lock!"

"Oh my, a professional lockpick?" Jane muttered to herself. Much could be learned there beyond the simple system of tension wrench and rake that she had mastered.

"Men only!" the announcer added.

"What?" Jane bellowed, "I could out-pick any of your damnable locks!"

Of course, no one heard; the place was a reflected and amplified roar. Jane moved on, scowling.

The machinery section was full of wonders of its own. A stove shaped like a suit of armor—how on earth did one put that together?—and a printing press about one-tenth the size of the *Voice's* immense press with a tired announcer continually declaiming how it could fit in one small room.

She passed steam-powered plows—"I suppose the mule and the plow are as subject to progress as anything," she muttered—but still no sign of Ridley Manufacturing, and Jane began to feel that her shilling and her time were wasted—

A woman in black brushed by Jane without comment. A woman in a mourning veil.

The woman stalked quickly through the crowd, despite her heavy, horsehide-bolstered skirts, with a walk that one could describe as wolfish.

And then she turned toward one display and vanished behind a curtain. Jane followed her, peered at the front of the display, and saw the stylized *R*.

Beverly Ridley.

She crept closer to the curtain but stopped. "Oh, dear."

Quite uncomfortably, the box she had tied just above her backside was now warm, like a frying pan pressed to her backside. "Why on earth . . ." Jane backed up, and as she drew farther away from the Ridleys' closed-off display, the box grew cooler.

She began advancing again toward the display, and the box grew ever warmer.

"There's something behind that curtain that has to do with you, fellow," Jane said. But there was no decent way, unless she could creep behind that curtain, to remove the box from where she'd hidden it, and it was about to turn her bottom redder than any paddle could.

Beverly Ridley crept out from behind the curtain and turned, sweeping through the crowd toward the exit with that wolfish walk.

Good heavens, this was a conundrum. If she sought to creep into the Ridleys' exhibition, she might find out more about this box. But if she followed the Red Princess, she might get closer to the secret of the new blood and perhaps gain another unexpected payday from Mister a-Lokk.

"I'll come back for you, fellow," she muttered to the exhibit.

The box mercifully cooled as she chased the Red Princess.

Four hours later, Jane was wheezing from catching omnibuses, following drivers, and running along muddy streets. Though the Ridley woman could well afford a carriage, she hadn't taken one, hiring instead a dizzying array of taxicabs on the way here, taking strange paths that cut away from the river and then back toward it, along the water and then startlingly north only to turn back toward the water again, until she came to the shipping yards.

"Well," Jane said to herself, "I sought to come here anyway."

The Isle of Dogs, the shipping center of London, was a great racket: all smoke and roar and clang, the great pounding hammers of workmen nailing things together, steam whistles, and even more coal dust settling into hair and clothing than anywhere else in London. Ships dropped their cargo on one side of the isle and passed through locks to the other side where they would pick up more material. Railroads roared and trains rattled by, bringing cargo out of the warehouses to the docks. Jane dodged great crowds of workmen, a press of humanity rushing through the streets as shifts ended. "Excuse me please!"

The carriage that Beverly Ridley rode took a turn, farther down between two great buildings in the warehousing districts. Jane ran after it, turning down the street just in time to see the carriage pulling away—the drapes open, revealing that it was without a passenger.

"Oh, curses and bother, where have you gone?" Jane put out a hand and leaned against a warehouse wall while she examined the street.

"Oy, miss, what's your dodge?"

"Excuse me?"

A bearded, dirty-coated man, pushing a wheelbarrow full of mortar, waited near her. "I've got business with the wall. I do. Don't think I en't seen your sort. Pretend to faint like you're all-overish and then snatch a man's reader straight out his back pocket!"

"I'm no pickpocket, sir!" Jane walked away from the wall. "Good day to you."

She paused as the man trundled his wheelbarrow up to the wall and began scooping mortar into the holes in the bricks. Jane couldn't help staring.

"If you're not of the rookery, get on all the quicker then. Nothing but trouble around here for the virtuous sort. These workingmen get knockered, they'll get rough. Or have yeh got the cholera?" He drew back.

"I am not sick, just a bit tired. What are you filling in there, sir?" Jane asked.

"Ratholes."

Jane turned to leave and paused.

The man turned back to her. "Funny thing," he said, "I en't seen a rat in a dog's age. Usually they're a blooming carpet underfoot here. Have to bring in a tun of cream for the cats if this keeps up."

"Hm." Half to herself, Jane said, "Was Professor Murgalak right?"

"What's that now?"

"Nothing, sir. Thank you."

Jane continued down the row of warehouses, back toward the place where she had lost Beverly Ridley at the head of the street. She peered around the bases of the warehouses. She saw numerous filled-in ratholes. But no new holes, and given the industrious nature of the rat, that was unusual.

"They can't be," Jane whispered to herself. "Rats?"

If there was one group that outnumbered unwanted children in London, it was unwanted rodents.

"They can't," Jane said. "Not even the Ridleys would be so terrible." And a moment later, she replied to herself, "They ate a fellow for losing a box."

She crept down a soupy mud alley between two warehouses. "Oh." Jane blinked. She'd nearly walked into a stagecoach, wheels showing under a great drop cloth. "I really am dead on my feet here. I might need to report to Mother, get some sleep after all, if I can't find the Ridleys' warehouse. Perhaps—"

She leaned against the stagecoach, and it shook and let out a great gout of steam: the drop cloth tore away, revealing an Iron Rider, its gleaming eyes fixed on Jane.

Chapter Fourteen

In which our Gnome's Newfound Convictions are Tested by Older Loyalties

GNOME!" THE FAUN PRISON GUARD PEERED AT CHARLES SUSPICIOUSLY over the spectacles perched on his snout. Dressed in a black uniform, the faun was one of the ineffectual "police" of the Otherworld, much supplemented by Iron Riders. "Gnomes are ba-a-ad business. Come to spring the poisoner like the last ten?"

"Are you cheesed—" Charles cut himself off. "That is not a reliable suggestion, sir."

The faun frowned at him.

"I have come to bring good cheer and reliability to me uncle."

Not taking his eyes off Charles, the faun reached for a ring of keys at his belt. "Sta-a-and back." He opened the main door and led Charles through a dark hallway into the main plaza of the prison.

A main plaza like some nightmare museum.

From the outside, Riordan's prison seemed a round building: two stories, built at the intersection of two bridges on one of the higher crossings in the Towering Market. One more rapidly built, Ridley-stamped piece of the new Otherworld.

From the inside though, the cells, all of them open to the air, were set up like a beehive around a great central plaza. And in that central plaza, an Iron Rider the size of a steam ship held court. Its enormous head screeched and danced about on wire and pulleys over a semi-spherical body the size of a house set right into the concrete of the ground. A good two dozen arms thrust from its body, moving constantly and crackling with alchemical light and fire. Two more standard-issue Riders rolled around the bigger one, making circuits about that central plaza.

The big central Rider's head turned, and it fixed Charles with those baleful gas-lamp eyes. Charles held the gaze for only one damned second before having to drop his eyes.

Like bathing in needles, that gaze.

After a bit, the eyes rotated on.

"Puck's tricks, Jane, I hope it's going better for you," he said under his breath.

The faun brayed. "See old Gearface over there?"

"He's hard to miss."

"One finger out of place and you'll go to his open arms, mate!" The faun walked off, muttering and stroking his beard.

Waiting, Charles shivered. The large Rider's head turned, continuing on its slow circuit monitoring of the cells. Charles pulled the *Manifesto* from his pocket surreptitiously, covering the title as he read it again, flipping through random pages. Oddly enough, his thoughts went not to Marx and Engels but to Jane. *An interview with the gnome who is going to pull down the Otherworld.* She'd blooming encouraged him.

He couldn't help recalling that flush in her cheeks when he stripped out of his jacket and shirtsleeves. It was a solid bet on good human coin that she'd never had a follower.

"Shame, that," Charles found himself saying. "She's got more spirit than half the Otherworld. If a gnome could keep up, why, that'd be a fine time."

He twitched. Where had that come from?

"Charles."

Riordan's voice shook with relief. Charles stood up, aware that the gaze of the great central Rider had turned on him, and met his uncle's eyes. "Uncle, you look ten years older!"

Riordan's usual creased, serious expression had been multiplied twice over. His well-weathered copy of *The Gnome God's Reliable Prayer Book* poked out from under one arm; Aunt Susan had brought that this morning.

Charles noticed all the other prisoners—bruised and bound trolls, ogres, a scattering of vampires—staring down at them from their beehive cells.

Riordan maintained his stolid expression despite what must have been his greatest test. "Susan mentioned that you would be coming by."

Charles took his uncle's hand, and Riordan, instead of protesting, smiled faintly.

"No touching!" the faun brayed

Charles pulled his hand away, glared. "I see they keep you right under a Rider's gaze."

"No, I'm quite fine," Riordan said. "It is un-gnomish to bemoan the ills of the world, for reliability is in solitary . . . hands . . ." He paused. "Is that correct?"

"Sounds just right to me, Uncle." If Riordan were off his platitudes, the prison really was getting to him.

"I await trial now, as soon as the Ridleys' mourning period is over, and there is plenty of time to study. For that, I say thanks to the gnome god. I feared that the wolves had done away with you. How did you get away?"

"Just ran, Uncle," Charles said. "I know I should have turned meself in, but there were three wolves like Fenrir's sisters coming at me, and I couldn't think to do otherwise."

"A difficult choice, but I am sure you could not have added much to the testimony."

He thought of the box, now gone with Jane, and the Ridleys chomping away. *Could have added a thing or two.* "I met a woman what works for the *Otherworld Voice*—you know, the newspaper. She'd like to interview you, get the real story out to the people. Vindicate you."

"I will not slander my employers, no matter how they have treated me."

Charles felt the *Manifesto* heavily in his pocket, like a reflection of the prayer book Riordan held. *Thirteen hells, he's ripe for Communism.* Charles instantly upbraided himself. *What am I going to do, start preaching to Uncle when he's at his lowest? Start preaching unreliable doctrine?*

Course, when else would Riordan listen?

"Ah, Uncle," Charles said, and before he realized it, he had the pamphlet out of his pocket and had set it on the table in front of Riordan. "I'd like to show you this."

Riordan picked it up, blinked at Charles. "Communists? Aren't they a human movement?"

"Yes," Charles said, "that they are. But not only—if I have my way. And that might be a key to bargaining your freedom."

"Your way? Charles, have you taken up with fey Communists? Is there such a thing?"

"No," Charles said.

"That is a relief."

"I mean, not yet. I'm hoping to start a fey Communist movement."

Riordan's expression cracked, the dour expression turned to shock.

Charles went on—because it was too bloody late to stop once he'd said that. "Just hear me out, Uncle. I was captured by these vampires, and I was sitting in their larder about to be et. And I prayed to the gnome god"—*And I agree with Marx that religion is a bunch of rot and superstition, which makes me a great hypocrite*—"and then, in that closet, there's this pamphlet and this candle to read it by. And suddenly, Uncle, it all comes together in me head."

Riordan remained tight-lipped.

Charles opened the *Manifesto* to an early page, one he'd read over and over in just the few short hours since they escaped the vampires. "There, read that bit about America and the Cape." He waited while Riordan read, silently until his uncle's eyes flitted above the book and back to Charles. "Who benefits when we turn out two dozen seven-league boots in the factory? Only the bourgeois who can afford to shop at the Towering Market. The rest of us rot in the Choke, in the cells, have to deal with the side effects of the alchemy. Or worst of all, run from Iron Riders when we don't step lightly enough." He opened the *Manifesto* again to the page that explained the proletariat. "Read that bit."

Uncle Riordan's eyes scanned the page one line at a time, expression never changing.

"Don't you see?" Charles said when his uncle looked up from the page. "We've been so focused on our own prejudices, our own traditions, that we never thought we could change our lot! We have to show the industrialists that the workers aren't the same as a hopper of coal or a river to turn a wheel—we're folk with rights! The vampires en't the problem, neither are the folk the vampires put out of work." Charles realized he was out of breath, and he inhaled deeply, so deeply he coughed on the faintly burning air. "And we gnomes, we let the world go right on by because we're so concerned with steadiness and decorum. Look at what they've done to you when it's obvious that you've got no motive and don't know John Ridley from Puck."

Uncle Riordan didn't answer.

"The solution is to make our own world, not to let the industrialists dictate for us."

Riordan let the silence hang for an age before he finally asked, "You are . . . speaking to others about this?"

Charles nodded. "There's a group of vampires coming to the Under-Market this evening to hear me speak. A bit of a dodge. If they don't like what they hear, I supposed I get et."

"And then what?"

"Cut off the supply of labor if I can convince enough of them to do so."

He waited, and the only sound was the creaking of the Iron Rider's massive gears in the eye of the prison.

Charles sat there with Riordan for an age of stinking alchemical wind, for an age of that turning, metal, gas-lamp head, for an age of watching his uncle's hands on the *Manifesto*. Was he going to speak?

Was he going to do anything?

Charles finally put a hand out. "I guess I'd better have me pamphlet back then."

And Riordan laughed. Only a small laugh but enough that Charles's heart lightened.

"Uncle?"

"Charles," he said. "I would say there is no gnome in all of the Otherworld who is so much like me as you are."

"You joking?"

His expression returned to its usual dour. "Joking is not reliable."

"What are you getting at, Uncle?" Charles asked.

Riordan nodded as if confirming something to himself. "You should know this. It is time to tell you. I was once enrolled in the clerics' school myself. Though I was not thrown out over a matter of indiscretion and lost virtue, I did leave over a matter of passion. That passion concerned a gnomette name Priscilla."

"What?" Charles had never been so shocked. "You never told me this!"

"This was at home in the dragon-coal mines. It was not like the Soundly Built Institute of Reliable Religion that you attended. This was a country school, not far from the mines. A hard-working gnome could work all the day and head to school in the evening, thus earning a fair wage while improving and striving toward greater reliability. Never a distinguished school, mind you. The books we had were limited, and the teachers had less in the way of education than surely any teacher so entrusted ever had. But we had a good life. We learned enough to know the gnome god in His Eternal Reliability." Riordan turned to look at Charles. "Elmont was there with me."

"So that's when you met him?"

"He was always one step ahead of me as a student. It caused me a great deal of very un-gnomish jealousy. But at least, I told myself, I had Priscilla."

"Puck's tricks." Charles made the connection. He'd heard the name last eve. "Is Priscilla Elmont's wife?"

"Yes," Riordan said. "Now she is. At the time, she was the model of everything I wished for as a gnome. Studious. Loyal. Always completing her tasks and reporting to her shift bosses and teachers on her progress. I was not a good student, Charles. I would let my passions get the best of me, I would argue points of doctrine, and I preferred drink to study. Once, the instructor taught that five minutes' lateness passes out of reliability, so I made a point of arriving four minutes late exactly all week. It was the talk of several gnomish communities."

Charles chuckled. "You cannot be speaking of the same gnome as yourself, Uncle!"

"I had been cursed with an unquiet nature, my skull filled with questions. Why such reliance on the prayer book? Why such acceptance of our lot, of the coal mines and the clergy? The very same questions you ask, Charles."

Charles knew the answers, but he didn't dare say. *Because the bourgeoisie want it so.*

"But Priscilla, ah, she was reliability personified, and she would balance me out! So I thought. And . . . and she was briefly taken in by my romantic spirit, Charles. As you know, women like that sort of thing."

Charles couldn't say why, but Jane's face came to mind, the questioning lilt of her narrow brows and her tense lips muttering to herself. "Oh, aye, some do."

"I was great fun for her at first, but once that novelty left, she did not want to drag a lesser gnome to reliability. She wanted one at her level. When she broke off our affair and I had to face my prospects myself, I realized there was no one I could truly depend on but my own self—that and the gnome god. I had many dark years, Charles, far from reliability, till I came to know Him fully and found Susan.

"When your parents wrote eight years ago to say you were already showing signs of unreliability, I saw my younger self in you. I wished to give you opportunities I had not had at a proper clerical school where you could recognize your talent, see a future." Charles had never seen Riordan's face fall so darkly. "And now I know it was useless. I have said it so many times, and you seem never to hear. The reliable gnome can stand at the center of a forest fire and only take a bit of char. The less reliable will burn away in the fire of passion."

"Uncle, come now," Charles began and coughed, once, twice. The words wouldn't come out.

"This Communism is no philosophy for a gnome."

"Well, this is no world for a gnome then!" Charles said louder than he meant to, loud enough that the Iron Rider's head creaked their way. "We have to get bargaining power with the Ridleys! No reliable wages without that." Riordan visibly winced at such a misuse of the word, but Charles plugged on. "I want to save the whole Otherworld from the madness the Ridleys brought, and I want to save you as well while we're at it! You didn't poison that blighter. Some other wastrel at that party had it in for him, no doubt." Charles gestured toward the *Manifesto* wildly. "I've been a right shame to the family for years, and you've been kind enough not to hold it over my head. But this is . . . this is different. I can force an answer from them! I might not be a reliable gnome, but I can be a reliable Communist."

Riordan waited for an eternity, Charles's last words hanging in the air. Then the older gnome actually smiled.

"Oy, what's that, Uncle? You giving me hope?" Charles said weakly.

"No, I am afraid I have entertained far too much hope for you, Charles." He stood. "I recommend you do not come see me again. The gnomes of Bredwardine have had far too much attention, and we do not need more."

Charles realized his mouth had fallen open. "But . . . but if you want, I . . ." He didn't know what he was about to say. A part of him wanted simply to toss the pamphlet on the ground, embrace Riordan and say, *I'm sorry, sorry, I'll work at reliability, I will, I truly will this time!*

The urge was so strong that he'd raised the pamphlet in the air before he stopped.

"You heard me quite well, Charles. And I must ask you, unfortunate as it is to deliver such an ultimatum, to find somewhere else to stay. Susan and George do not need any more attention. Elmont has seen to their needs while I await trial."

"Uncle . . . no, I . . ." Charles felt, quite against his will, two enormous tears glimmering in his eyes, the reflection of Riordan's own.

"Good night, Charles." Riordan stood up and signaled to the faun.

Charles couldn't say that he saw Riordan walk back to his cell or heard the faun telling him to get up—he could only look blurry-eyed at the *Manifesto*.

The eyes of the metal monster turned, and glowing gaslight caught the glimmer of tearstains across Marx's words.

Chapter Fifteen

In which our Vampire Experiences the Price of Curiosity, the Temptation of the Industrialist, and Achieves Feats of Daring

THE IRON RIDER HISSED, AND A GOUT OF GREEN STEAM SCALDED HER FACE. Jane stumbled backward and slipped in the mud, knocking her head against the wall of the warehouse. Her vision went black with pain. When it cleared, the Rider loomed over her, its spiderlike arms crackling with green alchemical light.

"Stop." A tall man stepped past her and held a hand up to the Rider. "Stop!"

The Rider slowed, raised an arm above the man.

"Do not test my patience," the man said.

The Rider slowly lowered its arms, and the alchemical fire at the end of each went out. Like a half-feral dog, the Rider merely shrunk away from the man, pulling the disguising cloth over itself with jerky movements.

Jane scrambled up onto her hands, about to flee, when the fellow turned around, away from the Rider, and she recognized the face below the hat, above that pressed, tight-waisted morning coat and vest.

Malcolm Ridley.

He doffed his hat to show that infamous white-streaked red hair, and his cold blue eyes lit up. "The reporter. I had heard of a vampire skulking about the party, asking questions. And then I saw the byline of the story in that troll's ridiculous paper. Of course. You were the pursuer who tailed Beverly here."

"I—"

"Don't be afraid." His smile was cold as frosted iron. Jane heard his voice echoing in her mind. *You're lucky I keep my stewardship well.* "I have no fear of the press, like some men. It speaks well of you that Beverly did not shake such a pursuit."

"She nearly did," Jane said, the words dry in her throat, and a part of her screamed, *Run! Don't stand here exchanging pleasantries!* "Just as I arrived, she lost me. It would have been easier with my own carriage."

"I suppose you're curious about the machine at the exhibition?"

"I . . . I am curious about a great many things." *Run, for God's sake! This man ate a fellow merely for dropping the box that hangs under your dress!*

But perhaps—just perhaps—the Ridleys wished to speak on the record. Perhaps she could present an exclusive interview with Malcolm Ridley to Mister a-Lokk.

"I imagine you came here to obtain our statement on some bit of business?" He laughed. "Spirit on you, girl, but I do despise newsmongers. They are interested only in rumor and scandal, and the daily grind of business is not exciting, so they make us businessmen sound like a great lot of villains."

"I've been among my fellow vampires," Jane said, still ready to bolt. "I've tasted of your new blood. Not exactly a delicacy. That story about the taste of what they call 'mudclots' is going to press in the Otherworld as we speak. Perhaps you'd like to follow up? If not, I will be left to conjecture."

He tilted his head, and his blue eyes narrowed. "You are an intelligent one for a vampire."

Jane clenched her hands behind her back to hide the shaking. *A story. Find a story.* "I'm half-human, sir. My mother."

"Indeed?" He raised his eyebrows and came closer, crooked his arm just as if he were offering her a walk in the park. "Then we are alike. Caught between Otherworld and the human world."

Jane looked down at the proffered arm clad in a fine linen suit.

"My arm is not my jaw, dear."

"What are you offering?"

Malcolm Ridley made a peculiar sound; a thing that reminded her of a dog's affectionate grumble. "We are alike as I said. I am also of both Otherworld and the human, and it was a great task for me to overcome the wolfish impulse and then to accept my stewardship. My dear, I want to show you the benefits of progress."

Run. You know what he can do.

The voice spoke sense, but . . . another exclusive. Another five pounds in her hand.

"Come now, girl. Many have called me mad, in my fifty years of overcoming the wolf. I know you must have suffered the same slights. It would be mad for any newspaperman to turn down such an offer for an interview. I will say that."

"I'm not mad," Jane said by reflex.

"Prove it to me."

That did it. She took Malcolm Ridley's arm. "An exclusive interview then."

"Lovely." They walked around the front of the warehouse toward a small door. Ridley spoke. "I know you have heard, as have I, of vampires stealing into London, taking children for their meals. I know that you yourself must feel somewhat of the hunger of the savage within and of the urge of every civilized man, especially every Englishman—and woman—to tame that savagery. It is our nature. The English are the noblest race on earth, destined to bring civilization to all worlds." He paused before the door of the warehouse. "What does the blood hunger feel like for you then, dear?"

"I . . ." Jane hesitated. "I feel a great ache. So much so that when I was a child my mother thought I had a stomach malady and feared ulcers and bursting sores. It was not un-excruciating."

"Indeed, hunger is torture for mankind but thrice so for the vampire."

Jane forced a smile. "I wish to hear about you."

"You do understand this, yes? What you felt is but a shadow of what a full-blooded vampire feels. I know you cannot doubt that. You have been among them, seen the lengths they will go to satisfy that hunger."

"Yes," Jane said, thinking of them carrying off Charles to their firepit.

"Upon finding myself in control of my situation and with the assets to prevent their predation, I felt I had no choice. I could not allow vampires to run rampant through London, committing savage murders and escaping back through madgekin doors."

"But they still do, don't they?" Jane asked. "Or they have recently."

Ridley's eyes narrowed. "Not since we closed the old doors. They should not be able to."

Interesting. Malcolm Ridley either was hiding what the cabbie had revealed to her or else he had not heard it. Nor did he know that at least one madgekin door still operated. "Go on."

"That is all, dear. Just keep that in mind as we go in."

He opened the door to the warehouse.

An enormous stench struck her nose. It was as though they'd bathed in the "mudclots" from the vampire village. A dull roar permeated the warehouse, the grinding groan of a machine.

The warehouse was dim save for a few gleaming gas lamps. And the eyes of more Riders, moving about between crates. They walked down a half flight of stairs onto a recessed floor.

Most of the roar came from one immense machine that took up half the warehouse: a great thing of steam pumps, conveyer belts, and a massive funnel at one end. It grumbled and groaned, letting out gouts of steam—the moisture in the air making the stink worse.

The smell was so overwhelming that Jane hardly noticed the woman in black or the immense Riders that closed in behind her and Malcolm. When she did, she found herself meeting the narrowed eyes of Beverly Ridley.

"I remember you," Beverly Ridley said over the low thrum of the machinery. She pointed at Jane as her vast skirt fluttered in the steam from the machine. "Insinuating terrible things! Insulting our reputation!"

"I'm . . . oh dear." *I'm terribly sorry,* she nearly said, but under the woman's cold gaze, Jane straightened. She had nothing to be sorry for. "I was seeking a story for the paper."

"Well, you found one. The help disposed of my brother John!" She growled, and her eyes glimmered with tears. "We spent all of yesterday arranging his funeral. And he barely twenty years old!"

Now, Beverly, claws in. I've made Jane the reporter an offer," Malcolm said.

"I am sorry for your loss," Jane said.

Malcolm and Beverly Ridley didn't answer but continued walking, and Jane, her arm clutched firmly in the crook of Malcolm's, went with them deeper into the warehouse.

Jane could not help but notice that the Riders closed in behind her.

Along with the smell of the gamey meat, now fresh and thick with the added stink of offal, there was a strange, nose-tingling stink—something that reminded her a bit of the smell of alchemy in the air near Ridleyville.

Several Riders were pushing wheeled hoppers nearly as big as train cars to the end of the conveyer belts. "We can only trust the Riders with such business," Malcolm Ridley said.

"What business—oh!" Jane drew back in initial horror at what was in the hoppers.

"You see, dear, you were right."

Each hopper was full to the brim with rats.

They appeared still alive but drugged. A faint green light came from the rats, the sign of alchemy. Their little claws moved, feebly clutching the air, and their tails hung limp, occasionally flicking.

"Now," Malcolm Ridley said and removed his arm from Jane's, moving to stand next to his daughter. "It seems you have your story."

"Yes, I do," Jane said. "A horrid story! You feed your employees ground rat!"

"A terribly scandalous headline it'll make, no doubt," Ridley said. "The picture of cruelty. Another condemnation of the heartless industrialist. But consider this." His voice rose, commanding. "The alternative to this was to let whole vampire populations prey on the rest of the Otherworld or to continue their plans to escape into the human world and live there, preying on humanity. What would you have done?"

"It's not as if vampires have discerning tastes," Beverly Ridley said. "They're ponderously stupid."

Jane glared between the man and the hoppers full of twitching, alchemically drugged rats. "I've been among vampires! They are no different than any other creature in their capacity. If they are stupid, perhaps it is from absorbing these soporifics you feed the rats! I—" Jane began, but Malcolm Ridley cut her off.

"Now. Pause, and consider. You return to the *Voice*, and you write up an account of this place. A great fuss goes through the Otherworld, and some vampires perhaps refuse to work for us. Given the number of employees we already have to manage, it will be no trouble to replace them. And other vampires, my dear, will work for anything that might quench their horrid hunger. Or . . ." He paused deliberately, voice still deep, echoing and commanding above the machine's roar. "Here is another scenario. I make a generous, anonymous donation to the fund for needy students at Guldenberg, your place of study. I allow but for one condition: this particular donation must go toward students who seek to complete their education but for whom circumstances have forced away from such. Students in their eighteenth, nineteenth, even twentieth year."

Jane, for the first time in days, couldn't find the words.

He was offering to pay her tuition. And with his money, it would not be a matter of five-pound advances. It would simply be "taken care of."

"Such an offer does not come with other conditions, I assure you," Malcolm Ridley said. "You are free to write as many polemical condemnations of the industrialist as you wish. Rant as you desire. But keep this fact quiet for the good of both worlds." He swept a hand across the hopper of alchemically drugged rats. And his face twitched. "Stop that!"

She spun around to see the Riders coming closer. "Sir, I came here in good faith!"

Ridley's face seemed surprised. "Stop!" He held a hand up.

There was an odd buzzing in the air, a crackling as if of electricity. Almost as if the Iron Riders spoke to each other. But they halted under Malcolm Ridley's glare.

"Harder to manage than rabid manticores," Malcolm said. "They don't seem to like news-peddlers."

Beverly Ridley put in her opinion. "A ridiculous trade for a woman. Look at you. You're nearly human. You could fetch yourself an excellent husband. No doubt you will when you tire of this as long as you focus on practical matters at Guldenberg instead of this fancy."

Jane glared at the other woman and turned to face Malcolm Ridley.

"Well?" he said. "Say the word, and your tuition is covered."

"An uncommonly generous offer," Jane said, and the words were as painful as if she'd just agreed to go back to the asylum. The words wrenched inside her: "But my profession is in the business of answering questions."

Malcolm Ridley's face twisted. "Do not test me, girl. I've just lost my son. Take the offer and go."

"Do you threaten me?" Jane said, more bravely than she felt. "I've seen your secrets, sir. I know about the children's bones and—"

Another Rider surged up to Malcolm's shoulder, reaching toward Jane. She backed away, found more Iron Riders surrounding her.

Beverly Ridley's nose twitched. "Father, they know something about her. What is this? Why are they so curious?"

Malcolm Ridley's cold blue eyes were even worse than the Iron Rider's bright gas lamps. "Children's bones? What nonsense are you speaking?"

"I have seen—"

"What are you hiding, girl?" He stalked forward. Jane backed up—right into Beverly Ridley. She whipped around and found a Rider closing in from a third side, creating a neat tri-point barrier around Jane.

"I can't smell anything in here," Beverly said, "but we could take her outside."

But something changed in Malcolm Ridley's face. Something lit up in those cold blue eyes, and his gaze widened, and he growled. "You have it."

"What?" Jane asked.

He advanced toward her, his hands raised in fists. "You have it. You have it on your person!" He bared his teeth. "A box. Oh yes, you do."

How did he know? Jane backed away, found a Rider just behind her.

"Give it to me."

"An exit would be very handy at the moment . . ." she whispered in case a man in a green suit was listening.

Nothing.

Malcolm Ridley was almost upon her, so close she could see the wolf's-head cufflinks trembling at his wrists. "I will tear you to shreds myself. Give me the power source."

Jane reached out, trying to grab anything that would help protect her from the werewolves and the Riders.

Jane's hand met the nearest hopper, full to the brim with rats.

She pulled herself behind the hopper and shoved it with all her strength.

It overturned, and the flood of twitching rats crashed into the two werewolves, a squirming, squeaking tide burying them to their waists.

She ran, dodging between the wheeled hoppers, keeping them between her and the Iron Rider just to her right as other Riders turned and drove at her. She ran and ran between the lines of rats till she reached the enormous grinding machine.

Jane seized a pipe but immediately pulled her hand away. It was scalding hot, channeling steam to turn mechanisms in the belly of the machine. She tried a protruding knob of steel—not too hot. She yanked herself up just as a Rider caught her.

Metal claws closed over her shoulders, pulled her back down to the floor. Jane twisted, yanked one shoulder free with a nasty slash to her flesh, but the Rider pulled her backward, and another seized her leg, throwing her face first to the wooden floor of the workhouse and—

Charles, she thought.

And then something struck her backside—no, not her backside, but it struck the box.

A high, ear-drilling whistle filled the air. Was the Iron Rider *screaming*?

She flipped around, now free from their hold, and scrambled to her feet. Four Riders waited behind her, but three of them had their eyes turned on the one that had struck her. Great coils of lightning crackled along its body, down its spiderlike arms, and arced between its gas-lamp eyes. Jane backed up till she was at the great grinding machine, but the Riders didn't follow her; they watched as their compatriot grew white hot, fused together, and then melted, the enchanted steel going to slag.

A scream echoed in Jane's ears, a gagging scream like that of a man hanged with his neck unbroken.

Jane didn't wait. She turned around, seized metal protrusions and scorching pipes, ignoring the burns on her hands, and scuttled to the top of the great machine through pipes and dials and gears, over a spur of metal, until finally falling onto a conveyer belt full of twitching rats.

Jane scrambled to her feet, kicked rats out of the way, and ran against the movement of the belt as it rose to meet the funnel and the grinder. Rats squirmed and feebly flailed around her feet. She waded through them to cross the conveyer belt, but she couldn't keep her footing. The belt under her feet began to slip, and she scrambled to seize the side of the funnel and pull herself up to where she could stand—

She made it to her feet. A small window, showing the blessed light of London outside, yawned a good ten-pace leap from her.

A Rider rose in front of her, spidery legs holding its bulbous body and wheels aloft.

The box.

Balanced on the edge, Jane reached for her backside. Her dress was torn, so her hand went through the rents and met the metal directly.

Jane ripped the box away from the makeshift hiding place.

The Rider raised one metal-clawed arm, crackling with alchemical light, and waited there, suspended, just staring at her.

Jane hurtled the box like a brick right at the Rider.

The box connected with an enormous flash and boom: lightning arced between the Rider and the metal of the machine, pipes broke and steam vented into the air, and the whole world shook. The box just bounced away and landed on the conveyer to her left among a pile of green glowing, twitching rats, and Jane jumped right into the mix, snatching it up. The box was red-hot, and she pressed it against her dress, wincing at the pain.

The Rider died, white-hot metal seizing up, its joints melting to slag, and fell to the floor of the warehouse.

The way was clear.

The machine clattered with more Riders, climbing away.

Jane hesitated on the edge of the conveyer belt, staring at the window. A great gap yawned beneath, wider than a tall man. With a fall farther than from the gable of a row house—a fall directly into Riders and werewolves. The recessed floor in here meant that the fall outside wouldn't be as far if she could just make it through the window.

"Help?" she whispered.

Had the green-suited man been her imagination?

The only sound was snarling. Below, among the Riders, two enormous red wolves waited, eyes glowing blue-gold.

Charles's words came into her head: *Puckish luck to you, Jane.*

She shut her eyes and jumped.

The Riders and the werewolves below her were a whirl. The air from outside met her nose, and her foot caught on the edge of the window as she toppled through it, the ground looming before her—

Jane landed smack in something wet, tumbled over, and rolled into the mud of the street.

The mortar-man looked dumbfoundedly at the girl who had just landed in his wheelbarrow of wet mortar.

Jane scrambled to her feet. No leg crumpled under her; her whole body was one huge bruise, but she could run. She clutched the box in her hand, despite the heat of it remaining from the Rider's strange death, and ran away down the street.

As she did, she bellowed out as if someone might hear and write it down, "The new blood is rats!"

Chapter Sixteen

In which our Gnome Lays Bare his Convictions and Formulates a Plan with the Aid of a Timely Arrival

THE UNDER-MARKET, AS USUAL, WAS A STUDY IN ECONOMIC DEPRESSION. A few bare booths selling only the piles of milk and straw stewed together to make "cheese." A drunk redcap lay on his side in the street, cheesed to the ears. A madgekin hawked his trinkets, little bits of carved wood no doubt blagged from the human world.

No sign of a vampire.

Charles turned the already-worn pages of the *Manifesto*. "Marx, Engels, you maniacs," he said. "Shouldn't have come here today. Shouldn't have trusted the vampire. Shouldn't have been so damn unrel . . ." Charles couldn't even bring himself to say the word, though Riordan certainly wasn't listening.

No vampires to be seen. Neither Billy and his compatriots nor Jane.

Charles thumbed through the *Manifesto*, idly read a page.

Where is the party in opposition that has not been decried as Communistic by its opponents in power? Where the opposition that has not hurled back the branding reproach of Communism . . .?

"Oh, that's bloody comforting," Charles said. "That's what I've got to look forward to? You want to rile up a brace of housewives, you call a thing Communist?"

A thick hand closed around his throat, yanked him backward under a tangle of blue vines. "Quiet, gnome," came the voice of the Irish vampire Billy Mac Baal.

Hot, rotten-meat breath swept across Charles's face. A dozen pairs of yellow eyes stared at him out of the dark under the vines. Vampires.

Billy leaned closer to Charles. The light from the Under-Market glimmered off the scars crisscrossing his head. "I've got a batch of fellows here interested in what's in your head, so they are."

"Oh, aye," called another vampire. "Brains in butter sauce!"

"Put him in boiling water. Softens up the innards, it does!" another vampire called out.

"Oy now!" Charles said through his choked throat, struggling against Billy's iron grip. "You came here to hear me speak on Communism, I thought! If we're going to go through this eating business again, I'll make you pay for every speck of gristle!"

Billy hesitated and withdrew his hand. "Will ye shut it?" Billy bellowed to the others. He coughed. "I, ah, I'm after a bet I made. Fair play to you, gnome, long as you can talk your way out of dinner."

"Blooming Puck's guts," Charles said, feeling his neck where the vampire claws had dug in. "You like what I say, or you eat me?"

Billy gave an enormous, broken-toothed grin. "It's no daemonsday today, stump."

The vampires all waited, the others' eyes turned on Billy, and while they did, more yellow eyes appeared in the darkness of the undergrowth. "There's more of you?" Charles squeaked.

"Franz!" Billy said with the first sign of warmth and friendship Charles had heard in the Irish vampire's voice. A thickset vampire, a head taller than Billy and with a thick black mustache, stood next to Billy. And damn if Billy didn't seem so excited he might embrace the fellow. "Franz, all of ye, here's that gnome that should have gotten et, I'm after telling you about."

"A gnome vith convictions," Franz the vampire said in a thick Bavarian accent. "And a bit daisy, Billy says."

"*Crazy*, you big Protty lug," Billy said with an affectionate rub of Franz's shoulder. "Gnome, this is Franz and his mates. Heretic Bible lickers, but they're not English, and we're after a long friendship." Billy leaned in closer. "If that mound of fleshy priest knew I was here. he'd eat me his own self, so he would. Now talk!"

"Well . . ." Charles flipped open the *Manifesto* and found he couldn't read a word of it in the dim light. "Well . . . the workingman . . ." He found his throat quite dry.

"Faster, gnome."

Hell and Puck's tricks. "It'll be a finer speech if, ah, I get a platform if yeh get me."

Billy motioned. "Climb up on whatever you like, English. It'll give us a better view of the calf meat."

Charles sprang out of the vines, and feeling like an exposed fox in a hunt, he ran to the nearest table at which a madgekin sat snoozing in the constant heat coming off the river.

The vampires didn't follow Charles, strangely, but remained under the shelter of the vines, glaring yellow-eyed at him.

He had no doubt they could catch him if they wished. But at least this was the way to properly address an audience. Charles leapt onto the table, turned around to all the Under-Market to face the vampires. "Working fey of the Otherworld!"

Two pixies giggled, and one squeaked, "Charles! Hullo, love!"

Charles held up the *Manifesto* and found his hand was shaking too much to read the thing. "Uh, hullo . . ." *What would Marx say? How to start?* "Brothers and, uh, sisters of the Otherworld. Redcaps, madgekins, brownies, badgebears . . ." He couldn't remember a damned word.

Uncle Riordan's face popped into Charles's head. That sad, confused look as he tried to recall the rest of an aphorism.

Charles found his words.

"My name is Charles. I am the nephew of Riordan, the gnome accused of poisoning John Ridley."

A whoop went up from the pixies, and two rock trolls, who had been sitting under a nearby tree chewing pebbles, let out a great groan, loud enough that the madgekin at Charles's feet woke up and started yelling.

"I know what you think!" Charles added over the noise. "Has the gnome some new information? Some insight into why his uncle did it? I do not!" Jeers now from the pixies and trolls. The vampires were still hidden under the cluster of vines. "I can tell you this—there was no more reliable gnome than my uncle!

How in the world could he come to poison his master, you ask? I have no answer. All I have is my own anger at the Ridleys and . . ." *And what? Bloody Puck, bloody Titania tupping the bloody donkey.* "And . . . and I have empty pockets."

They laughed. Good. Sweat dripped from Charles's cap into his eyes. He rubbed it away. "Well right! Each one of us is without work because the Ridleys found a cheaper way to make their seven-league boots, their time-tricking clocks, their invisibility cloaks. Because of the new blood."

The pixies booed drunkenly and yelled something about vampires.

Under the vines at the edge of the square, Billy moved enough so that the light coming through the vines could catch his bared teeth.

Don't rouse the crowd against each other. You're supposed to have a brain in that bonce.

"But what makes you think those vampires have it any better? You tasted their new blood?" He pointed to the rock trolls. "Have you?"

"I eat naught but onions," the rock troll said, "to keep meself healthy and windy—"

"Right," Charles interrupted. "Well, I'm told it tastes like the worst fen in the Choke! Most vampires can hardly hold it down!"

The pixies and trolls and scattered madgekins all went quiet at that.

"Don't believe me?" Charles motioned to Billy. "Come on, come out and tell us! There's a great army of yeh already!" Charles yelled.

Billy didn't move, but Franz did. The immense German vampire stepped forward from under the shelter of the vines.

Immediately, the Under-Market sprang more to life than Charles had thought it could. The sleepy madgekins, cheesed pixies, rock trolls, and two dozen redcaps and boggarts, having been hidden till now, roared. A rock sailed across the square, shattered at Franz's feet. A vinefruit, gleaming blue, sailed through the air and splattered his pants. The huge vampire froze, cowering.

And Billy sprang from the vines to his friend's side, hissing at the rest of the crowd.

"Stop!" Charles bellowed. "The lot of you! Quit that! They're here to help us!"

Billy and Franz scrambled to Charles's side while the crowd glared daggers at them. One redcap picked another glowing blue fruit from the nearest vine and reared back to throw it, but Charles shook his fist at the fellow and bellowed, "Speak, vampires! Tell them what it tastes like!"

Billy and Franz clung to each other, trembling below Charles's table.

Charles leapt down from the table and smacked Franz on the arm. "Go on, tell them what it tastes like!"

Franz lifted a hand. "Tastes?"

"The new blood!"

Franz coughed, nodded, and said in a thick and booming voice, "Das new blood tastes . . . vas ist das . . . like shallot. Shallot of a dog."

The rock troll yelled, "Nothing wrong with shallots! I have thirteen each night for the fine digestion of—"

"Not shallots!" Charles boomed. He leaned to Franz. "You mean, uh, shit?"

"Oh! Yes. Das is . . . the shit of a dog."

The crowd actually laughed. Charles saw more Otherworld creatures filtering in from the nearby avenues and alleys, even some he recognized from his time working at the factory. A couple of big, scarred badgebears, retired fighters, and one purple-warted ogre, arms crossed. They glared at the vampires, but they listened.

"Tell 'em more," Charles said.

"Many of us are sick from das new blood. The young, they cannot take it. Mothers having babies, they go dungy."

"Hungry," Billy clarified.

"It makes us slow, tired, sick," Franz said.

"Aye!" Billy said, emboldened. "I go days without food, to the point of death, so I do. And only then will I nibble a bit, and best to follow it with gin to kill the taste."

"Ve have," Franz said, raising his arms, "only poison for food and no money to purchase better food. Ve only took deal with verevolves because our children starve. All vampires know this."

Charles clambered back up the table. Now he could feel Marx's words burning inside of him. "They've made it just as difficult for the vampires as it is for us!" he yelled. "What is your purpose, people of the Otherworld? Why do you work?"

A pixie squeaked out, half-slurred, "Cheese!"

"No," Charles said, and the crowd laughed. "But you've hit on it, haven't you? If the Ridleys offered to pay you in cheese, well, it's better than nothing! So it goes for our brethren the vampires with this new blood! You were all ready to attack them, but they are held hostage by the whims of the industrialist! The Ridleys keep some of us drunk on cheap cheese and others hostage to this new blood, restrict our passage into the human world and tell us it is all for our good as if the Otherworld were not full of creatures who could decide their own destiny! I say *no more!*" Charles stomped on the table. "No more of this 'go here, go there, we can do anything we like because you need the wages!'" Charles raised his fist in the air. "We take the fight to them!"

The crowd went silent.

Billy blinked up at Charles. "You're mad, gnome. Bedivvah, how're we going to do that?"

"Simple!" Charles said. "You vampires, and any of you still working in Ridleyville, show at your place of work tomorrow. And simply don't go inside!"

"Vat?" Franz said. "Ve just . . . vait?"

"Nah, you make a ruckus and a nuisance of yourself and shame those who do go inside. This'll only work if the Ridleys lose a good portion of their workers. We'll join you. The rest of the Otherworld!" Charles motioned to the crowd. "We'll stand with you against the industrialist bourgeoisie!"

Faces in the crowd turned to each other quizzically.

"That means, ah—"

"Wait," Billy interrupted loudly. "Gnome, you haven't said a word about dealing with the Iron Riders."

At that, the crowd went restless, rustling and talking among themselves and then yelling at Charles. Bits of bread and vine flew through the air—toward Charles now. "What kind of idiot are you, gnome? You want us to be cut to bits?" A pixie squeaked, "Riders ran over my cousin!"

"We can't be afraid!" Charles yelled. "Protest and then sneak away! Sabotage machinery, supply lines—until the Ridleys hire vampires, pixies, badgebears, and gnomes alike to fill their factories and pay us fairly!"

"The Iron Riders, gnome!" Billy said. "They'll run us down, so they will. Don't matter how many we are, how much we sneak. They're built to hunt and kill Otherworlders!"

Charles opened his mouth but realized he didn't really have a response to that.

"Well, gnome?"

Charles swallowed. "Ah, surely mate . . . they can't get *all* of us . . ."

Billy snorted. "How many's enough now? Only *half* of ye'll be burned tae bones?"

Charles thought back to that group of metal-wheeled monstrosities, pouring children's bones into the river. One Iron Rider could make a good dozen Otherworld creatures disappear. Billy wasn't wrong about that.

Charles's hand tightened on the pamphlet. *What would you say, Marx?* Surely the Communists in the human world had dealt with police, but those were other humans, men with horses and guns.

Charles desperately turned around and flipped through the pamphlet as if it could offer a solution.

"You!"

Charles turned back and blinked. There was a new madgekin standing in the crowd. A familiar fuzzy face below those clouded goggles.

Oh, thirteen hells. It was Pedge.

"You promised! In the morning, blagging cheese for me! You didn't show, gnome!"

"Hullo, Pedge," Charles said, his voice squeaking. "Shouldn't you be watching your door? Anyone could come through with you gone."

The crowd rustled, laughed as the madgekin stalked forward, yelling, "I hear there was a gnome making a ruckus, and I knew right away 'twas you, and you owe me—"

And then someone knocked Pedge out of the way. A small someone with unusual strength for their size. Someone in a tattered, stained dress.

Jane!

"I'll tell you what you should do!" Jane stalked forward, exposing a dress and petticoats that had been ripped so badly she left no bit of leg to the imagination. She was bloody and muddy as a pit-fighting manticore. "I've been in the human world!" Jane bellowed. "Looking for answers from the Ridleys, and I found them! I can tell you what the mudclots are made of!"

At that, the rest of the vampires spilled out from underneath the vines, coming hesitantly forward toward Charles's makeshift pulpit, despite the grumbling from the rest of the crowd.

"The new blood . . ." Jane said and paused, swaying on her feet. "The new blood is rats!" When the vampires stared at her, disbelieving, Jane went on. "Think on it! What other creature could the Ridleys grind up without anyone noticing? I saw the machine! I saw the alchemical shine of the rats, drugged with their concoctions! Those same concoctions go into what you eat, vampires! Believe me, for I have vampire's blood in my veins, same as you!"

"They cannae be so cruel!" Billy said. "Not even the wolves!"

"They can," Jane said and faltered on her feet. Charles leapt down from the table, and she promptly leaned on him, digging the heel of her hand into his shoulder. Her fingers shook where she pressed them into him. "I have it from the mouth of Malcolm Ridley himself."

The whole crowd roared, and the vampires turned to each other, and their faces twisted into sneers. After a moment, Franz said, "I have eaten rats at the greatest constipation—"

"Desperation," Billy corrected Franz.

"Desperation! But not like this! Ja, ve cannot eat drugged rats for vages!" He gestured to the other vampires and to Charles and broke out into a long speech in German, catching himself at the end to add in English, "Ve must go vith the gnome!"

"The Riders!" said one of the other German vampires.

"I can kill the Riders," Jane said.

And that, more than anything Charles could have said, shut the crowd right up. Vampires, redcaps, badgebears, madgekins, all regarded Jane, rapt and silent.

She was holding something, Charles realized, and she raised it now. It was the box—the same box that had caused all the trouble—but now warped, twisted like it'd been left in a fire. "A Rider has only to touch this, and they burst like a bug under a boot."

The crowd erupted in noise, in shouts: "What? No!" and "We can kill them!" and "What about those fogs I hear?" and "Rats! Cannae believe I've lived off rats!" all at once.

Charles had eyes only for Jane. She mouthed, *They know we have this.*

It came to Charles for once, as if Marx and Engels had jumped into his blooming head. He bellowed louder than he ever had. "Listen! All of yeh! Go home and grab any boxes yeh've got! Jewelry boxes, anything of comparable size. How smart can an automaton be? Not much, I'll wager. We can fool them into thinking we've got a whole legion of the things! You understand? Tomorrow at the start of work! Show up, bring a box! We'll scare 'em off!"

Jane staggered, started to fall, and Charles propped her up. "Just a minute longer, love," he whispered. "On your feet a minute longer."

The crowd had gone silent, vampires, boggarts, trolls all. Even Pedge was stroking his furred chin although he glared at Charles.

And then Billy spoke. "Divvil take all of ye. I'll be there, so I will."

And then the Irish vampires as one yelled agreement. Then Franz and the

German vampires. And then from across the square, the redcaps and boggarts and trolls and pixies. Even the badgebears growled out their assent.

Charles's head swam and fluttered like a dancing water-nymph. *Marx, Engels, you goblin-minded maniacs. You ought to see what you've wrought.*

And then Jane fell. Charles just managing to catch her before she sprawled in the mud. Her pale-yellow eyes were just next to his.

"You all right?" Charles asked.

Her eyes were wide as full moons, her hands trembling in his. "I nearly died."

"Yeh're well all right now, Jane. Well—"

She kissed him.

If he hadn't been the only thing keeping Jane up, Charles might have fallen over himself. She pressed her parched lips against his and held the pose, both of them still with wide-open eyes, and then she pulled away—

"Oh, heavens," Jane said. "I think I really am mad."

Billy sniggered.

"Shut yer gut-munching trap," Charles snapped. "Help me prop her up, get her home."

"Charles," Jane said, clutching his shirt. "Wait. I am sorry . . . I am so . . . oh, dear, that was so improper, that—"

For the first time that day, Charles didn't wonder what to say, even as he wondered at himself for saying it.

"Nothing to be sorry about, love."

Chapter Seventeen

*In which Passions Torment our Gnome and Vampire
whilst they Attempt to Attend to Practicalities*

YOU DON'T WANT TO GO HOME?"

The two vampires and Charles escorted her through the now-shuttered streets of the Towering Market. Jane's breath came ragged, and her cuts burned where the Riders had slashed her, but she continued walking doggedly forward. "I need to go to the *Voice*. This'll have to go to print in the morning." She inhaled the alchemy-stinking wind, felt her lungs burn, and felt a strange tingling on her lips. *Oh, dear heavens. For once, I might not mind if I woke up in the madhouse.*

They reached the door to the newspaper office, and Jane turned the knob. And nothing moved, locked tight. Jane knocked at the hardened witchwood and called, "Mister a-Lokk?"

Nothing. There was no ground-shaking grumble from inside, which meant Mister a-Lokk had chosen tonight to go home early. Jane sank to her knees, took the lockpicks out of the bun in her hair, and started working on the door, cursing the half-light, cursing the ache all over, and cursing her foolishness.

"Hang on now," Charles said. "Hold still a bit, Jane."

"What is—oh." Charles pulled a twitching rat from the folds of her dress. It squeaked and tumbled to the ground and crawled off, leaving a trail of green slime.

"Must be a leftover from your adventures," Charles said.

"Thank you," she said. The world swam, and she put a hand on Charles's shoulder to steady herself. "One moment."

"Blooming hell, Jane, the story can wait!" Charles said.

"It cannot," Jane said, her balance returning. "It must be on the stands in time for your strike. You know this, Charles."

"Bedivvah," Billy snickered. "She's already treating you as her cocker!"

"Quiet, yeh lump," Charles snapped.

Jane flushed all over and redoubled her efforts to pick the lock, ignoring them. *I only have to get in, write the story, and then I can sleep. If I can ever sleep again.* The image of the Iron Riders, their gas-lamp eyes flashing and their wheels screeching, went through her head.

Jane's hand trembled. She forced it still.

And then she remembered kissing Charles.

Jane focused on the lock. Just the lock. Set the wrench, slip the picks in, find the catches, and lift them, so the door opens.

She wouldn't think about Charles, standing just at her left.

She wouldn't think about clutching his firm little body and kissing him as if he were the great anchor keeping her from drowning.

Nor about how good it felt—as though she'd been considering such a thing for ages.

There. The lock clicked, and Jane shoved the door with her bruised shoulder.

"So, ah, you got back through Pedge's door?" Charles asked as they went into the dark room lit only by a few floating white faerie lights.

"Yes, I thought to bargain with him or riddle with him, but all he wanted to know was where you were. Luckily, I knew. He was quite in a hurry to speak to you . . . Charles"—she swallowed the impulse to call him "dear Charles"—"so I simply followed."

"I do owe him a right load of cheese once this mess is all over."

Jane went straight to the largest desk, lit the candles Mister a-Lokk kept, and found a few blank pieces of foolscap.

Her eyes flittered across the words already written on the paper.

The chief characteristic of the Artist was a wan look, indeed, a wanness of spirit, a wannery of nature, a wanity of wanities . . .

She flipped the pages.

Oh, that the world could know that within this crusted outer shell resides the sweet yolkish egg! Why are the wise impenetrable to the kind arrows of my art?

"All set up?" Charles asked.

"Uh, yes," Jane said. Mister a-Lokk would need some proofreading for his novel. And perhaps an explanation of how arrows worked.

"Billy and Franz, they're going for something to help scrub the bad blood from your cuts. Said no one but a vampire can properly treat the blood."

"I am just fine, thank you," Jane said and looked up from the page.

Her eyes caught Charles's.

Both of them looked away.

"I'll write this story, and then . . ."

"Right," Charles said. "You'll need more paper. And ink. I'll gather it up."

"Thank you very much."

"You're welcome."

Jane almost asked why they weren't yelling "Mad!" and "Boor!" at each other. And then she remembered the kiss.

"Do not think on that now!" she muttered.

"What's that?"

"Nothing, Charles." The paper needed a story. Jane clutched a quill in her trembling hand and began to write. *Faithful reader, I come to you having escaped the very grip of death.* "Barely an exaggeration," she said to herself. *My tale is one that will tear the Otherworld apart. Prepare for an uprising the likes of which has never been seen in Faerie.*

As she wrote, her head cleared. The world may have been mad, and she may have done mad things, but she was answering questions as she'd been called to do. *The warehouse was patrolled by the fearsome Iron Riders who enforce the darkest whims of the werewolves. At its heart, an immense machine hummed and chugged, great gears that could turn the heart of the earth. One end crowned itself with a funnel, and the other spouted a half-dozen conveyer belts.*

She paused, gathered herself. The light was so dim and spotty in here. *And the purpose of the machine? None other than the bane of work in the City Beyond, the producer of the "new blood" that has given the vampires sustenance in exchange for free labor!*

She kept writing on and on until she reached the punch line—*The new blood is rats!*—and then the spotty light went quite suddenly dark.

Jane woke up facedown on the paper, a rough hand shaking her shoulder. "Jane! Oy! Wake up, love. Come on now."

She felt herself lifted from the chair by immense hands and moved to a pile of blankets. Then there was a furious stinging in the cuts on her arms. "Ow!" Jane's eyes shot open. "What is that?"

"Lush. Bit of wet. Drink this, you won't see a hole in a ladder." Billy was rubbing a cloth into her cuts.

"Why—*ow!*—why in the world would you put alcohol into my cuts? Stop that?"

Billy glared at her. "And who'll know more about blood than a vampire? Just settle down. Alcohol purges the blood. Helps it keep, so it does, when we're after a good haul of it."

It stung terrible, and Jane was not convinced that it was doing any good, but she could set up a basin of well water to wash it out when she returned to her mother's. "Let me up. Let me finish the story."

"I've got that, Jane," Charles said. "You just talk and let me write. My penmanship's not quite up to snuff, but it'll be readable."

"No, Charles, I couldn't—I say, stay away from my legs!"

"You're torn to bits, so you are. Don't worry. We're not concerned with your virtue here."

She had to admit that the burning pain in her cuts, now that Billy and Franz massaged alcohol into them, had the advantage of keeping her awake. Jane coughed and pulled her leg away from the vampires. "That is quite enough. Leave us to finish the story."

Billy and Franz raised an eyebrow to each other, but Jane held firm. "Go!"

The two vampires moved away from Tokk-a-Lokk's desk to the stairs down to the printing presses, leaving Jane and Charles alone.

"Where were we then?" Charles asked.

"What does it say?"

Charles peered down at the page. "I've got 'Rats. The dregs of the . . .' That's about where we get a fault line down the page."

"I-I was attacked by one of the Riders, Charles . . ." Again, that impulse to call him "dear Charles." "By providential luck, it struck the box, which I had hidden near my backside—oh, wait, don't write that."

"The box, yeh," Charles said. "Might be best to leave that bit out as we'll want our advantage over the Riders to remain a surprise." Charles reached into his pocket and withdrew the box, whistled. "Not much of a box anymore." It had warped and distended, the hinges cracked and the whole thing looking as though an ogre had stepped on it. "Ah, blooming Puck's bits. The thing inside is gone!"

"That little piece of meat?" Jane asked. "I'm not surprised. The whole thing was spitting lightning and fire."

"The key to the Ridleys' secret magic could be ground to mudclots, Jane. Thirteen hells. This is a rich development."

"My goblin professor said it wasn't enchanted though," Jane said. "No particular magic about the meat inside."

"Eh, the goblins're just concerned with whether they can look it up in some dusty volume."

"Professor Murgalak is a scholar!"

"En't he the one makes them Human Facts? How humans mate with the aid of bees and that?"

Jane sighed. "You have me there."

Charles whistled through his teeth. "How're we supposed to make this work? It's a damned big risk, it is, and no guarantee the Riders won't see right through it. What on earth was I thinking? Unreliable as winter weather, this is, and—"

"Come now!" Jane interjected. "I heard a few words of your speech! Have you given up on Marx so easily just because there are a few metal monsters to deal with? What about the . . . proleturtle and the . . . bousey-bee and . . ." Jane forced her eyes open, forced herself to stare at Charles, "I chased the Ridleys all over London and was nearly ground to mudclots"—*and turned down an offer to complete school, no questions asked*—"so risk is part of what we do! You shouldn't be such a goddamned boor!"

Charles chuckled. "I do believe I just heard you swear, Jane."

"Write my mother! She's very concerned about such things."

"Come on now. Let's finish this story up. I want to write my speech down after we've gotten you home. That is, uh, if you think the paper'll print it."

"Yes, I think that would make quite an excellent side-piece. Good thinking," Jane said. She flushed. Such romance. Swearing at him and talking about her mother. And she had called him a *boor* again.

She continued with the story, though her words were hardly as coherent as they would have been if she were putting them on the page herself. It didn't matter ultimately. Charles asked for clarification a few times, and once, after Jane had mumbled a long sentence of "injustice and social problem and not unlike the savagery of civilization," he chuckled and said, "A minute here. I'll just punch that bit up."

And then they were done.

"You'll head home as well?" Jane said. "The printing crew should be here soon, and Mister a-Lokk, to set the type."

"Nah," Charles said. "Need to write down me speech. Maybe I'll bed down on the floor in here if I get the time. You still have that pass for the Ridley doors?"

"If not, there'll be another in Mister a-Lokk's desk."

"Good," Charles said.

Jane stood, and all the black spots in her vision rushed together, and Charles ran to her side. "Oy, now! Take a nap in the boss's chair. He owes it to yeh."

Jane slumped against Mister a-Lokk's desk. "No, I'm all right. My mother will be terribly worried, and I must explain a few things to her." Telling her mother the truth wasn't so intimidating after the Riders and the possibility of joining ground rats in a mudclot packet.

"Lean on me then."

At the door of the *Voice*, Jane said, "It'd be best to send me with Franz, you know, as you've got to write the speech."

"Right. Don't know where he got to though."

And Jane realized they were quite alone in the office of the *Voice* and had been for some time.

And Charles's fierce, dark eyes under those bristling brows, so alive and intelligent, locked onto hers.

Her heart quailed. *Why on earth did I kiss him?*

And whatever other part of her spoke for her heart, whatever part of her had reassured her in the madhouse and told her to use witchwater on her mother—that part of her truest to her hopes—said, *Because you want him, you fool. He's alive and afire in a way no one in your life is.*

"Charles, I . . ."

You've offended the Ridleys. Your life is on a timer. You may never finish school or even finish out your eighteenth year of life. And here is the first man in your life worth a look!

She opened her mouth to speak, to let all the feelings that swelled in her out, and no words came.

After what could have been minutes or hours or days, she said, "Charles?"

"Yes?"

There was no way to say it.

"I, ah, I will see you at Ridleyville tomorrow."

And strangely enough, he tugged at her skirt.

"Excuse me?"

"Down here, love," Charles said. "There's no footstool handy."

"I don't—"

"Must I spell it all out for yeh?"

Jane knelt down.

Quite suddenly, Charles had his arms around her neck, and he was kissing her. Jane's whole body went aflutter, so much that she couldn't really tell whether she kissed properly or not—she thought she must be, for they were moving their lips, and that was proper kissing, wasn't it—and then she lost those thoughts as well. He was rough and hard like tree bark, his beard wiry against her lips, but she relished it. She opened her mouth to his, her teeth brushing his rough lips. She rather liked it and chewed gently—

"Ooh, felt that!" Charles pulled away and touched his lip. "A bit of a nip, eh? I might have figured you were a biter."

"Oh, I am so sorry, dear Charles, I—"

"No worry, love. Rather liked it, I did."

They kissed again. Jane truly didn't know what she was doing, but Charles was quite willing to show her.

When he finally pulled away, Jane's heart fluttered and danced like a bird's wings, and she gasped for air.

"One small matter, love." Charles said. "Next time, you swoop right in when you want a pash, eh? No more of this skirt-tugging business."

"I'll remember," Jane said, a flush of scarlet in her cheeks.

"Good night then. I'll fetch Franz." Charles kissed her one more time.

Jane managed to stand, putting more than half her weight against the doorframe, while Charles went to find Franz.

It seemed he was gone a long time, but perhaps that was just the feeling that she quite needed him here, next to her.

Chapter Eighteen

In which the Great Faerie Strike is Begun

IT WAS A FUNNY THING. CHARLES COULD HAVE SWORN HE FLOATED OVER the ground down the stairs of the *Otherworld Voice*, looking for Billy and Franz.

He'd put his lips on his share of the fairer sex, and it was always a fine time but not like this.

Jane.

The woman who'd made more trouble for his life than any other surely. And the one with more fire and grit than any other—man or woman for that matter. He'd met a lot of fellows who thought themselves daring, but she had a set on her, bloody right, bigger than a minotaur's—

Charles turned down a stairwell, nearly tripped on a number of letters scampering up the stairs, away from the printing press. He kicked an *E* and several *T*'s out of the way, and several letters swarmed him, throwing themselves at his shoes. Charles, chuckling, tiptoed more carefully through the escaped letters to a landing and stopped dead.

There was Billy, and there was Franz, and they were doing the same thing he and Jane had been. Kissing.

Billy caught a glance of Charles and shoved himself away from Franz. "Oh, angels burn me bits up! I really should have eaten you, yeh wee lump!"

Franz reacted quite differently. He snarled and leapt forward, clutched

Charles's neck in his thick right hand, and lifted Charles right off the ground. He barked something in German and then, "Nobody can sew!" He shook Charles, sending red spots through Charles's vision. Charles clutched vainly at the vampire's steel grip. "Nobody can sew!"

Billy waved a hand. "Nobody can *know*, love. Put him down for the nonce. He's after a good batch of secrets. Let's see if he can keep ours."

Franz dropped Charles onto the wooden landing. Charles clutched at his throat. "Blooming Puck's balls, you didn't have to squeeze the life out of me!" Charles coughed. "Just because I learned yeh're sods!"

"Sods?" Billy sneered. "Is that what you say, you sap-sticking wee stump, tupping that halfie vampire?"

Charles coughed, swallowed in a throat that definitely felt narrower than it had before. "Don't call her a halfie."

"Don't call us sods!"

"What d'yeh call it? Mandrakes?"

"Not sods! Not mandrakes! We're lovers." Billy took Franz's hand. "Same as you and the vampire girl."

Charles's neck felt like it had been in a vise. "Didn't know the word offended, mate. I never met any, ah, lovers of your sort."

"Course you have," Billy said. "You never knew a couple of bachelors who greatly enjoyed each other's company? A couple of spinsters with a great fondness for one another? Couldn't bear to be parted due to their great friendship? We're after three years of a *great* friendship, we are." Billy elbowed Franz with a ribald grin.

"Huh," Charles said. Billy was right. There'd been old Dorian and Bill back in Bredwardine, who just fit that description. Never connected with a woman to marry, either of them, so they agreed to live with one another out of great fondness. Now that Charles thought about it, there was his aunt Lilian and her great schoolfriend Gertrude, and . . .

"We don't go 'round showing it off, especially not to mouthy fellows like you," Billy said. "But we're here. Not just 'lovers.' There're fellows I know, you might call them women, so you might, if you knew their origins, but they say they're men, so that's what we call 'em. There're those you might say *he* or *she* to, but they don't fit either." Billy raised one of his great lumpy eyebrows. "And if you're going to go about calling us sods and mandrakes and buggers, pretending your movement only has room for straight-laced folk out of a corset and dress catalogue, you can stuff it, for we won't—"

"I've got it, mate," Charles said. "All are welcome in Communism. Apologies."

Billy swallowed whatever he was about to say and nodded. "Fair play then."

Charles realized he'd just apologized to a vampire.

Well, I kissed one a few moments ago. Suppose my relationship to vampires is going to be different from now on.

Billy seemed to realize it too. He nudged Charles with his boot. "Don't be a lump o'mush like. What's the business?"

"Oy now," Charles said. "Franz, I'll need your help for Jane to get to the door to the human world if you don't mind." Charles nodded. "Respect, mate."

"We'll see," Billy said.

They returned upstairs.

Jane still leaned against the doorway, her eyes bright in the light of the flaming stars and the eternal Otherworld twilight. "Cheers then," he said to Jane, taking her hand.

"Luck, ah, luckish Puck to you, Charles," she said, and her face twitched.

"Luckish Puck, Jane," Charles said. A smile big as sunrise cracked his face. "Luckish Puck."

He watched her go, leaning her slight frame on Franz, and couldn't help saying to Billy, "That's quite a girl. Angels take me. More spark than a whole factory."

"Come off it, wee schoolboy," Billy laughed. "Tossing flowers and dancing, so you'll be at this rate." He leaned back. "If I didn't know that chit to be such a straight one, I wouldn't trust her any thicker than her newspaper."

"Don't call her a chit, either," Charles snapped, and he winced remembering how often he'd said similar things.

"That box. You got more than one of those like?"

"Nah, mate," Charles said, still watching Jane walk off. "They're, uh, rare. That's why you're to bring decoys."

"That's your scheme? Boxes? Devil's arms, gnome, I really ought to just eat you."

"You can. And you can keep on eating rats after that. Or you can trust me."

Charles's eyes felt heavy as lead. But forcing them open, he took another piece of foolscap and wrote down every word he remembered of his speech today, minus the talk about the boxes.

He peered down at the page. Couldn't say where any of those commas and colons and periods were supposed to go, but other than that, it was well all right. He signed it, *Charles of Bredwardine*. And then added, *In the name of Communism*.

Blinking away tiredness, Charles crawled to a corner of the main foyer for the *Otherworld Voice* and closed his eyes.

Just before he went to sleep, he thought he saw Riordan's face, frowning at him.

"What is this foolishness?"

The ground shook under Charles. He rolled over, blinked. "I'm sorry, Uncle, I don't—oh, thirteen hells!"

A wood troll the size of a train car loomed over Charles. His scaly skin gleamed in the light coming through the open doorway, red eyes like two bright-burning coals. He was dressed in an approximation of a suit: a torn and tattered jacket and vest and pants that were far too tight.

"You! What are you doing up here? The printing crew is downstairs!"

The building rumbled, Charles realized, because the printing press below them was roaring away.

"Uh, sir," Charles said, springing to his feet, feeling the rush of the wood troll's rotten-meat breath, "Jane asked me, she did, to make sure you got her latest story."

"Jane?" The troll's enormous nostrils flared. "What has Jane to do with you? I have a story today on the moral virtues of fiction and the increase in readership among the Otherworld, penned myself since she turned nothing in—"

"It's the new blood, sir," Charles said. "She found out what it was. Announced it at a rally last night."

"What?"

Charles pointed toward the troll's desk, and the troll, with great lumbering strides, seized the papers from the table and yelled, "Is my sanctum not sacred? Is my muse so mocked?"

ᴏMurgalak's ᴏFun ᴏHuman ᴏFacts

Humans and rats have a great deal in common and once had a flourishing trade in grain—before cats took over the grain trade using their powers to hypnotize humans. A few sensible humans still eat cats and talk with rats but sadly most do the quite foolish opposite.

He went quiet, thank Puck, reading from one of two papers Charles had left out on his desk: one Jane's story and one Charles's speech. The troll held up Jane's story and bellowed, "Stop the presses. We must stop the presses!" He picked up the other paper. "What's this?" He shook it at Charles. "This reads like it is from a pamphlet!"

"From the rally last night," Charles said. "Where Jane announced the secret of the new blood, sir, and that's . . . um . . . that's the speech the fellow who led the rally gave."

"Really?" The enormous wood troll put the paper closer to his face. "This isn't copied from the pamphlet by Marx and Engels?"

"You've read it?" Charles said.

"I've read everything," the troll said. "And I can definitively say that this is the worst abomination of a sentence ever put before eyes, human or otherwise. My word. Punctuation abandoned like a forlorn child."

"Oy now," Charles started to say. "That's—"

"Nonetheless, I think it will set the whole Otherworld on fire." The troll grinned, showing enormous teeth.

Charles felt positively light-headed as though he'd imbibed a pound of cheese. Thirteen hells. After this, cheese might seem a bit pale.

Chapter Nineteen

In which a Mysterious Figure Reveals his Motives and Nature at the Last

JANE AWOKE TO NOISE OUTSIDE HER DOOR. PEOPLE WERE MOVING ABOUT downstairs in her mother's drawing room.

It had all been easy last night—despite her encounter with the Ridleys. The automaton doorkeepers hadn't stopped her, and she'd gotten to her mother's door and only seen a policeman in the distance, and her mother had been asleep, a Bible splayed out on her chest. Jane had gone to bed warm with thoughts of Charles, all well for once.

Now she crept to her door, turned the knob.

It was locked from outside.

"Mother, really?" Jane muttered. She put on the only dress left that the newspaper business hadn't destroyed, sank to her knees, and began to work at the door with her picks. It was quite a sight easier than the *Voice*'s door, with only two pin mechanisms.

From downstairs, she heard voices. At least one man's voice, which she faintly recognized, and a woman's voice. Jane crept down the stairs. "Mother?" Jane called. "I am sorry. I was out late for the paper—"

"Dear!"

Two men waited in the parlor, one wearing the collar of a preacher. Pastor Farnsworth and Deacon Bilibard. An older woman stood behind them—her mother's friend Doris.

She knew them all. They had been there the day Jane went to the asylum.

Run now, her instincts screamed, and this time, she listened. She bolted for the door, seized the knob, and the pastor shouted, "There's a policeman on the step outside, young lady!"

Jane froze. That policeman she'd seen last night then. Of course.

"Dear, I have been so worried!" Her mother said. "Four days home, and you running about, gallivanting and coming home hurt and dirty when your prescription was to be scripture and rest!"

"I've been home a month," Jane said, turning to face her mother.

Her mother's eyes twitched and went colorless, and for half a second, Jane had hope. But then her mother's eyes went dark and intense again, and she said, "Four days you've been home!"

Damnation. The witchwater had indeed worn off.

Her mother broke into a sob, and the pastor put a comforting hand on her shoulder. "You try to trick me as if I can't believe my senses?"

The pastor moved forward, letting out a harrumph, adjusting his tweed vest under his coat. "Your mother wishes you to return to the asylum, just for a matter of days, dear."

The two churchmen came closer, maneuvering past the staircase to corner her in the foyer of the home.

Jane bared her teeth, growled as viciously as Billy ever had. "Do not touch me!"

The pastor's eyes went wide, and he raised his hands. "Evil! Evil is in you! Bilibard, help me restrain her and fetch the holy water—"

Jane seized the doorknob to take her chances with the police. But before she could pull at it, the door opened.

No.

Opened was not the right word.

The door swept aside like a curtain. The knob melted away in Jane's hand. And as it did so, Jane became aware that she was moving slowly like she fought her way through water. Everything else had taken on the same pace, including the churchmen behind her. Her mother's sobs slowed down and became long low groans.

The whole world was trapped in amber. Except the man who came through the door.

A man in a green suit and with hair of flame.

"Oh, hullo!" he said. He straightened his bright, shining green lapels and adjusted the lace of a green-tinted cravat. Two gleaming green tails fluttered from the end of his coat around his boots. "You keep strange revels here tonight, dear."

"You!" Jane found she could speak and move in real time, though no one else did. "I thought . . . I was in such great peril, and I thought so many times that I could have used your help—"

"Ah." Fire danced in his green eyes, a twist of green and orange. "There is the problem. I cannot move directly against Malcolm, and each time you needed my help, you faced his opposition directly. I am . . . constrained." He grinned at the slow-moving friends of her mother. "And sometimes I am busy. There is a great deal of mischief to be made in two worlds." He raised three sharp fingers and two long thumbs, waggled them like a child imitating an ant-walk. "Like this."

All of a sudden, time ratcheted back into its normal speed, and Jane whipped around to see the members of her mother's church all abruptly falling to their knees.

"Oh, Heavenly Father! I see him!" the pastor said.

"I am so sorry about the puddings," the deacon said, falling to his knees as well. "So many puddings I ate!"

"Such a fine waistcoat you have, Heavenly Father!" the pastor said. "And an excellent chain for your watch—"

"Oh God, know this!" her mother's friend Doris called from behind them. "I don't regret poisoning me husband, only the circumstances that led to it!"

Jane blinked at Doris. "What's that? Doris?"

The green-suited fellow giggled, a high, piercing laugh, and his flame-hair moved with the laugh.

"Doris, my word!" Jane turned to the green-suited fellow, momentarily regretting that she couldn't follow up on that particular story. "What did you do?"

"I've given them a little taste of their true insides," the man said. "They think they see God." He giggled maniacally. "Any questions you would ask your mother?"

Jane paused.

Her mother, along with the others, had fallen to her knees, but her face was red and tearstained, puffy, and she let out only wordless sob after sob, clutching at her shawl and crumpling it in her fingers.

"She's under some powerful enchantment, isn't she?" Jane asked.

"No," the man in the green suit said. "Not that I can tell."

"And I suppose you are a great enchanter?" she asked the fellow in green.

"Thou speakest a'right."

"That's an odd way to say it." Jane waited there as if stretched between two poles. The strike would need her. And there was Charles. And this fellow— whoever he was!—could certainly be an asset. There wasn't enough time to ask her mother even if . . .

She couldn't help herself. "Mother, who was he? Who was my father?"

Her mother moved her mouth but made no sounds.

"Mother?"

Her mother reached for her face and clutched at her lips. And she cut her own chin open with her nails, scratching at her face. Red blood ran down the wrinkles in her mother's chin.

"Mother, no!" Jane said. "No, don't worry about it! Mother!" Jane seized her mother's hands, holding them still away from her. "Mother, it is all right. It is all right. You needn't tell me."

Her mother whispered, "Jane, I am mad."

"No, Mother, you're not. It's all right." Jane felt especially peculiar as she cradled her mother's head against her own breast as though she were the mother comforting the child. "You're not."

She cradled her mother like that while the churchmen blubbered about waistcoats and puddings and Doris muttered, "I didn't think that poison would work so well! Me husband fell right over!"

The green-suited man paced in the foyer and grimaced. "Will you remain here sobbing when I've offered you such a way out? Come now, I had plans."

"No," Jane said, getting up. Her mother seemed to have calmed although she would need a cup of tea, and Jane hadn't time to stoke the fire and put the kettle on. "But you must restore them to normal. My mother—"

"This is how she reacts when she sees who she truly is," the fellow said.

"Take whatever veil you've put from their eyes please," Jane said. "And then I would kindly follow your route out of here."

"If my meddlings have offended, just a twist, and all is mended," the flame-haired man said, sounding like a pouty child.

She knew that phrase from somewhere. Jane peered at the fellow. He was terribly familiar now that she thought it. As if she'd seen him in other places besides the two incidents on her first night home. "Indeed."

He waved a hand, and her mother and the others let out great gasps of air. Jane and the fellow ran out the door before anyone could say aught.

The green-suited gentleman waved a hand, and the carriage waiting to take Jane away twisted, turned, and swept aside like curtains, and they walked beyond it into the street. He waved another hand, and they passed through the next block of buildings, the bricks and mortar and wrought-iron folding around them, swinging open and closed as easily as a set of French doors.

"Ah, thank you," Jane said, quite flushed at the strange doings. "A door anywhere, I see."

"One of my many specialties."

"Can you make a gate to the Otherworld?"

"I can indeed," he said, "but there is one place Malcolm has me, that canny wolf. I have agreed not to carry living creatures through."

"I'll need to get to the Otherworld quickly then," Jane said. "I do appreciate the help. Have you any . . ." Oh, dear, what would Charles say? "Have you heard of, perhaps, this human notion called Communism? Perhaps you've noticed the inexcusable behavior of the industrialist toward the common man—"

"My dear," the man said with another giggle. "You do delight me with all this mischief. You are a thing like myself, I think, and you know what fools these mortals be!"

"I've heard that," Jane said. "Is that poetry? Or something you've said? Have we met before, my peculiar gentleman? Before the other night at the manor?"

He giggled without answering.

A little fellow in love with mischief who could make any sort of door and with a fondness for poetry. It was so familiar. It . . .

She wavered on her feet as if struck by a thunderbolt.

"Puck's tricks," she said and meant it. "*Puck!*"

"I am that merry wanderer of the night," he replied with another grin. "Give me your hands if we be friends."

Chapter Twenty

In which the Iron Riders are Confronted by the Great Faerie Strike

CHARLES, HOLDING A BUNDLE OF THE NEWSPAPERS UP ON HIS SHOULDER, took a flying leap from the ferry onto Coins-Teeth and landed on the dock. He ran for the streets.

Before the same gate where not three days past Charles had hurtled a brick at Malcolm Ridley, the vampires massed. Two distinct groups, in fact: those trying to get through the half-open wrought-iron gates and those trying to stop them. The line that sought to get through outnumbered the strikers and surged against the gate. The strikers stood off to the side for the most part, bellowing in lilting Irish or German accents, though a few ventured into the crowd of workers. Charles recognized Billy just as the big Irish vampire leapt forward and shook his fist in the faces of the others trying to get in the gate. "English mugs, all of ye! They're feeding us rats, so they are!"

"We've called Iron Riders!" an English vampire yelled from inside the gates.

"Gone running to mum, have we?" Billy yelled back.

A big vampire broke ranks from the group trying to get in and swatted a smaller Irish vampire on the head. An enormous vampire—Charles recognized Franz—yanked that troublesome vampire back by the ears and battered his face, crushing a pointed nose flat. The English vampire fell backward into the crowd, which rushed him inside the gates.

"Franz, no violence!" Charles bellowed.

Every vampire turned and stared at Charles.

He dropped the bundle of newspapers, opened it, and held up the first paper on the stack. "Hullo."

"What took so long?" Billy said.

"Ja, ve have been here for a shower now, and you see it is verrückt!" Franz added.

"Wait now!" Charles bellowed, walking forward. "Go on, you English bootlickers! Go on in there!" Charles waved at them with his free hand. "Just remember, nothing will change for you! Your lives, your children's lives, your children's children's lives, you'll be hunched over an assembly line with no reward at the end of the day but a packet of ground rat! Oh, yes! That's right!"

Charles held up the paper as he walked closer, proudly displaying the headline, "The New Blood Is Rats!"

"See this?"

Stupefied silence met his advance. Charles kept walking, holding the paper up, and realized, *Thirteen hells, there might not be a one of them that can read.*

Billy was squinting at the paper, mouthing the words. Franz shrugged. "I don't bleed English."

"It says—" Charles started and sighed. "Puck's guts, there has to be *one* of you who can read the thing."

"I can read it, so I can," Billy said. "One minute, you wee bastard." He peered at the words a bit longer, nodded his head as if they read what he thought they did. "I know, I do, that there're more of you English who can read than let on!" He raised a hand. "The new . . ."—he squinted at the paper again—"the new bl-uh-blood is rats! They're feeding us rats, so they are! There it is in the divvil-damned paper!"

A new flurry of shouts went through the crowd. Charles bellowed again, feeling his voice almost go hoarse. "Let the bastards go! Let 'em go in! Let 'em eat rats if that's what their lives are worth!"

He kept shouting, but the crowd was riled now, and Charles thought he was going to scream his whole throat ragged. "Let 'em go! You bastards, you thickheaded—"

The last word rang out in sudden silence.

Metal wheels rang on stone behind him.

Charles turned, and his innards went to pudding.

He had never seen so many Iron Riders in one place.

They made a wall of metal across the street between the warehouses. Their gleaming eyes beamed, blue and yellow, bobbing back and forth on bulbous heads. Gears and joints whirred and turned in their segmented necks. Their backs burst with appendages, spidery arms ending in hooked poles like pikes, scythes, clamps with sharp teeth, little fingers of lightning crackling at the ends.

The gas-lamp eyes all fixed on Charles, gleaming. The greenish air reflected off their steel, bulbous bodies.

Behind him, the vampires broke out into wails. Footsteps echoed of vampires scattering. "Wait," Charles called, forcing the words through a dry throat. "Wait!"

"Gnome," Franz's voice said, "we cannot place them."

Let Jane be right, Charles said, and that thought brought him strength. He reached under his coat and pulled out the box, using his hand to keep the squashed shape clamped shut. He raised it high in the air.

"You've got your boxes, yeah?" Charles asked.

Billy's strained voice sounded from Charles's side. "Yeah."

He chanced a look over his shoulder. Well over half the strikers had run, but those who remained followed Charles's lead.

The line of vampires lifted up all sorts of boxes: jewelry boxes, music boxes, shoe boxes, boxes woven from finger bones and sticks.

The Riders remained where they were, staring, bright gas-lamp eyes gleaming. Their metal arms didn't even twitch—frozen in place, gleaming alchemical fire.

Greenish-silver clouds formed overhead, and dark green rain began to pelt the Riders. It steamed away from the crackling lightning on their appendages, ran down the metal, and pooled on the ground.

Charles stood in the rain, holding up the box in front of a line of vampires doing the same.

The Riders faced him.

No one moved.

Chapter Twenty-One

In which our Vampire Enlists the Help of the Eternal Mischief-Maker

Puck?" Jane put a hand to her heart. Oh, my. Oh goodness. All of a sudden, it seemed as though the busy London street would all float away. "*The* Puck? Robin Goodfellow?"

He waved a four-fingered hand, making a *shh-h* sound. "Puck is fine. No need for formality, not between two leapers and dodgers such as us."

"Why, I . . ." Jane's breath raced in her chest, making it difficult to form words. "I have such questions to ask you! I have always dreamed of such a meeting where I could find out the truth of your exploits with the towers and the adventurers from Africa and—"

"All true," Puck said, grinning all the wider, showing red gums above sharp teeth.

"And what happened to the Otherworld! What has become of Oberon and Titania and the old ruling class in the face of the Ridleys, for—"

"Ahh," Puck said, "that's not needed now. Let's hurry! To your strike! You must go one way, and I another, but we shall meet there."

And like that, true to his reputation, he vanished, leaving only a green afterimage in her sight.

"Oh, sir—Puck—" Jane blinked. "Oh, come now! I have so many questions!"

Only the noise of the London street answered her.

Jane crouched out of sight.

The Riders—surely *all* the Iron Riders in the entire Otherworld!—waited in a line in front of Charles and his strikers. Green-tinted rain pinged off their metal bodies, steamed off their arms, and crackled at the alchemical fire rising from each claw. They formed a barrier between the strikers and the factory and docks but made no move.

"Puck, are you there?" she whispered.

No answer.

"If, ah, if you don't mind, we could use a trick to dispose of Riders?"

Nothing. Of course, he had said he couldn't move against Malcolm Ridley. Where had he gone then?

Murgalak's Fun Human Facts

The infamous William Shakesbeard wrote a chronicle of the Otherworld that was astonishingly accurate in its depiction of Faerie yet entirely a fabrication of human mating rituals. He didn't even include the tails.

And when would he be back? He'd spoken as though he'd rendezvous with her, and . . .

She peeked out again, and at the sight of the Riders, Jane's whole body shook.

Something tapped her shoulder.

Jane whipped around, punching blindly. Her fist connected, cracked something that felt like a face. Billy Mac Baal stumbled backward, clutching at his nose. "Lass! By Judas's last meal!"

"I'm sorry! Oh, dear!" Jane retrieved a handkerchief, wiped the blood from his nose. "Those Riders are a terrible scare."

Billy pulled away from her handkerchief. "I'll be fine, so I will. S'been broken before, anyhow. Not nearly as bad as when Franz did so."

"Franz broke your nose?"

"Twice now." Billy grinned, showing his crooked yellow teeth. "Careless when he's excited, so he is. Come on, I'll escort you to the wee nutter, our fearless leader."

"I, ah, very well." Jane got to her feet, shaking. She could still feel the sensation from yesterday of being yanked away from that machine, held down by the Iron Riders, nearly stabbed.

They circled behind the group of vampires. "Charles," Jane whispered, motioning for him to come near him.

Charles, still keeping the box raised in the air, turned and walked back to Jane, a deliberate, slow walk, looking back over his shoulder at the Iron Riders all the way.

Billy whistled. "Never thought I'd see the day the metal monkeys were afraid, so I didn't."

"Jane," Charles said as he reached her. He was wet all over, faintly glowing green from a rain that had mixed with the alchemical residue from the smoke. It made him look quite ragged, and rather dashing, like a soldier fresh home from the war. "Ah, hello," Jane said and flushed. She couldn't quite remember what she wanted to tell him. Perhaps how very much she loved his fierce eyes or his stocky chest?

No, that was not it!

"Let's blag us a moment," he said.

"Quite a good idea."

They walked around the side of the warehouse, still within sight of the vampires.

This close to Charles, the urge to kiss him was overwhelming. She noted his oaky scent, the musk of the day's sweat already on him, and though she'd never enjoyed the smell of a particular man before, his was rather intoxicating.

He raised one gnarled brow. "Well then, love?"

"Hello," Jane said and swallowed at the shiver she felt from *love*. "It goes well, wouldn't you say? I, ah, perhaps I should go among the strikers and take their comments and . . ."

Charles glared, his black eyes bristling under his great brows. "What's this now? You do remember last night? Thought I was clear that I won't pull a skirt again."

"Oh, ah, yes, yes, I do." Jane flushed. "It just doesn't seem proper to k-k-k—to do that in public."

"Oh, aye, I'm right worried about being proper in front of vampires and Riders," Charles snapped.

"Well, it would be best to keep our public interactions discreet in the name of the strike and the newspaper's interest."

"You ashamed? Blooming hell, Jane, I never met a girl so full of contradiction!"

"I am not ashamed! In private, we may do as we like." She flushed. "I mean, whatever's proper."

Charles groaned. "A fellow ought to be able to lay a pash on his girl when he wants to! Puck's tricks!"

His girl. Jane tried to ignore the rush of blood to her head. Charles was being quite thickheaded, and she must not be charmed by his willingness to name her so!

"Gnome," Billy said. "Company."

Charles turned around, grumbling something about pashes and women. And Jane groaned to herself. She had quite forgotten to mention Puck.

A figure made her way through the Riders, a woman in a black dress pressing her way among the metal men, through their ranks to the head to speak to Charles.

"In God's name, what sort of nonsense is this?" the woman asked.

Jane recognized her, and her blood went cold again. Beverly Ridley, daughter of Malcolm and grieving sister of dead John, eyes shining blue with flecks of gold, walking with the loping, threatening gait of a wolf beyond the Riders. "The reporter. I might have known you'd be involved. And what's this? A gnome?" She turned to the Riders. "What are you waiting on?"

"S'pose the Riders're on strike too!" Charles shot back.

He quickly pocketed the box, Jane noticed.

"Move aside if you're to be so useless," the woman told the Riders. The metal men nearest her wheeled backward, their steel-shod rims clicking on the cobblestones. Their glowing gas-lamp eyes remained fixed on Charles. Beverly Ridley's eyes took in all the boxes the striking vampires held up, and her gaze returned to Jane.

Jane forced iron into her spine despite her shaking hands and glared right back at the werewolf.

Beverly Ridley asked, glaring at Jane, "Who's the author of that terrible speech in the paper?"

"That'd be me," Charles volunteered.

She turned her gaze downward. "Not the reporter then? I thought it was even worse prose than her usual. A precociously unreliable gnome you are."

"Oh, never heard that one, have I? We must really bother you. Suppose the industrialist is just another bully. Right, lads?" A cheer went up among the vampires around them.

Beverly Ridley growled a little, and that seemed to only make the vampires jeer her more. "Whatever is causing these Riders to malfunction"—her eyes flicked to Jane—"I can overcome it. I can make more of them, have a new army here in a matter of hours."

The crowd went silent, and then into the quiet Charles yelled, "I'll call that bluff. Go ahead."

"I'm not eating another rat, so I'm not!" Billy Mac Baal added. "Take those mudclots to hell with all of ye!"

"Ja, you ditch of a she-wolf!" Franz bellowed.

Some vampire flung a piece of masonry, and it bounced off an unmoving Rider next to Beverly Ridley. "Stop that now!" Jane called, almost surprised to find her own voice. "You don't need violence to achieve your ends! You insist on fair wages and real food."

"That's right, Jane!" Charles bellowed. He raised one hand, and the vampires all turned their attention on Charles. "These Ridleys say they're protecting humans. They say that Faerie and the human world need to work in tandem, respect each other, but what have they done? Only disadvantaged the whole Otherworld in order to advance what they want! Seven-league boots! Invisibility cloaks! Potions and amulets, all for the bourgeois to take vacations and clean house! What blessing does that bring you, folks of the Otherworld—"

"Oh, hush," Beverly Ridley interrupted. "This gnome is paraphrasing, quite liberally, from a pamphlet called *The Communist Manifesto*. It was written by two humans. Yes, that's right, your leader here is a human-lover and feeding you human ideas."

The vampires' stares turned to Charles.

"You're quoting our bloody food at us?" Billy asked.

Beverly Ridley spoke again. "Here is what the Ridley family says to your ridiculous, half-cooked demands. The new blood is not made of rats. That is a sensationalist lie spread by that paper. If you must know, it is made from pigs and dogs."

"That's no pig, so it isn't!" Billy yelled.

"We had to resort to additives to preserve the substance, but they corrupt the natural meaty flavor. John was working on ways to improve the flavor the very day he died."

"All right then," Charles said to the vampires, "we'll accept that. You just bring us the pigs and the dogs, fresh from slaughter."

She settled back, crossed her arms. "That is not practical."

"We want fresh human blood!" a vampire called from the back. The other vampires cheered.

"I don't believe the human-loving gnome promised you fresh human blood!" Beverly Ridley said. "He asked me to bring you fresh livestock. What do you say to that, gnome?"

"Come here, Charles, Billy," Jane said. "Come, before you answer her again and make this worse."

The two leaned in close to her, Charles's musky smell quite pleasant but not strong enough to overcome Billy's rotten-meat smell.

"I thought I was doing all right," Charles whispered.

"Human talk?" Billy snapped. "I'm after a whole life of eating them, and now I'm following human philosophy?"

"Stop that," Jane said. "Charles is right. It matters not where the ideas come from. They are good ideas. More germane to us, however, she has a point. You'll have to sort out food for the strikers. We can't resolve this today, and they'll be without meals for the day. Possibly all week or month."

"Livestock then?" Charles whispered. "Can you bring some through yourself?"

"Have you money for it?" Jane said.

Charles grimaced. "Just blag it, eh? Maybe you could drive something to Pedge's door before anyone's the wiser?"

"Excuse me, Charles," she said, resisting the urge to comment on his nerve. "I am no cattle rustler. And farmers in the human world are still the proletariat!"

"I want human blood, gnome," Billy said. "Livestock's all well and good, but nothing does it like a bit of human blood."

"Can't do that, mate," Charles said. "Who could I bring through? No one deserves that."

"Find a raper, a murderer like!" Billy whined, "The sort no mother'll miss!"

"Am I supposed to snatch 'em from the stir? How short are these prison walls I'll be hopping? Sides, as Jane said, prisoners are also the proletariat. Gotta give them a chance to make good."

Beverly Ridley, apparently tiring of waiting for their answer, raised a hand. "Double rations to any vampire who leaves this ridiculous strike now!"

"Stay strong, mates!" Billy said. "She's only offering you twice the rat!"

Despite Billy's words, a few vampires, hiding their faces, crept away toward the factory entrance. Beverly Ridley, with a wolfishly satisfied smile, turned to walk away through the Iron Riders.

"Go on then!" Charles yelled after her.

"Oh, but this is highly interesting," said a voice near Jane's ear.

She turned and there was the green-suited man again, grinning and showing a mouthful of tiny, sharp teeth.

"You!" she said, and Jane found herself quite flushed. "The Puck!"

"Just Puck."

Think. Think like a reporter. The strike. She'd nearly forgotten what she was to speak to him of. "I wondered where you went. I mean, not that it is any of my business, but we are in great need of some aid. If you choose to give it. And give it freely, and . . ."

"In answer to your first question," he said, his grin widening even more, "here and there."

No one else appeared to see him. If only Jane could remember what she was going to say. "Ah, perhaps you might consent to an interview?"

"None of that, not yet. Let's keep our mischief secret." He stroked his chin. "My mistress with a labor union is in dispute. But it is not *my* dispute. And thus, I can help you in a roundabout manner."

Charles's voice raised above the rustling of the crowd. "We'll meet together at the Under-Market tonight, and everyone bring a scrap of something. We'll see what we can put together, eh? A bit here, a bit there, and the stewpot's full!"

She heard the desperation in his voice and wondered if anyone else did.

She fixed Puck with her gaze. "Perhaps we could form an agreement, one that honors your agreement with Malcolm. We find ourselves in need of food for the striking vampires, brought through from the human world. You said you could not bring any living creature through your portals. Could you bring a slaughtered animal?"

"I could," Puck said. "Of course, the Puck is in need of a favor. A favor I believe you can achieve with your unique skills."

A favor? From Jane? "What is this favor?"

He stomped up and down, frowning, looking quite the petulant child. "Must you make me say it? Simply do my work, and you shall have good luck!"

"Sir, no woman ever benefited by doing a strange man's will, questions unasked."

He let out a great groan. "Malcolm's potion!"

"What is this?"

"The potion! He has a potion that helps him control the wolf inside. He would like the world to think that he does it by force of will, but it is alchemy."

"Potion? Paid for by the blood of children?"

"Only alchemy, that cursed, mischief-free science." Puck spat, and the spit sizzled on the cobblestones like flame.

"Then you know nothing about a mass murder of children?"

Puck shrugged, a very odd gesture that flattened his flaming hair. "Such a thing would be a terrible sort of mischief."

Charles was now bellowing at the vampires to quiet down and settle in and reiterating that they could scrape up a meal together. "Send folk out all around the Choke, something'll turn up—no, you can't eat gnomes, yeh savages!"

Jane turned from the crowd back to the green suit and the smile. "You want me to get you the potion that lets Malcolm Ridley transform at will. How am I to do that?"

"I'll find the opportunity," Puck said. "Merely stay at the ready. As I am an honest Puck."

Hardly comforting, but it would have to be enough. "Very well, and you will . . ."

"I'll put a girdle 'round the earth!" He paused and nodded. "Ah, and there will be fresh livestock in the Under-Market tonight."

Riders, a warehouse, and wolves flashed through her mind. *No.* Jane steeled herself. It must be done. "Then I will do what you ask in regards to this potion."

It occurred to Jane, thinking back to her first meeting with Tokk-a-Lokk, that she might wish to make fewer grandiose promises.

Chapter Twenty-Two

In which our Gnome and Vampire Seek a Much-Deserved Reprieve and Find instead only Further Complications

"YOU TRUST THE PUCK HIMSELF?" CHARLES SAID.

Jane's face screwed up in that puzzled look she got so often. Were it not for the crowd of hungry vampires standing behind them and the dodgy prospect of provender, Charles might have taken a moment to enjoy her face.

"He helped me escape my mother's churchmen," Jane said. "And he helped me into the Ridleys' manor the night of the party."

"No one more famous for stirring up trouble."

"Dear Charles, lovely Charles, I must have missed the part where we had another option."

She had him there.

"I suppose the Communist thing to do," Jane added, "if the food doesn't turn up, is to let the vampires eat you."

"Out with that cheek!"

Jane chuckled. "I thought it a rather appropriate joke."

They turned the corner to the square where the meeting had occurred just the day before. As before, the street of the Under-Market was quiet, only a few stalls selling the lumps of straw-based fake cheese. A madgekin or two snoozed at their booths. But the faerie lights flitted all about like they'd been stirred up.

And a great purple tent, one Charles'd never seen before, took up space right in the middle of the street.

"Bloody blooming Puck's guts," Charles said. "It can't be. Where'd that come from?"

"You think that's—" Billy didn't have time to finish since the other vampires rushed past him, swung the tent doors open, and tied them back. The smell of blood and offal rushed out.

"Divvil take me!" an Irish vampire squealed in delight, and the German and Prussian vampires let out similar exclamations. "Pigs! Thirteen fat pigs, new-slaughtered!"

Charles just caught a glimpse of gray-furred pig carcasses, hanging from a stake-braced pole in the center of the tent.

The vampires all rushed forward. Even Jane, Charles saw, started forward but paused. "I should let the full-bloods drink first," she said. "I should . . ."

"Puck's tricks, no. Wade in, Jane," Charles said. "While you're at it, see if you can't save me a snout and ears. I'll pop 'em in the fire."

"If you think that's dignified . . ." Jane said, her eyes going glassy. "Very well. I will. Excuse me! I'm as hungered as any of you, so do be considerate—ouch! Fellow, I'm not a pig myself! Just a haunch, and a snout for Charles—dear me, let me through!"

Charles thought he might rush in to help Jane but then thought, *She can watch herself.* Better that he remove himself a bit from the crowd. Didn't want to be mistaken for a pig—they were not unalike gnomes in height and stoutness.

He went back a bit into the brush under a few swollen silver vines. The ground was soft and spongy here, littered with old leaves. Wasn't a terrible place to sleep if one was out one's bed.

"Right then," Charles found himself saying. "Mister Marx, Mister Puck, we're well set up to face down the industrialist."

It remained to be seen whether this would help his uncle.

It shouldn't have been possible, but the strike went on a full week.

Charles yelled himself hoarse every day on the line.

The Riders never moved, even when the vampires started showing up without their boxes. The next day and the day after and day after that, more vampires joined them on the line, though Charles thought it might be more for the rumor of livestock than Communist principles. A few half-hearted strike-breakers, ogres and big English vampires, started fights. They didn't last. Charles's vampires were better-fed and angrier.

The Riders' line blocked them from the docks, so they hadn't been able to stop goods from shipping to the Towering Market, though the factories' capability was reduced.

Every night, the tent appeared in the Under-Market, a new pack of livestock hung from a set of hooks each time. Three cows one night, more pigs another, sheep another.

Murgalak's Fun Human Facts

The Puck once crowned a gorilla the King of England, enchanted so that he would appear human. Humans, of course, found it a great honor to pick the king's lice and crush them between their teeth. The gorilla was quite heartbroken at this. Being a much more empathetic species, he'd named all his lice and considered them dear friends.

The seventh night, Billy patted his stomach while Charles roasted a pig trotter over the fire. "Ah, I'm after a week of mudclots and after months of nothing so fine as this. Gnome, how'd you do it?" He sank to the ground. "You must have fine friends, so you must."

"Fine friends indeed," Charles said. There was always a catch with the Puck in the stories, but after a week now, he couldn't figure what it was. The strike'd gone off well, especially with the Ridleys distracted by the funeral.

"En't human blood, but it'll well do. Aye, Franz?" Billy asked.

"You can get by on livestock," Charles said. The stories of vampires were coming more and more into sense. "You prefer human blood though?"

"It is like your vampire girl," Franz said, coming to sit with them, surreptitiously licking the blood from his mustache. "Ve refer the human flesh. Ve hunger greatly for it. She refers to glove the gnomes."

"What now, mate?" Charles said, sitting up.

Franz's face now bore a puzzled look. "She refers to glove the gnomes, or she gloves mothers?"

"Prefers. Love. Others. Divvil take me, might well stick a handful of screws in your mouth." Billy said. "I don't reckon they're a wee couple these days, Franz. Haven't spied a stolen kiss, and I been watching."

"Oy now!" Charles replied. "Don't go sticking your pointed nose in me business!" He motioned to Jane. "S'just better to put a professional face on it, it is. We're still . . ."

Were they? For three days now, he'd shouted at the crowd, and Jane had run back and forth to the *Voice*'s office carrying new stories, and they'd stolen a few pashes in secret but nothing worth taking to bed. Every night, he collapsed at starfall, having just salvaged a few bites to eat, usually from Jane's hand, before she had to rush to the paper.

Weren't exactly proper courting, were it?

"Mate," Charles said to Billy, "tomorrow morning you're managing the strike. It's the least you can do for subjecting me to all that bellyaching about food. I'll be along after lunch."

Billy nodded and waved a hand. "I've got it in hand, so I do, mate."

Nearby, Jane scribbled on some paper, her hands rapidly splaying out the story of the strike for the day. To bring color to the updates, she interviewed a new vampire every day or some of the non-vampires who occasionally sat in on the strike. Charles could hear her saying, *Otherwise, Mister a-Lokk says readers will lose interest, and that won't do.*

He stood there and watched her write, her thin fingers sweeping across the page. A fellow could watch that for a while. Maybe lie awake after a bit of fun, watching her write, sweeping across the paper under the light of a candle.

"Yes, Charles?" she asked, looking up. A strand of hair, limp and sweaty, had fallen across her forehead.

Charles couldn't help himself; he reached out and moved her lank hair aside, near the bun she wore atop her head. She smiled, showing the tips of those sharp teeth. "Thank you."

"Oy, Jane," he said. "I reckon we need to take a meeting, just the two of us. Tomorrow morning. I'll let Billy give the morning speech."

"A meeting about the strike? Have you clues about the nature of this box or about the children's bones or about the werewolves' transformation or—"

Charles chuckled. "Just meet me over by me family's tree in the Choke."

"I've got to maintain the stories as Mister a-Lokk says circulation is up with interest in the strike, but . . ."

"You can take the morning off, love. Won't kill yeh."

"You are right." She put down her paper. "I have greatly missed you, yet I've seen you every day. Tomorrow morning."

Next day, standing outside the tree under the green-tinted dew of the Otherworld, Charles looked down at the gleaming chokevine flowers in his hand, groaned, and mumbled, "Should've planned a picnic." It was bourgeois rot, a picnic, but Jane would have loved it. Some nonsense with sandwiches, though for her sake he'd have to get fresh meat for the sandwiches.

His face burned where he'd washed in the river. He felt the shape of the *Manifesto* in his pocket. "Don't give me shame, Messrs. Marx and Engels," Charles muttered. "You've got wives, and they'll want your time once in a while."

"Lovely to see you, dear Charles."

He blinked and was surprised to see Jane standing there. "Blooming . . . I must have been a bit dazed. Excuse."

She'd washed as well although she seemed to be restricted to the one dress he'd been seeing. She'd put on a fresh bonnet, looking as fine a vision as he'd ever imagined.

Puck's guts, she's a real bourgeois girl by upbringing. Charles coughed. *Ought to be treated better, but she chose me.* "Well, Jane, uh, I reckon even Marx and Engels take breaks."

"Is that so?"

"Thought we'd go for a walk along the sylph gardens. See if we might catch a dance."

"I didn't know this was a bit of proper courting," she said, and her smile grew wider. "I thought such a thing was far too bourgeois for you."

"Oy now, Jane! The proletariat can show his lass a good time by and by." Charles tipped his cap. "I didn't see anything in the *Manifesto* against it."

"Then I must insist on your elbow, sir, as the Choke is terribly rocky." She put her arm forward.

Charles, despite having to reach up over his head, clutched her arm. As it was, her crooked elbow came nearly down to his head. It'd be close enough. She leaned into him, pressing her hip against his ear just for a moment. He liked that.

It weren't like she was the first girl to put her hips near his face. But she did something to his belly the others didn't. She was clever, canny, and didn't dance around her meaning.

"You done aught besides writing for the paper?"

"Very little," Jane said. "Mister a-Lokk's made over one of the storage closets into a room for me. There's a washbasin and a cot, and when I lie down each night, I think, well, it will make excellent verve and fire for later stories. It's certainly better than sleeping with Mother and her asylum snatchers. Though I wake every morning with a terrible pain in my back."

"The Towering Market still affected?" Charles asked and then berated himself. *Talk about something besides work!*

"To some degree. There are queues for the goods that normally stacked up, and there seem to be fewer of these human tourists coming through. I do wish we could stop production altogether."

"And how's . . ." Charles couldn't think of aught that didn't have to do with the strike. "How's that old troll? Still liking your writing?"

"He's quite pleased with circulation." She reached into her handbag, produced a weathered novel with a torn cover. "He made it a condition of my lodging that I start reading Mister Thackeray."

"Oh, that's the fellow he rambles about?" Charles vaguely remembered from his one day in the office of the *Voice* that troll brandishing a great novel at the printing staff. "It's just wallpaper in print, is it?"

"No, madly enough! It turns out to be lovely stuff."

"Suppose it's the reader not the writer," Charles chuckled.

They went silent again, and Charles's gut churned. How she turned him around! What on earth was there for them to talk about besides the strike, Communism, and the paper?

But Jane interjected, "I rather like holding your arm on a quiet morning, Charles."

Well, that filled his belly with a mighty different feeling.

They turned at the entrance to the sylph gardens: a great sweep of silver grass that shifted in the wind, grass so high it closed over Jane's head. "Come on now," Charles said as they turned. "There's a path, though you'll have to duck a bit to get through."

"Oh my," Jane said, hunching down under the grass. The path made just enough room for a gnome. She near kneeled, crouching awkwardly. "It's a good thing I didn't wear a more heavily bolstered dress."

"There'll be a break up here," Charles said. "You just stay with me now." They reached a pile of rock, old stones raided from roads and houses and piled up here along a line of trees.

It was every bit the image of the wild Otherworld. Blue vines crept over the rock, shedding faerie lights, some of which revealed the form of a just-born slumbering pixie inside. Adult pixies, removed from the world of the factories where they often manipulated fine bits of machinery, tended the floating lights, stroking the babes and singing soft songs like ringing flutes.

Here, he could forget factories, forget Iron Riders and rat meat and mysteries. Charles held a hand out to Jane, helped her clamber up the rocks. From here, they could just make out the wide, dark pool fed by a tributary of the river, a star-reflecting jewel framed with the tall silver grass.

A rare cool wind parted the grass. It sent faerie lights dancing as well over the expanse of the dark water. The stars of the Otherworld flamed and glimmered purple in the sky above, and the Otherworld sky shifted, variegated with the dark hues of night and the lighter gleam of day in the human world.

And one sylph rose from the water.

She was slim and blue-black, all angles of darkness like moonlight caught through a cloud on dark leaves. She twisted and sprang up on a streamer of green-tinted water, reaching for the stars. One blue-black finger passed across the flaming stars, and she fell back into the water, dissolved.

Two more came up on the fringes of the pond, smaller, a kaleidoscope of light with each twist of their bodies, leaping across the water, skimming the pool, leaving soft ripples lit by starlight.

"Oh, my!" Jane whispered. "I'd heard of it. But I didn't think one could see it anymore!"

"Oh, aye," Charles said. "Long as you get up early, they'll give you a show, they will."

The sylphs were joined by the third, the tallest, twisting like a willow caught in the wind. As one, together, they reached an apex of water and collapsed.

"They'll only do it at this hour," Charles said. "Used to be there was a door here, and they'd slip into the occasional human pool, bring back fat trout and sometimes a poor farmer's son who'd fallen in love. Always the poor fella promptly drowned. The Ridleys shut that door down, but they still dance for our stars if not the human ones."

"It is too beautiful not to do such a thing," Jane said. She wrapped her hand in his, her slim, ink-stained hand in his knotty one. "Oh, Charles, so many wonders in the Otherworld, yet this is the first one I've truly seen since I was back."

"We'll see more, love," Charles said, patting her hand with his other.

"I was just thinking the other day how the strike has to break at some point. The Ridleys will have to give. Every day I talk to a vampire who's left the lines, joined the strike, because they're sick of eating that rot. They'll be with you, and . . ." Her face creased, her eyes opening in a strange puzzlement. "And there'll be the matter of you and I."

"What's that?"

"Well," Jane said, "I don't believe I've ever heard of a vampire and gnome courting, dear Charles. It will be quite a matter to speak of."

"Why bother with what others say?"

Jane continued. "I'd like to work things out with Mother once it's safe to return to the human world. I am not impatient, but I must know what the truth is around my father. And if so, what then?"

"What's that mean, what then?"

"Do I ask you to Christmas dinner? I'd like that. It might make Christmas bearable to have you there."

"What's Christmas now?" Charles had heard of this human custom, but it had been a while.

"End-of-year feast and celebration to celebrate the birth of the English god. Gnomes don't observe it?"

"A great gluttonous feast? Height of unreliability. Closest thing we've got to a holiday is the to-do on the first of the month. Extra bread with dinner. S'quite an indulgence." He nodded, and Jane giggled. "To celebrate the reliability of the new month, you know. Suppose you could come to firstday meal, if Uncle . . ." *Uncle.* Charles's throat felt tight.

Jane seemed to sense his distress and changed the subject to her own parent. "Don't worry about Mother, Charles. She might be relieved that I did not seek out another vampire."

Charles seized on the chance to talk about something besides Riordan. "She serve wine at Christmas?"

Jane raised an eyebrow. "That is the question on your mind?"

"I don't mind a bit of wine."

"You're a man driven by your need for justice, and you've not touched ale nor cheese in days. I've seen it. Alcohol dulls the mind and makes a man brutish."

"Oy now, it's one thing to hear a man out on Communism, but to tell him his business in drink, I . . ." Charles paused and shut up. "Why we arguing? It's a lovely morning."

"Had you something else in mind?"

Charles grinned. "I said I wasn't tugging no more skirts now."

Jane didn't need to be told twice. Clutching his hand, she pulled him into her lap, and Charles had a right good angle to kiss her now. With no vampires prying, he leaned right into her breast and gave her a few good pashes on the lips, and she opened up a bit to try kissing French-style, and that was even more pleasant, and then—

"Oooh," Charles said. "Nip on the tongue there! Bit more sensitive than the rest of me."

"I'm sorry," Jane whispered. "I cannot help it in the excitement—"

"Nip away, love. I don't mind."

They kissed a good while longer, and then Jane cut off to hold Charles closer, and she whispered in his ear. "Now, my dear Charles, the first day we met, you made an inquiry after fun to be had?"

"Oy, Jane," he said, pulling his head back to look in her eyes. "I was a real brute to you them first days, and—"

"Stop apologizing, dear. I think I could do with a bit of this 'fun.'"

Charles's whole body flushed. "Ah."

"Yes."

"Well, for starters, we ought to get down where there's a bit of privacy." Charles started to clamber down the rocks, Jane's hand in his—

And between two blinks, there was a fellow at the bottom of the rocks, a fellow wearing a green suit and grinning like a blooming idiot.

"Sod off—er, bugger off—I mean, get out!" Charles said, motioning with his hand and thinking Billy had a point about words used without thinking. "Nothing to see here!"

"Charles," Jane said with a great gasp of breath. "It's him."

"It's—oh."

She was right.

The Puck, shorter than Jane but taller than Charles, had hair like flame, orange-red strands flickering in the morning wind, and a bright green suit.

"Ah, hullo, sir—" Charles started to say and fell off. What did a fellow say to the blooming Puck?

"You've enjoyed your livestock, yes?" he asked with a sharp-toothed grin.

Jane spoke since Charles's tongue seemed tied up. "Yes, it's been quite timely. We thank you. How did you find us here?"

"I can always find you, dear," the man said. "As I told you, we are alike. Wild as a windy heath, neither one thing nor the other. The opportunity has come for the favor we discussed."

Jane grimaced. "Now? You need this now?"

"It must be now," he said. "The elder gnome has been moved from the prison to the very spot where we must find the potion."

"Me uncle's out of prison?" Charles said. "Where'd they bring him?"

The fellow ignored that inquiry. "Come now, Jane," the fellow said.

"One moment." She turned to Charles.

"On this hangs the food for your strike." Puck made a grand motion with his hands. "But if we shadows have offended? Call the deal, and all is mended."

"No, no, I'm coming!" Jane groaned audibly and left Charles's side to stand by the fellow. "I will inquire after Riordan and seek for an interview, my dear!" she called, looking back at Charles with a weak smile. "And I will be back, and . . ."

Charles was left standing there.

He yanked the *Manifesto* from his pocket and thumbed through the yellowed pages. "Marx, you got any writings about how to tell a woman you hope she'll stick around for good?"

Marx, for once, was not a bit of bloody help.

Chapter Twenty-Three

In which our Vampire Calls upon a Lycanthrope of a Different Sort

THE PUCK WAVED A HAND, AND THE TALL GRASSES SWEPT ASIDE, LEAVING a pathway for them.

"It's a very clever thing Malcolm has done, but I'm all the cleverer," he said. "For he made me swear a deal. No opening doors between worlds for living things, and no bringing a living thing through. But doesn't it all hinge upon whether or not I open a door? Yes, it does. If it's already open, well . . ."

Jane said nothing, particularly because her belly was still quite afire from kissing Charles with a distinct sensation that she should be off in a quiet patch of grass divesting herself of clothing.

That was rather quick and forward as a brazen street hussy. Jane pushed the thoughts away. The goblins didn't make a great fuss about marriage and reproduction, and as far as she could tell, it just made trouble for humans to dance around it. It wasn't as if a vampire could get with child by a gnome. She had quite made up her mind to have her way as Charles clearly had no objections.

The Puck drew a circle in the air and pronounced, "Behold!"

"What am I supposed to behold?" Jane asked.

"The remnants of a door Malcolm failed to close entirely. Oh, he worked his alchemy, but for once, the wild world resisted him."

Now Jane saw it. A small golden slash across the grass here. Had he not been pointing to it, she never would have noticed such a thing. She would have guessed it was but a golden variation of a faerie light.

"Interesting," Jane said. "How do you have such a knowledge of doors, my dear fellow?"

"It was part of our bargain that I help Malcolm make the new doors and shut down the old. Oh, yes," he continued before Jane could gather her thoughts, "yes, I helped the canny old werewolf make those metal men and those great bronze portals and all his ridiculous work."

"Oh, my. And your former masters?" Jane said. "What do Oberon and Titania think of this?"

"With great sorrow, I must admit that they are beyond my help."

What could that mean? "Dear Puck, will you tell me of the process of making those doors? It must be a powerful magic to create new passages between the Otherworld and the human world, and—"

"I cannot," he cut her off. The silvery half-light of the Otherworld made his face look as petulant as a child who had been sent to a corner. "It was in the deal with Malcolm not to speak of such things. I am bound by my bargains."

"Now just a tick," Jane began. "You cannot tease me with such a fact—"

"Take this." Puck pressed a vial of something blue into her hand, no bigger than the witchwater container she'd used after the asylum.

"What is this?"

"It is the gleaming jewel in a crown of mischief," Puck said and sniggered, his hair dancing wildly with his laugh. Before she could comment, Puck leaned down to peel up the corner of the golden slit in the air as though he were drawing curtains, and the air rushed around Jane. "You must go to Kensington. I cannot take you through. Go on, step lively!"

"I must insist—"

"Do you renege on your bargain?" Puck's face grew serious although he showed no fewer teeth.

"No." She stepped forward.

And she stood in human London.

Not in Kensington.

The lions of Trafalgar Square loomed behind her, and the street roared with commerce, louder and busier than the Towering Market. "Oh, good heavens," Jane said. "You will make me walk again? And . . . what's this?" Jane was clad in a clean dress, a finer dress than she'd ever owned: her corset stiff as if it were new and her skirt held away from her legs by the flared, stiff horsehair fabric style called crin au lin.

Puck did not answer, and he was nowhere in sight. But all of a sudden, his voice rang in her ear, his breath hot, *You'll need a better dress. We go among the high company of werewolves today.*

Puck or no, Jane didn't like the idea that a man other than Charles had access to dressing or undressing her. "Sir, I do respect your position, but it is hardly appropriate to clothe a woman without asking."

Distant giggling was her only answer.

Could a girl accuse the Puck of forgetting himself without causing offense? Likely not. "Very well, to Kensington. I do hope you'll guide me wherever I need to go once I get there." She tucked the blue vial into her corset and noted that at least he had not made it too tight.

Despite late afternoon daylight, the gas lamps had been turned on to illuminate the coal-dust haze. The rows of brick buildings seemed even more depressed and foreboding than the last time she had been here. Thankfully, the Puck had included high-heeled, clog-style boots with the dress, so although she had to hike the edge of the skirt well above her ankles to keep it out of mud, she didn't sink.

Hangers-on and dodgy characters lined the streets as Jane turned onto Piccadilly. "Hardly the way I wanted to return to the human world," Jane snapped. How on earth did any woman walk in this ridiculous fabric? And to think, there was talk of replacing the horsehair underskirt with a metal cage! Her steps were reduced by three-quarters of their range. She would need to hail an omnibus, but unless Puck had included a few shillings in this outfit, that would not be possible.

A woman yelled at Jane from a street corner. "Talking to the air, love? A bit mad, are yeh?"

"I am not!" Jane snapped back and felt foolish.

"En't you too swank for this borough, marm?" A boy spoke from her right. His face had been darkened by soot, and he wore a cap and held a ragged chimney brush.

"Wouldn't a chimney sweep be at work this hour?" Jane asked.

"Come on now," the boy said, coming closer. "Spare some of that 'oof, miss. You've got coin. I can see just looking at yeh." He fell in just behind Jane, and she walked faster. "Give us the handbag then."

"I have no time for this nonsense!" Jane bared her teeth. "Leave off!"

He stumbled backward, fell into the mud of the street, and scrambled to his feet. "Not you again! Leave off! I'm a good Christian, I am!" He ran down Piccadilly like the devil chased him. "I en't taking babes, I said. Not for a fortune!"

"Not you again? Hang on there, fellow—" Jane started after him but paused. She wanted to chase the boy down and find out what he knew about vampires since Billy and Franz's vampires weren't preying on anyone in the human world.

But no doubt if she followed a different course, Puck wouldn't keep the bargain.

"Save me from men and bargains," Jane snapped.

The suburban houses of Kensington lined up like toy soldiers, each one identical to the one next to it: a one-note symphony of coal-stained, white beveled windows and steep front steps, a paean to the human love of neatness and straightness.

Again she heard the Puck's voice and felt his hot breath on her ear. "There it is. The corner house." Jane continued, wincing at the sensation of whispering in her ear. "I will guide you once you are in the house. Gain audience with Mrs. Unsworth."

"How am I to do that?" Jane asked.

He didn't answer.

Of course.

She knocked on the clean white Kensington door.

A serving girl answered, to all appearances a typical human servant with the same lower-class accent Charles bore. She took one look at Jane and shrunk away, shivering. "Marm? What do you want? What's your business here? We don't want naught to do with your kind!"

My kind? "I'm here to see Mrs. Unsworth," Jane said. As the girl began to shut the door, Jane stepped forward, put a hand on it.

The girl whimpered.

"For the newspaper," Jane said, trying to sound kindly. "I mean you no harm. Look, I am part human, despite my eyes."

The serving woman coughed, cleared her throat. Her eyes remained big as two full moons. "Whom shall I say is calling?"

"Jane of Guldenburg from the *Otherworld Voice*. Ah . . ." Jane leaned forward. Interesting. Two in one day, both lower-class. "Have you an experience with vampires?"

"No marm!" The girl motioned for Jane to come in through a dark, plain hallway bereft of the usual end tables and knickknacks that Jane would have expected, so prevalent at the Ridleys' place.

The serving girl ran down the hall ahead of Jane into an equally plain drawing room where gauzy curtains let in more light than Jane had thought one could get in smoky London.

And then the servant ran into the back of the manor before Jane could get a word in about vampire sightings.

Again, a lower-class Londoner recognizing her. Yet she'd been among vampires for a week, and none of them gave any indication that they'd been to the human world.

"Who is raiding the human world?" Jane asked herself. "Some other vampires come from elsewhere?"

"You are the reporter."

Jane turned and stumbled backward at the sight of an older woman in a great white dress. The woman stood so close that Jane didn't know how she hadn't heard.

"Pardon me," Jane spluttered.

The noblewoman didn't answer.

Lady Elizabeth Unsworth—this must be her—was tall, rail-thin, and pale. Her sharp eyes, brown dusted with a glimmer of gold, gleamed from above a thick scar across her nose and below more scars emerging from the edge of her hairline. Her hair shone bright white even in the dim light.

"Lady Unsworth," Jane said, curtsying. "My pleasure."

She continued flatly, "You come here? Not to Malcolm nor to Beverly?"

"I heard . . ." *I heard from the Puck himself, a green-suited gentleman who walks through walls, that Riordan was here.* She swallowed. "My, ah, sources tell me that the gnome accused of poisoning John Ridley has been removed from the prison to this residence for safekeeping. I hoped to interview him for the sake of establishing the true story in the paper."

"Interesting. We hoped to avoid attention when we relocated the gnome. It was the entire point."

"My sources also tell me that you, ah, helped Malcolm Ridley to overcome the wolf within. Also a fascinating story for the paper."

Lady Unsworth *tsk*ed. "There's nothing for it with the help. Let's get some light in." Walking to the window, she pulled the drapes herself.

The fading sunlight blinded Jane, and her skin burned with an itchy pain as though she'd fallen into stinging nettle. It had been hazy in London; here she felt the setting sun. "Welcome to Marlborough."

"Marlborough?" Jane shaded her eyes against the new sun. The wide expanse of glass gave a view of a flower garden, a vast green lawn, and a carefully trimmed hedge under the golden light of autumn. In the distance, a row of downs caught the sunset, the light throwing hedgerows and fields into an orange and green relief.

She was well into the country.

It was beautiful, and the sunlight itched her skin terribly.

"The Swindon rail station is terribly convenient, but I've found a much easier way to London."

"So . . . the door in Kensington leads here."

"All of Malcolm's inner circle has such for their country estates," Lady Unsworth said. "It was part of the deal Malcolm made when the new doors were established. You may sit for now. I'll have the help bring tea."

Jane sat, trying not to show how the sun made her uncomfortable. It had been the same at the asylum in the walks in the garden, though she'd been better able to bear it there with so much time to rest.

"You were one of the first werewolves in Ridley's inner circle," Jane said, trying to make it sound like a casual question.

"Yes, Malcolm turned me." She offered no details. "Malcolm was always able to retain the man within the wolf. Many others could not."

Jane had a great deal of questions for that, but then the help spoke from behind her.

"Lavinia's taken a fright, mistress, and I will manage the tea for now." The voice sounded so much like Charles, despite a clipped and precise accent, that Jane leapt up and whipped around.

Uncle Riordan stood there, in a butler's outfit, just as he had been that

SPENCER ELLSWORTH   193

fateful night of the party when John Ridley had attacked his reliability. The
only difference was that he didn't bear the crestfallen look of a gnome accused.

Upon seeing Jane, his brow creased. She saw the light of recognition in his
eyes, but he didn't let on.

"Hello, sir," Jane said. "It's good to see you well. And out of prison?"

Riordan gave Lady Unsworth a particular look. She nodded as if giving
permission. "I am well," he said.

"He was quite unsafe there," Lady Unsworth said. "Inspired by your strike, a
number of unsavory elements sought to free him. I offered confinement here,
and he volunteered to serve. I think we'll take our tea in the garden, Riordan.
It'll soon be dreary winter, and we should make the most of the light."

"Very good, miss." Riordan bowed and hustled out of the room.

"To the garden?" Unsworth asked.

Go to the garden, Puck whispered. *There you'll be all the closer.*

"Ah, yes," Jane said. "The garden. We'll chat there." Riordan raised an eyebrow,
and Jane smiled. "It'll be quite reliable, I assure you."

Chapter Twenty-Four

In which the Great Faerie Strike is greatly Tested by the Lure of Violence

CHARLES ARRIVED AT RIDLEYVILLE, AND THE IRON RIDERS WERE GONE.

"Where've you been? They just up and rolled off!" Billy said when he saw Charles.

"They . . ." Charles stood and stared, right stupefied. "They're just gone?"

The wall of Iron Riders that had been there all week had vacated, leaving the factory gates, the docks, and the paved path, where handcarts and badgebear-drawn carts traveled to the docks, clear for the strikers.

"We've been waiting here to see if worse comes along, so we have. But we're after near a full day—a full day you've been shirking, gnome—and nothing."

"I told you I had plans, mate," Charles said, sitting on a nearby piece of broken masonry. His whole body still ached for Jane. They'd spent weeks on controlling one's passion in the cleric school, but Charles never paid much attention to such things, and now he wished he had. "Anything gone to the docks since they left?"

"Not yet, wee nutter."

"Ja, ve thought to block the shocks," Franz said.

"Form a line, mates." This was bloody it. "Today we disrupt the production of goods, and nothing reaches their little shops. Today we *make* the bastards listen."

The factory dock doors didn't open for ages, so the line stood there and waited in the heat and the madness of the day.

"They coming out?" Charles peered up at the Towering Market, the immense black towers lost in the ever-present green haze of the Otherworld air. "Surely some merchant's waiting for stock up there."

"Patience, gnome," Franz said. "Ve have but to force this confrontation."

Charles supposed if Franz didn't get a single word wrong, he was serious about this.

When the gates opened, instead of the three or four vampires that typically accompanied two handcarts loaded with goods, fifteen different vampires clustered around one handcart. Three big fellows, big as Franz, walked in front. Each one held a truncheon, a big spiky thing, gleaming with some kind of alchemical glaze.

"This is it, lads," Charles said. "Hold the line! Just hold the line!"

The three bruisers ran forward. Franz growled something and stepped forward himself. True to what Charles had said, he held his position, and six other vampires Franz's size came forward to form the vanguard of the strikers.

The opposing vampires spread out, but Franz's men spread out with them. Silence hung in the air, save for the rumble of the factories as the truncheon-wielding fellows glared murder at the strikers.

And then some vampire bellowed, "Ye'll get what ye deserve now, English! For Éire! Ireland up!"

Charles didn't see who struck first, but two massive cracks roared out, and black blood splashed over the road. The whole street became a blur of black as the vampires fought back, seized the truncheon-bearers, and yanked them into the crowd. A high keening scream rang out. "Cracked his skull! Make the bastards pay, so we will!"

"Hold the line!" Charles bellowed. "Just hold the line!"

It was no use.

Charles's vampires broke the line. They rushed the handcart full of goods, and hiding behind bigger English vampires, the vampires pulling the handcart tried to back it up the hill to the factories. And tripped.

Crates and barrels of goods spilled out on the street. One crate toppled down the hill and shattered, spilling out a strange blue shimmer that seemed more to wave through the air than to land.

"Invisibility cloaks!" an Irish vampire yelled. More yelling answered in German. With a swirl of blue, several vampires vanished. And then more crates smashed under unseen fists.

"Hold the line!" Charles bellowed. It was useless. They'd turned into a full-fledged riot, not at all the confrontation he'd imagined.

Charles scrambled under one fighting vampire and to another, looking for Billy. "Billy, stop them!" he yelled out.

He caught a glimpse of Billy's face through the crowd, looking as flustered as Charles felt. He could tell by looking at Billy that the vampire was yelling, *Stop it!* But all words were lost in the din.

And someone screamed, the ringing scream of something much worse than a truncheon on the skull.

A silvery mist crept out from between the factories, and tentacles of fog wrapped around one vampire who had fallen to the ground, sucking him right into the fog bank. A horrible, garbled scream rang out from within, ending in a hideous gurgle.

Then the fog sent out three more fingers toward the crowd. Two fingers of fog caught at what appeared to be empty air, yanking an invisibility cloak from a vampire who screamed as he was pulled away.

"Scatter!" Charles yelled. "Run! We'll meet in the Under-Market! Get away from that!"

He doubted anyone heard the command, but they scattered just as readily. Charles bolted down to the docks. The ferry that took goods to the Towering Market had pulled up to see chaos and was rapidly disembarking.

Nothing for it.

Charles ran like the werewolves themselves were after him, down the central hub of the dock of Coins-Teeth, and along one of the docks. He didn't look back, didn't pause, just gathered speed.

He leapt out over the water. The blackish-green river swirled beneath him, and some part of his brain squeaked, *I'm sorry, Uncle!*

His hands met the railing of the ferry, and Charles seized it and slammed against the side of the boat so hard he near pulled his arms out of the blooming sockets.

The inhabitants of the ferry didn't try to stop him clambering up. They watched in horror as the fog ate its way through what few vampires had been unlucky enough not to make it.

And Charles whispered, "Puckish bloody luck."

The sort that went bad.

"Lost two of me cousins to that bastard fog!"

Billy was furious, and though Charles couldn't blame him, he also had no words for it.

The vampires who had regrouped in the Under-Market were much diminished. They sat around on the rocks and the vine clusters, wiping sweat from their heads. A couple of them who had just escaped the fog with one touch bore visible scars—long, twisting green marks like burns.

"Hell and damnation. And angels come for me with flaming swords and all seventeen wings out. I can't face that, so I can't."

Charles didn't know how to answer. After a long silence, he just said, "It's not sent by the Ridleys. Seems to just be a result of the alchemical waste in the air. You start messing with alchemy and . . ." He waved a hand. "I don't know, mate. I don't know."

"You'd best know! I en't going back there, so I'm not."

Charles couldn't blame him.

"Let's see what's on the menu at least," Billy said, standing up to head to the food tent. The other vampires formed a queue.

A strange green glimmer fluttered in the air. And before anyone could run, it twisted into the shape of a man, standing at the crest of the food tent.

No, not a man. Too short. Taller than Charles but still too short to be a man.

He bore hair of flame, a row of small sharp teeth, and a green suit, glimmering in the dim dusky light of the Otherworld as if it had been specially made to catch the light of the flaming stars.

"You!" Charles said and nearly bellowed, *Where's Jane?*

"Welcome, you poor souls! A tragic day it was," the Puck said, grinning despite his words. "I've got a real treat here. To honor your great labor against

---

Murgalak's Fun Human Facts

Goblins know from scholarship that vampires, when feeding upon humans, grow hot-blooded and brutish with a great imbalance of the humours. This is why we sometimes hear of romance between vampires and those humans between the ages of sixteen and eighteen.

the industrialist, against"—he grimaced—"Malcolm Ridley who overthrew the old order and denies you hard-working vampires what you've earned."

"What is this?" Charles said and walked closer, so he was within an arm's length of the tent. "Where's Jane gone to?"

"She made a deal with me, fiery gnome," the Puck said. "She is off fulfilling her end of the deal." His eyes lost focus, and he shook his head. "Forgive me. It is not easy to be in two places at once, but I am terribly clever and will manage it."

"What is this? Why're you helping us? What happened to serving Oberon and Titania?"

"My mistress to a werewolf fell prey," the Puck said. Charles thought he saw something like pain on the creature's face. "They were not wise enough to outsmart Ridley, more fool them. I offered my . . . talents to Malcolm Ridley, but I seek a way out of his grasp."

"Right, I'm supposed to take your word for it. You, the Puck—Robin Goodfellow—who fed a whole legion of the British Army to a hungry tree . . ."

The Puck giggled.

"And took the King of Elfland for all he was worth . . ."

The Puck clutched his stomach for the giggles. "Such a devotee you are of my work!" He wiped his eyes.

"And tricked your mistress into tupping an ass."

"That was such merriment!" The Puck shrieked with laughter. "I must say though that the antics of the last few days rival it!"

"S'no laughing matter, mate. This is a mess today, it is," Charles said. "You know anything about those Riders leaving? And that fog?"

He winked. "I thought you might enjoy that. The Iron Riders were a terrible difficulty to you, were they not?"

"You made them blag off?"

"I gave a slight whisper in their metal ears."

He could command the Riders? That information hadn't been in what he revealed before. Before Charles could speak, Billy came forward. "We're after a terrible day! What's this you speak of for dinner?"

"An excellent treat!" the Puck said. "But first, I must make one request of your leader. You frightened the Iron Riders, poor creatures, with a certain box?"

Charles became aware of several dozen vampire eyes turned on him. "What of it?"

"If I could but examine it for a moment to put my mind at ease?"

"Mate, you've got no business—"

"Don't hold up dinner, gnome," Billy growled.

Charles hesitated. He wasn't about to put the weapon that had made their whole strike possible in the hands of the trickiest creature in the whole Otherworld . . . but on the other hand, said creature had also made the whole strike possible.

And there was what he'd heard in the chamber where the Ridleys ate a man. *That box was our only advantage over . . .*

You know well whom.

Had they meant Puck? Who else could challenge the Ridley bastards?

Charles removed the box from his pocket. "Found the blooming thing when Ridley's messenger dropped it. It was Jane who discovered it could kill the Riders."

"And yet not magical at all?" The Puck touched it and winced. "Oooh. Burns a bit!" He juggled it like a hot potato, grinning all the while. "But Malcolm underestimates my strength." Wincing, the Puck clenched the box in his fingers, though his fingers smoked a little at the touch. He opened the now-warped box, hinges twisting and groaning at the effort. "It's taken a bit of punishment, hasn't it? And nothing inside."

"There was something inside," Charles said. "A bit of flesh. A withered heart." A voice in his head, a voice that reminded Charles a good bit of Uncle Riordan, kept saying, *Don't tell him so much!*

"Flesh?" The Puck's eyebrows shot up. "Oh, ho ho ho. That's an old bit of magic, that is. Clever, Malcolm. Very clever. Old and dark magic. But if you've lost the heart . . ." The Puck's eyes unfocused a bit, and he muttered, "Yes, dear vampire girl, through there, through the roses."

"What do you mean, vampire girl? You talking to Jane?" Charles asked. "Where is she?"

The Puck handed the box back to Charles without a word, and Charles snatched it up, shoved it in his pocket. He didn't answer any questions about Jane. "Useless now without the flesh," the Puck said. "But oh, Malcolm thought himself clever! Such a jest this is. His son dead of an accidental poisoning!"

"Accidental?" Charles said.

"And your little strike, upsetting all his factories and his real work! And the Iron Riders! It's been a long while since they felt fear, felt anything other than hunger." Puck shrieked with laughter. "Oh, my mischief on Malcolm will be sweet! You have no idea the mischief I'm planning!"

"Speaking of hunger, fellow, we're after a rough day!" Billy said.

"Of course!" The Puck leapt down to stand in front of the warehouse door, took the handle. "I've brought you . . ."

Charles had a good three dozen questions but bit back on his tongue. *His real work? Accidental poisoning? What's this blooming mischief?*

He forgot them all when the Puck pulled back the flaps of the tent.

Four men lay dead inside.

"I've brought you the dregs of humankind. Vicious men who steal and belittle women, who murder in shadows and betray their brethren. But I am told, just as delicious as any virtuous man."

The corpses lay there with eyes wide open and staring, their necks twisted at hideous angles—expertly broken.

"Still fresh!" the Puck said. "Not a drop of blood shed in their slaughter."

"Hang on!" Charles put a hand out. "I said no humans! No one deserves to die for the strike!"

"Bedivvah, they smell right," Billy said. "I mean, I'm with you, gnome, but they smell all right, so they do."

"Ja," Franz agreed. "My mouth full of clobber."

"Help yourselves," the Puck said.

"Hey now, a point's been made, divvil save," Billy said. "We don't need folk to die even if they deserve it . . . even if they smell the world of amazing . . . what was I saying?"

"Don't help yourselves!" Charles shouted. "We don't know! We have only his word about these men—the word of Puck, the king of trouble!"

"Why, these came straight from the noose," the Puck said. "Else the Puck a liar—"

"Well right, I'll call you a liar," Charles said. "I don't see any rope marks on their necks, mate, and I reckon there's more going on here, I do—"

Something knocked him out of the way, something unseen. And then a great slurping noise as one of the corpses' necks burst in a shower of blood. The first vampire to feed shed his invisibility cloak, and the rest rushed forward, and the smell of gore rose in the air.

"No!" Charles cried in despair. He ran forward into the carnage, seized Franz's arm just as Franz bit down on the arm of one of the dead men. "Franz, you cannot give in to this! We don't know! They're the prolet—"

Franz turned around, his eyes more clouded than any drunk man's, and he roared at Charles, blood dripping from his maw.

Charles didn't back up. He stood his ground, staring up at the German vampire now quite transformed. "Leave off, mate. Come on now. For Communism, bloody leave off!" He snatched the gore-covered arm out of Franz's grip. "Leave—"

Charles didn't see which vampire picked him up and tossed him out of the warehouse, but he went flying over the vines until he crashed into a madgekin's stall and tumbled through a patch of branches, which clung to him, keeping him from falling for one heart-stopping second.

Then the branches gave way, and Charles dropped into the river.

Chapter Twenty-Five

In which our Vampire Meets with Two Figures of Import and is quite Challenged by her own Heart

IT WAS RARE TO GET MUCH SUNLIGHT IN DREARY, SMOKE-CHOKED LONDON, especially in fall. The golden sun lit the whole lawn of the Unsworth Estate and the scattered oak and chestnut leaves that the autumn breeze blew across the walkway. It was gorgeous, the sort of sunset painters and lovers sought out.

It itched Jane quite horribly. Had she been alone, she would have scratched her skin till it was within an inch of bleeding.

The air was fresh at least, smelling of vegetation instead of coal.

They passed a row of roses attended by bizarre ant-like creatures of a sort Jane had never seen. Garbed in suits like the butler, they bobbed about the gardens slurping at the flowers, insectile heads twitching and segmented bodies lurching along.

"Malcolm's latest experiment. Attempting to create servants by alchemical treatment of insects," Lady Unsworth said. She walked sedately, dignified, without the swaying, hunting pace of the Ridleys. Jane found it easy to keep pace with her despite the discomfort of the sunlight. "They're quite hopeless, but he's ordered us all to cease relying on gnomes. When I offered to take Riordan in, I did not tell Malcolm it was for want of a good butler!" She laughed, a laugh that seemed honest, open, as if they were merely friends taking tea.

"And that is permitted? To simply take a prisoner from the jailhouse?"

"When his life is in danger, yes. Another subject: I've been reading your stories in the *Otherworld Voice.* I had no idea that anyone of vampire blood could write so. Malcolm's always said your kind are dullards."

That explained a lot. If the Ridleys were telling all their compatriots, their fellow circle of werewolves and sorcerers, that vampires were too stupid to protest a diet of ground rat, none of their subordinates might think to offer an alternative.

"You are silent, dear. Are you insulted?" Her tone said that she wouldn't care either way about Jane's feelings.

"Do you think me unintelligent?" Jane's irritation got the better of her. "Do you think me worthy only of rats for dinner? I am half a vampire, but I can say, after being among my fellows, any vampire could do what I do."

Looking Jane up and down, Lady Unsworth nodded. "Yes, I believe that." She resumed walking, and Jane resumed trying to ignore the itch. "Rats. An ugly thing to feed your employees rats, and uglier still to keep it from us, his confidants in business."

Interesting. Malcolm Ridley had *not* told his inner circle the contents of the new blood. "It is an insult to working men. Even if you reduce it all to 'meat,' there is not the nutrition needed for a man to work all the day."

"And yet you've managed to feed them," Lady Unsworth said. "The strikers are not just tossing scraps in a stewpot but are fed well each night. That fact quite attracts our workers to Communism, more than your message."

Jane didn't answer. It wouldn't do for anyone to know about the source of food for the strike. Puck had made that clear.

Lady Unsworth added, "You've also published a speech by a very interesting fellow. A gnome, nephew of the very gnome accused of poisoning Malcolm's son, and influenced by the Marxist pamphlet."

"Ah, yes, an interesting fellow." Just thinking about Charles made heat rise in Jane, almost distracting her from the terrible itch of the sunlight.

"But what is the end result? Fair wages from Malcolm? Fair food? You don't know Malcolm." There was something in those words. A long, perhaps frustrated level of experience. "I've followed the Communists for some time. I find them fascinating in their optimism and vastly deficient in their understanding of an industrialist."

"Malcolm Ridley will have to bend," Jane said. "It's been an entire week."

"Malcolm will wait you out much longer than a week, dear. He may grind the Otherworld to a halt. He may allow the strike to damage his business for years. But he will have victory, no matter how blood-soaked or grueling. He would rather see the Otherworld a slag-heap than admit defeat to one tenacious gnome."

Lady Unsworth stopped and sat in the fading sunlight at the edge of a planter on a carved stone seat among three planters that formed a small garden of flowers. Jane sat on the rim of another planter—in the shade, thank Providence.

Gathering the enormous skirt was quite difficult with lace spilling over her hands, but she finally managed to prop it against her buttocks and the backs of her legs and sit without the dress flaring up too badly.

She sighed with relief at the shade. Cursed sunlight.

"You asked about our initial experience as werewolves," Lady Unsworth said. Jane sat up. "Yes. I would love to hear."

"There is not much to hear. After the initial bite, Malcolm hired many an alchemist, seeking to control the wolf within. Most of his potions were unstable, but a few took hold. I helped him perfect that which we use now. We drink it once a month before the full moon, and all the month we are able to control the transformation."

"Interesting." The blue vial Puck had given her felt all the more conspicuous where she'd tucked it in her corset. "And still you manufacture it?"

"I have a gift for alchemy, and Malcolm would not trust a factory with that task." She didn't shift, gaze still fixed on Jane with all the focus of a tailor taking measurements. "Had I been born of a lower class, alchemy could have earned me a living, I imagine."

Riordan arrived with their tea, and the picture of an excellent servant, served Jane first.

"You know a butler should not deign to serve tea, Riordan," Lady Unsworth said.

Riordan turned a bit red in his oaky cheeks. "The reliable must take up the task when others do not."

"Well said," Jane added. "As they say, one good gnome's word is the worth of all the less reliable world."

Riordan raised a bushy eyebrow. "Indeed. The truly reliable intention is embodied in the truly reliable action."

"Yes." Shouldn't have wasted her only platitude on an introduction. "We haven't met properly. I am Jane of Guldenburg, reporter for the *Otherworld Voice*. I would love to ask you questions about the night of the poisoning."

"You were there, were you not?" Riordan asked. "You heard me serve the master wine. You know what I have told my masters, and the honest gnome need not speak more than his meaning."

"Yes, but . . ."

The voice in her ear chose that second to whisper, *The insect creatures are guarding the repository of potion in the roses. I will distract them. You slip the vial into the potion!*

Jane muttered under her breath, "No, wait! I need this interview!"

"Excuse me?" Riordan asked.

"Sorry," Jane said. "I have a terrible habit of talking to myself."

Riordan raised an eyebrow.

Hurry up! Puck whispered.

She tried to ignore him, though the hot breath in her ear was terribly annoying. Jane wished she had brought scrip. "You are accused of putting maradoth root in the wine of Lord John Ridley. If you stood before a jury now, what defense would you give?"

"You, miss, are not a jury," Riordan answered.

"I would like to know exactly what happened," Jane said.

Riordan didn't speak.

Lady Unsworth sat back, took a sip of tea. "Riordan, you serve me as a free agent. You may choose whether or not to answer her. It may be the answer could help illuminate the actions of your nephew."

Riordan pondered for a long moment and addressed Jane with all the icy politeness of a perfect butler confronted with a disreputable guest. "As you well remember, the master was in a distemper. I bore a clay pitcher meant for the help, and he mistook it for something meant for him and drank it."

"Did the help often drink wine on the job?" Jane asked.

"Employer's grace. They set out a small amount of weak wine for servants for the purpose of quenching thirst. Water in London is hardly drinkable, even for the fey." Riordan's face was carved disapproval.

"So whoever put the maradoth root in there," Jane said, "meant it for a gnome?"

"It would not trouble a gnome," Riordan answered, "as long as a privy was nearby."

Jane almost asked, *Did you do it?* But looking on him, she believed Charles.

Riordan wasn't capable of misplacing his cufflinks, much less playing a cruel joke on a co-worker, which appeared to be the source of the root. "All an accident then? The entire poisoning? There was no conspiracy?"

"I've told you what I know. Honesty is breath for the reliable," Riordan said and screwed up his eyebrows. "No, that is not right. Honesty is . . ." His beard bunched up in a frown.

"You are upsetting my butler, miss," Lady Unsworth said. "The interview should finish."

"Yes," Jane said. "Yes, I've got quite enough."

And Riordan spoke up. "Mistress, if I may, I would ask a question of Miss Jane about my nephew."

"Of course," Unsworth said.

"You know he leads the strike," Jane said.

Riordan pursed his lips. "Indeed. I saw the substance of Charles's most recent speech."

"How did you find the speech?"

Riordan pursed his lips. "Miss Jane, let me make a few things clear for your sake. You are, no doubt, filled with a great deal of pluck and savvy and all traits that serve you well as a reporter. However, you are not familiar with Charles, not nearly enough. I know that Charles is fired up with passion for his movement. I believe that Communism has stirred something in him that nothing else has. Normally, his passions extend as far as nymphs, succubi, and water sprites."

"Succubi?" Jane's stomach began a slow fall to the bottom of her legs. "He consorts with succubi?"

"You see, Charles is passionate, and the nature of passion is change."

Jane didn't answer. She was trying to get her racing head around it. *Succubi? How many women has he been with? I thought perhaps one or two in the past, and . . . I must look such a fool!*

"I believe that his actions will make good fodder for your paper," Riordan said. "I believe he will pursue this Communism he told me of and this great bluff against the Ridleys. But his passion will turn as it always does." Riordan's face softened. "Always, passion is our undoing."

Jane found herself getting up. "I . . . excuse me, I think it is best I go." *I was so direct! Is that how he likes women? Would he be done with me once he had a taste?*

Puck chose that moment of all moments to yell in her ear, *The potion!*

Jane brushed the back of her hand across her face. "I'll see myself out. If you please. You may finish your tea. Lovely sunset."

"Oh no, I must insist—" But before Lady Unsworth could gather her skirts and stand, Jane walked away.

Now go right into the rosebushes, Puck whispered.

Jane wanted to curse him and get along, but looking behind her and seeing no pursuit yet, she ducked between two rows of rosebushes, pushing through the thorns to reach the repository of the potion.

She passed two of the ant creatures, but both were occupied slurping nectar from enormous yellow flowers that hadn't been there before, no doubt Puck's work.

This was all the more difficult for the damnable tears clogging her eyes. *What he must think of me.* No. She couldn't think of that now. She couldn't bear it, not now, and . . .

A shed just in the center.

Thorns snagged at the enormous skirt, but Jane pressed on, letting the thing rip and leave bits in the brambles.

Sure enough, the row of rosebushes terminated in a small shed, the sort of place she would have guessed carried tools for tending these roses.

Or so she would think if there wasn't a faint whiff on the air, a smell like the nose-burning stink in the rat facility but different.

The sun slipped further, illuminating the garden with red light. Jane, gathering the enormous skirt, went down in a crouch. Her skirt groaned at the shape it was forced into. It was all she could do to keep from ripping the skirt away and going in petticoats.

Suppose Charles would like that in a woman! Just to rip away her petticoats and get what he wants and be done! Oh dear. Now was not the time to think of Charles, to think that she might be no more than a plaything to one like him. *Focus!*

Open the lock, Puck's voice whispered.

She'd hoped for a padlock, but it was one of the new Yale locks like the one she'd picked in the vampires' larder, gleaming with beaten, mold-poured steel. "Tension wrench and rake, no different," she said through snuffling. She withdrew the tools from her hair and bent over the lock. The Yale locks had to be levered with a tension wrench, and then the rakes could align the pins, and . . .

"Damnable tears!" She wiped them with the lace-adorned sleeve of the fancy dress. She just managed to insert the tension wrench.

And the lock snarled.

Jane was so startled, she let go, and the lock, now the metal face of a werewolf, shook the wrench back and forth while glaring at her.

"Oh, dear."

It seemed she'd found the enchantment on this lock.

The wolf bared steel teeth in a steel face.

"What am I supposed to do about this?" she snapped.

Puck didn't answer.

The metal wolf in front of her dropped the tension wrench and growled again . . . and then, oddly, sniffed at her. It seemed unsure whether to be friendly or to do its duty and drive her away.

"Are you lonely here, fellow?"

It whimpered and then growled. Perhaps a side effect of the enchantment—one could hardly expect a dog to do nothing but guard all day with no play.

It opened its mouth and panted, and she thought she saw, in the depths of its gullet, the pin mechanism.

"Want the wrench, fellow?" Jane picked up the tension wrench and held it in view. "Want to play?"

It blinked, eyes following the wrench as Jane moved it back and forth. Very slowly, Jane dipped the bent end of the tension wrench into the mudclot from her pocket and held it out for the metal wolf.

The wolf, as playfully as a dog, nipped at the wrench, shook it away from her hand, and dropped it for her to pick it up again. It panted happily, revealing a row of pins right between its teeth.

Now! Jane thrust the rake into the wolf's mouth, and it snarled and bit down, but it froze as the rake met the pins.

Its steel teeth, sharp as any grinder, hovered just on the skin of her fingers, about ready to bite down.

Jane had never so quickly lined up the pins in a lock in her life. She yanked her hand away, and the lock became just a lock as the door slid open and revealed the secret of the Ridleys' wolfhood.

It was only a small tun, silvery liquid dripping from the tip of a long tube like whiskey from a still. A hair-curling stink rose from it.

The vial! the voice whispered, and Jane pulled it from where she'd stored it down the front of her corset, uncapped it, and tipped it into the tun. She closed the door.

Jane turned and heard someone calling her name. No wolf howling, not yet. No voice from Puck.

It was too much to hope that Unsworth had been so lost in thought she believed Jane had left. The woman seemed far too canny for that. Bolting through the roses, she came out near the house along another row of planters.

And found herself facing Riordan.

"I was lost," she said.

Riordan's knotty fists came up as if he was afraid she would attack, but he hesitated. "The mistress is quite angry with you. I've been sent to search the grounds and bring you to justice."

"Please, for the love I bear your nephew," Jane said. "Let me go."

Riordan said something to himself, looked down, and then back up at Jane. "You should not put such faith in Charles."

Perhaps, Jane said, but it didn't bear thinking about, so she shoved the thought away.

Riordan frowned again. "I . . . I yet love my nephew as well. I would not have you think otherwise."

"Please," Jane begged.

"Through the house! Now!" Riordan took her hand and pulled her inside, rushed her through the manor as fast as she'd ever been rushed through a house, despite the tables she rocked with the enormous skirt and the knickknacks she knocked to the floor.

Love. The very word she'd been on the brink of uttering to Charles, and now . . . Jane's eyes clouded again, and she hardly noticed when she went through the door. "Thank you, sir—"

Riordan slammed the door.

Jane let out a heavy breath, turned, and gasped in horror.

A lawn stretched before her to a wall and a country road. She was still in Marlborough.

"Puck?" Jane asked.

Only the cool evening breeze answered her.

Chapter Twenty-Six

In which our Gnome Sees the Consequences of the Chaos Incurred at the Docks

CHARLES WENT DOWN INTO THE BLACKISH-GREEN, SWIRLING WATER. *No! Jane! Uncle!* He tried to call for help and swallowed half the river, burning in his lungs.

A knotty fist caught the back of his shirt and yanked him up. Charles scrabbled about, caught the edge of the riverbank, dug his fingers into a muddy sward of grass, and pulled himself out, coughing and retching all the while. When he could find words finally, he couldn't swear, just whimper, "Uncle. Jane. Uncle."

"Cousin Charles, are you all right?"

Charles blinked twice and cleared the green-glowing water from his eyes before his rescuer came into view. "George?"

Riordan's son waited next to him, clutching a thick vine that had allowed him to get a grip on his cousin. George's knotty little face was screwed up in the same concern he'd borne last time they talked. "I saw you go flying. I—"

"Blooming hell, George," Charles said and started coughing again. "I mean, goodness gracious. I mean . . . er, something reliable . . ." He hacked and coughed more.

Half the river came up in a surge of vomit. Charles groaned. "Oy, that's a bit better."

"I saw the vampire throw you, and I ran as quick as I could," George said. "I mean, it's not reliable to run so fast, but . . ."

"What are you doing here?"

George colored a bit, visible even through those ruddy, knotty cheeks. "Ah, my mother, she sent me. She wanted to see how you were getting on."

Just then, the vine that George held snapped at him, blue teeth emerging from a blossom. "Off now!" Charles smacked the vine. "Be off!" He grabbed George, and they began walking. "She sent you, eh? Just today?"

"No . . ." George looked away, knotty cheeks turning red as persimmons. "Four days back. I've been coming back to hear you speak about Communism, Cousin."

"Oh, no," Charles coughed, spraying more river water everywhere. "That's all I need." He reached into his pocket, yanking out the *Manifesto*. "Oh, hell!" He held the soggy, battered pamphlet up. "I'll have to get this dried."

"That's the pamphlet?" George's eyes widened. "That's the one about Mister Markles?"

"No!" Charles groaned, which turned into another cough. "And it's Marx! George, you've been listening in? Does Susan know?"

"Mother is distraught, and it's better for her that I keep an eye on you as worrying about you is familiar but worrying about Father is not but—" George leaned in and whispered. "Cousin Charles, I want to be a Communist! I want to be unreliable like you!" He clapped a hand to his mouth as if he had just realized what he said.

"Bloody well not! You keep reliable!"

"You say the whole Otherworld isn't reliable! The industrialist—"

"I know, mate," Charles said before George could repeat his own speech back to him. "I know how it feels, all right? But as long as Uncle's in the stir, you've got to keep your head and keep reliable. For Auntie. We'll chat more once this is all sorted with Uncle, all right?"

"Yes, Cousin," George said, unable to keep a very unreliable disappointment from his voice.

Charles saw George back to a vine bridge—one with troll-sized bites dotting the railings—and headed back toward the Under-Market.

Other than a massive black stain, attracting flies as big as Charles's arm, there was naught where the food tent had been. The whole Under-Market was deserted without even the usual skeleton crew managing the tables.

Charles, his gut sinking, noticed a stream of white smoke from the Towering Market far above.

He borrowed a couple of seven-league boots and made the leap up to the bridges, avoiding the commotion on the stairs. From here, he could see the enormous port that served the Towering Market. Any pretense of orderly trade had ceased there. None of the big wooden lifts were working. Two smaller cranes made of alchemical black glass had toppled and left shattered bits all over the waterfront.

Masonry from bridges far above had toppled with the cranes and lay in the water, rocks scattered about the shore like new islands. Crates of goods had broken open on shore: seven-league boots littering the ground, golden watches and heaps of shimmering blue invisibility cloaks falling into the water, swirling around in eddies. Charles whistled.

The Ridleys would notice this.

Along the bridges of the Towering Market, stalls had been broken, and awnings leaned haphazardly on the ground. Some were torn, bearing the obvious claw marks of trolls. Fauns and madgekins and a few humans attempted to clean up. A boggart and a phooka bolted past Charles, giggling. "Cheese, guv!" called the phooka, snatching a wheel of the stuff right out of the hands of a nearby human. "Cheese for everyone!" Loaves of bread littered the ground, running like confused insects.

"Humans!" A boggart leered at the nonplussed human, a fellow in a black coat and hat. The boggart showed a great gaping mouth of sharp cheese-coated teeth. "Humans go home! Out of the Otherworld with yeh for good!" Its toadlike tongue flicked out, swatting the man's leg and face. He stumbled, fell against the table. "Out! All of yeh, werewolves too!"

"Oy!" Charles bellowed, running at the cheesed crowd. The boggart turned toward Charles, red eyes lighting up. "The gnome! This is the gnome that—"

"Off! Before I kick yeh off the bridge!" Charles bellowed. He backhanded the boggart and yanked the cheese out of his hand. The cheese itself squealed and jumped away.

"The gnome! We love you! Communism forever!" squeaked a pixie.

Charles picked up a flailing loaf of bread, tossed it at the pixies. "This en't the way, damn you!"

He stalked away, stopping only to give the human a hand up. Charles grimaced at the fellow as he brushed himself off. "Cut your stick and off with yeh, mate, and tell all your kind to stay out of the Otherworld. For your own safety."

The human, apparently not a werewolf or blessed otherwise with natural defenses, ran.

A faun policeman, who Charles recognized from the prison, galloped round the corner, hooves ringing, blowing a whistle. "Out! Out! We've called the Riders!"

"They're not coming! They buggered off!" the pixies called.

"Gnome!" The faun's eyes went wide. "Get the gnome!"

The boggarts and phookas squealed and tossed cheese at the fauns' eyes. Charles ran, fast as his stubby legs would carry him.

The office of the *Voice* would be safe if he could just hole up there. Whole Otherworld was mad, far beyond Marx and into the law of the bloody gorilla.

He clambered up stairs and ducked behind a splintered stall when more fauns rushed by. The farther up Charles went, the smokier it got. Some rioter'd set more of the market on fire, no doubt. What a mess.

Had Marx and Engels said anything about rioting? Charles couldn't remember. He fished in his sopping pocket but found nothing.

Oh, thirteen hells.

George had nicked the pamphlet!

Charles slapped his own face. "To think I wanted Communism to catch on among gnomes! Did it have to start with me blooming cousin?"

The smoke grew thicker as Charles approached the *Voice*, making his eyes gush into his already soaked beard. More smoke, and Charles hacked up a gut-rattling cough as he inhaled some of it.

That smoke's coming from the direction of . . . oh, no.

Charles ran even harder.

Jane's editor was on his knees in front of the building, the massive spiky form of the wood troll silhouetted by green alchemical flame and white smoke. The fire shot out the window; white smoke poured into the sky. The bricks had cracked and crumbled now in the heat, tumbling into heaps of ash as they hit the ground.

The wood troll coughed up smoke. Great tears rolled in thick trails down his face between the rough stubs along his cheeks, and he raised his clawed hands to hide his face. "My printing press. My newspaper. My manuscript! By Oberon!"

Charles opened his mouth to rage against the Ridleys who had no doubt ordered this but choked on the smoke. *They must have ordered it. But who would know in the heat of a riot with stolen invisibility cloaks everywhere?*

They watched the building burn until a faun fire squad arrived, and then Charles ducked out of view into the troll's shadow, though it didn't much matter. They didn't see him.

The fauns pumped water on the building from a great tank and threw sand, but by the time they were done, only a black skeleton of charred bricks stood.

The wood troll finally got up when the building was out. Wiping the enormous tears from his face, he said, "I will take this as a sign. I am meant to be a writer and naught else. I will go to the human world and live as one of them, one of the humble. I will find art or death."

Charles nodded. *Makes about as much bloody sense as anything I've done.*

After a while standing and staring at the ashes, Charles noticed a faint blue shimmer near him. "Oy, take that off," he spat.

The cloak shimmered, revealing Billy. He'd scrubbed a bit of the bloodstains from around his mouth, and his eyes glimmered.

"What're you doing here? En't you got some hole to crawl into?"

Billy's eyes glimmered.

Were those bloody *tears*? In a vampire's eyes? It didn't change Charles's anger. "Come to gloat about what you've done? Yeh think this is helping the strike? Set it back months, we did."

"Mate," Billy said, his voice breaking. "I'm sorry. That smell of human blood, it, ah, it does a thing to us. I didn't start this fire, so I didn't—"

Murgalak's Fun Human Facts

Many humans pursue art, a vocation proven to drive them mad. However, artists benefit by wearing very little clothing with some divesting themselves of bothersome ears and toes, which allows them greater communication with the universe. Other humans seem unable to learn from this practice.

"If I can stay off cheese, you can—"

"En't a thing like cheese, divvil knows!" Billy said. It was half a growl, half a sob. "It makes us blooming mad. Bedivvah, I can't stop thinking about it. Could still go for a wee taste. Watch that vampire girl. She'll feel the hunger too."

"That Puck knew such a thing, did he?"

"I figure the Ridleys were waiting for us to break out into a riot," Billy said. "Wouldn't be surprised if they brought out invisibility cloaks a'purpose. And maybe that fellow brought us humans a'purpose as well. The Puck would well know about the hunger."

Charles couldn't argue with that. Nor could he say why the Puck did anything—save that it was not for the good of the strike.

Billy sank to his knees, put his head in his hands. "Well sorry, so I am. I believe in your strike, gnome. Tis the only hope we have, and we're after a long life without hope. Being Irish and being an angel-cursed *sod* on top of it, my whole life—"

"Oy, don't use that word," Charles said. "I won't have you insulting me friends."

Billy gave a little smile, showing a hint of teeth. He put a hand covered in dry blood on Charles's shoulder. "I'll do me best to make today up to you like. For Communism. Haven't got a divvil's prayer without it."

Charles took a deep breath, winced at the heat of the fresh-burned building, and stood. If there was one trait he'd learned from Marx and Engels, it had to be optimism in the face of insane odds. "Oy, let's put this back together."

Chapter Twenty-Seven

*In which our Vampire at last Receives
Answers to Questions, albeit the
Answers are quite Problematic*

THE SUNNY DAY TURNED OF A SUDDEN INTO A RAINY NIGHT AND POURED on Jane not a mile from Unsworth Manor. Soaked through, she might be, but it would mask her scent. She found a stand of trees and tore away the immense, stiff underskirt. "I do hope that's a passing fashion," she said, tossing it happily into the hedge.

Once she joined the main road, she caught a ride in a farmer's cart—a farmer whose assessment of Jane was, "Oi've naught seen such a lady along the rood, aye."

"Yes," she said. "I've got to get back to London. I appreciate your willingness."

The farmer asked her questions about London, but Jane gave only the most perfunctory answers. She was busy looking back over her shoulder. Despite her roaring stomach, she hardly noticed the pigs rooting about in the back of the cart.

They drove half the night, and the farmer pulled the cart over to bed down a few hours. Though he gave her a blanket and let her sleep in the front of the wagon, Jane didn't close her eyes. All the while she stared at the road as if she could make out the eyes of Unsworth in the rain.

Had the werewolf noblewoman missed what Jane did to the potion?

Had Riordan kept her secret?

It couldn't be this easy. Any moment now, a huge wolf would leap from the underbrush, she was sure, and Unsworth's jaws would rend her to pieces or worse, drag her back to where the Ridleys and Riders were—

Nothing.

"Well," Jane found herself saying. "At least there are things to think of other than . . ."

She couldn't say *Charles*.

In particular, it was better not to think of his . . . experience. And what he must think of her. And why he didn't tell her. And whether she'd been a complete fool or mostly a fool. And whether he'd changed, for true, in that closet with the pamphlet, and how far that change extended . . .

Jane rubbed at her cheeks, wet with rain. "It is a good thing there is a wolf after me," she muttered. "A good thing there are other things to think of!"

At dawn, as the rain slackened and the pigs rooted about, she closed her eyes. She dreamed of pork, bacon, and great heaps of lard. And of Charles, laughing at her as she ate them. "Stop laughing at me," she kept trying to say, but her mouth was too thick with meat.

Jane woke to a hollow stomach and the great stink of London and air so thick she could have chewed it. A silvery curtain closed all around her, thick with the smell of coal dust and wet as if rain had gotten into the furnace. Still soaked, Jane shivered, ran her hands up and down her arms.

"A pea-souper, tis!" the farmer called. "Have to rely on the horses, oi, I do, marm, to find the market." He mumbled a bawdy song to himself in his thick brogue, "Oooh, burr, oi've got an uncle has a thing, a marvelouz thing, oi, his thing is ten feet long!"

Jane side-eyed the farmer. "Pardon, sir?"

He shrugged. "Oi don't know naught but them songs, marm."

"I'll thank you to take me near Shoreditch if you head that way," Jane said.

"This'll be the closest you get, marm. Got to get to market, oi do. En' see the exhibition, oi will, on the morrow. Oi bin hearing it, nae a day gone by, burr—"

"I'll buy a pig!" Dear heavens, they smelled so good. She'd never known how difficult it was to be so hungry until she'd been well-fed every night. "I've got money—just take me to my house."

The farmer eyed her askance. "Oi believe that, oi do, marm, you walking the rood all poor and draggled."

Jane had no choice. She exited at a street corner where she couldn't even see the signs for the mad fog. As he pulled away, Jane added the farmer to her list of folks to curse. "He did give me a ride," she muttered to herself as she started walking. "I'll curse him lightly."

Her head throbbed, and her whole body shook with cold. It might as well have been night as day with the thick, sour fog filling the air. Pale, faint-yellow gas lamps gave the only light. Jane clenched her teeth to keep from chewing her lips to bits. "The market's in Spitalfields," Jane said. "So that's where I must be."

Rumor made the neighborhoods of the Fields into a rough place. She could feel eyes on her. Shapes lurked in the fog behind her. A carriage rattled by, and a dark shape came out from behind it, started following her.

"Eh, love," a man's voice rang out from behind her. "Fine dress, that is."

"Excuse me, sir."

"Moment of your time."

"I can't be bothered," Jane said. "I must get home."

Something sharp shoved into her back just below her corset. "I believe you can," the fellow said. "I've got a knife to yer nancy, I do, lass. Turn 'ere."

Jane, now shaking worse than ever, turned into the nearest muddy alley. *What can I do against a knife at my back? What will he . . . what will he do when he sees I've no money? What—*

Oh, this was ridiculous.

She could do plenty against a man with a knife.

"No funny business," he said. "Or I'll do worse, and a lady like you don't want that, do you?"

"Let me just turn around, fellow," Jane said. "You are not so unkind?"

"No," he said, "yeh'll stay right there—"

Jane whipped around so fast his knife cut her corset but caught on the underwire, and she bared her fangs. She caught only a brief glimpse of eyes going wide in a mustachioed face before she shoved him back against the wall and bit through his neck.

Her teeth went right through the soft skin like it was butter on warm toast, shredding the muscle beneath, spraying hot blood down his throat. The gristle of his neck tasted of fresh ground nutmeg. His blood tasted of sweet grapes. Jane tore away more of his flesh and gulped it down.

When she finally came to herself, he lay slumped against the wall, most of his face and neck gone.

She had eaten his eyeballs and his ears and his lips.

She'd drank his neck arteries dry.

He was an abuser of women, a blaggard, a . . . a very nice meal.

The worst part was, she wanted more. She wanted to eat the marbled muscle from his arms and legs right off the bone and his liver, pickled with drink, but oh, it would be tender nonetheless, and oh my, livestock had never tasted like this. Humans were indeed a delicacy and . . .

"Stop it!" Jane said to herself. "You are a civilized woman! No more! Get a hold of yourself! This *is* mad!"

She bent down, hands shaking, and just managed to keep herself from eating more. She tore away a piece of his coat and started wiping her hands, muttering to herself, "I must look a horror. Like a vampire in a penny blood—"

An idea struck her.

She dropped the cloth and had to resist the urge to clean herself any further. As repulsive as the hot blood was—*and delicious! oh, dear, don't think that*—she left it smeared on her chin and face. She pulled the knife out of the fellow's twitching hand, kept it tucked into her own sleeve.

Creeping back into the street, masked by the thick fog, Jane waited. Soon enough, a boy came along dressed as a chimney sweep. Perhaps the same boy who'd tried to rob her at Piccadilly the day before. An omnibus rattled by, wheels clattering, horses champing, throwing up clods of mud that the boy ignored.

Jane leapt from the alley and seized him by the arm.

He started to scream, and Jane shoved a blood-soaked hand over his mouth. "Quiet, meat," she growled. He struggled, but her grip was iron. *Dear me, I think I'm all the stronger for having eaten a man.* "Take me to where the others are. Where they trade in children."

The boy whimpered. Jane slowly took her hand away, but he let out a yelp, so she shoved the hand over his mouth again. "Do it!" she said, trying to keep her voice as close to Franz's growl as possible. "Take me, or you'll be my meat."

He nodded his head, whole body shaking. He pointed back the way he had come along the street. Jane didn't let go of his arm but let him lead her toward an alley so narrow they had to press themselves between the walls just to get through it. It joined up with a wider alley.

A weathered, wooden cellar door waited there.

"That's where my kin go?" Jane asked.

The boy stuttered. "Not an hour gone, they mizzled down there. They—" His voice trailed off in a squeak.

The cellar door creaked and opened.

The boy bolted, jerking his arm away from Jane before she could do aught. She pressed herself against the wall.

A vampire emerged from the cellar door, moving with a strange, lurching sort of awkwardness. He was the size of Franz, looming in a black cloak, the only visible features his glowing yellow eyes and thick fangs jutting from his lower jaw. She backed up along this strange alley.

The vampire came toward her, jerking with each step.

"Why have you left the mission?" The vampire had a clean, precise accent that could have been the Queen's. Even the English vampires Jane heard at the strike had all shared Charles's rough cockney

Jane cleared her throat and enunciated as if she were the Queen. "Good day."

"Are you off the mission?" The voice, despite the accent, was flat, inhuman in a way Billy's and Franz's weren't.

"I'm part of the mission." Jane said in a precise accent. "I was rained on, you see, and the cloak so sodden that I would like to get a new one. Have you come for a batch of children?"

The vampire cocked his head. "Yes."

This was it. "Lead the way."

The vampire started to turn awkwardly, but it spun back and seized Jane's neck. An iron-hard grip clutched her windpipe, cutting all breath. *You're going to die!* something shouted, and Jane kicked at the vampire, her feet meeting iron-hard flesh, and then stabbed at its chest with the dead man's knife—

The knife screeched as if meeting metal, slid to the side, punctured something. Whatever it was, it burst, and hot steam sprayed Jane, scalding her face and hand. The vampire's grip jerked open, and she pulled away.

The vampire—if it was a vampire—gripped her with the other hand, lifted Jane with freakish strength, and threw her against the brick wall. Her vision swam and went black for just a second, but she forced herself up, clutching the knife.

Even in the dark of the alley, metal gleamed through the "vampire's" clothes.

A long appendage like a hooked pole, green with alchemical fire, tore through the front of the black cloak and snapped at her like a vise closing. Jane knocked it away with an elbow, stabbing with her other arm right at the "vampire's" eyes.

Glass shattered under the knife. Jane pulled away just in time to avoid an arc of electricity between its head and the wall. The flash blinded her. She reached up, felt a shock run through her, but she didn't stop; she seized the "vampire's" head and twisted as it tried to buck her off. Jane twisted until something gave, pipes and connections breaking, and more steam rushed out. The flailing appendage dropped.

It fell to the ground and shed sparks and steam.

"Oh, God—" Jane's vision swam.

When she came to her senses, she was back eating more of the dead man.

"Gah!" She pulled away, wiping her lips furiously. "No more!"

But his heart was only half-gone, and there was a great deal left, and it would just go to waste . . .

"Stop that!" Jane snapped at herself. "Go look at that vampire!"

She retraced her steps to get a good look at the vampire-disguised construct. Touching it, she found that the vampire "flesh" was a rather convincingly woven fabric, realistic even to her sharp eyes, and in the dark would fool any human.

Jane tore the cloak and the disguise fabric away.

Two round, lamplit eyes, one shattered by her stab. A neck made of pipes and gears, now twisted, the steam pipes wrenched beyond repair. And a segmented body of riveted metal spheres. "Good heavens," Jane said.

The common folks of London had not been seeing vampires. They'd been seeing Iron Riders disguised as vampires.

Chapter Twenty-Eight

*In which our Gnome Leads a Great
Rally, entirely without Preparation*

HERE WAS A RALLY IN THE UNDER-MARKET.

Rally was the wrong word. It was a whole bloody revival.

Every creature imaginable from the Otherworld was there. Pixies fluttered through the air, swarming blue crowds dropping crumbs of real cheese, cheese raided from the Towering Market. Phookas howled and danced in backward circles. Boggarts and redcaps danced together, and badgebears roared and tussled in circles laid out for amusement.

The Under-Market had come alive again, this time from stolen goods. Redcaps played peek-a-boo with invisibility cloaks. Folks tumbled in from the sky on seven-league boots. And the whole place stank of cheese. Madgekins— including Pedge—sold whole plates of the stuff to Otherworlders who were already swaying on their feet.

Pedge shook a furry fist in Charles's direction but seemed otherwise content with his lot.

There were even three gnomes, sitting on broken masonry, smoking pipes and trying to look reliable in the midst of what must have been a high-water mark for unreliability in the City Beyond.

A few Irish and German vampires huddled at the edge of the market under the gleaming blue vines with the look of caged pigs awaiting slaughter. Franz stood with them, a thick bandage across his nose. He and Billy exchanged glances that Charles couldn't suss out.

"The gnome's here!" a pixie squeaked.

Words rushed through the crowd, and they turned and cheered. At Charles. He felt naked. "Oy, now! Calm down!"

"I think they'll be expecting a speech," Billy said. "Divvil knows you'd best have one, so you should. Otherwise . . ." He shivered. "I don't like how they're looking at us, so I don't."

"What?" Charles said. "What are you afraid of?"

"The vampires are outnumbered, bedivvah! We're after a long history of snatching and eating Otherworld folk when we can, and I reckon they're about to pay us back."

"Don't worry," Charles said, making his way toward a table, which several creatures cleared off to give him room. "I won't eat you till the strike is over."

Billy groaned. "Been saving that one up, have you?"

Charles clambered up on the table. The crowd roared, their babbling turning into a cheer. Cheese flew up in the air, and the pixies fluttered around trying to snatch it, a storm of blue light and white cheese.

Charles surveyed the mad crowd and made his voice as loud as he dared. "Working fey of the Otherworld!"

A cheer resounded back.

"At last, you've come to hear us out, we who've held the line against the Riders all the week?" He raised a fist. "Well listen good! We won the victory against the Ridleys by slowing down their factories, not—"

"How d'ya kill the Riders?" a badgebear roared.

"Didn't kill any! They Iron-Rode right off. Far as I can tell, the Riders went on strike too. Can't blame them if they're paid what we are, right, me mates?"

That led to a round of chuckles.

"Now, we've got to change some things!" Charles said. "I won't have rioting, you understand? I en't saying you've got to return everything you took from the bourgeoisie . . ." That let up a strange combination of cheers from the drunker, more cheesed crowd, and "What's a boujer-bee?" from the sober ones. "Ah, from the Towering Market, but we cannot count on a spree of destruction! Ridley'll come himself and tear us to pieces, we keep this up."

The crowd booed. Charles held up a hand, but it took near a blooming minute for them even to quiet enough to shout over. "We showed them today, we did! Right, mates? We showed them we were in solidarity with our vampire brethren." That provoked an awkward silence. "And that we need fair wages! What are our demands?"

"Cheese!" someone yelled.

"No!" Charles said. "Our goal is no less than the fair and equal employment of every fey in the Otherworld for fair wages."

"No, gno-o-o-ome!" a nearby faun bleated. Charles was surprised to see that, though he was trying to hide it with a cloak, he wore a police uniform underneath. "We want the Otherworld to be-e-e back to the way it was!"

"You all hear him?" Charles pointed to the faun. "You all want the Otherworld to go back?"

A roar went up from the crowd. "Humans go home!" a cheesed boggart yelled. "Go home forever!"

Charles waited for the uproar to subside. It never really did, though it got quiet enough for him to shout. "Mates, if the humans go home and we find the old doors and open them again, the damage is still bloody done. You think the bastards will leave us alone, now that they know there's money to be made? No. World's changed. We can't go back, and I like having coin in me pockets. We need to focus on our message, and that is no less than the fair and equal employment of every fey in the Otherworld for fair wages!"

"How's that work?" a pixie squeaked. "There en't enough factory jobs!"

"There's plenty to do around here!" Charles had his head worked up now, sure as a horse. "The Choke is swarming with waste from the Ridley factories, and if ye've seen the witchfogs, ye know it's killing us! Here's one demand: the Ridleys create more jobs by disposing of waste proper-like, well outside the City Beyond!"

The crowd went silent. *Puck's guts, I came up with that off me head. They're thinking about it harder than I did.*

Billy broke the silence.

"Who's going to handle the waste now?" Billy asked. "I dinnae want that job."

Charles turned to Billy. "And if we demanded full-spelled suits of protection?"

"That's big money, so it is, gnome. Years of cleanup."

"I'm going after every werewolf penny," Charles replied.

"Excuse me, well, this isn't quite the place to discuss it, but . . ." One of the gnomes raised his hand, stumbling through a question.

"Out with it," Charles said.

"Well, it seems to me that if we seek reliable wages, there is, in the meantime, a question of reliable food. There is a rumor that the vampires have eaten well each night? Perhaps such sustenance could be available to all if we seek to stop the factories?" He sputtered. "I mean, it is not a terribly reliable suggestion—"

"Course it is," Charles said. "A growling stomach every night when you're out your wages, well, that's reliable but in all the worst ways. Ah, well, the source for the vampire's food is . . . not as reliable as we'd hoped."

The crowd let out a great murmur. Charles held a hand up, but they continued to make noise. "Workers!" Charles called. "Come on now. We've all got a bit stored away, haven't we? We can pull together for another week!"

"I vill not bear vith the hunger again, gnome," Franz said. "It makes a man daisy."

Charles spied Pedge and gave the madgekin a pointed look.

Pedge glared right back.

All right, that's how he would do it.

"Lots of us have more than we're willing to admit, and if this is going to work—if the whole Otherworld is going to grind to a halt—we've got to share when we can. Say there's a madgekin stocked up on coin and goods, got a nice burrow tucked away, an enchanted oven making curried eggs each morning? That fellow ought to bring out what he's got." Charles kept his gaze turned on Pedge. Half the crowd followed that gaze. *Good. Let him sweat. He's sitting on a heap of human goods that could save us.* "The strike doesn't work, then none of the Otherworld has coin. The Ridleys have learned they can't rely on the Riders anymore, but they'll find some kind of enforcement. That's for sure. Let's make a barricade, settle in at Ridleyville, show them we en't going anywhere, that all the Otherworld is for our cause. Tomorrow morning!"

The crowd cheered. Charles clambered down from the table. "Franz, I'll need you to speak to old Pedge there. Help convince him."

"Convince?" Franz made a fist. "Vith the physical horse?"

"Nah, no *force,* just . . . loom a little," Charles said. "I'm full coopered, I am. Billy, you . . ."

"Come now, what's this?" Billy peered into the vines beyond the crowd. "There's one of your wee bourgeoisie, right there."

"What?"

He was right. The faint twilight of the Otherworld outlined a woman in heavy-skirted dress, her hands crossed in front of her.

"Quite an audience," Billy said.

"Come with me," Charles said.

As Charles got closer, he could have sworn her eyes glowed gold, flickered in the faint light. An older woman with white hair. Familiar. Had he seen her at that party? Maybe served her a drink off the tray?

"Hello, Charles of Bredwardine," she said as he got closer. "I was hoping we would have a chance to talk. Your Uncle Riordan is doing well."

Charles's hand curled into a fist before he could think. "What are you doing, making threats against me uncle?"

"Threats?" Her smile didn't touch those cold, dark, gold-flecked eyes. "No threats. He was quite threatened in that ridiculous prison if you want to speak of threats. I took the liberty of having him removed to my country estates. He's much happier, let me assure you."

"You trying to hold me whole family against me, you bourgeois—"

She grimaced. "That's not how you pronounce it."

"What?"

"Bourgeois." She pronounced it *boozh-WAH*.

"It's spelled bourgeois," Charles said, pronouncing it *bur-jee-OYS* as he had been. "That's how it's bloody spelled!"

"One mustn't trust a French spelling, my good gnome. They're terribly tricky."

"Why would you . . . you read Marx?" Charles stammered. "And you're a werewolf too. You one of the Ridleys?"

"Not a Ridley but a werewolf, yes," she said. "I've followed these developments since the night John Ridley was poisoned and now have had a conversation with your vampire reporter that has confirmed my suspicions. I would like to take you someplace more private for a discussion." She paused. "You are right. Malcolm Ridley's approach to the Otherworld is unsustainable. But so is yours. Follow me and find a third way." She turned and began to walk away.

"Come now!" Charles called. She didn't stop. "Can't trust that," he said to Billy. "Bourgeois threatening me family . . ."

"We cannae, aye, but . . ." Billy cast a glance behind him at Pedge, now in the center of a group of Otherworlders that oddly did not include any vampires.

"Out with it, mate."

"That madgekin, he whom you called out, he en't got fresh-slaughtered pigs, do he?"

"No."

"Not a bit of fresh meat?" Billy's voice was hopeful.

"Dried stuff, mate. All cooked."

"It was right clever, so it was, to shame the furry bastard. Fair play to that. But for us," Billy said, "with no fresh flesh, it'll be sickness and hunger again. Or mudclots and that what we can beg."

Hadn't even thought of that. Charles deserved a right good smack. "All right, we've got to address that for surely. But . . . right into the jaws of a werewolf?"

"Getting et don't scare me," Billy said. "It's starving that do."

Charles couldn't argue with that. "Off we go then."

Chapter Twenty-Nine

In which our Vampire Learns of Long-Withheld Truths

ONE SLOW, GROANING, HEAVY INCH AT A TIME, JANE WORKED THE CLOAK off the construct. Its body weighed more than a horse, and to even shift the limbs, Jane had to get under them and brace them with her shoulders. By some Puckish luck, nothing else came out of the cellar door while she got the cloak settled.

She swept herself up in the now muddy, torn cloak, and steeled her nerves.

Riders. A whole cellar full of Iron Riders disguised as vampires and stealing children. And no box.

Her heart thundered, and her whole body shook. "You must do it," she said under her breath. "For the sake of everything decent, you must go in there."

It seemed to take half the night before she forced her feet to move, before she crossed the small muddy alley to the cellar.

Warm, golden light spilled up from the open cellar doors.

Jane's hands shook again, and she couldn't help thinking of the Riders seizing her, pulling her down, about to grind her up with a batch of rats.

But *children*.

She went down the stairs.

The lamplight illuminated thick wooden beams holding up the roof, a stained and stinking privy in the corner, and seven or eight black-robed figures in the center of the cellar.

A dirt-smudged man and a woman, dressed in tattered clothes, stood by eyeing the black-clad figures with obvious terror.

Each black-robed figure held a baby. They fed the babes from green-tinted bottles, glowing green just as the rats in the Ridleys' warehouse had glowed.

Jane walked closer, trying to imitate the jerky gait of that Rider she'd killed. One of the constructs was conversing with the man in that perfect clipped accent, the same voice as the Rider that Jane had killed.

"There are not enough. We need more children."

"Bleeding hell!" the man cursed. "We've emptied out the orphanages! Every bloody one in London's sent you their unwanted babes, and don't think the bluebottles aren't sniffing around!"

"We will give you money tonight if you can find more babes." The sinister words sounded so odd in that perfect accent.

The man and woman looked between each other, their sallow faces a portrait of fear. "Can't just blag them out of a pram in the park."

"Manchester?" the woman said. "I heard there're baby farms up there, take in ten, twelve babe a week. Have to be disappearing some of them."

The man shuddered. "Black dealings, these are."

"We will give you money," the Rider-as-vampire said again.

The last vampire construct in line turned to Jane. "You are on sentry," it hissed. "On sentry."

"People in the alley," Jane replied, thanking her mother, for once, for drilling proper pronunciation into her. "We must go."

"I will open the door," said another, lurching forward and handing Jane both baby and bottle. Trying to imitate its jerky movements and also avoid dropping the child, she took it and cradled it in her arm. The child slurped sluggishly at the bottle, drool falling out of the corner of its mouth.

These children were dosed-up, just as the rats had been.

"Next week then?" the man said.

"Tomorrow night," the first construct said. "Or you are punished."

The "vampires" gathered around something set into the wall like a coal-chute door. One of the constructs twisted its handle and opened it—

And Jane, baby and all, was sucked into the Otherworld.

It was the worst of the doors she had ever been through. The air screamed and whistled in her ears, high and piercing, and by the time it stopped rushing around her, she was sure her ears must be bleeding. The baby at her breast cried low, groaning drugged sobs.

Other cries reached her ears. Many others. More than had been in the cellar.

She blinked away spots and saw above her the dim purple sky of the Otherworld and the flaming stars. And around her more sky.

She stood on the edge of an immense platform with no guardrail on the top of a high tower. The wind battered Jane like a wall, the black cloak flapping and threatening to pull her off her feet.

Below her, so far below they could have been the workings of ants, tiny spots crowded along lines between towers.

"That's—" Jane gasped. "I am looking *down* on the Towering Market?" She stood atop the Old Towers?

Jane turned around.

A pile of gears and pipes and vents stretched up into the open sky, spouting a pillar of smoke, rattling and chugging along. It was like a machine from the exhibition, multiplied by ten and Otherworldly—an immense mess of metal pipes and gears and steam, gleaming bronze and gold, pipes pumping green alchemical substances.

Riders were everywhere up here. Jane was goaded into moving by the sight, stumbling along after the vampire constructs, pushed by wind and fear, pretending to be one of them. The Riders clambered spiderlike up and down the great apparatus at the center of the tower and rolled around the borders of the platform, patrolling. Some, smaller and one-eyed, flew around the tower on spar-and-cloth sailing wings. Some walked on two legs like men, the vampire constructs shed of their cloaks. Most were the familiar bulbous, wheeled spiderlike creatures that had faced off with the strike.

The constructs Jane followed, still clad as vampires, moved toward where prams had been set on a track like a railroad, leading into the machine. Glass jugs hung above the pram-carts, trailing tubes full of green substance for the babes' mouths.

The first black-clad figure laid a child down in the pram-cart, put the substance in its mouth, and wheeled it toward the machine.

Heavens. No!

To the right, a group of Riders, like several spiders clattering around the same fly, rolled a round metal object out of the opposite end of the machine. It took

Jane a moment to recognize one of the Ridley doors. Just like the one she'd seen her first night back: a great round thing, gleaming steel.

A Rider with a particular arm extension set rivets along the rounded edges of the door. Another welded a handle to it, wrapped the handle in leather.

They kill children to make the doors. Professor Murgalak's words resounded in her head: *flesh for flesh, blood for blood, both for magic.* The darkest magic she could imagine. "No!" The word burst out of her. She clutched the child to her breast.

The Riders, with a creak of gears and a hiss of metal, stopped to look at her.

"Well. I hoped you would be impressed."

Jane turned around.

A green-suited figure stood at the edge of the tower, grinning that sharp-toothed grin, the wind blowing his flaming hair about like a bonfire.

"You," Jane said, and the wind chilled the tears on her face. "This is your doing?"

"Thou speakest aright. Else the Puck a liar call."

Chapter Thirty

In which our Gnome Receives an Offer

UNSWORTH, BELYING HER MASSIVE DRESS, DARTED THROUGH THE VINES, scrubby trees, and broken masonry that surrounded the Under-Market, like a walking white bell. Charles dodged crumbling brick walls and immense vines and tripped over roots, trying to keep up with her. Billy grumbled and swatted away branches and vines.

"Fast for a woman dressed in that layer cake," Charles said.

"Can't see a damn thing!" Billy said, crouching down, ducking under the twisting, blue-gleaming vines. "Where do you suppose she's going to?"

"I'm clueless as you," Charles said. But the lacy dress had stopped, he saw. Stopped at an old, crumbling wall marked with a wide circle in green moss—

Unsworth looked back, the faint light catching the gold flecks in her eyes. "Yes, a door. But not to the human world." She traced the circle, and warm golden light followed her hand, spreading in a lazy arc to the center of the circle, opening a door much like Pedge's, a door that pre-dated the Ridleys.

Hitching up her skirts, Lady Unsworth stepped through to somewhere else. Beyond the door, gray swirled, enclosing Unsworth until she was lost to view.

"Ah, thirteen hells," Charles said, pausing. "What d'yeh suppose is there?"

Billy whistled between his lower fangs. "Franz'd say some rot about how they'll feed us to tree-horned feasts and shit us out in the depths of the tea."

"We can go back."

"Not trusting that Puck again," Billy said, "and there's no fresh blood coming elsewhere."

"The depths of the tea it is." Charles walked forward, stepped through the old door—

He lurched and fell into an enormous dune of ash. Stumbling to his feet, flailing through the fine gray stuff, Charles caught a better glimpse. The world here was coated in ash. It fell in a thick mist, settling around them. Dunes of fine ash rose in varied peaks, some as small as Charles, some the size of a badgebear. Charles coughed, inhaling the dry, throat-burning stuff, and lifted the collar of his shirt to breathe through it. Above, Charles just saw a faint silver sun, sickly yellow in the gray sky.

Behind him, Billy stumbled through the door and let out a litany of curses interrupted by coughs. The noblewoman, who had similarly wrapped her shawl around her face, waited, pointing down the hill ahead of her.

Where she pointed, the faint light illuminated a crumbling castle.

That castle reminded Charles of nothing so much as loaves of bread shoved against each other. The walls were crowned by battlements thick as Towering Market bastions but irregular and all skewing in one direction or the other, nothing standing free. Fat towers clustered inside the walls, lurching on their foundations in the same way.

"Where in thirteen hells are we?" Charles asked.

"A place beyond the City Beyond as the city is beyond London," Unsworth said.

"And why are we here?"

The woman didn't answer, just trudged ahead toward the castle.

They descended the hill through increasingly soggy ash piles, and Charles struggled to keep his balance, going down on his hands at least ten times. This time it was Billy's turn to keep Charles going, yanking him up by his armpit and picking through the least ash-filled walkway.

The ash diminished as they approached the castle, the piles down to Charles's shoes by the time they made the drawbridge and portcullis. The portcullis stood half-drawn, and the woman walked over the drawbridge and ducked under the metal prongs.

Charles and Billy followed into a courtyard also choked with ash and populated by tall statues, gleaming even in the poor half-light. He recognized those depicted in the statues, those who had roamed the Under-Market in the days before Ridley. Tall, wispy-haired, their eyes vast and empty, now captured in black stone.

"Yes, they are sidhe," Mrs. Unsworth said.

"They built statues to themselves?"

"This is no memorial," Unsworth said. "These *are* the sidhe. They've been turned to iron."

Charles reached out, but just putting his hand close to the statue made him draw back. Hot, skin-itching iron.

"King Oberon and Queen Titania are over there if you wish to see them," Unsworth said, pointing.

Charles made out the tall, regal statues at the end of the courtyard. Oberon's square-jawed face was a mask of surprise and horror, his hands up to protect himself from something, his fine robes captured the very second some force blew them back. Titania was similarly shocked, her once-crystal crown askew forever.

"Malcolm Ridley did this," Charles said.

"No, in fact," Unsworth said through the shawl around her face. "A disobedient servant turned on them because he saw a better opportunity with Malcolm."

"The Puck. You called us here to warn us about him?" Charles shook his head. "Already figured that out when he brought four dead men to dinner."

"Now you trust the tales of his true nature? Come inside," she said.

"What's inside?" Billy asked.

She didn't answer but passed through the large, half-open portal of the castle.

Charles exchanged glances with Billy, and they followed.

Inside the castle, lights shone faint silver from far overhead, illuminating a massive banquet table set with the wreckage of a giant feast.

Charles had to restrain the urge to grab the apple cores and chicken bones off the table and devour whatever was left. Billy eyed the remains of a suckling pig but didn't touch the crispy, grease-glistening skin. The apple cores were crisp and white, but the food had to be years old.

At the end of the table, Unsworth pushed open a door. "In here," she said. "Away from this damnable ash and smoke."

Charles and Billy followed her . . . into as respectable a parlor as one might find anywhere in London.

A fire blazed on a cheery hearth, the mantle bearing a single piece of bric-a-brac—a porcelain white wolf. An end table held a kettle of tea. The woman sat in an overstuffed chair and motioned Charles and Billy toward two smaller chairs.

Charles didn't sit. "Why here?"

She placed a warming plate in the fire casually as if she'd been doing so without servants for years. "I use this place when I do not want Malcolm looking for me."

"Bloody quiet," Charles said. The only sound—only sound for miles, he reckoned—was the crackle of the fire.

"Like a tomb," she said. "Because it is. This was once a fine, twilit world of never-ending feasts, food always unspoilt, great sidhe manors where mute humans flitted about as slaves. A place where the royalty of the Otherworld could go to escape the drudgery of the commons. Malcolm broke it. He brought alchemy to burn it and sorcerers to counter spells, but he could not have done it if Oberon's greatest servant had not turned."

"So the Puck has been helping Malcolm Ridley," Charles said. "I know they made a deal."

"My dear, the Puck made everything possible. He made the Iron Riders. He made the doors to the human world."

"He made the blooming doors?" *That* detail the Puck had left out.

"Sit! Can you not tell by now that we are alone?"

Charles finally sat. Taking his cue, Billy sat as well.

"I'll have tea ready in a moment," Unsworth said. "Know that I have attended a Communist lecture, my good gnome, and read the pamphlet. I find your interpretation quite interesting, and I would have you know there are other economic theories to be considered. Be a good fellow and remind me to loan you Adam Smith's book."

Charles crossed his arms. "I'm well without, thanks."

Billy spoke. "We're after quite a week, so we are, a week I've had my soul burned by the angels. You spoke of an offer."

"Yes," she said. "At first, your strike made little impact, but now, it will take a month for the Towering Market to recover, and that's only if Malcolm can rehire enough vampires willing to eat rat."

"You come here to negotiate on his behalf now?"

She shook her head no. "If we are careful, we can both restore stability and undercut Malcolm. I have purchased several factories, both in the human world and the City Beyond. I propose to employ a great number of Otherworlders, vampires and others, for fair wages and offer good livestock at a company shop." She took three small sips from the steaming cup. "In short, I will give the strike exactly what you want."

Chapter Thirty-One

In which our Vampire Takes a Great Leap of Faith

"YOU MURDERED CHILDREN?" THE CHILD WRIGGLED AGAINST HER AS IF PROOF of the crime. The cold wind turned the tears on her cheeks into ice.

Puck waved a hand, and the carts with the children ceased rolling on the track behind him. "There are an awful lot of these little children in London," he answered, grinning the sharp-toothed grin. "A terrible great deal, and so few care to attend them. Malcolm called for deep, darkest magic, and I told him the price. Flesh for flesh, blood for blood, both for magic."

"You monstrous creature!" Jane said and held the sluggish child all the tighter to her breast. "You're worse than Ridley!"

Puck burst into laughter.

"How dare you laugh at this?"

"It's—it's—" He snorted, waved a hand. "It's just that old Ridley wanted this!" He could barely speak for choking with laughter. "Let my friends explain."

Just then, one Iron Rider grew a mouth, a hole like a fish's mouth in its metal face. "Why would he do this? What has he to gain?" The voice sounded like steel plates scraping together.

Another Iron Rider grew a similar mouth. "He is the Puck, my dear! He jests with Oberon and deals with werewolves, always seeking merriment!"

The other wailed, "But Ridley wanted everything! He got Oberon and Titania's land by deceit and sorcery. He controlled his wolfishness by alchemy!

He built factories to control the flow of magical objects! But he could not do what Puck does!"

"How clever is the Puck!" the other one squeaked. "What a piece of work is Puck!"

"Will you stop with—" Jane's tongue froze between words.

"Do go on. So right you are," Puck said to the talking Riders.

The Riders spoke into the roaring wind atop the tower. "Only one creature knew of the making of doors between Otherworld and the human world! The Puck alone could spin a door between realms, and this was what the werewolf wanted! And so the deal was made, and flesh and blood were needed. Only the most innocent could fuel such magic!"

"Now you see." Puck held his hands out. "You distracted Malcolm with your clever strike. I have always loathed the bargain I was forced to make with that vile werewolf. Everything I made had a barb in it for Malcolm. See the Iron Riders? Oh, it's clever how I made them." He snapped a finger, and the nearest Rider groaned from its makeshift mouth. "Tell her what you are!"

"He tore my flesh!" one Iron Rider cried. "All because I failed! I lost the power source, the metal focus!"

Jane's head snapped toward the Iron Rider. Tore flesh. Because he lost a power source, which was what Malcolm Ridley had called the box. "That's . . ."

"Yes!" Puck giggled. "Malcolm requested animated mechanical machines. He did not say what need animate them. Each Rider is powered by the spirit of a man wronged by Malcolm Ridley."

This Iron Rider was animated by the spirit of the very fellow she'd witnessed being eaten, hiding under that bed? It seemed to be so. Who could have a better claim on being wronged by the Ridleys?

"In my last act, as a spirit moved by vengeance, I returned the metal focus to the unreliable gnome!" The spirit wailed.

And *that* was how the box returned to Charles's pocket the night of the party? "My word." A vengeful ghost, exerting his last physical act. But he had said *the metal focus*—Jane just stopped herself from asking for clarification.

Her mind went back to the Great Exhibition, to the box warming against her backside.

She'd thought the magic came from the heart inside, but Professor Murgalak had said there was no magic in that piece of flesh.

The box itself was a well. It could hold anything. Maybe even serve as a prison.

A prison . . . made to contain a creature who could make a door of anything?

If the Iron Riders are made by Puck's magic, then the box killed them precisely because it is meant to negate that particular magic. An alchemically infused substance could negate magic for anything that touched it. If Puck had animated the Iron Riders and they were rendered inoperable by the touch, then . . .

Perhaps the box was meant to *imprison Puck.*

And she hadn't ruined *anything* by losing the scrap of flesh within.

Jane's mind raced as fast as the wind.

"Now are you ready to speak, dear?" Puck asked. "To compliment our genius?"

Jane found her tongue unfrozen. "You are planning some vengeance against Malcolm Ridley?"

"Let my friends explain it," Puck said. "I cannot speak of it without great fits of laughter!"

"Malcolm Ridley does not know what the Puck plans!" The second Rider wailed. "Tell us!"

"You see the doors!" the other Rider wailed. 'But that is not all this machine does. Look, and behold!"

Several Riders, their spidery arms hurrying along, wheeled out a whole new shape from the machine. It joined several others of such a shape, piled on the far side of the platform. They glowed a dull bronze, but all bore the rounded shape of a wheeled cylinder with a wide lever set into the top.

Puck burst into a fit of giggling. "You see it?"

"Are those . . . cannons?" What a strange thing. The machine made doors and cannons?

"They are cannons!" yelled the Iron Riders. Puck danced with glee. The Riders wailed, "A cannon. And a *door*!"

Puck squealed. "Oh, I am clever!"

"I'm missing the joke," Jane said.

"They fire *openings* between worlds! I fire them upon the sky and make the greatest door of all! And all sorts of pieces of London will fall right through onto the Otherworld!"

"What?" Jane cried. "What? You cannot be serious."

"I never lie about mischief, my dear."

London, crashing down onto the City Beyond? "What on earth would that achieve?"

Puck's face twitched into a puzzled expression. "I don't know."

"You don't know."

"It will be a great piece of mischief!"

"It will kill thousands!"

"Ruining Malcolm's plans for both worlds in the process. Imagine"—he broke into a shriek of laughter—"the look on his face!"

Jane stood silent in horror.

"Will you not enjoy such a thing?" Puck's tone softened. "My dear, your very nature is trickery. I can taste it on your words, smell it in your blood. You are like me, a thing of neither world, wild, blessed and cursed with luck."

"I cannot let you do this," Jane cried, holding the child close against her breast.

"You would truly rather dance about earning coin?" Puck's fingers glimmered, and shillings rained from his hands. "I have always dealt in coin! Travel with me, be the wild creature you are, feast on human blood, and make magic sing! I will not hurt your loved ones if that is your concern."

"No!" Jane said, the wind stinging her tear-streaked cheeks.

Puck grimaced. "You'd rather scribble and grope with a gnome? All for the sake of the oak root between his legs?"

Jane flushed. "Excuse me, sir, you forget yourself in the worst way!"

"It's true. It looks like an oak root."

"I find oak roots rather lovely," Jane said, and when he just giggled, she yelled, "And I will stop you! All of this! It will end now!"

Puck held his four-fingered hands up with a sigh of futility. "I suppose that would also be a lovely piece of mischief if you can." And with that, the carts bearing the children began running along the track again toward the machine.

Jane rushed to the machine and the track of baby prams. Iron Riders perked up and began closing in all around her.

She still had the knife she took from the man she ate. Running as hard as she could as Riders on every side wheeled closer, she took aim and hurtled the knife at one of the steam pipes that snaked up the side of the machine, hoping to puncture it.

It bounced away harmlessly.

The wind increased and yanked at her cloak. Jane lost her footing, just making it to the railway in time to seize a pram-cart and stop herself. Regaining her footing, she leaned against the cart, tried to derail it. No luck. Too heavy. And the sluggish, drugged babies were all getting closer to the machine that would murder them as they rolled along the track.

A Rider wheeled close enough to slash at her. Jane dodged, tumbled against the machine, nearly dropped the child in her arms.

They were backing her in, forcing her to block the babes with her body.

If I have to die to stop this machine, I will. Jane could throw her body into the gears—

Hang on. Several of the Riders, interrupted mid-task by Puck's unsaid command, had left a lone cannon waiting halfway between the fracas and the other completed cannons, neatly stacked.

She could just see what she needed to do in a matter of seconds.

Jane laid the babe into the cradle with his fellow. "I will save you!" she promised.

And then she leapt over the rail line, letting the wind catch her cloak. She went tumbling across the open space until an Iron Rider caught her dress with a clamping arm. Jane twisted away. The Rider tried to yank her back but succeeded only in tearing her dress. Jane rolled across the ground, helped by the wind, and fetched up against the cannon.

A slash of pain ran down her leg and another down her arm. A jolt ran through her, her vision dancing with sparks. *No, do not fail.* Jane kicked out, connected with an Iron Rider's eye, and glass shattered under her foot. She scrambled up, pulled herself behind the cannon. Like the Riders, it was on wheels, and as she seized the lever with one hand and the wheels with the other, she turned it—

She yanked the lever back, wrenching it with all the force she could muster.

The air distended, and the cannon shrieked, the screams of thousands of children who had died for this horrid thing. A screeching wind erupted from the enormous barrel, knocking the crowding Riders aside. The shot struck the towering machine just where the babes were fed into it. The air itself tore. Jane smelled sulfur, horse droppings. London smells.

The shot did not wreck the machine but rather tore a hole in the air just before it, a door to the human world right where the babes should have fed into the machine. A hole that led to a grassy lawn in London, a park, where two women were walking along the path and staring in horror—

The first child's pram-cart rolled off the rails into the human world. And another one. And another. The women in the human world didn't run, bless them, instead pulling the first child from the pram.

The Iron Riders paused as if unsure whether to pursue the children into the human world.

Puck groaned. "Now that's no mischief at all. Mothers and babes? The very opposite!"

The wind tore at Jane's hair, blew it about her face, made it difficult to see anything. The children were safe. And—

And the Iron Riders decided to go after her. They turned and closed, forming a barrier, wheeling closer and closer until her back was to the great drop.

They came close enough to touch. "What do I do?" Jane muttered to herself. "What can I—" Sharp appendages caught Jane, slung her around. Blades slashed her chest, tore her dress. She toppled to the ground, wind catching in her cloak, attempting to blow her into the great open sky.

The children are safe. That is all that matters.

Charles's face came into her mind, and her heart quailed. *I want to see him again.*

The Riders paused like cats letting their prey catch its breath

Jane forced herself to stand at the edge of the tower. The whole of the Otherworld wheeled around her, and Puck's shrieking laughter joined the wind.

Above her, a one-eyed, flying Rider unfurled its own long, sharp appendages and dove for her.

Charles.

She heard him whisper, *luckish Puck.*

Jane jumped.

The flying Rider's arm slashed across her ribs, a deep, bone-scraping cut. Jane flailed for its wing.

Her right hand closed on empty air.

Chapter Thirty-Two

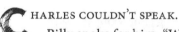
In which our Gnome Learns the Tale of Lycanthropy's Great Success and Receives an Offer via the Hated Bourgeoisie

CHARLES COULDN'T SPEAK.

Billy spoke for him. "What are we making? Boots? Amulets?"

"To start," Unsworth said. "We must restore Towering Market trade. It's an important source of profit. In time, I am intrigued by your proposal for cleaning up the river and the rest of the Otherworld. I suggest a general fund. Whatever the workers can contribute to the cleanup fund, I will contribute in duplicate and put my alchemical talents to work on better waste treatment."

"What's the wages?" Charles narrowed his eyes.

"The same Malcolm paid, dear. With a company shop, offering livestock in kind, but prices will reflect the convenience of shopping near work."

Charles snorted in anger. "A company shop? You're proposing to *own* us!"

She withdrew the warming plate from the fire, placed it under the teakettle, watched it for steam, and finally poured some. 'My dear gnome, when I say it will take a month to recover, I also mean that in a month you will feel Malcolm's vengeance. Tea?"

"No!" Charles snapped. "What vengeance is that?"

"You identified the problem yourself. Too many humans know of the Otherworld, let into ever-widening circles of Ridley influence and tourism. If the Otherworld is not profitable to him on current terms, he will expand knowledge—and access—to all other humans. Outside investors are the best way to restore equilibrium."

"How do you know?"

"I am not unknown to members of Parliament and military leaders. I know how they think." She set down the tea. "Imagine if the entire British Empire knew of the City Beyond. You become but another colony. Another India or China to be raped in the name of 'stewardship.'"

"En't that what you bloody want?"

"You think I am proud of the atrocity behind 'progress?'" Lady Unsworth's neutral, pleasant tone grew dark. "British cotton bears the blood of American slaves, and British spices are extorted from a China soaked in opium—opium that our troops forced into their mouths at gunpoint. I am in no hurry to see the Otherworld go thus. I am a capitalist, yes, but an ethical woman."

"No such bloody thing."

Unsworth leaned back, narrowing her already tight, cold blue-gold eyes. "Do you know how Malcolm became a werewolf?"

Charles groaned, but Billy said, "I'm after a long time wondering this."

Unsworth sipped her tea again. "It was no accident that bite that turned him. As a young man, Malcolm made a foolish bargain with one of the sidhe. A typical man's bargain—land, wealth, the woman he loved—and in repayment, the sidhe would collect a favor from him. Two years later, they came to collect.

"But Malcolm was, among his other talents, a man of the law. He found every English law relating to any deals with 'savages' and 'lesser races,' and the sidhe could not deny his argument that in the human world, on English land, he bore stewardship over them.

"So in repayment, the sidhe let the werewolf loose on his grounds. It was seen as a bit of rapacious justice. Would he call them savages? He would see true savagery. But Malcolm—well, you know his nature. He spent years and millions of pounds regaining control of the wolf inside. Then he moved to control the entire Otherworld by purchasing land from sidhe and using alchemy to destroy them when they were all here"—she flourished with her hand, indicating the ruins—"planning their retaliation. He calls it stewardship. I, who shared his bed long enough to know, call it a longing for control. He still works at alchemy, seeking potions to extend his life, and he must have every drop of profit he can to do so." She leaned forward. "He will not hesitate to burn the whole Otherworld. You have the evidence here around you."

"It's a fine offer," Charles said, "and the fact that a committed bourgeois is making it, well, that makes me all the more barbed."

"My dear gnome—" Unsworth began.

He cut her off. "My dear wolf, every word you say's a drop of poison! You started by insinuating business against me uncle, and now you offer us the same deal as Ridley, but there's a hook in it for a company store? You'll have the wages back not ten minutes after you disperse them. I won't lift a plate for your filthy deal or for any of you wolves."

The place was silent, as silent as the grave with the ash muffling the sound from outside. Finally, Unsworth nodded and stood, carefully straightening her massive dress and rising with more grace than should have been possible in such a ridiculous thing. "That is an impasse for sure."

"We'll take it," Billy said. "The vampires will."

"Billy, what?" Charles turned to him.

"I won't see me people starve, gnome." Billy shook his head, staring at the ground. "I won't see wee wains crying for a drop of blood again, and I won't cry myself with thankfulness for a packet of ground rat. Fair play to Communism, but you're forgetting this's for all folks, and it's for the purpose of good wages. Or are ye Otherworlders after working with suckabuckets and sods?" The last words came out bitter as vinegar.

"Billy, how could you think such a thing? I just called you a mate!"

He looked up, meeting Charles's eyes with his own pale-yellow ones. "You needed us yesterday. I saw that crowd, so I did. You don't need us today when you were talking that rot about food from madgekins. And I had to point out to you what vampires need?"

Charles stumbled on his words. "I-I-I need all the working folks of the Otherworld."

"Prove it," Billy said.

Charles lowered his head, so he couldn't see Unsworth. *Bloody hell, Marx, I can't make peace with the bourgeoisie. I can't.*

But this wasn't about Marx, was it? Marx was human, and Charles an Otherworlder, and Billy was right. The Otherworlders had to eat, had to have coin in their pocket, had to have newspapers to read and warm homes and clean water. Progress would kill them or be roped to them, but it would go on.

Charles finally looked up at Unsworth. "I'm with him. But you advance the livestock tomorrow. That's firm!"

"The deal is done on two conditions," Unsworth said. "Firstly, you will curb violence among your followers. You may be fey, but you are British fey. You will not conduct yourself like French nationalists."

Charles hadn't a blooming clue what a French nationalist was. "Right."

"Second, you will return whatever you have that gives you power over the Iron Riders."

"Hell and damnation I will!" Charles stood up. "That's what got the Iron Riders off our arse. What's to stop Ridley sending them in?"

"They appear to have quite abdicated their activities, my dear gnome," Unsworth said. "They have even abandoned the doors. I would not worry about the Iron Riders."

"When Ridley tosses them on the slag heap," Charles said, "then we deal."

"Oy now," Billy said. "I'll take me chances with the Riders, Charles. We'll be back at work anyway with things well in order."

Charles put his hand in his pocket and on the box. He wasn't convinced. "Why does Ridley need this? I didn't think it would do a thing as we lost the bit of flesh inside of it."

"He has not chosen to share the details of this item or what it does, but I suspect it can be used against the Puck. I worked that out after hearing the details of what it did to Iron Riders suffused with his magic." She stood. "This is not a condition of my bargain but a condition of your uncle's life. Malcolm came to my house just after your vampire girl did and collected Riordan. He asked me to arrange a meeting with you if possible to talk about the exchange. I took this opportunity to discuss my own interests first."

Charles felt as if he'd been hit in the gut, and his air all let out. "Y-you could've bloody led with that—"

"I thought it might color your emotions when we spoke of the strike."

"Well right, it does! Yeh bourgeois liars! You said he was at your house!" They were holding his uncle's life over this negotiation? "Yeh've taken me for a fool!"

Her face, strangely, softened. "Not in the least. I offer you a path out of your dilemma because you have, to some degree, convinced me of the rightness of your cause. I believe we can work together. Meet with Malcolm, secure your uncle's life, fulfill your strike, and preserve the Otherworld."

"Mate," Billy said. "I can't see how we've got another choice after this week."

"Me uncle!" Charles spat. "Me family!"

"As I said, I seek to preserve it," Unsworth repeated.

Charles glared at her. "I don't trust you bourgeois further than a drunk troll." But after a long silence, he drew the box out of his pocket. "Here you bloody go."

Chapter Thirty-Three

In which our Vampire's Leap of Faith is Consequential

HER LEFT HAND CAUGHT A SUPPORT STRUT ON THE WING.

The wind hammered her, catching her cloak, twisting her grip, but she clung. With her right hand, she seized its slashing appendage, holding on desperately just above the blade.

Puckish luck.

The Rider's wings flapped and flapped, struggling as Jane's weight pulled them down. The City Beyond spun dizzily below her, the towers like walls, as she and the flying Rider whipped faster and faster like rodents sucked into a whirlpool. The Puck's shrieks of laughter followed her.

Jane's arms wrenched in their sockets as the small Rider jerked and twisted, trying to rid itself of the weight. The Towers rose huge and black around them, and all the lights below gleamed, getting closer, closer, faster—

Something flashed below them—a long path. A bridge of the Towering Market, Jane recognized through her blurry vision. The Rider yanked its appendage from Jane's right hand, and her left arm lurched with all her weight, but she clung, her grip a ball of pain. She only had to make it to the ground, to find something to land in—

The Rider tore her dress, gashing her leg.

Down, down, down—too fast—Jane caught a glimpse of fauns and humans scattering, of awnings and goods scattered across the street—

Her grip gave out just as they plunged into the Towering Market.

Jane bowled into an awning like a cannonball, crashed against a stack of bread, knocked her head against the metal of a railing, and rebounded against a merchant's table, which crashed to the ground.

Everything hurt. The whole world swam. Blinding, burning darkness. She thought she saw her mother's face and then Charles, grimacing and muttering with his nose in the pamphlet. She thought she saw a light and darkness and heard a train . . .

And slow as the dawn, the dim Otherworld sky came through her eyes.

Jane blinked away stars. "I'm alive." She felt her chest, legs, and stomach. "I'm alive!"

Alive, and . . . Puck was going to drop London onto the City Beyond.

Head swimming, she got to her feet. Blood ran down her legs and arms, but she lived. Feeling the cuts, she noted none of the heavy rush of blood that would mean the Rider had cut a vein.

She could mend herself later.

It took a good few minutes before she recognized the Towering Market around her.

It was quite ruined. Stalls had been smashed apart. Enchanted food lay torn to crumbs in the street, and enchanted objects were scattered about. "Well . . ." Jane started to say and realized she had no words even for herself. Had it been Charles's strike that did all this?

"Charles, say you're all right," Jane said. "Say you . . ." She had been angry with Charles, and she couldn't even remember why. "Charles?"

Another voice babbled along with her. "Oh, my soul. Oh, my soulfullest of all soulful souls . . ."

Jane recognized the thunderous voice. She ran ahead, turned a corner, and found none other than Mister a-Lokk, sifting through fragments of paper from an ink-and-paper stall. His characteristic ragged suit was now scorched.

"Oh, my muse, dear musiest of all mysteries . . ."

"Mister a-Lokk!" Jane stumbled forward, caught him by the arm. "Mister a-Lokk, I am so glad to see you! I must reach the human world! I am missing my pass, and—"

"Jane!" He seized her, pulled her close enough that the spikes on his skin quite scratched her up, and he wept great black tears onto her shoulder. "I am so sorry! Oh, my heart weeps, and my spleen drips bile—"

"What?"

"For the *Voice* is gone! It has been burned!"

Jane's heart felt again flung into a gulf as wide as death. The *Voice* was gone?

"I sought to go to the human world," he said, briefly containing his sobs. "I wished to study art! But the doorkeepers are gone, and the metal doors will not open!"

Jane shook her head. She could mourn the *Voice* later. She had to get to the human world. The metal doorkeepers were gone along with the Riders, summoned by Puck. "It's all right. I know where a madgekin keeps a door just outside Ridleyville," Jane said. Hopefully Pedge, Charles's erstwhile employer, would be there. "We just need to convince him to let us through."

Mister a-Lokk nodded. "Perhaps he'll be sympathetic"—two great black tears rolled down his cheeks—"to art! Oh, my soul!"

"Yes," Jane said. "Or you could just ask. I imagine people find you hard to refuse."

"Yes," he said, wiping the tears with enormous claws. "There is that. Many see only my intimidating outward appearance, not knowing the sensitive yolkery within the shell. But is this the path the muse—"

"Yes," Jane said, and though all her body groaned in pain, she seized Mister a-Lokk's hand and started walking. "This is the path the muse wants for your yolkery. Hurry!"

Chapter Thirty-Four

In which our Gnome Confronts the Wolf at the Last and Finds the Wolfish Nature not all that was Promised

H OT AS THIRTEEN HELLS," CHARLES SAID. THE BOX MIGHT BURN HIM SOON. "What's wrong?" Unsworth asked.

He glared at her and didn't answer.

"You've no reason to be petulant as I can see, dear gnome. I dealt fairly if not in the order you'd have preferred."

He glared harder.

The London fog was thick tonight, a right impenetrable curtain, so one couldn't see farther than a few dull gas lamps in the distance. Except for the stink of coal instead of pulverized trees and grass, it wasn't much different from the netherworld Unsworth had led them into.

Billy had gone back to the Otherworld proper to arrange things while the vampires waited on the distribution of Unsworth's promised livestock, and Unsworth had led Charles through another door into the human world.

"I suppose there'll be no answer?" Unsworth asked. "After tonight, a better future awaits both of us. Greater goodwill all round."

Charles didn't like answering this blatant bourgeois, even now, even if Billy'd acceded to her, but there was no point in keeping it in. "That box is getting hot as a poker in me pocket." With one hand, he held his jacket away from his body. It was tough to tell in the greenish, smoky light, but he could have sworn curls of smoke rose from the pocket where the box sat.

"It'll do that, I imagine," Unsworth said. "We are close to the exhibition where the great machine is, and there will be sympathetic resonance."

"I don't reckon this thing should be magical at all. We lost the bit of flesh. I thought that was magic."

"No, my dear fellow. The box isn't magic. It's built to contain magic by the alchemy woven into its construction."

Charles was dumbstruck. The box, not the flesh inside?

"You have not figured this out?"

"Right clueless, I am," Charles said. "What's it do?"

"I told you, Malcolm did not make me privy to his plan. I've had to fill it in via hearsay. A box, likely a well, and a machine, hidden in plain sight at the exhibition—all meant to contain the Puck."

"Thought you were proper kith with Ridley. Close enough to chat in his bed."

"I suppose it's quite useless to upbraid you for being so vulgar?"

Oy, this bourgeois lass would be the death of his tongue. "Why wouldn't you know?"

"We were close for many years, yes," she said. "My husband did not bear well with the transformation to a wolf, and I sought solace from the one man who seemed to understand. I am not ashamed of it."

"Can't imagine you're ashamed of much," Charles said.

Unsworth let that one pass with no comment.

As they walked through the smoke and fog, something emerged. The dull gas lights themselves were reflected, showing a structure, a glowing grid of reflective glass. As they got closer, Charles's mouth fell open with wonder. More and more, the structure revealed itself, an endless, tall expanse of glass on a grid. A huge building, all made of glass. An immense archway—more glass—rose over the entrance, wings extending out to either side. Flags hung limp in the smoky air along the entrance. Signs everywhere read some variation on "Great Exhibition of London."

"Is this a trade fair?" Charles asked.

"Where better to hide a thing you don't want an Otherworlder to find than in a great conflagration of humans?" Unsworth answered.

Charles yanked the jacket pocket farther from his body. "This is the place," he muttered. Now, holding it away from himself, Charles could see the red-hot box even through the fabric.

A group of red-coated soldiers marched about the place with irritating regularity, but Unsworth just nodded to them, and one of them motioned for her to go ahead through a side entrance meant for merchants.

Bloody bourgeoisie and their bloody privileges. Hang on. Charles tapped Unsworth's arm with the hand not occupied in keeping him from burns. "How d'yeh pronounce it again?"

"What's that, my dear gnome?"

"The words. From Marx. How d'yeh pronounce them?"

"Ah. *Boozh-WAH*, singular. *Boozh-wah-ZEE*, plural."

Charles nodded. "Ah . . . thank you."

"Oh my. A thank you? Don't spoil me, dear gnome."

"Blooming hell, I've had enough sarcasm for a lifetime."

"I can't imagine how you provoke it so."

Charles glared.

They entered the massive glass palace through a dark area, stacked with crates all around, a place that reminded him of nothing so much as Pedge's burrow. They emerged from the back of the booth into a vast hall lit by irregular gas lamps, enough for Charles to see the shapes of the things around him and whistle. "Thirteen raging hells."

No human was supposed to have an imagination this . . . crowded.

The vast crystal hallway was packed with knick-knackery. Vases as tall as a troll. Two rearing white horses, statues about three times the size of the biggest horses Charles'd ever seen, kicking their great marble legs out toward each other. Statue after statue of benevolent maidens in flowing robes. Looms so big they could have been designed for ogres. Fountains every few paces, and in the distance, a king fountain stretching the height of ten gnomes.

He'd never seen so many human oddments. Crystal chandeliers and fine dining ware and inventions for shoveling manure and picking cotton. Some so bizarre that he hadn't seen the like in the City Beyond. One thing, hanging above their heads, took the prize: a little black carousel with a couple of glass containers filled with leeches that scrambled in their glass prisons for bells.

"Leeches? Bells?" Charles said.

Unsworth didn't answer.

And trees! Full-grown trees right there along the pathway, sprouting as if this were the Choke. Exotic trees with immense, spreading palm leaves atop stalks that extended from bulbous bases. Regular old London trees, shedding autumn leaves onto the mud-stained stone path.

"Impressed?" Unsworth asked.

"So this is what you bourgeois want the Otherworld to be?" Charles asked. "A mess of knick-knacks?"

"Not quite what we want," Unsworth said, "but you cannot deny that the production of these goods has both created new inequalities and new opportunities." She pointed ahead of them. "Now is hardly the time for a debate. There they are."

Charles saw first a drop-cloth-covered machine, the cloth bearing a stylized *R*. And then noticed the smaller figures standing in front of it.

Malcolm Ridley, tall, wiry, straight as a bayoneted rifle. His red-dusted white hair shone, same as it had the day this all started behind the factory gates.

And with him, Uncle Riordan. Looking none the worse for the wear, though his eyes were wide with fear.

"Uncle—" Charles held himself back.

"Elizabeth, lovely to see you." Malcolm Ridley came forward and kissed Lady Unsworth on both cheeks. Charles just caught sight of her slipping a tiny corked bottle into his hand before Ridley turned his attention to Charles.

"Uncle." Charles stepped forward. "Uncle, you well? They treat you all right?"

Riordan didn't answer, keeping his lips tight.

"Ah, not yet," Ridley said, stepping away from Unsworth. "Gnome, you know what I want."

Charles frowned, grumbled, and reached into his pocket, touched the blazing-hot box but stopped. "I don't trust you, bourgeois swine." He made sure to pronounce it as Unsworth had indicated. "Not an inch. Give my uncle over, and then you get your box."

"Give him over?" Malcolm Ridley raised a faded red eyebrow. "My dear gnome, that was never part of the deal. I offer to spare his life. You should take that offer."

"What's this now?" Charles glared at Unsworth.

"Malcolm speaks the truth," Unsworth said. "I never said we bargained for his freedom, dear gnome. He must remain in custody."

Charles's vision went red with anger. "Yeh'll kill him? Just kill the fellow, no questions asked, unless I hand the box over? Whole Otherworld will make yeh pay for that!" Charles's fists hurt from clenching. Nothing would feel better than to pop this swell one in the face right now. He didn't think he could stop himself. "I'll bloody—"

"It is a benefit of stewardship," Ridley said, "that my judgment in such matters is trusted. And who would deny it is deserved? A life for a life. But not, gnome, if you give me the box."

Charles's vision went red. He had to pound this swell, he deserved it and—

He didn't throw the punch. Charles forced breath after breath, one at a time, into his furious body. *There is a better way, bloody hell. Marx knew it.* "He didn't poison your mean little cub, yeh thick mug!" Charles finally said.

"He didn't poison my son?" Ridley's eyes were aflame now. "How many lies has that Puck been feeding you? How much nonsense have you heard? Speak, Riordan. Reliably tell your nephew the truth about that night when my son died."

Riordan's already-wide eyes seemed to get wider, but he did not open his mouth, a firm black line between his knotty lips.

"Uncle?" Charles said. "You all right now?"

Riordan shook his head and wouldn't open his mouth, but something seemed to be *pushing* out. Something green.

"By heaven," Unsworth whispered.

"Oh, Puck's bloody tricks," Charles said.

Literally.

Despite Riordan's best efforts to keep his lips closed, a green-jacketed elbow jabbed its way out of his uncle's mouth and unfolded, grabbing the top of Riordan's head, and yanked the rest of itself out. Stained by gnome slobber, Puck fell to the ground of the Great Exhibition like a newborn babe from Riordan's mouth.

"*You!*" Malcolm Ridley cried.

Three things happened at once.

Puck leapt to his feet, giggling like a madman.

Lady Unsworth seized Riordan and pulled him away toward the shelter of the booth, leaving Puck between Charles and Ridley.

Malcolm Ridley swallowed the potion Unsworth had slipped him.

"You," Ridley growled, tossing away the bottle, the white-red fur of his sideburns growing, his ears extending. "You, dealing against me! Trying to play your trickery, taking advantage of my period of mourning and—" Ridley let out a strange noise, halfway between a wolf's growl and a . . . if Charles hadn't known better, he'd have said it was a mule's snort. "You who made me a deal and now seek to—"

Ridley's snout was lengthening, becoming more wolfish in his transformation.

But no, something was off on the wolfishness. His nose shifted, elongating into a thin snout, capping in a soft black nose and ragged fangs beneath whiskered pads. And then it widened, flaring out the front fangs, flattening them. A whole different sort of nose—thick and blunt with wide, heavy nostrils and enormous squared-off teeth. "Traitorous—*hee-aww!*" Ridley bellowed.

"Oh, thirteen hells," Charles said, backing away.

Puck shrieked with laughter as Malcolm Ridley transformed not into a wolf but into an ass.

The angry donkey reared up and kicked out, seeking to bite the Puck who ran around the exhibition squealing in delight. Puck led the ass on a wild chase until they both crashed into an enormous loom, sending a massive steel spinning wheel flying across the floor.

In the distance, Riordan and Unsworth ran for the exit where he'd come in. The Puck was now between them and Charles.

His green suit gleaming, the trickster rose into the air above the exhibition. His flame-tossed hair lit up, fluttering well above his head, and the trees around him burst into flame. "Oh, gnome," he said. "It was such mischief to work with you! I did love the vampires! Now see the great mischief I've planned!"

A great boom sounded, and the air shuddered. The ground underneath Charles changed, becoming translucent, and he looked *down* on the City Beyond. The Towering Market was a handful of jutting black dots. The Choke and the glowing green of the Black Fork were a wide, endless expanse.

"Thirteen hells!" Charles called as the vision passed. "What're yeh doing? What is that?"

"Charles?"

He whipped around, looking for the source of the voice, and saw her just beyond where Puck floated, standing in the center of the aisle. "Jane?"

"He's going to drop London onto the City Beyond!" Jane called. "I . . . I hoped to tell you before now."

"Well right," Charles said. *I suppose I need to turn this bloody machine on myself.* Gritting his teeth, Charles ran for the machine—

With a wave of Puck's hand, a wall of Riders appeared.

Chapter Thirty-Five

In which All Things Come to a Final Reckoning

JANE RAN FOR CHARLES, AND CHARLES RAN FOR THE RIDLEY'S EXHIBIT.
Puck's high giggling filled all the exhibition, ringing from the statues around them, and with that, the exhibition came alive. An enormous marble horse reared up, stomped a cart-sized hoof down near Jane's head. She dodged it but was thrown to the ground by a heavy tapestry that tried to suffocate her, wrapping around her like a dozen snakes—

She tore the tapestry open as it screamed like a wounded man. Charles's hands, as rough as ever, were there to yank her up. "Come on now!" They ran and tumbled under the lee of a fountain, out of the way of massive rolls of paper barreling out of the printing press. Pushed against each other as they were, Jane felt the heat from the box in his pocket.

"You'll not delay my mischief!" the Puck yelled in a sing-song voice. "I fired the test cannons, and any minute now . . ."

"Charles," Jane heaved. "Why did you bother with me? Get to the machine!"

"Right impossible with those Riders in the way," Charles said. "Can't kill them all at once, even with this box. I figured I'd get up on those balconies, maybe try to jump on it." He fished two tiny boots from his pocket, and they instantly grew to full size. "Nicked these back in the riot. Land one proper on a Rider, he'll sail all the way to France."

"Right," Jane said, "I'll—"

She had no chance to finish since Charles grabbed her by the front of her dress and kissed her furiously, a rapid, lip-smashing kiss. "In case this is it," he said. "I love yeh, Jane. Always will."

She nodded, and the words spilled out. "Your uncle—he said—"

Charles laughed. He laughed with the world going mad around them! "I imagine he told you about all kinds of other girls and said I'm three kinds of unreliable?"

"Ah . . ." Jane had not thought it would be so hard to say. "Not in so many words."

Charles squeezed her hand. "I have me past, but weren't none of them like you."

She flushed. "I'm sorry, Charles, but that's what any man would s—"

"You got steel in you, my girl Jane. If yeh don't know you're one of a kind, well, let's save our lives, so I can spend the rest of them convincing you."

She clutched him close, and despite the mania around her, the ache in her heart, she believed him. "I love you, Charles my dear."

He eyed the balconies. "And I you, Jane. Now, any chance you can toss me up there?"

She leapt up from the fountain, lifted Charles by the scruff of his jacket and pants, and threw him hard as she could. As he sailed through the air, a massive marble horse stampeded right into him. Charles clutched at its tail while it tried to kick him off.

Glass shattered nearby with a frantic pealing of bells as three immense leeches, purple and fat with red-rimmed mouths of quavering teeth, slithered across the exhibits, coming straight for Jane.

Jane threw a seven-league boot at one leech and quite missed. The boot landed on a nearby tree branch, sending the tree crashing through the ceiling. Cursing, she tossed the other, this time into a leech's maw, and the enormous, slimy thing flew through the glass panes to their side.

"Charles!" Jane yelled. "Toss the box!"

To the sound of more glass breaking, iron bending, and Puck's shrieking, Jane bolted for the machine, the Riders in her way. Charles hurtled the box through the air. Jane dove for it and caught it just before it thudded into the ground, hot as a poker fresh from the fire. A second later, the mouth of one of the two remaining leeches appeared on her right, and Jane rolled away and scrambled to her feet, part of her dress tearing away, and she ran forward, toward the great drop-cloth-covered Ridley machine.

Riders made a barrier. Jane held the box out toward them despite how it blistered her fingertips.

A living statue of a maiden leapt forward, her arm outstretched, and knocked the box away. It slid right under one of the Riders, and the Rider in question lit up with arcs of lightning.

Jane changed direction, ran toward the dying Rider, and shoved it out of the way, seizing the now red-hot box from the ground as she ran toward the machine.

The massive marble hooves came down in front of her, and she just caught sight of Charles clinging to strands of marble tail, bellowing, "Throw it!"

She hurtled the box.

Charles let go, sailing through the air, caught the box, and crashed into the machine, seizing the drop cloth and pulling it away, revealing a vast heap of gears and boilers and brass and steel with a gap in the center just made for something the size of the box.

He landed on the ground near a Rider.

The Rider seized Charles by the foot with one of its gleaming appendages. He screamed in pain as he was swallowed up in green fire and clutched at the drop cloth where it had fallen. Turning around, his entire body smoking like a tree in a fire, Charles just managed to bring the box down on the Rider's arm, and it wheeled away, pulling back from the box and arcing lightning like unraveling string.

But Charles fell back to the floor, unmoving, skin pouring smoke.

The air smelled of burning oak.

"No!" Jane cried and sank to her bloodied knees.

Puck came down next to her and giggled. "Oh, dear! This is the end! You were glorious, my dear. Almost equal to the wolves."

The whole of the exhibition calmed, all magic ceasing save the fire in Puck's hair.

"It can't be," Jane whispered. "Charles—"

Charles's hand twitched. Twitched and clasped the box. He moved. Just a bit, crawling along the ground toward the machine.

She looked at Puck. "Fine mischief this is?"

"The finest!" Puck giggled. "Oh, dear me, I knew it from the start! I knew from the moment I observed you trying to clamber into the Otherworld that you were made for mischief, so dedicated, so single-minded—"

"It's a terrible shame it's not real," Jane said.

"What?" Puck's face for the first time bore a confused look.

Jane emptied her face of expression. "This isn't real. The Otherworld? The doors? The living exhibition? No, it is too much. I am back in my room at the asylum."

Saying it wasn't enough. He would know. She had to *feel* it. He'd said he smelled things on her; let him smell this if he were so devoted to her life as a trickster.

Jane closed her eyes and went back to the feeling that had tormented her in her darkest thoughts for the last year: that horrible feeling that the quiet was all there was, that the hunger was a sickness, and that she had imagined all of her life . . .

Puck's voice grew higher. "A fine jest! Admit it! Why are your words flavored with doubt? We are weavers, duckers, creatures of mischief!"

She pictured the asylum halls, the soft voices of the matrons. "Merely the quiet," Jane said. It was strange. It felt so accurate to say. Of course, she was still in her room. Of course, she had imagined this—all her imaginings had become a problem. One could imagine so many things in a cold, spare room. "Not real."

Puck's voice was shrieking now. "You shouldn't speak of common, stupid human things! You have trickery in your blood!"

Jane said the words she'd sworn not to say.

"I am mad."

She *knew* what she would see when she opened her eyes. White walls. A wrought-iron grill over the window. Her cold bed frame and Bible on the nightstand.

She opened her eyes.

The exhibition lay shattered around her, the floor thick with slime, the statues frozen in unnatural positions, and the trees afire.

And in the distance, beyond Puck's reddened face, Charles crawled an inch at a time toward the machine. He made it to the base and clutched at the metal spars, pulled himself up, clinging to the white-hot box.

A thought swam up through Jane's mind, a single thought like a bubble in a stream. *Oh, I'm not mad after all.* That was a relief.

Puck stared at Jane as if trying to puzzle out what was wrong. "I thought you would make such a trickster in your time." He sounded almost sad. "So fine. Never you mind." He snapped his fingers, and for half a second, the ground turned clear as glass, and again the City Beyond loomed—

A howl roared through the hall. The ground turned back to stone, and Puck screamed.

Charles had jammed the box in place, and the Ridleys' machine turned on.

Jane crumpled to the floor, hands over her ears, and it was a good thing too, for the Riders broke apart with great screams of tortured metal, making her head ring even with her ears plugged. Their gas-lamp eyes burst, pouring forth white smoke; their appendages melted, dripping away like ice in sunlight; and their great bulbous bodies tore away from their wheels and rolled along the ground as if they'd been hit by an invisible hammer.

Puck himself swelled to an immense size, filling the exhibition hall from crystal ceiling to floor. His green eyes, immense now, flashed on and off like lamps. "It would have been such a jest!" he called out. "You must admit it!"

With an enormous slurp, the machine roared and whirred and sucked him down into the box that Charles and Jane had carried for so long. From white-hot to yellow-hot, the box changed, fading to a charred-black piece of metal, all one piece now, fused shut at the center of the machine.

The Great Exhibition went silent.

Charles sprawled out on the ground, looking all the world like a fire-charred stump.

Jane ran to him. "Charles! My dear Charles! You must awaken! Please!" His skin sizzled, burned black all over. "Please!" She lifted him up, and parts of his skin came away like coals, brushing into ash. "My dear Charles! Please wake up!" She kissed him on his burnt lips, swallowed half a mouthful of ash. "You must . . ."

"Oy, Jane," he said. "I'm . . . I'm all right."

Tears clouded her vision. "Charles, what happened?"

"Got a bit singed is all," he coughed and reached out, clinging to her hand. "Not too bad. Uncle says the most reliable gnome could stand at the center of a forest fire and only take a bit of char." He stood up, brushed his beard, and most of the hair went flying, turned to ash. "I didn't think it was literally true! Might have to learn me aphorisms after all."

"It's odd though since you're not quite the most reliable gnome," Jane said.

"Although you did just save two worlds, and I suppose that's exactly the sort of person one can rely on. Oh—"

Charles grabbed her and pulled her down for a proper kiss. Despite the ash in his beard, the racing in Jane's lungs, neither of them stopped for a good long time until they were out of breath and the sun shone through the windows around them.

Chapter Thirty-Six

In which a Truth is at last Revealed

THE WHOLE BLOODY EXHIBITION REPAIRED ITSELF A PIECE AT A TIME. THE horses stomped back to their places. The leeches shrank to normal size. The trees swayed in the changing air currents as though they'd never been burned.

"Oy, that's a strange thing." Just saying that caused him to choke on a cloud of ash, flying up when his beard moved with the words.

Jane rubbed away the soot that their pash had left on her face and prodded a remaining patch of leech-slime on the ground with her foot. "I think we'd best remain on good terms with Pedge. I suspect most of Puck's magic is undone today, including the doors to the Otherworld."

"I'd better bring him that cheese after all," Charles said with a sigh. He filled Jane in on the plan.

Outside, Lady Unsworth spoke to a guard who, wide-eyed, glanced between her and Riordan.

"Trust me, dear fellow," Unsworth said. "A jackass got loose in the exhibition and caused a great deal of trouble. That is all. You'll find the beast quite unconscious in there. Do me a favor, and revive the ass, and give it any amount of carrots and hay as is appropriate. I'll send someone to retrieve the poor thing."

The soldier seemed unconvinced, but Lady Unsworth pressed a whole ten pounds into his hand, and he saluted. "Yes, marm, right away."

"Well done." She turned to Charles and Jane. "It is done then?"

"You knew?" Charles tried to say more, but he choked on a bit of ash from his beard.

"I didn't know any of that would happen," she said as the soldier moved away, casting suspicious looks over his shoulder. "But given what Riordan has told me and what Miss Jane proved when she came to visit me, I suspected that you two would be able to take care of yourselves in there. I'll have that box containing the Puck removed to a vault, quite protected."

Jane narrowed her eyes. "You knew about the potion?"

"That Puck had poisoned it against Malcolm? No, I did not know."

"Truly," Jane said in a tone that said she was unconvinced.

Unsworth's face was blank as a blooming brick wall. "It is fortunate I have not had any of the potion today. I'll have to have the whole batch thrown out. I'll be quite at an advantage over those other werewolves or, ah, were-asses who've already had it distributed to them as I sent the latest portion out just before now."

"That's your official statement?" Jane said.

"I would be happy to give a full interview if you wish, dear vampire girl. Perhaps even a contribution to a new printing press and to your living in the meantime."

Charles tried to say, *You've a right dodge going on, so you do! Taking over everything!* But all he could do was hack up ash. *I've enabled a whole takeover of the economy. Via Communism!*

"Bloody well n—"

"Are you trying to speak, dear gnome?"

Charles could only cough. The burnt-toast feeling had moved into his chest. *Speak!* Damned if he'd spend the rest of his life on the down side of this push-pull with Unsworth. Charles tried three times to clear his throat and finally managed to croak out, "Livestock for the vampires today. And a shilling more a week! For that!" He pointed at the exhibition.

"Now is not the time—"

"It's going to be two shilling more, we stand here much longer!" Charles fell to horrible hacking, coughing that shed coals from his skin. "We bloody—" He coughed again. "We saved your bourg—" More coughing. It was like trying to get around a bonfire in the chest, it damned well was.

Jane spoke for him. "We saved both worlds, Lady Unsworth, and you will not be ungrateful but will pay your workers accordingly. A shilling more a week, and you will agree that the company store will raise the prices no more than five percent of normal market value."

"Fine," Unsworth said. "For conquering the Puck, a shilling more a week per worker."

"And a regulated company store. No more than five percent."

"Agreed. I'll see you in Ridleyville. Wednesday afternoon after Riordan's made me a morning tea." She put a fond hand on Riordan's shoulder. "Now, my dear Riordan, you must see a doctor as must your nephew. I insist. Your jaw is quite distended, and Charles will need care for his burns." She pressed two-pound coins into Riordan's hand. "I'll give you two days off to recover and expect you all the earlier on Wednesday."

Riordan's eyebrows shot up, and for the first time, he spoke, "Mistress, no, I am under guard, I am in prison, I—"

"I do not think Malcolm can be trusted as a gaoler when he was threatening to privately execute prisoners. We must reevaluate your situation. For now, I give you into the care of these respected community leaders and business partners, trusting them to see you don't escape while you seek medical care. Be at my Kensington door fresh Wednesday morning."

Riordan stood confused. "This is a double standard and doubly un . . . er, un . . ."

Charles coughed and hacked three times before he managed to say, "Off with it, Uncle, be reliable for the new boss."

Unsworth's cold, gold-flecked blue eyes caught the dull smoky light of London as she regarded Charles. "There is a saying, dear gnome, about the devil you know. I suggest you observe it and we regard each other with good faith tempered by skepticism."

The devil you know. Charles nodded to this particular devil and with Riordan and Jane at his side headed through London's awakening streets.

"I came through Pedge's door, dear Charles," Jane said as they crossed from Hyde Park along a street already full of awakening humans. Charles didn't even bother to hide his face. They would just think he was a chimney sweep.

"How'd yeh manage—" Charles couldn't get any more out.

"I found a fellow who was willing to convince Pedge to keep it open." Jane's forehead furrowed. "Although by now, he may have put the poor madgekin to sleep. And oh dear, I lost his book." She clutched Charles's hand, and despite the pain of the burns, it felt right nice to have her next to him again. "I found out a number of things, dear Charles. There were Riders stealing children from the human world to power the doors the Ridleys made. Vengeful ghosts powered the Riders, including the ghost of the man we heard murdered and—oh!—that ghost returned the box to your pocket. The Puck was helping with that, always playing us against the wolves, for his greater scheme of mischief."

Might've known, Charles wanted to say but couldn't get it out. He clenched her hand, hoping that would speak for him.

Jane looked over at Riordan. "Well, sir, it is good to see you hale if with a bit of a distended jaw. I suppose the Puck must have been the one who poisoned John Ridley then?"

Riordan actually stopped mid-step, and a suited man hurrying to work dodged around him with a shout. "Oh, young man, keep walking!"

"Thick human!" Charles snapped. Riordan still stood in the center of the walkway unmoving. "Uncle?" Charles managed to choke out. "We've got to go before the traffic. Don't want to be recognized by any humans."

Riordan didn't answer.

"Uncle?" He'd never seen such a look on his uncle's face, not even when the young Ridley'd called him unreliable. "What on earth's the matter?"

"Charles, how have you not seen it?" Riordan said. "My dear nephew, do you judge me so well?" He turned to Jane. "And you with all the instincts of your profession?"

"Charles . . ." Jane's mouth seemed stuck open. "He told me you weren't capable of misplacing your cufflinks."

Riordan said, "I poisoned John Ridley."

Charles's mouth fell open wide, and forget the ash and coals that fell in from his charred beard, he stood there dumbstruck as an Iron Rider.

"It was meant for Elmont. Hence the clay pitcher. I wanted to take some petty vengeance on him, so I added a whole packet of maradoth root to send him to the privy just when the company would be calling for their horses and thus prove him unreliable in the eyes of his employers. The clay pitcher was . . . intercepted."

Charles clutched his aching chest, wheezed for breath, and managed, "Uncle, that's so so so un-gnomish!"

"I know," Riordan said and resumed walking with them. "All those years, I gnawed on my resentment for Elmont, even after I met Susan and ceased to pine for Priscilla. Always he was a more upstanding, reliable, and centered gnome and acting as though it came without effort! And myself an itinerant servant while he was a full driver for a family. I brought the maradoth to the party despite its danger to humans, for I worried that you might overindulge in cheese. But there you were, Charles, the picture of reliability—well, for a bit—and Elmont refusing even to lend a hand, and I saw the wine meant for the help, and I was unreliable and passionate, and the gnome god has punished me for it." Riordan raised his head up to an uncharacteristically clear London sky. "It feels somewhat of a relief to tell you, though of course confession is the wine of the unreliable and restitution the reliable gnome's—"

"I cannot believe it!" Charles bellowed, forcing the words out through the coughs. This was more bloody shocking than meeting the Puck or getting kissed by Jane or seeing Malcolm Ridley turn into an ass. "It's . . . it's . . ." He hacked and coughed like a man on his deathbed, swallowing more chunks of burnt beard.

"It's . . . not un-surprising," Jane finished. "We were blinded by your good nature, sir"

"I am a creature of passion in my own manner," Riordan said. "And it may be that in the long run, Charles, you have conquered your passions more effectively than I ever did." He cast an eye at Jane. "You may not put this in your newspaper!"

"I don't think that will be a problem," Jane said with a sigh.

They were silent. The only sounds were the neighing of horses and creaking of machinery that marked morning in London as they walked through the morning haze headed back to the Otherworld.

"Uncle," Charles said when he was sure he could talk.

"Words will not comfort me at the moment, Charles."

"What's that platitude about friends?"

Riordan furrowed up his knotty brow and said, "A gnome without companions is a shorn stump indeed."

"Uncle," Charles said, his throat a little less dry now, "no matter our flaws, everything that I've done right—hang reliable for a moment, just think about what's right—was all because of you." He clasped his uncle's hand, and Riordan didn't move away, just looked at Charles with two tears glimmering behind gnarled eyelids. "Without you, Uncle, I woulda been the shornest of stumps."

"Speak properly, and the world will note the extra care."

"See, you'll be all right."

Chapter Thirty-Seven

*In which there are Reconciliations,
Introductions, and at last a Parting
as we say Fare You Well, Reader*

THIS TIME, NO ONE WAITED OUTSIDE HER MOTHER'S HOUSE. NO POLICEMAN, no sign of guests. Jane turned the knob, and for once, she needed no lockpicks as it swung open to reveal a dusty parlor.

"Think she's home?" Charles asked, peering into the house.

"She would have locked the door if she went out." As before, the parlor was bare, end tables missing some favorite knick-knacks, and the fireplace heaped with cold ashes. Jane's dress, mended from the adventure in the rat processing facility, hung from the banister across from the fireplace.

"You're after a great fight like?" Billy asked, his voice muffled by the scarf and hat that hid his features. "Blagged off, did she? Got out of London?"

Franz added, equally muffled, "Or she has took long valk on green sass to enjoy the bunshine."

"I'm starting to think you do that on purpose," Charles said.

"I am highly pretended by this suggestion, gnome."

"Jane, she en't here. Mayhap we ought to get back, get Pedge his cheese. Unsworth's going to have the madgekins open that company store again after five, and no doubt, she'll say the market's up again, that blooming robber, and . . ."

"My dear Charles," Jane said. "You have faced the Puck, the industrialist, conducted a successful strike, and saved two worlds. Do not tell me you are afraid to meet my mother."

Billy and Franz chuckled.

"None of that!" Charles grumbled something under his breath and stepped inside the front hall. "You stay here and remember your blooming oath!"

"Lend some fair play to us now!" Billy said. "No more human blood. We swore. Anyone comes around, we'll just loom a little." Billy clasped Charles's shoulder. "For the good of the workers, our brothers."

"For the workers." Charles tipped his cap to Billy and Franz. "Well right, brothers."

Jane removed her muddy boots as did Charles, and they stepped into the parlor. "Mother?"

No answer.

Jane went into the kitchen, which was cold, the oven crowded with old ashes. No one. She wasn't in her bedroom downstairs nor was she in the larder. Jane returned to the parlor where Charles was sweeping the old ashes from the main fireplace. "Just a tick. I'll have this clean and a fire laid."

Jane, her hand down the skirt of the mended dress, admired the thorough job. Her mother had stitched it so that the Riders' slashes and the stains of rat blood were not noticeable and the mending only visible up close. It was still warm from her hand.

Jane crept upstairs to her own room and opened the door.

Her mother sat on Jane's bed, holding her hands out as if she were afraid of them. The old woman's hands shook. Blood glimmered on her chin.

"Mother!" Jane rushed to her side, opened her bedside-table drawer, and fished out a handkerchief. "Mother, you've cut your chin!" Jane held up her mother's hands and saw the dark stains of blood under her ragged fingernails. "Mother, what are you doing?"

"Jane, I am mad," her mother whispered. "They are coming because I am mad." She patted Jane's arm. "I am so sorry, dear. I should have gone to the asylum with you. I knew I should have."

"Mother, no!" Jane said. "You are sending *yourself* to the asylum?"

"I must."

"Mother, I—" Jane paused. Other than the cost, her mother would rather like a routine of Bible verses and steam baths, and it would stop her from clawing herself. But . . . "How will you pay for such a thing? Are you not still in debt?"

"I've found one run by wardens of the state. It should do—"

"No," Jane said. "No, do not go there. Let's wait until I've saved for a private institution, yes?"

"But I am insolvent, Jane," she said. "I cannot pay for the house, and I must go somewhere."

"Don't you worry," Jane said and winced. She supposed she would take Lady Unsworth up on that interview and the investment in a new press after all. *But I will be honest about the industrialist!* "I'll have funds within the week."

"They are coming now to get me. I was to wait for them. I did not—" She began to sob. "I did not know you would come back!"

Jane held her mother while the older woman, in a curious reversal of roles, wept into Jane's breast. After her mother had calmed a little, Jane stroked her hair and said, "One moment please, Mother. I need but to step into the hall."

She did so. "Charles?"

"Oy, love?" he called up from below.

"There may be men coming to the door after all. See that Billy and Franz . . . run them off."

"I'll do that."

Jane went back into her room and took her mother's hands.

Her mother sniffled, shedding two tears that tracked through dirt on her cheeks. "My girl. You look so strong, so confident. I wish the hysteria did not torment me so."

"Mother, listen," Jane said, feeling more and more desperate. "You're not mad. Your memories, whatever they may be, are true." Her own voice broke. "Mother, you need not admit it nor speak of it, but whatever you saw with your own eyes, it was real."

Her mother began to sob again, leaning into Jane's chest, into the wet spot she had made by her weeping.

Jane stroked her mother's hair.

And then her mother blurted out, "Your father was a Mormon!"

Jane stammered, "What? A-a morlock?"

"No, a Mormon." And she burst into tears again and buried her face in Jane's chest. Jane sat there dazed. There was nothing to do for her mother but let her soak the lapel of Jane's dress for what felt like half the hour while she held back her questions. *Is a Mormon a breed of vampire? A sorcerer?*

When the tears subsided enough for her mother to talk, Jane asked, "Mother, what is a Mormon?"

"A kind of preacher. An American."

"My father is an American preacher? And a vampire?"

"I-I did not see him . . . in another form . . . but once." She had the tone of a condemned man, stammering through a last speech on the gallows. "He came preaching to Manchester after your grandfather died. I was working in a factory before Aunt Rebecca took me in. I bought one of his new Bibles—the book of the Mormons—and let him preach to me, but as a foolish young girl, I was less interested in his religion than, well, him." Her hand began to shake. "I-I—"

"Don't stop!" Jane said. "You're doing so well, Mother. Mormons are wandering preachers? With a new bible?"

"Americans. I was . . . I was . . . I was indiscreet. The plan was to go to Liverpool, take ship for America, and be wed on the boat by one of his fellow preachers. Of course, he said that in Heaven's view we were already married. Men say a great deal when they think you're willing."

"You didn't go with him."

"Your Aunt Rebecca came to visit and convinced me of the madness of my decision. When I told him, he grew wroth, and though I begged him to stay in England, I thought—" She shook all the more. "Here is the peculiar thing, Jane. If he was . . . was what you said, then he must have been behind some sort of glamor. I thought in his anger that I saw the glamor slip. I thought . . ." She clutched at her chest. "Oh, God, I thought I saw Satan himself!"

"Not quite," Jane said. "Gray skin, bald head, yellow eyes like mine? That's a vampire." Her mother whimpered. Jane pressed on. "They're like men, but where men can eat both vegetable and meat, vampires can only subsist on meat, and they avoid sunlight."

"I . . . he did mislike sunny days. Preferred the gloom of Manchester cloud. And blood pudding as often as he could get it."

"And he looked a normal man?"

She nodded. "Save for that one moment."

"I see." So her mother had known he was a vampire but refused to trust her eyes.

"You were born sickly, but that is not so strange. Aunt Rebecca left us half her inheritance, and I moved you to the city hoping to find a doctor who understood your malady, but then . . . then this talk of . . . devilish things." She started to cry again. "I thought I must be mad and passed the madness to you!"

"Shhh, shhh, Mother." Jane took her hand, the anger melting away. It all made sense.

And something inside Jane, something still wound tight and knotted from the asylum, relaxed.

It had been too easy still, as in the exhibition, to convince herself. Every day in the Otherworld, even over the length of the strike, she'd thought, *If I but close my eyes long enough, I'll awaken in the asylum.*

No. She was not mad. And she wouldn't need to reassure herself again.

It took ages before she could even speak. "Why did you not tell me when I was younger? At least, you could have told me that my father was a wandering preacher and you guilty of an indiscretion."

She swallowed. "Dear, you were hardly ready to hear about the ways of men and women, much less know that I fell into sin in such a manner."

"Mother . . ." Jane laughed. Oh dear. "I know what goes on between men and women! I am eighteen!"

"Eighteen is young yet! I thought to tell you when you were older!"

"How much older?" Jane asked.

"I don't know." Her mother clutched Jane's hand. "Thirty?"

"Oh, dear." Jane stood. "Mother, I have someone to introduce you to. A man. And one I'm quite familiar with and I hope you will also become familiar with him. Though not in the same way." Jane grimaced. There was a terrible way to begin things. "Come downstairs."

"What? There is a man downstairs? Jane, I . . . oh dear, I haven't had a girl out to clean in ages, I—"

"Come downstairs. You'll like him . . . well, I like him." Jane winced. "I suppose we mustn't have any more falsehoods. I quite hope you like him, though you may not."

Step by quivering step, they descended the stairs until they saw Charles, rubbing away at the stones of the fireplace with a bristle brush. "Bloody black-leading, applied sloppy as a mug," he grumbled, "just when I got this damnable char off—"

"There's a child? You have a *child*?" her mother squeaked, stopping on the third step up. "You—oh." She caught a better glimpse of the gnarled face and the scruffy beard when Charles turned around.

He doffed his cap. "Marm."

"Mother, this is Charles. Charles is a union leader, my beau, and a gnome."

"Charmed," Charles said. He extended his right hand, cap clutched in his left.

Her mother looked down at the hand, the stumpy little hand covered in gnarled, whorled patterns like an old tree trunk. There were still char marks across the surface of his skin. "And . . . you are one of God's children, same as I?"

"Oh, indeed, marm. Was in the clergy for a bit, you know, seeking the reliable old profession, but now, I represent the workers' interests."

Jane guided her mother down the last few steps within arm's reach of Charles. "Gnomes are known for being trustworthy and upright. Charles employs those traits in service to the workers of the Otherworld, creating transparency between labor boss and worker."

Her mother bent down and put out her own trembling hand to take Charles's. "I suppose it's quite admirable to ensure a fair workplace. The world has turned wicked and un-Christian with these industrialists taking advantage of common people and pretending all the while to Jesus's good graces."

"Mother, I . . . indeed." Jane had not expected to hear that. That was quite near Communist talk in and of itself. "Mother, was that *your* copy of the *Manifesto*?"

"You've read Marx then?" Charles asked.

"I . . . do consider him a man of principle." Her mother stammered onward. "And for you to have studied theology, even if only for a bit! Very admirable."

"Right you are, marm." Charles clutched her hand.

And Jane couldn't help a laugh. Her mother had some hidden leanings, it seemed. She might get along better with Charles than they'd thought.

"I should . . . I should put the kettle on," her mother said. "I've got good tea somewhere, fresh from India, though I suppose . . . does your kind drink tea?"

"I don't mind a bit of something hot," Charles said. "Long as I'm not in the fire."

"Good, very good . . ." Her mother looked away, fixed her gaze on the Bible on an end table. "I don't . . . do not ask me to believe in everything at once, Jane, and this talk of other worlds . . . but perhaps . . . perhaps we could agree to abide together for a time, and if you attend church with me—oh, I do miss having you in the pew—then perhaps we might one day speak of these things."

"Vampires," Jane said. "Mother, Father was a vampire, and I am half-vampire. If we're to make our peace, you mustn't be ashamed to say that."

Charles clutched his hat and looked down, but Jane stood up straight and faced her mother.

Her mother made a small, strained noise in her throat. "We could . . . we could . . . we could call them something else: those carnivorous men of which you contain some breeding?"

"That is quite a sentence, Mother."

"A lady welcomes an elocutive sentence as a challenge." Her mother peered off to her left, toward the door. "Oh, dear, the men from the asylum will be here soon . . ."

"I think they've been delayed, marm." A shout came from outside, and Charles raised an eyebrow. "No harm done though."

Jane put an arm around her mother. "You need not go to the asylum. I will stay tonight. We can make up my bed together, and I will bind your hands to prevent scratching. And yes, I'll come sit in church with you." Jane took her mother's hand again. "Although we should watch ourselves around Doris."

"I'll get the kettle," her mother said, "and clean the oven and . . ." She scuttled away to the kitchen.

"That weren't as bad as it could have been," Charles said.

Jane sank into a chair. She knew. At last, she knew.

"Jane, love, what is it?"

"She told me who my father is," Jane said.

"That's well, en't it?" Charles stood next to the chair, holding Jane's hand.

"It's so peculiar to think that, after all we went through, there was no enchantment, no force but Mother's own mind that kept her from telling me. Can you believe it?"

"Jane, who's your blooming father?"

"Ah, yes, that." Jane clutched Charles's knotty hand, pressed her thumb against the comforting ridges of his knuckles. "He was a . . . Mordred? A wandering preacher from America with many wives."

"Oh yeah, Mormons," Charles said.

"You know?"

"Read a penny blood the other day that Pedge nicked off some human. Had wicked Mormons in it what stole young women."

"Yes." Jane put a hand to her forehead. "Oh my. It is a great deal of information to take in. Where do they live in America?"

"Blagged off to some desert if the book told the truth."

"Indeed." Jane shut her eyes. At last, she knew. "What must one do with this information?"

"Feeling a bit tempted to run off to America?"

"Can't do it now," Jane said. "We've got Riordan's trial to attend to and the printing press and Lady Unsworth must be called to account and . . . I suppose it would be terribly unreliable, even after we've taken care of all that, to gallavant off to America's great West."

Charles grinned. "Terribly unreliable? You trying to entice me?"

Jane laughed and, checking to ensure her mother was still in the kitchen, gave him a swift and thorough kiss. "In a few months, I think we'd best check steamboat prices."

"I'll do that."

"And tonight . . ." Jane whispered as softly as possible in his ear, "I'll need another dose of the oak root."

It was lovely to see Charles turn so red under his gnarled skin.

He coughed, peered at the kitchen, starting at the sound of a teapot clanking. "So this is it for the nonce? Tea and church with Mother on Sunday, and the Otherworld the rest of the time? Thought I was done being caught between two worlds."

Jane couldn't help reaching out to brush away a bit of char still in his beard. "I don't belong to the human world or the Otherworld. My whole world is right here, standing at my side."

Charles pressed her hand in his. "Aye."

And at last, neither of them sought any other answer.

Glossary,
and a
Note on Victorianisms

ACTUAL VICTORIAN COCKNEY WAS A BIZARRE DIALECT THAT USED RHYMES as synonyms and endless biblical references, and if Charles (and Billy for that matter) spoke accurately, this book would probably be unreadable by a modern audience. When in doubt, I made them sound as Dickensian as possible. I used James Redding's 1909 book *Passing English of the Victorian Era* to source the phrases, which means they may not have all been in use in 1851, but one does what one can.

Contemporaneous slang and common terms used in this book include:

* **Bird:** girl
* **Black-leading:** the process of rubbing black lead into a fireplace to polish it
* **Bit of wet:** an alcoholic drink
* **Blag:** steal or snatch
* **Blower:** girl
* **Chumpy:** mad, crazy
* **Cut your stick:** get out of here
* **Glocky:** mad, crazy
* **Gooseneck bar:** crowbar
* **In a state of hugger-mugger:** muddled
* **Jimmy:** crowbar

- ❖ **Leg:** dishonest person
- ❖ **Lush:** alcoholic drink
- ❖ **Mandrake:** homosexual
- ❖ **Mizzle:** quit, vanish
- ❖ **Mug:** idiot
- ❖ **Papist:** Protestant term for Catholics
- ❖ **Sod:** homosexual
- ❖ **Swell:** a well-dressed and preening fellow

Acknowledgments

FIRST AND FOREMOST, THANKS TO A BRAINSTORMING SESSION WITH CAT Rambo in the long-ago year of 2007. Cat talked through this idea, the worldbuilding, and many of the plot twists, when I was a young writer excited by a cool idea and unsure how to wrangle it.

No book I've ever finished, so far, had such a long gestation period as the eleven-year journey of *The Great Faerie Strike*. Thanks to everyone in my life who read a draft of the book and critiqued it during its long journey to publication: Emma and Bill Jones, Tina Connolly, Nikki Trionfo, Chrissy Ellsworth, Rebecca Ellsworth, Jessica Holdaway, Langley Hyde (twice!), Cory Skerry, Marta Murvosh, Sam Bailey, Leslie Copeland, Claire Eddy, and apologies to anyone I inadvertently left out. Thanks to my agent, Sara Megibow, who read the book before she was my agent and gave invaluable feedback. Thanks to Effie Seiberg and Codex, for help with the dreaded lock-picking scene.

Huge thanks to Scott and Caroline at Broken Eye Books for taking a chance on this weird little story, a story I had pretty much given up on, and for being patient with me while I ripped it apart and re-stitched it.

Charles and Jane bear a transparent debt to the writings of Karl Marx, Friedrich Engels, and Nellie Bly. Thanks for your courage and your attempts to make sense of a vicious world.

Other primary sources included Queen Victoria's own journals, accounts of the Great Exhibition, Dickens's and Thackeray's own editorials and novels, and Henry Mayhew's accounts of the fléneur in London. I owe an immense debt to the aforementioned *Passing English of the Victorian Era*, Liza Picard's *Victorian London*, Judith Flanders's *The Invention of Murder*, Ruth Goodman's *How To Be A Victorian,* and Jürgen Osterhammel's *The Transformation of the World*. The Victorian Web resources on slang and pricing were particularly helpful, as were the Great Courses' audio lectures *Victorian Britain* and *The Rise and Fall of the British Empire* series taught by Patrick N. Allitt.

(Did you know the leeches at the Great Exhibition were real?! They were part of a nineteenth-century barometer—called the tempest prognosticator, or leech barometer—and when the barometric change of an approaching storm irritated them, they climbed farther up in the machine and struck a bell. Humans, amiright? Goblin-minded.)

Finally, all my love to Chrissy, Adia, Sam, and Brigitta, for making my wondrous worlds.

{{

Spencer Ellsworth is the author of *The Great Faerie Strike* from Broken Eye Books and the Starfire Trilogy from Tor.com, beginning with *A Red Peace*, as well as numerous works of short fiction. He lives in Bellingham, Washington, with his wife and three children and works as a teacher at a small tribal college.

BROKEN EYE BOOKS

The Hole Behind Midnight, by Clinton J. Boomer
Crooked, by Richard Pett
Scourge of the Realm, by Erik Scott de Bie
Izanami's Choice, by Adam Heine
Never Now Always, by Desirina Boskovich
Pretty Marys All in a Row, by Gwendolyn Kiste
Queen of No Tomorrows, by Matt Maxwell
The Great Faerie Strike, by Spencer Ellsworth
Catfish Lullaby, by AC Wise

COLLECTIONS
Royden Poole's Field Guide to the 25th Hour, by Clinton J. Boomer

ANTHOLOGIES
(edited by Scott Gable & C. Dombrowski)
By Faerie Light: Tales of the Fair Folk
Ghost in the Cogs: Steam-Powered Ghost Stories
Tomorrow's Cthulhu: Stories at the Dawn of Posthumanity
Ride the Star Wind: Cthulhu, Space Opera, and the Cosmic Weird
Welcome to Miskatonic University: Fantastically Weird Tales of Campus Life
It Came from Miskatonic University: Weirdly Fantastical Tales of Campus Life
Nowhereville: Weird is Other People

Stay weird.
Read books.
Repeat.

brokeneyebooks.com
twitter.com/brokeneyebooks
facebook.com/brokeneyebooks
instagram.com/brokeneyebooks

CPSIA information can be obtained
at www.ICGtesting.com
Printed in the USA
LVHW011241170120
643988LV00002B/25